THE ILLUMINATED

THE ILLUMINATED

OR THE PRECURSORS OF SOCIALISM

TALES AND PORTRAITS

GÉRARD DE NERVAL

TRANSLATED BY PETER VALENTE

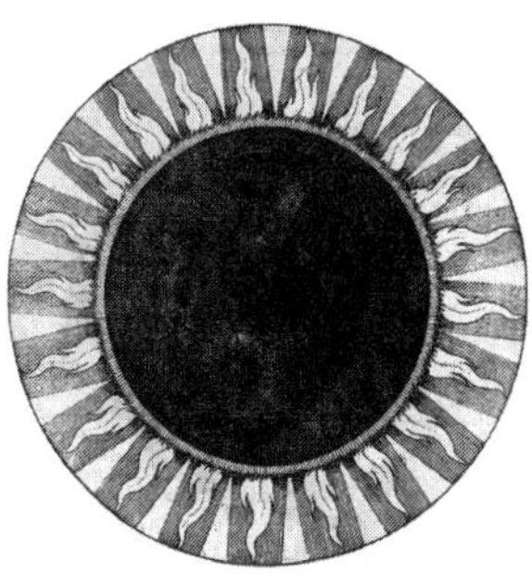

WAKEFIELD PRESS / CAMBRIDGE, MASSACHUSETTS

Wakefield Press, P.O. Box 425645,
Cambridge, MA 02142

Originally published as *Les Illuminés: Recits et Portraits* in 1852.

Images on cover and title page from *Utriusque Cosmi Maioris Scilicet et Minoris Metaphysica* by Robert Fludd.

This book was set in Garamond Premier Pro and Helvetica Neue LT Pro by Wakefield Press.
Printed and bound by McNaughton & Gunn, Inc., in the United States of America.

ISBN: 978-1-939663-74-0

Available through D.A.P./Distributed Art Publishers
75 Broad Street, Suite 630
New York, New York 10004
Tel: (212) 627-1999
Fax: (212) 627-9484

10 9 8 7 6 5 4 3 2 1

This translation is in memory of Gerrit Lansing (1928–2018)

CONTENTS

A NOTE ON THE TITLE

Nerval's use of the word *Illuminés* is complex and suggestive of multiple meanings. In one sense, it refers specifically to the Order of the Illuminati, a secret society founded by Adam Weishaupt (1748–1830) on 1 May 1776, distinct from Freemasonry and other secret groups. But it is also used generally to refer to those individuals who were "enlightened ones," or "visionaries." The first individual in the series of Nerval's portraits, Raoul Spifame, is an eccentric, a visionary, an enlightened madman; the abbé de Bucquoy, Restif de la Bretone, Jacques Cazotte, Cagliostro, and Quintus Auclur are also eccentrics possessed with a visionary sense. Therefore, the title, *The Illuminated*, refers to these individuals. I have used the term "Illuminati" when it refers to the specific secret society.

TRANSLATOR'S INTRODUCTION

Les Illuminés by Gérard de Nerval (the nom de plume of Gérard Labrunie, 1808–1855) was published in May 1852. He was traveling in Belgium and Holland at the time; that winter the play he had co-written on the invention of printing, *L'Imagier de Harlem* (The image-maker of Haarlam), proved a disaster at the box office, despite his initial hopes. As a result, Nerval suffered a severe mental breakdown and accompanying physical illness, which required him to stay in a hospital for three weeks. At this time in his life, he was trying to avoid creditors and signing contracts for books that were not yet written, all at a time, following Bonaparte's coup d'etat, when there was severe censorship of books in France. It was a period of intense production for Nerval, and he was also taking stock of his writing life; he was forty-four years old. He had started to compile his writings, and to identify those of his works that he hoped would survive the test of time. He had started publishing early, and by now he was used to seeing his name in print; but much of his output had been in the form of theatrical reviews and writings that described contemporary cultural events and personalities, which were published in a variety of newspapers. *Les Illuminés* was one of Nerval's first true books, coming a year after *Voyage to the Orient* (1851).

The first portrait in *The Illuminated* is entitled "My Uncle's Library," which serves as something of a preface. Nerval mentions the books in his uncle's library, acquired "during the time of the old revolution," when there was "a certain tendency to mysticism, at a time when there was no official religion to speak of." His uncle relegated these books, presumably "books dealing with the Cabala and the occult sciences," to the attic, and changed his thinking about religious matters, opting for a "moderate deism." Nerval concludes the essay in this way: "I absorbed at a very young age much of this indigestible or unhealthy food for the soul; and even later, my judgment had to defend itself against these primitive impressions." *The Illuminated* thus traces the trajectory of Nerval's thoughts as they fluctuate between a faith in dreams and magic and his realization of the harsh realities of daily life. It is important to note that the first portrait (Raoul Spifame) dates from 1839, just following the height of the Romantic movement in France, and the final portrait (Quintus Aucler) dates from 1852, a period of artistic disillusionment and intellectual alienation that followed the coup d'etat and the renewal of strict censorship in France.

Unlike his contemporaries, Nerval had read extensively the German (he had translated Goethe's *Faust*) and British Romantics; he saw traces of spirituality behind the blasphemies of Bryon or Shelly: "Byron's sneering still belongs to religious sentiment, as does Shelley's materialistic impiety. But who today would deign to be impious? No one dreams of it!" Nerval also explored the past writings of alleged madmen, dreamers, and visionaries. In this we can see a reflection of Nerval's psyche. This uncharted land was symbolized by the Orient, and also by the marginal utopian visionaries throughout history who have been excluded from representation in the canon. One of these, Quintus Aucler, the subject of one of Nerval's portraits, writes, "There is something more frightening in history than the fall of empires: it is the death of religions." This theme is central to *The Illuminated* as a whole.

In the portrait of Raoul Spifame, a mad lawyer who imagines himself to be Henry II, Nerval shows a man in conflict with himself, much as Nerval had been in conflict with his doctor father because the latter wanted the young man to follow in the family tradition. If Henry II represents his father, as well as the patriarchal world, then Raoul represents Nerval, his son. In the end, the king pities Raoul and lets him live in his own dream world, but Nerval's father, "active, strong, realistic in his outlook, accustomed to the sight of horror, suffering, and death, hardened by the rigors of war, had no patience with his son: a dreamer, withdrawn and relatively passive in his approach to life."[1]

Nerval's portrait of the abbé de Bucquoy presents him as a man whose amazing escapes suggest someone with magical powers; he is like a neophyte who, with each escape, ascends to a higher grade in some mysterious occult order. Bettina Knapp, in her study of Nerval, writes, "Methods of escape, whether on a physical or spiritual level, always struck a responsive chord with Nerval, who was himself so victimized and imprisoned by his own emotional turmoil."[2] The abbé is against the reigning monarchy and in favor of a more liberal one where the leader would be a "wise" man able to guide his people to a more profound understanding of themselves as well as the beauties and pleasures inherent in life. But Nerval does not explain how the abbé was able to escape from so many prisons; Nerval, at this time, was still attempting to discover a way of life that would allow him to be truly free.

Of particular interest to Nerval was the figure of Restif, the subject of another portrait, who was an eighteenth-century novelist, theosophist, sensualist, and pantheist. The term *retifism* for shoe fetishism was named after him. It was only five or six years after his marriage that Restif emerged as an author, and from that time until his death he produced hundred volumes, many of them printed by his own hand, on many different subjects. He has been seen as both a social realist and a sexual fantasist, and differed from his fellow visionaries in that he defined God not in spiritual terms, but in human ones: "The Sun is that Great Animal's Mind, the Moon are his testicles; in the planets repose his intestines."[3] Author of many novels as well as various books on politics, sociology, and criminology, Restif was one of the most paradoxical figures of the eighteenth century: a figure in fierce opposition to the so-called Age of Enlightenment, and who has puzzled scholars and psychologists in their attempts to sort out the complexities of his mind and his mysterious escapades. Brought up in a strict religious household, Restif did not believe in sin (which he thought was destructive to one's pursuit of pleasure) and founded instead a religion of "voluptuousness"; he was well known in his time for his numerous sexual escapades. Nerval's essay on Restif consists of a series of love episodes; the women are portrayed as in a painting: ethereal, delicate, mysterious, yet cruel. Nerval may have had in mind the actress Jenny Colon, with whom he was obsessed, when he wrote the following:

> Nothing is more dangerous for people who are natural dreamers than the serious love for a person of the theater; it is a perpetual lie, the dream of a sick person, the illusion of a madman. Life attaches itself entirely to an unattainable chimera that one would be happy to preserve in a state of desire and aspiration, but which vanishes as soon as one wishes to touch the idol.

Nerval's identification with Restif was based on the theory of resemblances: Restif believed that one fell in love with only one woman in a lifetime. Nerval shared such a view at this time since he was still in love with Jenny Colon, who had become for him the embodiment of an unattainable goddess, the essential female archetype, whether he imagined her as Astarte or the Virgin Mary.

Nerval also explores the lives of three other visionaries from the eighteenth century: in the portrait of Count Alessandro di Cagliostro, the famous magus and alchemist, the reader encounters a kind of love feast based on occult ideas; the French writer, Jacques Cazotte, author of *The Devil in Love* (1772), created a synthesis between hermetic ideas and Catholic thought; and Quintus Aucler, a lawyer interested in the mysteries of antiquity, sought to revive paganism during the ideologically unstable world of French society in the immediate aftermath of the Revolution of 1789.

A feeling of optimism permeates Nerval's text on Cagliostro. In this narrative, Nerval tells of a pagan vison of the unity between all men and women, which gives "an idea of the movement then taking place in minds that were gradually freed themselves from Catholic dogma." The portraits of Raoul and the abbé also suggest an alternative view of reality, one that favored a dreamlike and magical universe over one ruled by reason.

But in these narratives, Nerval also explores and critiques his own sense of disillusionment with the French society of the nineteenth century. Nerval became disenchanted with the political paralysis and hypocrisy of the Louis-Philippe monarchy, as well as with the Second Revolution that resulted from Napolean's coup d'etat. The poet's role in the political life of the country was next to nothing, and Nerval's utopian dreams of a better society were shattered in the wake of the Revolution. His sense of alienation is reflected in the texts on Restif, Quintus Aucler, and Jacques Cazotte, where optimism will eventually be tempered by misunderstanding (Aucler), revolution (Cazotte), and the suffering one encounters when their love is not returned (Restif).

But Nerval does not see Cazotte's life, for example, as a failure because he supported the monarchy and was unable to realize his dreams. Nerval writes that Cazotte's final words were, "I die as I have lived, faithful to God and to my king," and also that "His heroism has since rendered him forever illustrious." Like Nerval, he "experienced the text of the Cosmos as fully as his individuation allowed."[4] The same can be said of Quintus Aucler and Restif.

Nerval's aesthetic project brings to light a Romantic conception of knowledge, which denies boundaries and offers an alternative to what Coleridge called the "barren dualities" of Western thought. Nerval's aesthetic and spiritual quest was centered on the Middle East throughout his entire life. From 1842 to 1843, he traveled to Greece, Egypt, Lebanon, and Turkey, and wrote a book, *Voyage to the Orient* (1851), based on his observations and experiences. According to Louis Massignon (1883–1962), a Catholic scholar of Islam whose work focused on creating better relations between Catholics and Muslims, Nerval "wished to Islamicize his Christian heterodoxy by going to live in the Arabian Orient."[5] In his portrait of Quintus Aucler, Nerval writes about the Eastern origins of Western occultism:

> The Templars were among those Crusaders who endeavored to achieve the broadest possible alliance between these Eastern ideas and those of Roman Christianity.
>
> In the desire to establish a link between their order and the Syrian people they were responsible for governing, they laid the foundations for a new kind of doctrine that was engaged with all the religions practiced by the Levantines, without abandoning in essence the Catholic synthesis, but by often making it bend to the requirements of their position.
>
> These were the foundations of Freemasonry, which were connected to similar institutions established by various Muslim sects and which still survive persecution, especially in the Hauran, Lebanon, and Kurdistan.

Nerval had an extensive knowledge of ancient mythology, religions, and their rituals. For him, the underlying nature of reality is based on the complex patterns of myth contained in the holy documents of various religions, and to understand these hermetic texts would be to understand the complex reality of ordinary life and the truth of God's revelation. One such holy document is Quintus Aucler's book, *La Threicie* (The Thracian), excerpted in Nerval's portrait of him.

Collectively, these narratives show Nerval's attempt to map out an alternative history of France through examining the lives of six visionaries. Nerval's descent into the abyss of madness (he suffered from periodic bouts of madness throughout his life) was followed by an ascent back to reality, however brief, that resulted in a clearer vision of truth: he would write, in "My Uncle's Library," "Is there not something of reason to be extracted from madness . . . ?" Nerval did extract "something of reason" in the portraits of each of these visionaries as they confronted, in their own ways, and across centuries, the abyss opened up by their direct experience of "the death of God." Like the writer Jacques Cazotte, Nerval "had few illusions as to the triumph of his cause." Said another way: "We can trust Nerval's flotation as we can't Melville's gloomy ongoing after *Moby-Dick*—he didn't cut his intellect in 'twain' like Mark or Herman, didn't give his soul to live in distinguished and divided worlds, but remained centered in the heat of the process, his eyes bent on the only target worth a man's Will, apotheosis."[6]

The importance of *The Illuminated* has been overshadowed by the works that came after it in rapid succession as Nerval worked in a feverish state to stave off creditors, culminating with *Aurelia* in 1855. Nerval would take his own life on the night of 26 January 1855. In the years since then, critics have primarily seen *The Illuminated* in terms of the light it sheds on Nerval's later masterpieces; with this first complete translation, this important book can now be seen as a complex work of art in its own right.

NOTES

1. Bettina Knapp, *Gérard de Nerval: The Mystic's Dilemma* (Tuscaloosa: University of Alabama Press, 1980), 16.
2. Knapp, *Gérard de Nerval*, 181.
3. Bettina L. Knapp, quoting Restif from *Les Sources occultes du romantisme* by Auguste Viatte, in *Gérard de Nerval*, 182.
4. Gerrit Lansing, "Test of Translation IX: Nerval's 'Horus,'" in *A Caterpillar Anthology*, ed. Clayton Eshleman (New York: Doubleday, 1971), 238.
5. Hichem Djaït, *Europe and Islam* (Oakland: University of California Press, 1985).
6. Lansing, "Test of Translation IX," 238.

MY UNCLE'S LIBRARY

It is not given to everyone to write *The Praise of Folly*; but without being Erasmus, or Saint-Evremond,[1] one can nevertheless take pleasure in drawing from the clutter of the centuries some singular figure whom one will endeavor to dress again ingeniously, as in restoring old paintings, whose strange composition and worn-out paint cause the vulgar amateur to smile.

In this present time, when literary portraits have had some success, my wish has been to paint a portrait of certain eccentrics of philosophy. Far be it from me to attack their successors who today suffer from having tried too foolishly or too soon to realize their dreams. These analyses, these biographies, were written at various times, although they ought to be linked to the same series.

I was raised in the countryside, at the home of an old uncle who owned a library formed in part during the time of the old revolution. Since then he had relegated a great number of books to the attic; most were anonymously published under the monarchy, or had not been deposited in the public libraries at the time of the previous revolution.[2] A certain tendency to mysticism, at a time when there was no official religion to speak of, had doubtless guided my uncle in choosing these kinds of writings: he has apparently since changed his ideas, and remained content, for the sake of his own conscience, with a moderate deism.[3]

Having rummaged through his house until I discovered the enormous mass of books piled up and forgotten in the attic—most of which had been attacked by rats and were rotten or wet from rainwater dripping through the spaces between the tiles—I absorbed at a very young age much of this indigestible or unhealthy food for the soul; and even later, my judgment had to defend itself against these primitive impressions.

Perhaps it was best to give it no more thought: but I believe it's good to rid oneself of the excessive burden that confuses the mind. And yet, is there not something of reason to be extracted from madness, if only to preserve oneself from believing again in what is very ancient?

These thoughts led me to develop a particularly amusing and perhaps instructive way that I could present the life and character of my *eccentrics*. Analyzing the variegations of the human soul is moral physiology—well worth the effort of a naturalist, a paleographer, or an archaeologist; my only regret, having undertaken the work, is that I've left it incomplete.

The history of the eighteenth century could probably do without this annotation; but it can gain some unforeseen detail that scrupulous historians should not overlook. That period has rubbed off on us more than we could have predicted. Whether this is good or bad—who knows?

My poor uncle often said: "Always think twice before you speak."

What should we do before writing?

THE KING OF BICÊTRE

(Sixteenth Century)
Raoul Spifame

I. The Image

Let us tell you now the story of the madness of a singular character, who lived around the middle of the sixteenth century. Raoul Spifame,[1] seigneur des Granges, was an overlord without a domain, as there were so many already in this period of wars and ruins which struck all the high houses of France. His father left him only a small sum in terms of an inheritance, and the same small amount to his two brothers,[2] Paul and Jean, who have since become famous, in different ways; as a result, Raoul was sent off to Paris at a very young age, where he studied law and eventually became a barrister. When King Henry II succeeded his glorious father, Francis I, this king came in person, after the judicial vacations that followed his accession, to attend the return of the Houses of Parliament.[3] Raoul Spifame held a modest place in the lowest ranks of the assembly, mingling with the throng of the lower legists, and only his waistcoat gave any indication that he was a Doctor of the Laws. The king was seated higher than the first president and wore his royal blue mantle woven with the fleurs-de-lis, and everyone admired the nobility and agreeableness of his face, despite the sickly pallor that distinguished all the princes of this line. The Latin speech of the venerable chancellor was very long on that day. The distracted eyes of the king, weary from counting the leaning foreheads of the men in the assembly and the sculpted beams of the ceiling, finally focused for a while on a single assistant placed at the far end of the room, where a ray of sunshine fell directly on his figure; so that gradually all eyes were directed toward this one who seemed to excite the attention of the king. It was Raoul Spifame who was thus examined.

It seemed to King Henry II that a portrait was placed before him that reproduced his whole person exactly, save for his splendid regal vestments, which had been transformed into black clothes. Each of those present made the same remark, that the young advocate looked prodigiously like the king, and, because of the superstition which suggests that some time before the king's own death his image will appear dressed in mourning, the king appeared anxious during the rest of the session. Upon leaving, he obtained information about Raoul Spifame, and reassured himself simply by learning the name, position, and origin of his ghost.[4] However, he showed no desire to know more about him, and the Italian wars resumed shortly after and occupied him to such an extent that he no longer had time to dwell upon this singular impression.

As for Raoul, from that day onward he was referred to as *Sire* and *Your Majesty* by his companions in the bar. This jest was so prolonged in all manner of variations, as often happens among these young men of learning, who seize upon every opportunity to amuse themselves and have some fun, that according to some, this was the chief cause of the disturbance of spirit which led Raoul Spifame to engage in various bizarre activities. Thus, one day he allowed himself to address a remonstrance to the presiding judge concerning a decision that was, according to him, poorly rendered, concerning matters of inheritance. As a result, he was suspended from his duties for a time and fined. On other occasions, in his pleadings, he ventured to attack the laws of the kingdom, or the most respected judicial opinions, and often even went entirely beyond the initial subject of his case to express very bold remarks concerning the government, without always respecting the authority of the king. This was taken to such an extreme that the superior magistrates thought they were merely indulging him by barring him entirely from the exercise of his profession. Nevertheless, Raoul Spifame visited the halls of Justice on a daily basis, where he stopped passersby to put before them his ideas for reform and his complaints against the judges. His brothers and his own daughter[5] were eventually forced to apply for a restraining order, and it was thus as a defendant that he eventually reappeared before the court.

This produced a serious revolution in his entire personality, for his madness was hitherto only a species of common sense and logic; there was no aberration except perhaps in its recklessness. But if the man called to appear before the court was simply a visionary whose name was Raoul Spifame, this Spifame who emerged from the audience to appear before the judge was a genuine madman, one of the most elusive minds that ever required the padded cell of an asylum. In his capacity as barrister, Raoul had permitted himself to harangue the judges, and he had amassed certain examples such as Sophocles and other ancients accused by their children; but chance disposed of it differently. As he was crossing the vestibule that led to the courtroom, he heard a hundred voices whispering, "It's the king, here's the king, make way for the king!" This sobriquet, whose mocking spirit he should have appreciated, produced on his disturbed intelligence the effect of a jolt that releases a fragile spring: his reason deserted him and flew off in a singsong fashion, and the true madman, truly of "unsound mind," as had been said of Triboulet, entered the hall with the barrette on his head, and his fist on his hip, and placed himself in his seat with a dignity worthy of the king.

He addressed the councilors as *loyal subjects* and honored the prosecutor, Noël Brûlot,[6] with a *God be with thee* full of amenity. As for himself, *Spifame*, he scanned the assembly, regretted not seeing himself there, inquired after his health, and always mentioned himself in the third person, qualifying himself with: "Our friend Raoul Spifame, of whom all must speak well." Then there were general catcalls mingled with taunts, where the jokesters seated behind him tried their hardest to confirm him in his follies, despite the efforts of the magistrates to restore the order and dignity of the court. A swift verdict, easily rendered, recommended the poor man to the solicitude and skill of medical physicians; then he was taken, well guarded, to the asylum, as he continued distributing greetings to his good people in Paris.

News of this judgment stirred the court. The king, who had not forgotten his Double, asked to be informed of Raoul's speeches, and as it was learned that this impromptu king had imitated the royal majesty exactly: "So much the better," said the king, "since he has the honor of being in our very image, let him not dishonor such a likeness." And he ordered the poor man to be treated well, though he expressed no desire to see him again.

II. The Reflection

For more than a month, fever dominated Raoul's still rebellious reason, which sometimes roughly shook his golden illusions. If during the day he remained seated in his chair, aware of his sad identity, and if he could then recognize himself, understand himself, get a hold of himself, at night the situation was different: his real existence gave way to extraordinary dreams, and he suffered a completely different existence, an entirely absurd and hyperbolic life, like that Burgundian peasant who, during his sleep, was transported to the palace of his duke and awoke there surrounded by honors and attentions, as if he were the king himself. Every night Spifame was the real King Henry II; he held court at the Louvre, inspected his troops on horseback, held important council meetings, or presided over splendid banquets. Then, occasionally, he remembered a lawyer from the palace, a barrister by the name of seigneur des Granges, for whom he felt a strong affection. The sun would never rise without this barrister having obtained some brilliant testimony of the king's friendship and esteem: sometimes the ceremonial mortier worn by chief justices, sometimes the seal of the Crown or the ribbon of one of its orders. Spifame was convinced that his dreams were his life and that his prison was only a dream; for we know that he often repeated in the evenings: "We slept badly last night; Oh, what horrible dreams!"

It has since been thought, in collecting the details of this unique existence, that the unfortunate man was the victim of one of those magnetic fascinations, the science of which is better understood today. Identical in appearance to the king, a reflection of his other self, and confounded by this similarity which everyone thought was astonishing, Spifame, by directing his gaze into that of the prince, suddenly felt conscious of a second personality; that is why, after assimilating himself by his gaze, he identified himself with the king in his mind, and now he was the one who, on the sixteenth day of June 1549, had entered the city of Paris by the gate of Saint-Denis, which was adorned with very beautiful and rich tapestries, and with such a noise and thunder of artillery that all the houses shook. He was not sorry either to have deprived of their office Messrs Liget, François de Saint-André, and Antoine Ménard, chief justices of the Parliament of Paris. It was a small debt of friendship that Henry was paying to Spifame.[7]

We have noted with interest all the various aspects of this madness, which can be of value to the study of the science of the phenomena of the soul, so arduously pursued by philosophers, but which has, alas, only produced the effects and the results of madness, reason being insufficient to determine the causes which God hides from us! The following is a strange scene that one of the guards reported to the head doctor of the asylum. This guard, to whom the prisoner made a royal largesse from the little money he acquired from his sequestered income, liked to adorn the cell of Raoul Spifame as best he could, and one day he placed there an antique mirror of polished metal, the others being forbidden in the asylum because of the fear that the insane would hurt themselves by breaking them. At first, Spifame paid little attention to it; but when evening came, as he paced back and forth in his room, lost in melancholy thoughts, the appearance of his face reproduced in the mirror made him suddenly stop. Forced, during this moment of wakefulness, to believe in his actual identity, confirmed all too well by the triple walls of his prison, he nevertheless thought he had suddenly seen the king approaching him from a distant hall and stopping at last to speak to him through the iron bars, as if showing compassion for his fate, at which point the monarch hastened to bow deeply. When he arose, casting his eyes upon the supposed king, he distinctly saw his image rising too, a sure sign that the king had bowed to him, from which he conceived a great joy and infinite honor. Then he launched into immense recriminations against the traitors who had put him in this situation, having undoubtedly blackened his name in the eyes of His Majesty. He even wept, the poor gentleman, protesting his innocence, and asked the king to avenge the wrongs done him by his enemies; about which the king appeared singularly touched, for a tear shone, following the contours of his royal nose. At this sight, a flash of joy illuminated Spifame's face; the king was already smiling affably; he held out his hand; Spifame reached out his; the mirror, roughly struck by his hand, detached itself from the wall, and crashed to the ground with a terrible noise that caused the guards to rush into the room.

The following night, in his dream, the poor fool ordered the king to immediately release Spifame, who was unjustly detained and falsely accused of having wanted, as a favorite, to impinge upon the rights and duties of the king, his master and friend: he also issued an edict, creating the high office of *Director of the Royal Seal** on behalf of said Spifame, charged from now on to put in order the affairs of the wretched kingdom. Several days of fever followed the profound shock that all these serious events had produced on such a brain. The delirium was so severe that the doctor was worried and had the madman transported to a larger room, where it was thought that the company of other prisoners might occasionally divert him from his flights of imagination.

III. The Court Poet

Spifame's tale clearly demonstrates the truth of the portrait of that figure, so famous in Spain, who was a madman in one aspect of his brain and very sensible when it came to the rest of his logical faculties;[8] he was clearly still conscious of himself, unlike those vulgar fools who forget themselves entirely and are constantly convinced that they are characters of their own invention. Spifame, before a mirror or in his sleep, recognized his individual self and yet judged himself apart, changing his adopted role and actual identity in turn, so that he was both double and distinct; however, this is often the case when one feels oneself living in a dream. Moreover, as we noted above, the adventure of the mirror had been followed by a very intense crisis, after which the patient had exhibited a melancholy and dreamlike mood, and where it was decided that he might profit from the company of other prisoners.

They brought into his room a short, balding man with green eyes, who thought himself the king of poets, and whose folly was to tear up any piece of paper or parchment not written in his own hand, because he thought he saw in it the rival productions of the bad poets of the time who had robbed him of the good graces of King Henry and the court. It was amusing to bring these two original madmen together and see the result of such an encounter. This character was named Claude Vignet, and he took on the title of *Royal Poet*. He was, moreover, a very gentle man, whose verses were well turned and perhaps deserved the place he assigned them in his mind.

---

* See the *Memoires de la Société des incriptions et belles-lettres*, volume XXIII.

On entering Spifame's room, Claude Vignet was amazed: his hair was bristling, his eyes were transfixed; he had taken but a step forward before falling to his knees.

"Your Majesty!" he exclaimed.

"Rise up, my friend," said Spifame, wrapping the free sleeve of his doublet around himself; "Who are you?"

"Do you not recognize the humblest of your subjects and the greatest of your poets, O great king? . . . I am Claudius Vignetus, *one* of the Pléiade, and the illustrious author of the sonnet addressed *to the billowing waves* . . . Sire, I ask that you punish the traitor who has defamed my honor! His name is Mellin de Saint-Gelais!"[9]

"Do you mean my favorite poet, the guardian of my library?"

"He robbed me! He stole my sonnet! He took advantage of your kindness . . ."

"Is he really a plagiarist? . . . Then I will give his position to my brave Spifame, now on a trip in the interests of the kingdom."

"Give it to me, instead, Sire! And I will spread your name from east to west over the whole earth.

O Sire! Let my rhymes immortalize you! . . .

"You will have a pension of a thousand crowns, and my old doublet, for yours is threadbare."

"Sire, I see that all my sonnets and my epistles addressed to you have been hitherto intercepted by traitors. Such is the way of these courts . . .

This heinous stay of treacherous deceit.

"Honorable Claudius Vignetus, you will remain here; you will be my minister, and you will render in verse my judgments and my ordinances. This is the way to immortalize memory. And now, this is the hour our Diana visits us. You understand that it is time for you to leave us alone."

And Spifame, after having dismissed the poet, fell asleep in his chaise lounge, as he was accustomed to do an hour after his meal.

After a few days the two fools had grown inseparable, each understanding and fostering the thought of the other without ever opposing their reciprocal identities. For the one, this poet provided the praise that multiplies in all forms around kings and confirms them in their high estimation of themselves; for the other, this incredible resemblance confirmed the presence of the king himself. Their asylum was no longer a prison, but a palace; no more rags, but glittering vestments; their ordinary meals were transformed into splendid banquets, where harmonious rhymes rose above the strains of viola and trumpet.

After his reveries, Spifame was communicative, and Vignet proved to be especially enthusiastic after dinner. The monarch once told the poet of all that he had to endure on the part of those schoolchildren, those unruly hecklers, and he developed plans for a war against Spain; but his greatest solicitude, as will be seen below, was the organization and embellishment of the principal city of the kingdom, whose endless roofs unfolded in the distance under the prisoner's windows.

Vignet had lucid moments, during which he was aware of the metallic sound of the cell door slamming shut or the jangle of the jailer's keys. This led him to think that His Majesty was locked up in a cell from time to time, and he communicated this judicious observation to Spifame, who answered mysteriously that his ministers were playing a big joke on him, that he divined all their plots, and that on the return of his chancellor, Spifame's fate would take a different turn; that with the help of Raoul Spifame and Claude Vignet, his only friends, the King of France would be released from captivity and revive the golden age sung by the poets.

In response, Claudius Vignetus composed a poem that he offered to the king as a sign of his future benediction and glory:

You are the heat that turns all the fields green and warm,
You give life to the lamb, the bird in its aerie,
You are the sun that helps the snowy slopes transform
Into harvests and the lush, beautiful prairie!

But with his release being so long in coming, Spifame thought it his duty to warn his people of the captivity in which treacherous councillors held him; he composed a proclamation, urging his loyal subjects to rise up on his behalf; and at the same time, he issued a number of very severe edicts and ordinances: here the word *launched* is more exact, for it was through his window, between the bars, that he threw his *charters*, rolled up and weighted down with small stones. Unfortunately, some fell on the roof of a pigsty, others were lost in the thick grass of a deserted courtyard beneath his window; only one or two, after being tossed and carried by the air, went perching, like birds, in the branches of a linden tree beyond the walls. Nobody noticed them in any case.

Seeing that all these public demonstrations were producing no effect, Claude Vignet imagined that they, being simply handwritten, were not inspiring confidence, so he decided to found a royal printing office that would serve in turn for the reproduction of the edicts of the king and his own poetry. Given the limited resources available to him, his invention had to revert to the primary elements of typographic art. With infinite patience, he managed to cut twenty-five letters out of wood, which he used to spell, letter by letter, the ordinances, which were of course very brief: the oil and the soot from his lamp furnished him with the ink he needed.

From then on, the official ballots multiplied in a much more satisfactory manner. Several of these documents, preserved and reprinted several times since, are very curious, especially one which declares that King Henry II, upon due council, having acknowledged the citizen's pathetic cries of protest against the perfidies and injustices of Paul and Jean Spifame, both brothers of his faithful subject of the same name, condemned them to be flayed, skinned, and boiled alive. As for the ungrateful daughter of Raoul Spifame, she was to be flogged on the whipping post and then locked up with all the other repentant girls.

One of the most memorable ordinances that have been preserved from this period is one where Spifame, still irritated by the judges' initial decision to ban him from the bar because of his careless and exorbitant perorations, issues a royal order by the authority of the king to all bailiffs, guards, or judicial agents, to let his friend and foe Raoul Spifame freely enter the halls of justice; forbidding all lawyers, litigants, passersby, and other scoundrels to interfere in any way with either the flights of his eloquence or the unparalleled enjoyment of his intimate conversation with respect to the political, as well as other matters on which he wished to express his opinion.

His other edicts, judgments, and ordinances that have been preserved, as rendered in the name of Henry II, deal with justice, finance, war, and especially policies having to do with the management of the city of Paris.

Vignet printed several epigrams against his enemies in poetry, whose notable positions, benefits, and pensions he conferred upon himself. It must be said that, seeing themselves alone in the world, the two companions were tirelessly busy, one in requesting favors, the other in lavishly granting them.

IV. The Escape

After many edicts and appeals to the loyalty of the good citizens of Paris, the two prisoners were astonished in the end to not witness any popular uprising, and to always wake up to the same situation. Spifame attributed this lack of success to the supervision of the ministers, and Vignet to the constant hatred of Mellin and du Bellay. The printing press was closed for a few days as they dreamed of more serious resolutions; they meditated on the possibility of a coup d'état. These two men, who had never thought of freeing themselves simply to be free, at last drew up a plan of escape with the intention of opening the eyes of the people of Paris and provoking their contempt for the *Sophonisbe* of Saint-Gelais and the *Franciade* of Ronsard.[10]

They began to loosen the bars of the window, slowly, but all while making the traces of their work disappear, and this was all the easier since they were quiet, patient, and content with their destiny. Once the preparations were over, the printing press was reopened, the four-line libelles, the incendiary proclamations, the commissioned poems formed part of the baggage, and toward midnight, after Spifame addressed a short but vigorous address to his confidant, the latter tied the king's bedsheets to one of the remaining bars, slipped down to the ground first, and soon helped Spifame back to his feet after he fell two-thirds of his way down into the thick grass, not without garnering some bruises. Vignet did not delay in finding the old wall overlooking the countryside; more agile than Spifame, he managed to climb to the top, and stretched his leg from there to his gracious sovereign, who made much use of it, placing his foot on the stones protruding from the wall. A moment later the Rubicon was crossed.

It was around three o'clock in the morning when our two liberated heroes at last reached a densely wooded region that could hide them for a while; but they were not duly cautious, secure in the knowledge that they only needed to be out of captivity to be immediately recognized: the king by his subjects, the poet by his admirers.

They needed to wait until the gates of Paris were opened, however, which did not take place until five o'clock in the morning. Already the road was crowded with peasants who were bringing their provisions to the marketplace. Raoul found it prudent not to reveal himself until he reached the center of his good city; he drew his coat over his mustache and recommended that Claude Vignet likewise veil the rays of his Apollonian face beneath the flap of his gray felt hat.

After passing through the gate of Saint-Victor, they followed the banks of the Bièvre river, crossing the green *cultures* that stretched out on either side. Before arriving at the edge of the Île de la Cité, Spifame told his favorite that he would not have embarked on such a painful expedition and would not have adopted such an embarrassing incognito were it not a greater matter than that of his freedom and his power. The unhappy man was jealous! Jealous of whom? Of the duchesse de Valentinois, of Diane de Poitiers, his beautiful mistress, whom he had not seen for several days, and who perhaps was engaged in many escapades far from her royal knight. "Patience," said Claude Vignet, "I am sharpening my mind with a series of epigrams worthy of Martial which will punish her flippancy, but your father Francis I said it well: Often does a woman change her heart!" Speaking in this manner, they had already made their way through the crowded streets of the Right Bank and soon found themselves in a rather large square, situated near the Church of the Innocents, and already crowded with people, because it was market day.

Noticing the commotion in the square, Spifame could not hide his joy. "Friend," he said to the poet, who was quite occupied by the shoes he had lost on the way, "look how these bourgeois and these knights are already filled with emotion, see how these faces are inflamed with anger, see how the seeds of discontent and sedition float through the lower firmament! Do you see this one with his halberd . . . Oh, I sense these poor people will provoke a civil war! But how could I command my arquebusiers to fire on all these innocent men today since they desire to help me with my projects, even though tomorrow they may be guilty of no longer respecting my authority?"

"Mobile vulgus," said Vignet.[11]

V. The Marketplace

Looking at the middle of the square, Spifame felt a sense of surprise and anger. Vignet asked him what was wrong. "Don't you see," said the angry king, "that lantern on the whipping post which has been left in contempt of my orders? The whipping post has been abolished, and that will cost the provost and all the aldermen greatly, if we hadn't limited our royal authority over them. But it is up to our people of Paris to take the matter into their own hands."

"Sire," observed the poet, "don't you think that the people will be even more outraged to learn that the couplets engraved on this fountain, which are by the poet du Bellay, contain two prosodic errors: a hexameter with the words *humida sceptra*, which, contrary to Horace, prosody disallows, and a pentameter with an incorrect caesura."

"Hear ye!" shouted Spifame without worrying too much over the poet's observation, "Hear ye! Good people of Paris, gather together, and listen carefully."

"Listen closely to the king who wants to speak to you in person," added Claude Vignet, shouting with the full force of his lungs.

Both were already mounted upon a large rock, which supported an iron cross: Spifame standing, Clade Vignet seated at his feet. Many people crowded around them, and those closest initially imagined that their subject had something to do with selling ointments or singing ballads or carols. But suddenly, Raoul Spifame took off his cap and flung open his cloak, revealing a shimmering necklace made of clinking glass beads whose pendant contained the royal insignia, which he was allowed to wear while in prison in order to flatter his incurable mania, and there, standing high above the people with a sunbeam illuminating his face, it became impossible to ignore the true image of King Henry II, who was seen on occasion traveling through the city on horseback.

"Yes," cried Claude Vignet to the astonished crowd, "it is King Henry whom you have in your midst, as well as the illustrious poet Claudius Vignetus, his minister and his favorite, whose poetic works you know by heart . . ."

"Good people of Paris, hear me!" interrupted Spifame, "I will tell you of the darkest treachery. Our ministers are traitors, our judges are felons! . . .

Your beloved King was held in captivity and treated harshly, like the first kings of his race, like King Charles IV, his illustrious grandfather . . ."[12]

At these words, a long murmur of surprise traveled a great distance through the crowd; everyone repeated: "The king, the king! . . ." The people commented on the strange revelation he had just made; but some still had their doubts when Claude Vignet drew from his pocket the roll of royal edicts, judgments, and ordinances, and distributed them to the crowd, adding his own poems to the pile for good measure.

"See," said the king, "These are the edicts we have written for the good of our people, and which have not been published or put into effect."

"These are," said Vignet, "the divine poems treacherously pillaged, altered, and spoiled by Pierre de Ronsard and Mellin de Saint-Gelais."

"The bourgeois and the people are being tyrannized in our name . . ."

"The *Sophonisbe* and the *Franciade* are printed and circulated without the approval of the king, and without his royal seal!"

"Listen to this order which removes the salt tax, and this other which abolishes tallage . . ."

"Hear this sonnet whose syllables obey the rules of Latin prosody . . ."

But already the words of Spifame and Vignet were lost amidst the growing commotion; the papers that were distributed among the people and read in individual groups were receiving overwhelming support; there were endless cheers. The monarch and his poet were lifted and placed on a hastily arranged platform, and there was talk about marching to the Hotel de Ville and waiting there for enough people to attack the Louvre, the stronghold of the traitors.

This popular emotion could have been pushed very far, if on the same day Mary of Scotland, the new wife of the Dauphin, had not been scheduled to make her solemn entry through the Porte Saint-Denis.[13] That is why, as Raoul Spifame was walking about in the market, the real King Henry II was riding on horseback along the ditches of the Hôtel de Bourgogne. At the sound of the great commotion not far from there, several officers went to inspect the scene, and immediately returned to inform him that a king was being proclaimed in the marketplace. "Let us go and meet him," said Henry II, "and, if he is a gentleman (he swore like his father) worthy of us, we will challenge him to combat."

But seeing the halberdiers of the procession advancing through the streets to the square, the crowd stopped, and many fled through some of the side streets. It was, indeed, a very imposing sight. The king's household regiment took up position in the square; the lansquenets, the arquebusiers, and the Swiss guards lined the neighboring streets. M. de Bassompierre[14] was near the king, and from the breast of Henry II shone the diamonds of all the sovereign orders of Europe. The dismayed people were no longer detained except by their own mass, which blocked all the exits; many shouted at witnessing such a miracle, for there were two kings of France before them; both pale, proud, and dressed in much the same way; except that the *good king* was less resplendent.

As soon as the cavalry moved toward the crowd, there was a general panic, and the people made way for them, while Spifame and Vignet stood boldly on the strange platform where they had been placed; the soldiers and sergeants seized them with ease.

The impression which the appearance of the king himself made on the poor madman when he was brought before him was so strong that he was immediately overcome by one of his most intense fevers, confused as to his true identity, whether he was indeed Henry or Spifame. The king, who was soon informed of the whole episode, took pity on this unfortunate seigneur, and had him brought to the Louvre, where he received medical attention, and where, for a long time, he became an object of curiosity to the members of the court, and sad to say, a source of entertainment for them.

The king, having observed how harmless Spifame's madness was and how he was always respectful of His Majesty, did not want him to be sent back to that asylum, since was not fond of the idea of having the perfect image of the king exposed to ill treatment, or to the jeers of visitors and valets. He commanded that Spifame should be housed in one of his country castles under the attendance of servants who had been appointed for that purpose, and who had orders to treat him as a real prince, and to call him *Sire* and *Your Majesty*. He was provided with Claude Vignet's companionship as before, whose poems, as well as the new ordinances Spifame composed from his retreat, were printed and preserved by the order of the king.

The collection of edicts and decrees made by this famous madman were printed in their entirety during the following reign and titled:

Dicœarchiæ Henrici regis progymnasmata. There is one copy in the Royal Library under number VII, 6,412. One can also consult *The Proceedings of the Society of Inscriptions and Belles-Lettres*, volume 23. It is remarkable that most of the reforms proposed by Raoul Spifame have since been implemented.[15]

HISTORY OF THE ABBÉ DE BUCQUOY

(Seventeenth Century)

I. A Tavern in Burgundy

The *grand siècle* had come to an end: it had suffered the fate of all waning moons and suns. Louis XIV had exhausted the brilliant era of his victories. He was losing what he had gained in Flanders, in Franche-Comté, on the banks of the Rhine, and in Italy. Prince Eugene triumphed in Germany, Marlborough in the North.[1] The French people, unable to do better, avenged themselves with a popular song.[2]

France had exhausted itself serving the family ambitions and the obstinate system of the old king. Our nation has always been too willing to support belligerent sovereigns, and both Henry IV and Louis XIV of the House of Bourbon were only too ready to oblige this spirit, though the latter had occasion to complain that it was only "his grandeur that binds him to the shore."[3] If need be, these sovereigns took refuge in their vices. Their loves kept up the castles and the cottages, and they realized from afar that gallant and chivalric ideal which has always been the generous dream of the French.

Nevertheless, there were provinces that did not share in this admiration, and which always protested in various forms, either under the cover of religious ideas, or in the obvious form of peasant revolts, rebellious leagues, or a *Fronde*.[4]

The revocation of the Edict of Nantes had been the great blow struck against these pockets of resistance. Villars had just triumphed over the rising of the Cévennes people, and those people of the Camisards, who had escaped the massacres, fled in small groups to Germany, joining the millions of Protestants in exile who had been forced to carry abroad the remnants of their fortune and the various industries in which they excelled.

They had burned the Palatinate, the chief refuge of the Protestants: "Such are the games of princes."[5] The sun of the great century could still be comfortably mirrored in the ponds of Versailles; but its luster had significantly dimmed. Mme de Maintenon herself no longer struggled against time: she only applied herself to infusing devotion into the soul of a skeptical king, who answered her with the numbers brought daily by Chamallard:[6]

"Three billion in debts! What can Providence do about that?"

Louis XIV was not an ordinary man; he may well have loved France and desired its greatness. His personality, coupled with the family spirit, only abandoned him when age weakened his strength, and when his entourage managed to dominate his will.

Some time after the loss of the battle of Hochstedt,[7] which deprived us of a hundred leagues of country in Flanders, Archambault de Bucquoy[8] was passing through Morchandgy, a small village in Burgundy, two leagues from Sens.

Where did he come from? . . . We do not know much . . .

Where was he going? We shall see . . .

A wheel of his carriage having broken, the wheelwright of the village asked for an hour to put on a new one. The count said to his servant: "I only see this tavern. You will come and let me know when the wheelwright has finished."

"The count would do better to stay in his carriage."

"Come, come! . . . I am going into the tavern. I am sure that I will find only good people there . . ."

Archambault de Bucquoy entered the kitchen and asked for soup. But first he wanted to taste the broth.

The innkeeper consented to this request. But Archambault, having found it too salty, said: "I see that salt is cheap here."

"Not really," said the innkeeper.

"Then I imagine the salt smugglers have brought a large amount here."

"I don't know those people. They wouldn't dare come here, in any case. His Majesty's troops have just defeated them, and their groups have been cut to pieces, save for some thirty carters who were led, weighted down with iron shackles, to the prisons."

"Ah," said Archambault de Bucquoy, "so the poor devils were caught. If they had had a man like me as their leader, their affairs would be in a better state!"

He went from the kitchen to the dining room, where bottles of a certain little vintage were being emptied, which wouldn't have aged well elsewhere or at a later time.

Archambault de Bucquoy took his place at a table, where they brought him his soup, and he still found it too salty. We know the hatred of the Burgundians for this reference, which has been renewed since the fifteenth century, when the greatest insult was to call them *salty Burgundians.*[9]

The stranger found he had to explain himself.

"I mean," he replied, "you are generous with the salt in the dishes you serve here . . . which proves that salt is not uncommon in the province . . ."

"You are right," said a man of colossal strength, who rose from amidst the drinkers and slapped his shoulder; "but brave men are needed . . . if you want to have inexpensive salt!"

"What's your name?"

The man did not answer; but a neighbor said to Archambault de Bucquoy: "He's the captain."

"Well," he replied, "I am in the company of honest people. So, I may freely speak my mind! . . . You men are obviously the ones who smuggle salt . . . You do well."

"These are difficult times," said the captain.

"Well, my children! God rewards those who act for the good of all."

"He is a Huguenot," said some of the drinkers in a low voice.

"That's all over," resumed Archambault; "The old king is passing away, his old mistress is breathing her last breath . . . He has exhausted the genius and strength of France; so much so that these days, the most significant battles that take place are between Fénelon and Bossuet! The former maintains that 'the love of God and neighbor can be pure and disinterested.' The other, 'that charity, *qua* charity, must always be founded on the hope of eternal bliss.' A serious question, gentlemen!"

An immense burst of laughter from everywhere in the tavern welcomed this observation. Archambault lowered his head and ate his soup without saying another word.

The captain slapped his shoulder again: "What do you think of the religious ecstasies of Mme Guyon?"[10]

"Fénelon has said that she is holy, and Bossuet, who had attacked her at first, is not far from believing her at least inspired."

"Squire," said the captain, "I suspect you are familiar with some theology."

"I have renounced it . . . I have become a simple quietist, especially since I read the following, in a book entitled *Contempt for the World*: 'It is more profitable for a man to cultivate himself with the intention of doing God's will, than to cultivate the land, which is nothing to us.'"

"Yes," said the captain, "these days this maxim seems to be followed everywhere. Who cultivates anything anymore? . . . We fight, we hunt, we do a little salt smuggling on the side . . . ; goods are introduced from Germany and England, and prohibited books are sold. Those who have money speculate on the good of the farms; but cultivating the earth is a job for ignoramuses!"

Archambault understood the irony of this speech: "Gentlemen," he said, "I came here by chance, but I don't know why I feel like I am one of you . . . I am one of those sons of the ancient military families who fought against kings, and who are always suspected of rebellion. I do not belong to the Protestants, but I am for those who protest the absolute monarchy and the abuses it perpetuates . . . My family had made me a priest; I threw the frock to the stinging nettles and regained my freedom. By the way, how many of you are there?"

"Six thousand," said the captain.

"I have already served in the military for some time. I have even wanted to organize a regiment ever since I abandoned the religious life. But the expenses incurred by my uncle hampered me regarding certain resources I had expected from my family . . . M. de Louvois has caused us great sorrows!"[11]

"My dear lord," said the captain, "you seem to me like a brave man. All can still be repaired. Do you live in Paris?"

"I am on a journey to visit my aunt, the Dowager Countess of Bucquoy."

One of those present stood up and said to the others at his table, "This is the one we're looking for." The man was known to be a bailiff; he went to fetch an officer of the constabulary.

Archambault de Bucquoy, forewarned by his servant, was about to enter his carriage when this officer, accompanied by six gendarmes, announced that he was under arrest. The people of the tavern came out and tried to oppose this. He wanted to use his pistols, but the constable had received reinforcements.

The traveler was placed in his carriage between two officers; the gendarmes followed. They soon arrived at Sens. The provost judge questioned everyone with impartiality, then said to the traveler:

"You are the abbé de la Bourlie?"[12]

"No, your honor."

"You come from Cévennes?"

"No, your honor."

"You are a disturber of the peace?"

"No, your honor."

"I know that in the tavern you claimed to be from Bucquoy; but if you are the abbé de la Bourlie, also known as the Marquis de Guiscard, you can admit it now, you'll be treated the same: he has mingled with the affairs of the people of Cévennes; you have compromised yourself with the salt smugglers . . . Whoever you are, I am forced to have you taken to the prison of Sens."

When Archambault de Bucquoy arrived, he found himself in the company of some thirty salt smugglers, who were going to be tried by the presidial court of Sens;[13] the provost came from Melun for this case and regarded his arrest as imprudent and light. However, several charges already weighed on him.

He had been a soldier for five years, then he had become what they call a *man of the world* . . . and then, "with no concern for the Christian religion," he got involved with those "that some claim to be honest people," who were then called deists.

An adventure, the details of which are not well known, but which seems to have had something to do with love,[14] threw the comte de Bucquoy into a sort of devotion too exaggerated to have appeared solid. He joined the order at La Trappe and endeavored to observe that law of silence which is so difficult to maintain . . . One day, he grew weary of this discipline, resumed his officer's outfit, and left the Trappists without saying farewell.

On the way, he quarreled with and wounded a man who had insulted him. This unfortunate chance encounter led him to reenter the religious life. He thought he should divest himself of his regular clothes in favor of those of a poor man, and it was then that, despite the doctrines of St. Paul, he founded a community or seminary at Rouen, which he directed and called *Le Mort*. This name symbolized for him the forgetting of the pains of life and the desire for eternal rest.

Nevertheless, he was an eloquent speaker, which was perhaps a result of his having learned the discipline of silence, which he underwent with the Trappists: so much so that the Jesuits wanted him to join their order; but at the time he feared that doing so would "expose him too much to the world."

II. The For-l'Évêque[15]

Such were the stories that, if they had come to light while he was at Sens, would have been harmful to the abbé de Bucquoy's case if his identity had not already been confused with that of the abbé de la Bourlie, who was greatly compromised in the revolts of the Cévennes people.

What particularly aggravated the abbé de Bucquoy's position was that they found in his carriage "books which dealt only with revolutions, a mask, and a number of *little caps*,"[16] and, moreover, tablets that were all encrypted.

He gave a satisfactory explanation for these objects, and his affairs took a *fairly good turn* when, bored by his stay in the prison, he got it into his head to plan an escape, and sought to engage the help of the thirty salt smugglers who were with him in the prison at Sens, as well as certain individuals arrested for various minor infractions, who had been forced to enter the regiment of the Count de Tonnerre. At that time, there was a sort of *levy* employed along the highways to provide soldiers for the wars of Louis XIV.

These escape plans were not successful, and the abbé de Bucquoy was accused of having enticed the concierge's daughter to help him. At two o'clock after midnight, they entered his room and *very civilly* put chains on his hands and feet, then *stuffed* him into a *van* escorted by a dozen constables.

At Montereau he invited the constables to dine with him, and although they watched him closely, he managed to rid himself of certain compromising papers. These constables paid little attention to this detail; but *joking around* that evening at supper, they dared him to escape.

He was put to bed, with one foot chained to the bedpost. The constables bedded down in the entrance room. The abbé de Bucquoy, when he judged them to be almost fully asleep, managed to lift up the canopy and slip his chain over the top of the bedpost to which it had been attached. He was trying to reach the window when one of the guards, whose boot he had struck, awoke with a start and called for help.

He was bound more tightly and brought by coach from Sens to the Hôtel of the *Silver Key* in Paris, on rue de la Mortellerie. Not being one to hold a grudge, he again gave the constables something to eat.

He was closely guarded and brought by two constables to the *For-l'Évêque*, which was situated on the quai du Louvre.[17]

The abbé de Bucquoy remained a week at the For-l'Évêque without being interrogated. He was free to walk in the courtyard, where he reflected on his means of escape.

Upon entering the prison, he had noticed that the facade of the For-l'Évêque had a series of grated windows arranged in tiers up to the attic, and that the gratings naturally formed ladders, except for spaces formed by the gaps between the floors.

After his interrogation, in which he proved that he was not the abbé de la Bourlie but the abbé de Bucquoy, and though he had been imprudent in his conversations, "he was nevertheless in a position to rely on the support of some people with influence," so they lessened their guard on him and he was allowed to walk the corridors of the prison unsupervised.

Since he still possessed a few gold coins, the jailer allowed him to go breathe the air in the attic during the evenings, which he said was indispensable to his health. During the the day, he passed the time braiding ropes out of his linen bedsheets and towels, and eventually, under the pretext of daydreaming, he managed to have them forget about him one evening in the highest corridor of the prison.

Forcing the attic door and opening the mansard window was no easy affair. When he cast his eyes on the quay in the moonlight, he was frightened by the number of *branches* covered with spikes and wire entanglements, and other obstacles which, he said, "formed a most hideous spectacle . . . for it looked like a forest bristling with iron spears."

However, in the middle of the night, when he no longer heard the noise of the town or the passage of the patrols, the abbé de Bucquoy, using the ropes he had fashioned, succeeded, despite all the spikey points on the iron bars, in reaching the quay, which corresponded to a vast site that was then called the Valley of Misery.[18]

III. Other Plans of Escape

We have not given more details of the escape of the abbé de Bucquoy from For-l'Évêque for fear of interrupting the principal narrative. When he had imagined escaping through a small attic window, he realized that the door to the gables that he had to get through first was padlocked. He lacked the tools to deal with it, so instead he had the idea of burning down the door. The concierge had allowed him to cook in his room and had sold him eggs . . . charcoal, and a tinder box.

With these means he was able to set fire to the door, hoping to create an opening through which he could pass. But as the flames reached too high and threatened to burn the roof, he found a bucket of water to extinguish the flames, but the smoke nearly suffocated him and burned some of his clothes.

We have thought it good to mention these details to explain what happened to him after he had set foot on the quai du Louvre. His descent through the spiked iron gratings and the wire entanglements tore his already singed clothing. So much so that several merchants, who opened their shops at daybreak, noticed his disordered state. But no one breathed a word; only a few rascals followed him, *jeering*. A heavy rain came and scattered them.

The abbé, thanks to this downpour, which moreover kept the sentries in their boxes, took rue des Bourdonnais, reached the Saint-Eustache quarter, and finally came to la halle where he found a tavern that was open.

The state of his clothes, to which he had not yet paid much attention, led to some taunting; he didn't respond, paid his bill, and sought a safe haven. It would not have been good for him to go to his aunt, the Dowager Countess of Bucquoy; but he remembered one of his servant's relatives who lodged at the Enfant-Jésus near the Madelonnettes.

The abbé arrived at this woman's home early in the morning and told her that he had come from the provinces, and that while going through the forest of Bondy he was attacked by thieves who had put him in this state. She sheltered him and gave him something to eat. Toward evening he sensed that she was growing suspicious and felt he should find a safer place to stay . . . He had already met some of those fine minds in the Marais district who frequented the salon of Ninon de Lenclos, then nearly eighty years old, and who still had her share of lovers, despite what Mme de Sévigné's letters claim.[19] The great houses of the Marais were the last asylum of bourgeois and parliamentary opposition. Some of the nobles, the last remnant of the Fronde, were occasionally seen in these old homes, the deserted buildings of which still recalled the days when the councilors of the Grande Chambre of the Hôtel des Tournelles passed through the crowd in their red robes, greeted with applause like the Roman senators of the popular party.

There was a small establishment on the Île Saint Louis called the Café Laurent.[20] There the modern *Epicureans* got together, those who, under a cover of skepticism and gaiety, concealed the remnants of a muffled and patient opposition, just as Harmodius and Aristogiton hid their swords under roses.

And this was not insignificant, when these philosophical points were sharpened by the disciples of Descartes and Gassendi. This party was closely watched by the police; but thanks to the protection of such nobles as d'Orleans, Conti, and Vendome, and thanks also to their spirited and gallant manners, which charmed even the police and easily deceived them, the *neo-frondeurs* were generally left in peace; only the court thought to denigrate their name by calling them *the cabal.*[21]

Fontenelle, Jean-Baptiste Rousseau, Lafare, and Chaulieu had occasionally appeared at the Café Laurent.[22] Even Molière had appeared there at one time; Boileau was too old. The older regulars spoke of Molière, Chapelle, and those suppers at Auteuil, which had been at the center of those first meetings.

Most of the café regulars could still remember that beautiful Ninon, who lived on rue des Tournelles, and who died at the age of eighty-six, leaving a pension of two thousand pounds to the young Arouet, who had been introduced to her by the abbé de Chateauneuf, her last lover.

The abbé de Bucquoy had long had some friends among the members of the cabal. He waited for them to emerge; and, pretending to be a poor man, he addressed one of them, took him aside, and told of his predicament ... This man took him to his house, gave him fresh clothes, and put him in safe keeping, from where the abbé was able to warn his aunt and receive some needed help. From his hideout, he made several petitions to the Parliament, requesting that his case be dismissed. His aunt herself sent the petitions to the king. But no decision was made, even though the abbé de Bucquoy was willing to return to the prisons of the Concierge if he could be assured that his case would be dealt with fairly by the law.

The abbé de Bucquoy, seeing that all his solicitations were ineffective, decided to leave France. He took the road to Champagne, disguised as a merchant. Unfortunately, he arrived at La Fère right when a party of allies who had captured M. le Premier had been cut off in the vicinity of Ham and forced to disperse.[23] The abbé was considered one of the fugitives, and although he protested that he was a merchant, he was taken to the prison of La Fère as they awaited orders from Paris ... His sharp gaze, which had helped him find ways of escaping from For-l'Évêque, led him to discover a certain pile of stones that could be used to reach the ramparts of the prison.

Before entering his cell, he asked the concierge to get him something to drink, and in his absence, began climbing up onto the ramparts from which he jumped into a water-filled moat that surrounded the prison. He was swimming across it when the concierge's wife, who had seen him from a window, sounded the alarm in the prison, which led him to be seized again wh he was on the other side and brought back, exhausted and covered in mud. This time they took care to put him in the dungeon.

They had a difficult time rousing the poor abbé de Bucquoy, who was unconscious for a long time following his plunge into the water, and the words he pronounced on Providence, which had abandoned him in his design, made one think he was a Calvinist minister who had escaped from the Cévennes; so he was sent to Soissons, a prison that was more secure than that of La Fère.

Soissons is a very interesting city for those who visit it in liberty. The prison was then situated between the bishop's palace and the Abbey of St. Jean; on the northern side, it abutted the fortifications of the town.

The abbé de Bucquoy was placed in a tower with an Englishman who had been taken prisoner during the expedition to Ham. The turnkey who gave them their meals allowed the abbé, who was still pretending to be sick, as he had done at For-l'Eveque, to get a breath of fresh air in the evening atop the tower where he was imprisoned. This guard had a Burgundian accent, which the abbé recognized from having heard it near Sens.

One evening, this turnkey said to him: "Monsieur l'abbé, it will be a lovely evening to see the stars from the dungeon."

The abbé regarded him but the man's face showed only indifference.

There was a fog on the dungeon.

The abbé descended and found the door of the dungeon wall open. A sentry was pacing back and forth. He was withdrawing when the soldier, passing near him, said in a low voice: "Abbé . . . it's a lovely night . . . Why don't you go for a walk: who could possibly see you in this fog?"

The abbé de Bucquoy saw in this nothing but the kindness of a brave soldier putting aside his orders for a poor prisoner.

At the end of the parapet, he felt a rope, and as he took hold of it, he found it to be equipped with a strap and some knots.

The sentry had his back turned and the abbé, who was experienced in this kind of thing, descended, seated in the strap like a house painter.

He found himself in a ditch, which was dry and full of grass. The exterior wall was too high for him to think of going back up. But while looking for some crack in the wall that would enable the ascent, he found himself by a sewer opening, surrounded by gravel and freshly cut stones, which indicated it was being repaired.

A stranger suddenly looked out from the open sump and whispered:

"Is it you, abbé?"

"Why do you ask?"

"Because it is a lovely evening; and yet the weather's even better down below."

The abbé understood what was meant and began descending a ladder into this rather fetid shaft. The man led him silently to a spiral staircase and said to him: "Now go up until you encounter resistance . . . knock, and they will open up for you."

The abbé went up a good three hundred steps, then his head struck a trapdoor that seemed heavy, and which wouldn't give even against the pressure of his shoulders.

A moment later, he felt it being lifted, and someone addressed him with these words:

"Is that you, abbé?"

The abbé said: "It certainly is; but who are you? . . ."

The stranger replied with a *shush*, and the abbé found himself on a solid floor, but in the deepest night.

IV. Captain Roland

Feeling his way about, the abbé de Bucquoy encountered some tables that extended, but he still did not understand where he was. But the man who had spoken soon lit a dark lantern that illuminated the whole room. Silverware glittered in display cases, and a thousand jewels of gold and precious stones flowed over the tables . . . which were clearly counters . . . There was no question about it. They were in a goldsmith's shop.

The abbé thought for a moment, then said to himself, as he saw the face of the man holding the dark lantern: "It's clear this man is a thief; whatever his intention toward me, my conscience obliges me to awaken the merchant who is to be robbed."

Indeed, a second individual emerged from under the other counter and was rushing to grab as many precious jewels as he could. The abbé shouted, "Help! Help! A thief!" They covered his mouth and threatened him, but in vain. Because of the noise he made, a frightened man in his nightshirt came from the back, a candle in his hand.

"Monsieur, you are being robbed," cried the abbé.

"Stop, thief! Guard!" cried the merchant in turn.

"Will you shut up?" said the man holding the dark lantern, threatening him with a pistol.

The merchant stopped talking; but the abbé began to strike violently at the outer door, continuing to shout.

A quick marching could be heard outside. It was obviously a patrol; the two thieves hid themselves again under the counters. A noise of rifle butts could be heard at the door.

"Open, in the name of the king," said a rough voice.

The merchant went to fetch his keys and opened the door. The patrol entered.

"What's going on here?" asked the sergeant.

"I'm being robbed," cried the jeweler; "they're hiding under the counters . . ."

"Monsieur sergeant," said the abbé de Bucquoy, "people I don't know, and whose intentions I cannot understand, hatched a plot to have me escape from the Soissons prison. I realized that these people were criminals, and being myself an honest man, I cannot consent to make myself their accomplice . . . I know that the Bastille awaits me; arrest me . . . and take me back to prison."

The sergeant, who was a man of great stature, turned to his soldiers and said, "Begin by seizing the jeweler, and apply the pear of anguish to him so that he keeps quiet. Then do the same with the abbé . . . he's getting on my nerves."

The pear of anguish was a sort of gag whose center consisted of a leather pocket filled with bran, which could be chewed at leisure without allowing for any discernible articulation.

The abbé de Bucquoy, reduced to silence by the gag and the pear of anguish, did not understand why the goldsmith who was being robbed had received the same treatment. His surprise increased when he saw that the soldiers on the patrol were helping the two thieves ransack the shop. A few slang words exchanged between them finally explained the situation to him. They were a fake patrol.

The sergeant, of Herculean size, was recognized by the abbé as that same leader of the salt smugglers with whom he had already talked in Morchandgy, near Sens, and who was called the Captain.

The bags were filled when a great commotion, mingled with musket-shots, could be heard outside.—"Let's load everything up," said the captain.

The bundles were swiftly removed, and the abbé himself, who was tightly bound, was carried on the back of one of the thieves. They all went out through the door of the shop, which opened onto rue de l'Intendance.

The light of a great fire was visible near the Porte de Compiegne . . . There was fighting across the way. The small troop forced the door of the garden of the bishopric, and were met there, among the trees, with a great many other people, loaded with bundles, who entered the city as the others, exchanging signs of recognition, descended the rampart with the aid of ladders and then climbed the outer wall where it had deteriorated. It was then necessary to pass the river Aisne to reach the heights of Cuffy and the outer edge of the forest.

It has since been supposed that the people who had attempted to help the abbé de Bucquoy escape the prison at Soissons were a party of those same salt smugglers he had met in Burgundy, and whom he had offered to lead . . . A rich nobleman, as adventurous and powerful as he was, with his relations in France and abroad, was exactly what they needed.

As for Captain Roland, the former leader of the partisans of Cévennes, he had escaped through the Eastern countries after the surrender of Cavalier.[24] While the latter, who had obtained forgiveness at the price of the shedding of his brethren's blood, paraded at Versailles as the leader of a vanquished tribe, Roland, aided by the bands of salt smugglers—a mixture, as one knows, of Protestants, deserters, and peasants reduced to a state of poverty—tried to reach the North and take refuge there if necessary. Meanwhile, his followers engaged in salt smuggling, secretly aided by the population and the poorly paid soldiers of the royal troops.—They set fire to a house, and the whole town would come to watch. While that happened, the numerous and well-armed salt smugglers brought sacks of salt in through some badly guarded rampart. Then, if necessary, they would fight and flee to safety in the woods. Here is what we learned from other accounts of the time.

At the time when the Protestants left France without having time to settle their affairs, very expensive jewels had been deposited with this goldsmith, who dabbled in usury and loaned out various sums that were far inferior to the actual value of the collateral. Since then, people sent by the refugees had come to reclaim the jewels by repaying the amount that was due. The goldsmith found it very simple to discharge himself of any responsibility by denouncing these claimants to the Law. Hence the motive for the expedition in which Captain Roland participated.

The salt smugglers, who had tried to help the count abbé de Bucquoy escape, found the road blocked beyond the Aisne. A great number of them were captured, and were hanged or crushed on the wheel, according to their rank. History no longer speaks of Captain Roland—and the abbé de Bucquoy, now under more suspicion than ever, headed for the Bastille.

When he was removed from his seat, he had time to glance to the right and left, "either to the drawbridge or to the outer wall . . . but they didn't leave him time to give more thought to it," for he was quickly taken to the tower known as La Bretignière.

V. The Living Hell

There were eight towers to the Bastille, each of which had a name and consisted of six floors, each lighted by a single window. A grate on the interior and exterior of the walls revealed a single square room, defined by the thickness of the walls, at the far side of which one could breathe some fresh air.

The abbé had been placed in the tower of *La Bretignière*.

The others were called the tower of the *Bretaudière*, of the *Country*, of the *Pit*, of the *Treasure*, of the *Corner*, of *Liberty*. The eighth tower was called the tower of the *Chapel*. Prisoners were generally released only to die, unless they were taken downstairs into the darkness of those famous *dungeons*, the traces of which were found at the time of its demolition.

The abbé de Bucquoy remained several days in the lower rooms of the tower of La Bretigniere, which indicated that his affair seemed serious, since prisoners were usually better treated in the beginning. His first interrogation, over which d'Argenson presided,[25] removed any suspicion that he was an accomplice of the salt smugglers of Soissons. Moreover, he relied on his family's highly placed connections; such that Governor Bernaville paid him a visit and invited him to lunch, which was customary for prisoners of a certain rank when they arrived at the prison.[26]

The abbé de Bucquoy was placed in a higher chamber with better ventilation, and with other prisoners. This was at the tower of the Corner: a privileged place guarded by a turnkey named Ru, who was regarded as a very gentle man and attentive to the prisoners.

Upon entering the common room, the abbé was astonished, seeing the walls painted in fresco, to find there a picture of Christ strangely deformed.

Red horns had been drawn on his head and on his breast was a large inscription bearing the word *Mystery*.[27]

A charred inscription below read: "Great Babylon, mother of the indecencies and abominations of the earth."[28]

It is evident that this inscription had been formulated by a Protestant who had previously been a captive in that place. But no one since had erased it.

On the mantelpiece was an oval painting, representing the figure of Louis XIV. Another prisoner's hand had inscribed around his head the words *spit bucket* and one could barely distinguish the features of the sovereign, effaced by a thousand insults.

The abbé de Bucquoy said to the turnkey: "Ru, why are such degradations of respected images allowed here?" The turnkey burst into laughter and replied: "If it was necessary to chastise all the prisoners' *crimes*, we'd be *breaking and burning* all day long, so it's better for the intelligent prisoners to see how far fanatics could take exaggerated ideas."

The inhabitants of this tower enjoyed a relative freedom; at certain hours, they could walk in the governor's gardens, situated in one of the strongholds of the fortress, planted with linden trees, with bocce courts and tables where those with money could play cards and drink refreshments. Governor Bernaville had handed this concession establishment over to one of the prison cooks for a fee.

The abbé de Bucquoy, who at this time no longer posed any threat of escape, and who had caused powerful friends to act, found himself part of this favored circle. He had been given gold, which was always well received in prison, and after losing a few louis at cards, he became friendly with Corbé, the nephew of the previous governor (M. de Saint-Mars), who still retained a high position under Bernaville.[29]

It is relevant, perhaps, to describe the latter, according to the physical description given by one of the prisoners of the Bastille, later a refugee in Holland.[30]

"He has two green eyes sunk beneath two thick eyebrows: when he looks at you it's as if you were pierced by the gaze of a basilisk. His forehead is wrinkled like the bark of a tree on which some mufti had engraved the Alcoran . . . The yellow pallor of his complexion suggests years of worry and the pain of envy. His face is so emaciated that it's the very portrait of the anxiety and restlessness caused by Greed, and his creased cheeks are like purses for coins or a monkey's *buns* . . . The stubble of his beard is of a dark red chestnut color.

"When he was a *knight of the mandille* (lackey), he wore his hair flat and curled into rolls like candlesticks.[31] He gave up this affectation.

"Though he seldom speaks, he no doubt listens to himself talking, for his grin extends from ear to ear. However, his mouth opens only to pronounce monosyllabic rulings, executed punctually by the minions he has surrounded himself with . . ."

It was Bernaville who had actually been in the service of the maréchal de Bellefonds, and had worn the *mandille*, that is to say, the livery of the house; but after the maréchal's death he managed to gain the good graces of the widow,[32] whose children were still young, and it was through his highly placed protection that he obtained the management over the hunts at Vincennes, which was very profitable as it involved the stewardship of the hunting lodges and the eating establishments, where the people of the court spent a good deal of money. This explains the term of contempt used for him when he was called a *grease pit* . . . The prisoners said, behind his back, that he was the best example of a lackey who, by dint of climbing up behind the carriages, had dared to plant himself inside one . . . But we cannot comment before having appreciated the acts of this Bernaville, and it would be unjust to confine ourselves to the exaggerated accounts of prisoners.

As for the aforementioned Corbé, his supporter and accomplice, here's his portrait, traced with a hand that somewhat resembles the school of Cyrano:

"He had a little gray coat from Nimes, so threadbare that he scared thieves when swinging the noose under their noses; miserable blue trousers, all worn out, patched on the knees; a battered hat whose old faded black plume had almost lost all of its feathers; and a wig that had turned red from being so old. His downtrodden appearance, which gave him the look of someone below his station, caused him to resemble a lowly prison guard rather than an officer."

The abbé de Bucquoy, playing piquet with Renneville, one of the prisoners, under a trellised arbor, said to him: "But we are all doing very well here, and with the prospect of being released soon, who would want to try to escape?"

"That would be impossible, anyway" said Renneville . . . "But, as for judging the treatment that you receive in this castle, just wait a bit longer."

"Are you not doing well here?"

"Very well for the moment . . . I'm reminded of a honeymoon, which is where you still are . . ."

"How did you end up here?"

"Very simply; like many others . . . I don't know why."

"But you must have done something to enter the Bastille?"

"A madrigal."

"Read it to me . . . I will give you my honest opinion."

"What happened was that this madrigal was followed by another, *parodied* on the same rhymes, and which was wrongly attributed to me . . ."

"That's more serious."

At this moment, Corbé passed by with a smile and said, "Ah, you're still speaking of your madrigal, M. de Renneville . . . But it's nothing; it's charming."

"It's the reason they keep me here," said Renneville.

"And do you complain of the treatment?"

"How could I? When one is dealing with such honest people!"

Corbé was satisfied and went to another table with his implacable smile . . . He was offered refreshments that he always refused. From time to time, he glanced through the windows of the prison, where the vague forms of the female prisoners could be glimpsed, and he seemed to find that nothing was more charming than the interior of this state prison.

"And how," said the abbé de Bucquoy, to Renneville, while playing cards, "was this madrigal formed?"

"It was a traditional tribute. I had addressed it to the Marquis de Torcy, so that he might show it to the king.[33] It made allusion to the combined power of Spain and France fighting the allies . . . and at the same time it referred to the principles of piquet."

Renneville proceeded to recite his madrigal, which ended with the following words, addressed to the *allies* of the North:

In fighting against Spain and France,
You won't win any tricks . . . A Fourteenth and Fifth in hand!

This referred to Philip V (fifth) and Louis XIV.

"It seems quite innocent! . . ." said the abbé de Bucquoy.

"Of course," replied Renneville, "this fall in octave and alexandrine was admired by everyone. But some malicious people have parodied these verses in favor of the enemies, and here is their version:

> *Let's do a repique . . .*[34] *and outsmart Spain and France*
> *Who'll have no choice but to fold . . . A Fourteenth and Fifth in hand.*

"Now, Monsieur le Comte, how could I possibly have written this parody of my own madrigal . . . while still not keeping the measure of the penultimate verse?"

"That seems unlikely to me," said the abbé, "I'm sure of it, since I'm a poet as well."

"Well, it was enough evidence for M. de Torcy to send me to the Bastille. Yet I was supported by M. de Chamillard, to whom I have dedicated my books, and who continues to offer me his services."

"What!" said the abbé, pensively, "can a madrigal really get a man thrown into the Bastille?"

"A madrigal? . . . A couplet alone can open its doors. We have here a young man . . . whose hair is beginning to turn white, it's true . . . who, for a Latin couplet, was retained for a long time in the islands of *Sainte-Marguerite*; then, when M. de Saint-Mars, who had put both Fouquet and Lauzun in prison, was appointed governor here, he brought him along for a change of scenery. This young man, or, if you like, this man, had been one of the best pupils of the Jesuits."

"And they didn't support him?"

"Here's what happened. The Jesuits had inscribed a Latin couplet on their headquarters in Paris, in honor of Christ. Wanting later to secure the support of the court against the attacks of certain powerful gentlemen of the robe, or *cabalists*, they resolved to stage a great tragedy with choruses, in the style of those formerly given at Saint-Cyr. The King and Mme de Maintenon were sympathetic to their invitation. Everything in this celebration was designed to remind them of their youth. In the absence of young girls, which the house could not supply, the younger male students were dressed as women, and the choirs and ballets were executed by individuals from the Opera. The success was such that the king, dazzled and charmed, allowed the reverend fathers to inscribe his name on the door of their headquarters. It bore the following inscription: *Collegium claro montanum societatis Jesu*;[35] these words were replaced by the following: *Collegum Ludovici magni*.[36]—The young man of whom we are speaking inscribed on the wall a couplet in which he pointed out that the name of Jesus had been replaced by that of Louis the Great . . . It is this crime for which he is still paying here.

"But," said the abbé de Bucquoy, "it's impossible for us to complain much of the rigors of this state prison. I suffered a little in the dungeon . . . but now, under this arbor, enjoying the warmth of a full-bodied Burgundy wine, I feel inclined to be patient."

"I have been patient for four years," said Renneville; "and if I told you what had happened to me . . ."

"I'm interested in knowing what they can do to a man guilty of a madrigal."

"You wouldn't hear any complaints from me if I had not left my wife in Holland . . . But let's drop it. I was arrested at Versailles and taken to Paris. As I passed the Samaritane, I pulled out my watch, and observed by comparing it to the sundial at the fountain that it was eight o'clock in the morning. The officer said to me: your watch works well. This man was not lacking in a certain education: 'It's unfortunate,' said he, 'that I've been forced to arrest you, which is entirely against my inclination . . . But I had to carry out my job's responsabilities before becoming what I am now, which is to say, an equerry of the Duchesse de Lude.[37] My name is *De Bourbon* . . . My employment as officer ceases from today, and henceforth, refer to me should you need anything . . .' This officer seemed to me an honest man, and as we were passing the Pont Neuf, I offered him something to drink, as well as the three *hacquetons* accompaning us, who wore on their coat of arms the representation of a body covered with spikes with this motto: *monstrorum terror*.[38] I could not help saying, as I drank with them: 'You are the terror . . . and I am the monster!' They laughed and we all arrived at the Bastille in good humor.

"The governor received me in a room hung in yellow damask with fairly clean silver fringes . . . He gave me his hand and invited me to lunch

. . . His hand was cold, which seemed to me a bad sign . . . His nephew, Corbé, entered the room and flitted about, telling me of his exploits in Holland . . . and of the success he achieved afterward, in the bull rings of Madrid, where the ladies, admiring his bravery, threw him eggs filled with perfume. When lunch was finished, the governor said to me: 'Make use of me as you please,' and he added to his nephew: 'We must take our new guest to the pavilion of the princes.'"

"The governor held you in high esteem . . ." sighed the abbé de Bucquoy.

"You can see the pavilion of the princes from here . . . It's on the ground floor. The windows are furnished with green shutters. Except there are five doors to pass through to get to the room. I found it sad, although there was a straw mattress on the bed, and the sleeping alcove was furnished with a curtain of crisp brocade; moreover, three armchairs upholstered in tailor's canvas."

"I don't have it so well here as you did!" said the abbé de Bucquoy.

"I was only worried over not having towels and sheets, and then I saw the turnkey, Ru, with linen, blankets, vases, candlesticks, and all that was necessary for me to establish myself comfortably in this pavilion.

"Evening had come. I was sent two more boys from the prison canteen, led by Corbé, who brought me *dinner*.

"It consisted of green pea soup with lettuce, simmered well, with a side of chicken, a slice of beef, a godiveau[39] and sheep's tongue . . . For dessert: a biscuit and pippin apples . . . Wine from Burgundy."

"I would certainly be satisfied with that," said the abbé.

"Corbé saluted me and said, 'Are you paying for your food, or will you be indebted to the king?'

"I replied that I would pay.

"Not being very hungry after the breakfast which the governor had offered me, I had asked Corbé to sit down and help me finish the dish; but he replied that he was not hungry and would not even accept a glass of the Burgundy wine."

"It's his custom!" said the abbé de Bucquoy.

A bell warned the prisoners that they had to return to their rooms.

"Do you know," said Renneville, returning back from the garden with the abbé de Bucquoy, "that this Corbé is a *womanizer*?"

"What? That monster!"

"A seducer . . . a little pushy toward the lady prisoners only . . . Yesterday we had a very unpleasant scene on the staircase. A loud noise was heard in the dungeons, at the base of the tower. This noise finally subsided . . .

"We saw Ru, the turnkey, come up with his breeches covered in blood. He told us, 'I just saved that poor Irish woman, whom M. Corbé wanted to please . . .' He had sent her to the dungeon because she refused to receive his visits; and as she again refused to receive him, he decided to place her on a lower floor.

"She resisted when they tried to take her down, and the people who carried her dragged her so awkwardly that her head struck the stairs . . . I was stained with her blood. They took her from her bed half-naked . . . And Corbé, who directed this expedition, tortured her without mercy."

"Is she dead?" said the abbé de Bucquoy.

"She strangled herself that night."

VI. The Tower of the Corner

The third floor of the tower of the Corner gathered quite an elite group. It was there that the *governor's favorites* were housed. There was, besides Renneville and the abbé, a German gentleman named Baron de Peken, arrested for having said that "the king saw only through Mme Maintenon's glasses"; then a man named Falourdet, compromised in a matter relating to false titles of nobility;[40] then a former soldier named Jacob le Berthon, accused of singing racy songs in which the name of the king's mistress was not respected.[41]

Renneville pitied him a great deal for being detained over such a minor offense and said that Maintenon ought to have followed the example of Queen Catherine de Medici who, opening her window one day in the Louvre palace, saw, on the banks of the Seine, soldiers roasting a goose and passing the time by singing a song directed against herself. She simply cried out to them, "Why do you speak ill of poor Queen Catherine, who treats you so well? It is thanks to her money that you're roasting that goose!" The king of Navarre, who was at that moment standing next to her, wanted to go down to chastise the rascals, and she said to him: "Stay, this it too far beneath us."[42]

There was also an Italian abbé named Papasaredo.[43]

When supper was brought, Corbé, following custom, accompanied the staff and asked if anyone had any reason for complaint. "I must complain," exclaimed the abbé Papasaredo, "that there are already too many people here, and the number has grown with the addition of a second abbé . . . I would much prefer women, and there is no lack of them available here."

"It's entirely against the regulations," said Corbé.

"Come, my little Corbé, put me in a cell with a female prisoner . . ."

Corbé shrugged his shoulders.

"Come, give me Marton, Fleury, Bondy, or Dubois, just one of your leftovers . . . Why not even that pretty Marguerite Filandrier, the wig-seller in the cloister of Sainte-Opportune, whom we can hear singing all day long?"[44]

"Is that how an abbé should talk?" said Corbé . . . "I appeal to the decency of these gentlemen! As for the Filandrier girl, we put her in the dungeon for having exchanged words with an officer of the watch."

"Oh!" said the abbé Papasaredo, "there's also another reason . . . You've punished her for having spoken to that officer . . . You are cruel in your jealousies, Corbé!"

"That's not true," said Corbé, flattered by the remark. "This girl has a mania for raising birds and training them. She had been allowed to keep some sparrows. Her window overlooks the garden. One of her birds escapes and is grabbed by a cat. She then cries to the officer, 'Oh, save my bird, it's the prettiest one, the one who dances the minuet!' The officer had a weakness for the girl and ran after the cat and couldn't even save the bird; now he's under arrest and she's in the dungeon, and that's that."

Corbé turned on his heels and left, escaping the sardonic invectives of the Italian abbé. Moreover, he was in an extremely good mood because one of the prisoners had bribed him with a sapphire ring, and the abbé de Bucquoy, dissatisfied with his usual dinner, had decided to get his meals from outside at his own expense. M. de Falourdet commented that he had seen things improve when he decided to pay for his own food. However, it was expensive and the service mediocre; he would ask for champagne at a livre and would get in return wine at six sous and the same thing went for the rest.

He had therefore said to Corbé: "I'm willing to pay double, but I want the best." Corbé had replied: "You're right, the suppliers are deceiving us . . . I'll take care of the wines and victuals myself."

After that, everything was first rate and of good quality.

The conversation grew animated after Corbé left; the Baron de Peken alone remained pensive before his plate, with a concentrated anger that eventually fell on Ru, the turnkey.

"Damn it!" said the baron, "why do I have only a half-bottle in front of me, while the *newcomer* has a whole bottle?"

"Because," said Ru, "you are five livres, whereas M. le comte de Bucquoy has a pistole."

"What on earth . . . Can't one get an ordinary bottle with five livres?" exclaimed the baron. "Bring back that rotten *grease pit* Corbé and ask him whether an honest man can be content with half a bottle of lousy wine! If I see this bottle again, I'll break it over your head!"

"Monsieur le baron," said Ru, "calm down, and be careful what you wish for; M. Corbé would immediately throw you in the dungeon . . . It's in his interest, because the food of a prisoner in a dungeon is only a sou a day, and accommodation amounts to nothing because it's the king who provides it . . . As for the profit on the food, a third enters M. Corbé's pocket, and the rest goes into that of M. Bernaville!"

Ru, as can be seen, was a diplomatic man, and the prisoners only reproached him for making certain food items disappear, notably the little pâtes of which he was fond.—He had the service for himself, which ought to have made him more moderate in this respect.

Renneville and the abbé de Bucquoy declared that they drank very little wine, and poured the rest for the Baron de Peken, who ended up eating his dinner in peace. Renneville then recounted the troubles he had suffered when put in isolation after an outburst of just the same kind, and the brilliant invention he had for communicating with prisoners above and below him.

It was a simple alphabet he had created, which consisted of striking a wall with the rod of a chair, with a single blow for *a*, two blows for *b*, and so on. His neighbors finally caught on and responded in the same way, only it took a while. Here is how, for example, the word *Monsieur* was rendered:

M (13 blows), *o* (15), *n* (14), *s* (19), *i* (9), *e* (5), *u* (21), *r* (18).

In this way he learned the names of all his companions in the same tower, with the exception of that of an abbé who had never wished to make himself known.

In prison, one speaks only of prison, or of the means of overcoming one's troubles. De Falourdet recounted how he had managed to communicate with a friend in the same prison in a manner no less ingenious than that of the alphabet invented by Renneville. He had been lodged in one of those upper chambers of the towers called *calottes*, and which had the disadvantage of being as hot in summer as they were cold in winter. And yet there was a beautiful view. Before being separated from his friend, M. de la Baldonnière (detained at the Bastille for having found the secret of making gold and not wanting to communicate it to the ministers), he had learned that the latter was housed on the ground floor of the same tower, overlooking the small garden in one of the bastions. He made a writing utensil with pigeon bones, ink with some diluted soot, and he wrote letters which he threw out of his window and which fell to the bottom of the tower with the aid of a small stone's weight.

Baldonnière, for his part, trained one of the governor's dogs who was often roaming in the garden to bring back to him, through the bars of his window, any papers that might be found there. By initially throwing her the remains of his breakfast, he ended up training the animal well . . . Then he sent the dog to look for the little packages Falourdet had sent him, which she faithfully brought back to him. He was eventually found out. The correspondence of the two friends was seized, and they received a certain number of blows from a bullwhip, administered by *soldiers*. Falourdet, as the guiltier of the two, was then put in a dungeon, where there was a dead man they didn't come to get until the third day. Later, having received some money, he was able to regain the good graces of the governor.

When he was still in the *calotte*, he had also found a way to correspond with his wife, who had rented a room in the first houses of the Faubourg

Saint-Antoine. He wrote very large letters on a board with coal, which he set behind his window; then, by erasing the letters and forming others, he managed to convey whole sentences outside.

Someone else told him that they had found an even better system by training pigeons, caught at the tops of the towers, and attaching letters under their wings, which they would then carry to houses outside.

Such were the principal conversations among the prisoners of that tower of the Corner, where Marie de Mancini, the niece of Mazarin, had formerly dwelled—who, as we know, created the *Academy of Humorists*—and later the famous Mme Guyon, who simply passed through the Bastille, but whose confessor was still living there at the age of eighty, at the same time as the abbé of Bucquoy, our hero, who, unlike his companions, took scant interest in seeking a means of correspondence.[45] Not seeing his affairs take a turn for the better, he was even thinking openly of an escape. When he had sufficiently studied his plans, he probed his neighbors, who at first thought it was impossible; but the ingenious spirit of the abbé gradually solved all the difficulties. Falourdet declared that the abbé's proposal seemed like it could work, but that money was needed to lull the surveillance of Ru and Corbé.

Whereupon the abbé de Bucquoy pulled out some gold and precious stones from who knows where, and which gave the impression that the enterprise was becoming a reality. It was decided that they could make ropes by ripping up the sheets and use the metal sawhorses supporting the beds and a few nails from the fireplace to make iron hooks.

The work was progressing when Corbé suddenly entered with soldiers and declared that he knew everything. One of the prisoners had betrayed his companions . . . It was the Italian abbé Papasaredo. He had hoped to obtain his pardon by means of this treachery; he only obtained the advantage of being treated better for a while.

All the others were thrown in a dungeon; the abbé de Bucquoy was taken to the lowest dungeon of all.

VII. Other Escape Plans

Needless to say, the abbé comte de Bucquoy took little pleasure in his dungeon. After a few days of penance, he took recourse to something which had already served him well on other occasions: pretending that he was sick. The turnkey who served him was alarmed at his condition, which was divided between a sort of feverish exaltation and a dejection which then overtook him and made him resemble a dead man; he even mimicked this situation to such a degree that the physicians of the Bastille were barely able to detect any signs of life in him, and declared that his malady was degenerating into paralysis. After this consultation, he pretended that half of his body was so and moved only on one side.

Corbé came to see him and said: "We'll take you somewhere else. But you see now what your escape plans have brought about."

"Escape!" cried the abbé. "But who could escape from the Bastille? Has it ever happened?"

"Never! Hugues Aubriot, who had worked on the construction of this dungeon, and was later imprisoned in it, only emerged after a revolution brought on by the Maillotines. He is the only one to have left against the will of the government."[46]

"My God!" said the abbé, "apart from this illness that plagues me, I would have no reason to complain of anything . . . save for the toads which leave their slime on my face when they pass over me as I sleep."

"You see what is gained by rebellion."

"On the other hand, I take some consolation in training the rats to whom I give the bread from the king, which my illness prevents me from eating . . . You will see how intelligent they are."

And he called out: "Moricaud?"

A rat emerged from a crack in the stone wall and presented itself by the abbé's bed . . .

Corbé could not help laughing and said:

"We'll put you in a more suitable place."

"I should like to be with the baron de Peken again," said the abbé. "I had undertaken to convert this Lutheran, and as my mind has now turned to holy things because of this illness with which God has struck me, I would be happy to accomplish this work."

Corbé gave the orders and the abbé was transported to a room on the third floor in the tower of La Bretaudière, where the Baron de Peken had been with an Irishman for a few days.

The abbé continued to act like a paralytic, even in front of his companions, for what had happened at the tower of the Corner had showed him the danger of too much frankness. The German didn't get along with the Irishman. It didn't take much for him to annoy the abbé as well. But the Baron de Peken, who was even more irritable, insulted the Irishman in such a way that it was resolved a duel should take place.

A pair of scissors was separated, the two parts of which were sharpened and made into little swords, and the duel began according to the rules. The abbé de Bucquoy, who at first believed it all a joke, saw the matter getting heated and the blood flow, and began pounding on the door, which was the only way of getting the turnkey to come.

When questioned about this affair, the abbé blamed the Irishman, who was taken elsewhere, and so he remained alone with the baron. Then he confided to him a plan of escape, better conceived than the other, and which consisted in piercing a wall that communicated with a rather foul locale, but from which, through a long opening, one descended naturally to the sewers of rue Saint-Antoine.

They both began to work diligently, and the wall was already entirely pierced . . . Unfortunately, the Baron de Peken was boastful and indiscreet. He had found a way to communicate through the holes made in the chimney with prisoners in the room above. The two recluses took turns climbing into the chimney and conversing at a fair distance with these unknown friends.

As the baron chatted, he told them he hoped to escape with his friend, and either from jealousy or from a desire to be pardoned, one, someone named Joyeuse, son of a magistrate of Cologne who was housed in that chamber, denounced the project to Corbé, who informed the governor.[47]

Bernaville summoned the abbé de Bucquoy, who was carried in as a paralytic, and who launched into a spirited defense of his position. He claimed that the Baron de Peken, having drunk a few too many glasses of wine, took it into his head to tell some ridiculous tales to this Joyeuse, who was really nothing but a *half-wit*, and that it would be unfortunate for such a foolish denunciation to separate him from the baron, whose conversion had made much progress.

The baron spoke in the same way, and Joyeuse's claims were disregarded. Moreover, the two friends, warned in time by the turnkey, who had been given enough money by the abbé to become an ally, had been able to repair the damage made to the wall in time so that nothing was noticed.

The abbé de Bucquoy was put into another cell which was part of the tower of *Liberty*. He continued to work on converting the Lutheran Baron de Peken, and yet he did not abandon his plans to escape.

The turnkey had mercilessly mocked him by telling him the ease with which a certain Du Puits had escaped from Vincennes by using skeleton keys.

This Du Puits had been secretary to M. de Chamillard, and he was called the *golden quill* on account of his excellent handwriting. He was just as good at counterfeiting the door keys, which he melted and forged with the tin plates on which his meals were served.

With the skeleton keys he thus manufactured, this Du Puits left his room at night and went to visit some prisoners, and even female prisoners, several of whom welcomed him with as much astonishment as courtesy.

He finally escaped from Vincennes and took refuge at Lyons with a man named Pigeon, his cellmate. "Never," Renneville later said in his memoirs, "never had Doctor Faust been deemed as a great magician as this Du Puits."

He was, however, arrested again at Lyons, where, to procure money, he had forged a number of treasury bonds issued in the king's name.

At the Bastille, Du Puits was less happy than at Vincennes. He had managed to descend into a ditch where they mowed weeds all day long, and he had noted that these workers retired in the evening through an underground gate, which they left open. So he went in that direction; but it was still daylight, and a sentry fired at him with his arquebus, after which he was taken back to the Bastille where, after a long illness, he was no longer seen to walk without a *bracket* under his arm.

The end of this story was not reassuring. Yet the abbé de Bucquoy did not abandon his plans. He had taken care to strip the bottles served to him of their wicker casings, claiming before the turnkey that he'd use them to light the fire in the morning. He spent his day weaving this wicker into a rope with the thread he extracted from his bedsheets, his napkins, and the canvas cover of his mattresses, taking care to sew them back up together so that nothing would be suspected.

The Baron de Peken, for his part, was working to make tools with pieces of iron taken here and there from the remnants of pots and nails. All this scrap was sharpened, put in the fire, then placed into the sandstone pitchers that held water.

The ropes of wicker and thread were very cumbersome. The abbé de Bucquoy lifted some tiles in the room and managed to secure a hiding place to hide these materials. One day, by digging too much, he caused the floor to crack because the joists were so rotted, and he plunged, along with the Baron de Peken, through the hole in the ceiling onto the floor in the cell below, which was inhabited by a Jesuit . . . whose mind had already been disturbed, and this adventure ended up driving him mad.

The abbé de Bucquoy and his companion had received only slight contusions. The Jesuit cried out, "Help, help!" so loudly that the abbé engaged him in Latin, telling him to be still, promising to include him in their escape plans. The Jesuit, feeble in mind as he was, believed that they were going to kill him and shouted even louder.

The turnkeys arrived, and the abbé de Bucquoy and the baron, each in turn, complained loudly about their fall, which had been caused by the weak ceiling.

They were returned to their room, and they were able to remove the rope ladders hidden under the tiles, along with the ironwork needed for their escape; except one day they saw a carpenter arrive who was to make a window in the door . . . The abbé asked the reason for this work and was told that the window was to be used to feed the mad Jesuit they would be housing there. As for them, they were to be moved to a much nicer room . . . This was not what the two friends wanted, given that they had already succeeded in sawing their iron bars, and whose preparations were soon bound for success.

The abbé asked to see the governor and told him that he liked his room, and that furthermore, if he were to be separated from the Baron de Peken, the latter's conversion would become impossible, since he only had confidence in his friendly exhortations . . . The governor was inflexible; and the abbé, on his return, warned the German of what had taken place.

He then advised the baron to feign great melancholy over leaving the cell, and to make as if he might kill himself. The baron played the part so well that instead of drawing a little blood, he cut open the veins in his arm, so that the abbé, alarmed at seeing so much blood, called for help. The sentries alerted their superiors, and the governor himself came, showing great pity for the baron's suffering.

But the chief reason for this conduct was that for some time already he had received the order to set the baron free . . . But to profit further from his prison fees, he had extended his captivity as much as possible.

After this adventure, the abbé de Bucquoy was again moved, not to a dungeon, but to one of the top floors of the towers they called *calottes*. Previous prisoners had taken it upon themselves to draw frightening figures on the walls of this cell, along with sentences from the Bible "proper for preparing for death."

Other prisoners, more political than religious, had inscribed this epigram on the wall:

Under Fouquet,[48] *now sadly missed,*
A Golden Age did once exist;
And then the Age of Silver came,
Brought on by Colbert;[49] *and grief came to pass:*
Vapid Pelletier,[50] *his conduct to blame,*
Followed it with the Age of Brass;
And France, today poor and hungry en masse,
An Iron Age must now lay claim
With the swinish Pontchartrain![51]

Another more fearless individual had carved these four verses on the wall:

Louis must take comfort for losing through the war
The Netherlands, Milan, Naples, Sicily, Spain;
He has La Maintenon: with her, loss becomes gain;
A king could not want more!

The abbé took no pleasure in this octagonal cell and its ogival vaults, in which he was alone. They offered to give him the company of a Capuchin named Brandenburg;[52] but after having accepted, he complained of the monk taking on great airs and wanting to be treated like a prince. He asked the governor to put him with some good Protestant boy he could convert. He even spoke of a man named Grandville, of whom the prisoners in the previous cell had already spoken to him.

He was an enterprising man, this Grandville, and far less interested in conversion than in developing ideas of escape; he and the abbé de Bucquoy got along well.

VIII. Final Attempts

The abbé and Grandville worked on breaking through the wall and were succeeding in demolishing an old window blocked by the masonry, when two new guests suddenly arrived, one of whom was the chevalier de Soulanges, a trustworthy man whom the abbé de Bucquoy had known previously.[53] They embraced each other. As for the fourth, he was a sort of lunatic named Gringalet, who was suspected of being an informer, for there was always one in the large cells.[54] They managed to make his life so miserable that he asked to be removed and was replaced by someone else.

The four prisoners, recognizing themselves as men of honor and true brothers, held council on the means of escape, and the plan proposed by the abbé de Bucquoy was unanimously approved from the outset.

It was simply a matter of filing the bars of the window and descending at night into a ditch by using cords of thread and wicker. The abbé had managed to hold on to some of those he had woven with the Baron de Peken, and taught his companions how to make more, as well as how to forge the spikes.

As for the question of filing the bars, he revealed a small file he had managed to hold on to, and which was sufficient for all they had to do.

His previous attempts had made him wary, though, and he still wanted each of them to swear an oath not to betray the others. He wrote out passages from the Gospel with a pen of straw and diluted soot and had his companions make a solemn vow.

But a difficulty arose regarding the location from which they would scale the outer wall, once they were in the ditch.

The abbé favored climbing up the outer wall by the Saint-Antoine quarter; the others were for "passing by the half-moon into the moat that leads out of the gate."

Opinions were so divided that they had to appoint someone to preside . . . They finally agreed on this one important point: once in the ditch, it would be every man for himself.

It was on the 5th of May, at two o'clock in the morning, that the escape took place.

To support the rope, a spike had to emerge sufficiently far enough out from the window to provide the necessary clearance. They had constructed a makeshift sundial, held by a rod outside the window to get the guards accustomed to seeing the apparatus sticking out. It was still necessary to dye the ropes black with soot and tie them to the spike emerging from the window. As they risked being seen when they passed the room below, they took the precaution of hanging out a large blanket under the pretext of drying it.

The abbé de Bucquoy went down first. It was agreed that he should watch the march of the sentries and alert his comrades by means of the rope, which he would tug to indicate if the moment was dangerous or not. He stayed hiding in the tall grass for over two hours without seeing anyone descend.

The problem was that Grandville, because of his large frame, could not pass through the opening between the bars, which they were trying in vain to enlarge.

Two of the prisoners eventually descended and informed the abbé de Bucquoy that Grandville had sacrificed himself in the interest of all, saying: "It was better for just one to perish."

The abbé was only worried about the sentry; he offered to go and grab him, as his marching back and forth greatly interfered with the plan of climbing over the outer wall by rue Saint-Antoine. His friends were not in agreement and wished to escape via a different side by taking advantage of the tall grass to hide themselves from the gaze of the sentry.

The abbé, who wasn't one to give in so easily, remained on his own in the same spot and waited until the sentry was far away, and began to climb the wall, beyond which he came upon another moat. This moat was also crossed, and he found himself on the other side atop a drainpipe that gave onto rue Saint-Antoine. He had only to climb down the roof of a building that housed butcher stalls.

As he was about to come down the drainpipe, he wished to find out what happened to his comrades; but he heard a gunshot, which made him think that they had tried unsuccessfully to disarm the sentry.

When the abbé de Bucquoy leapt off the drainpipe, he split his arm on the hook of a stall. But he ignored this inconvenience and quickly went down rue Saint-Antoine, then reached rue des Tournelles, crossed Paris, and came to the porte de la Conférence where one of his friends from the Café Laurent lived. The latter hid his friend for a few days. Then he avoided the mistake of remaining in Paris and managed, in disguise, to gain entry into Switzerland through Burgundy. There is no record to show whether he was arrested there again for giving speeches to salt smugglers.

The abbé's escape had very serious consequences for the prisoners who had remained at the Bastille. Until then it was a popular saying that no one could escape that fortress . . . Bernaville was so disturbed by this adventure that he cut down all the trees in the garden and in the streets just beyond the ramparts. Then, informed by Corbé of the means employed by certain prisoners to communicate with the outside world, he had all the pigeons and ravens that had nested at the tops of the towers killed, along with the sparrows and robins that had made the prisoner's time easier to bear.

Corbé was suspected of being lax in his surveillance because of the gifts he had received from the abbé de Bucquoy. Moreover, his conduct with the prisoners had already made him the subject of reproach.

He had fallen very much in love with the wife of an Irishman named Odricot, who was imprisoned in the Bastille without her husband even knowing she was so close by.[55] Corbé and Giraut (the chaplain) also courted this lady, who ended up getting pregnant . . . and it was impossible to know whose child it was.[56]

Nonetheless, Corbé persuaded himself that he was the father, and through his connections managed to obtain a pardon for the lady Odricot, who was very beautiful, although slightly red-headed. Corbé was very miserly, so much so that he was blamed for the death of a Protestant minister named Cardel, whom he had let starve to death just so he could inherit some pieces of silver the poor man possessed.[57] But the lady Odricot knew how to dominate him to the point that he ruined himself by giving her a carriage, servants, and all the trappings of great wealth. Well-founded complaints finally resulted in his dismissal, and everything would suggest that he came to an unhappy end.

Bernaville, so greedy for gold that it was calculated he made six hundred thousand francs a year off his prisoners, was replaced by Delaunay around the time of the death of Louis XIV.[58] The last prisoner of note he had received was the young Fronsac, duke of Richelieu, who was one day discovered hiding under the bed of the Duchess of Burgundy, the wife of the heir to the crown . . .[59] Gossips of the time remarked that it was sad that the laurels of the Duke of Burgundy had not saved him from such an affront.[60] He died a short time afterward, leaving to Fénelon the regret of having wasted many fine thoughts and phrases in instructing his pupil in the duties of royalty.

IX. Conclusion

We have shown the abbé de Bucquoy escaping from the Bastille, which was not easy; it would now be tedious to recount his travels in the German-speaking lands, where he made his way after leaving Switzerland. The comte du Luc, to whom J.-B. Rousseau addressed a famous ode, was the ambassador of France there, and he endeavored to make peace with the court. But he failed, as did the abbé's aunt, the Dowager Countess of Bucquoy, who addressed to the king a letter beginning thus:

> The widow of the Count de Bucquoy very humbly reminds Your Majesty that the honorable abbé de Bucquoy, the nephew of my husband, the count, had the misfortune of being arrested near Sens, mistakenly taken for the abbé de la Bourlie, an alleged agent of M. de Marlborough sent to encourage the *salt smugglers* throughout Burgundy and Champagne and to endeavor to initiate some sort of rebellion there.

The countess then pointed to the false claims of this arrest and portrayed the sufferings endured by such a faithful subject as the count abbé de

Bucquoy, who had been confused with the rebels and had first been held in the prison of Soissons, with the men guilty of kidnapping M. de Beringhen.*

The countess then endeavored to show the courage of her nephew in escaping from the Bastille, *without any splendor*, on 5 May, at the cost of much sweat and labor . . . Yet once arrived in a foreign country, he asks that his innocence be recognized, protesting that he is one of the most zealous subjects of the king, "one of those subjects *à la Fénelon*, who go straight to the truth, a truth in which the king discovers that glory that owes its splendor to virtue . . ."

The countess also noted "that it would be good if her nephew's prison records be expunged at *Sens, Soissons, the For-l'Evêque, and the Bastille*, and that he be restored all his rights, honors, privileges, and dignities, and that the six hundred pistols confiscated from him through his various imprisonments be given back to him." She also pointed out that her nephew's valet and maid, Fournier and Louise Deputs, made off with the two thousand écus he possessed at the time of his escape.

The Dowager Countess of Bucquoy concludes by asking for an honorable employment for her nephew, whether in the armies of the king or in the church, he himself being open to any *order* that would have him, disposed, as he is, "to accept his position, provided he is able, in such a role, to contribute to the common good."

The date is 22 July 1709.

There was no response.

When in Switzerland, it is very easy to travel down the Rhine, either by ordinary boat or timber raft, which often carry entire villages on their planks of pine. The many canals that emerge from the branches of the Rhine further facilitate access to the Netherlands.

We do not know how the abbé de Bucquoy traveled from Switzerland to Holland, but it is certain that he was well received by the *grand pensionary Heinsius*, who, as a philosopher, welcomed him with open arms.[61]

The abbé de Bucquoy had already drawn up the plan of a republic that would apply to France, which showed ways to eliminate the monarchy! He

* Michaud's *Biographie universelle* refers to a M. le Premier. This semi-German book, published in Frankfurt, which contains the original history of the abbé de Bucquoy, provides us with this other name.

had titled it: *Anti-Machiavellism, or Metaphysical Reflections on Authority in General and on Arbitrary Power in Particular*.

"It may be said," he observed in his *Memoirs*, "that a republic is but a temporary reform of the abuse which the passage of time creates in the government of the people."

The abbé de Bucquoy, probably in a spirit of fairness, conceded that the monarchy also sometimes serves as a violent remedy against the excesses of a republic ... "*Nature* expresses itself in these two governments, republican or monarchical, but not as *willingly* in the latter as in the former."

He confesses that monarchical power, in the hands of a wise man, would be the most perfect government of all, but where to find this wise man? ... The republican state therefore seems to him the least defective of all.

"The *arbitrary authority* (according to the abbé, this is the government of Louis XIV) appeals too much to the grace of God, but to what end? To cover up its injustice ... It can surprise the multitude, or stun them with visions of *Gehenna* in such a way that their speechlessness seems a form of applause; but one must still beware of it[62] ... One needs only a few men of a certain temper, a certain manner, a certain moment, a mere nothing to rouse what in the people seems to be asleep."

And how can you be sure, the abbé adds, about these *secret atheists* who, no more than you, think only of themselves. Don't expect them to come to your aid when things heat up. "They will follow the movement of the times, leaving you in shock when you realize that they were the first to abandon you."

Our work here has been merely to sketch a portrait of the abbé de Bucquoy and to suggest that he was one of the precursors of the first French Revolution. The work above, the general spirit of which we have just seen, is followed by an *Extract from a Treatise on the Existence of God* in which the author seeks to demonstrate, in opposition to materialist philosophers, that *matter* is not in possession of its existence and its movement by its own virtue.

"Does each part of matter," says he, "exist by itself? There would then be as many necessary gods as parts ... This would produce gods without number, as in the imaginations of the pagans." Bodies, according to the abbé, have neither existence nor movement by themselves ... Will it be claimed that "at the center of matter one atom pushes another, and that order results from their acting upon each other?" This is what the abbé cannot accept without the intervention of a God.

"Bodies can no more explain their ability to move as they can their existence. Is this all a matter of *chance*? By the same token, this movement must be contingent upon something. Or does it exist by itself, in violation of everything we have been told? Then it would be God. Is it neither one or the other? Then it is nothing!"

The author, we see, struggles here against certain Cartesian ideas which were already preparing the way for Holbach and La Mettrie; he cannot help but make a final criticism of the court of Louis XIV, saying: "O Lord, you hear enough confessions from the mouth, but who is it that confesses to you from their heart? Is it that you, Lord, have no credit among men, save as a pretext for man's injustices toward one another?"

The government of the Netherlands took great interest in the abbé de Bucquoy's plans; but it was difficult to establish a republic in France; and moreover, this could only have been done through the triumph of the *allies*.

The abbé, therefore, only had success in the salons of Holland, where he was considered a profound metaphysician. He was listened to favorably at gatherings and received the applause of *that France* dispersed abroad by all sorts of persecutions, and which consisted of fearless Catholics as well as Protestants. The two parties were united in the hatred of he who answered to the epithets *Viro immortali or fit regio divo*.[63]

With regard to the petition his aunt addressed to the king, the ladies of the Hague blamed her lack of success on its tone. It was no longer, they said, the fashion in France to speak so loudly and so naively... "It had cost M. de Cambray dearly, who had otherwise *comported himself with style*..."[64]

At the time of Louis XIV's death, the abbé de Bucquoy wrote these four verses with this title:

His Final Performance
(The scene is Saint-Denis)

Here he is now, deep in the ground;
This is the end of his story;
Those who would add to his glory,
Would do well to not make a sound.

Perhaps there was some exaggeration in the abbé's remark. "His reign was a true novel," he said later, "I want it, I do it!": such was his motto.

"What did he do? Nothing.

"How restore the lives of those thousands of people he sacrificed to his ambitions!"

It was to the *mother of the Regent* that the count de Bucquoy addressed these observations from his exile in Hanover on 3 April 1717.[65]

The abbé de Bucquoy, while living in Hanover, published some reflections on the *unexpected death* of the King of Sweden. In an attempt to make princes consider their position, he wrote the following sentence: "What a disgrace and what a scandal it is that those whom Providence has brought to light appear no better than if they had been covered by a bushel." He added: "The soul of a particular wretch wearing princely attire strangely shocks me."

As for his Swedish majesty, he reproaches him for having read Quintus Curtius too young.[66] "Beware," he adds, "of a man who has only one book in his pocket.

"He was a definite soldier in every respect, a grenadier par excellence, but his reading of Quintus Curtius led him astray. From his triumph at Nerva, he was reduced to flight, abandoning the siege of Pultava, and afterward hiding out at Bender, and then he gets himself killed for no reason at Fredrichstahl! . . ."[67]

Such was the political reasoning of the abbé de Bucquoy in Hanover around 1718. But in 1721 he grew concerned only with women, making incidental observations "on the malignity of the fair sex." In this new book we find this sentence:

"O woman, extracted from a rib, the daughter of night and sleep:[68] Adam slept when God made you . . . If he had been awake, perhaps there would have been better work done; or else He would have prayed to the Lord to make the bone of his bones more supple, at least in the region of the head.

"Adam could also have said to God: 'Leave my rib at rest: I prefer to be alone rather than in bad company . . .'"

The abbé de Bucquoy was well received at the court of Hanover, where he was given lodging in the palace. But he did not expect to find a lady named Martha there, who was the caretaker's wife, and who caused him to suffer on several occasions. This woman was very greedy and took all she could from the abbé.

He had gone to Leipsic, and money had been sent to him during his absence. On his return, he heard nothing about it; but a letter alerted him as to what was sent. Then he complained, and the caretaker's wife replied that in his absence she had used the money, but that she would return it to him later. He simply replied in German: *Es ist nicht recht* (This is not right).

However, having complained to the husband about his wife, she came to the abbé's room in the morning, dressed in a white shirt and bare legged with a very short cotillion . . . "How can we know," said the abbé, "that this wasn't a *Phaedra* furious with love and rage . . ." It was at this point that he ran to get his pistols "to put a bullet in her. The lady took care to escape very quickly . . ."

The abbé de Bucquoy was very sensitive to these last persecutions, and several times complained of them to His British Majesty, on whom the government of Hanover depended. It may be supposed that in his final years, which is to say when he was close to ninety years old, his mind weakened and led him to exaggerate many things.

We have no further information concerning the final years of the abbé de Bucquoy.

This writer seemed remarkable as much in his escapes as in the relative merit of his writings. We must not, however, confuse him with a man named Jacques de Bucquoy, whose book is in the Bibliothèque Nationale and is entitled *Reise door de Indiën*, door Jacob de Bucquoy, Harlem: *Jan Bosch*, 1744.[69]

The Count de Bucquoy, after his escape, remained either in Holland or Germany, and did not go to India. One of his relatives perhaps made an excursion there around that time.

THE CONFIDENCES OF NICOLAS

(Eighteenth Century)
Restif de la Bretonne

PART ONE

I. The Hôtel de Hollande[1]

In 1757, during the month of July, there was in Paris a young man of twenty-five years of age, exercising the profession of a typesetter at the printing house of the galleries of the Louvre and known around the workshop by the simple name of Nicolas, because he reserved his surname for the time when he could form an establishment or attain some distinguished position.—However, do not imagine that he was ambitious; love alone occupied his thoughts, and he would have sacrificed to it even fame, of which he was perhaps worthy, and which he never managed to obtain. Anyone at that time who frequented the Comédie-Française would not have failed to see in the first row of the stalls a long face with an aquiline nose, brown skin marked by smallpox, dark eyes full of expression, and an air of boldness tempered by much finesse; he was a handsome rider as well, with a slender waist, an elegant and nervous leg, carefully dressed, and redeemed by the grace of a man accustomed to shine during the public balls, yet whose setup was a bit modest for a viewer in the Royal Theatre. This was Nicolas the worker, who dedicated, almost every night, a large part of his earnings made during the day to the pleasures of the stage, cheerfully applauding the masterpieces of the comic repertoire (he disliked tragedy), and making his enthusiasm known especially during the passages delivered by the beautiful Mlle Guéant, who at the time obtained great success in *La Pupille* and *Les Dehors Trompeurs*.[2]

Nothing is more dangerous for natural dreamers than the serious love for a person of the theater; it is a perpetual lie, the dream of a sick person, the illusion of a madman. Life attaches itself entirely to an unattainable chimera that one would be happy to preserve in a state of desire and aspiration, but which vanishes as soon as one wishes to touch the idol.

Nicolas had been admiring Mlle Guéant for a year under the deceptive light of the chandelier and the footlights when it occurred to him to take a closer look at her. He went to stand at the actors' exit, which then corresponded to a passage leading to the crossroads of Bussy.[3] The little door of the theater was crowded with lackeys, porters carrying chairs, and unhappy suitors who, like Nicolas, burned with a modest passion for one of these young ladies. Here, one would generally find shop stewards, students, or shameful poets escaped from the Procope café, where they had written a madrigal or a sonnet during the intermission.[4] The gentlemen of the robe, the farm clerks, and the publishers of gazettes were not reduced to these extremes.[5] They penetrated the society of the theater, either by favor or because they were rich, and it was they who more often accompanied the actresses to their homes, to the despair of the attendants outside.

It was here that Nicolas came to intoxicate himself on the sterile happiness of admiring the slender waist, the dazzling complexion, the charming foot of the beautiful Mlle Guéant, who usually climbed onto her post chaise at this point and was transported directly to her home. Nicolas had been accustomed to following her just so far as to see her get out and had never noted her being accompanied by any horseman. He often indulged in this childishness to the point of walking part of the night beneath the windows of the actress's home, watching the play of lights and the shadows on the curtains, as if he imagined he had a chance; he, a poor child of the people, living on a manual worker's wage, who would never dare aspire to she who barred her door to financiers and lords.

One evening, on leaving the theater, Mlle Guéant, instead of climbing directly into her seat on the coach, set off on foot, giving her arm to one of her companions, crossed the passageway and, when they arrived at the rear, suddenly climbed into a carriage that was waiting for her, and which quickly departed. Nicolas started running after it; but the horses were going so fast that he was soon out of breath. In the streets, he was still able to follow them; but soon they reached the long series of quays, where his strength was necessarily to be conquered. Fortunately, as the night provided cover, he had the idea of jumping onto the carriage from behind where he could catch his breath, and though delighted with this position, his heart was distressed by jealousy. It was obvious to him that the couple were heading to some *petit maison*.[6] The innocent *pupille* he had just admired in the theater was bound this time to mysterious nuptials.

And what right had this foolish spectator, still full of the illusions of the evening, to inquire into the nocturnal activities of the beautiful Mlle Guéant? If, instead of acting in *La Pupille*, she had acted in *Les Dehors Trompeurs*, would the feeling Nicolas experienced have been the same?[7] Therefore, it was an ideal woman he loved, since he never dreamed of approaching her; but the heart is made of contradictions. From that day, Nicolas felt love for the woman and not only the actress. He was determined to penetrate one of her secrets, and felt determined to join this adventure if need be, as it sometimes happens that the feeling of reality is roused in dreams, and one wants at all costs to realize them.

The carriage, after crossing the bridges and again riding along the streets of the Right Bank, had finally stopped in the courtyard of a hotel in the Temple district. Nicolas slipped to the ground without the concierge noticing him and found himself for a moment embarrassed by his position. Meanwhile, the gently modulated voice of Mlle Guéant said to her companion: "Come down first, Junie."

Junie! At this name, an already vague memory passed through Nicolas's mind. It was the nickname of the young Lady Prudhomme, a dancer at the Opéra-Comique, whom he had met at a party in the countryside. He approached to give her his hand as she stepped down from the carriage. "Well, so you also belong to this party?" she said, recognizing him. He was about to reply when Mlle Guéant, who next stepped down from the carriage, leaned lightly on his arm. The impression was such that Nicolas was speechless. At that moment, a colonel of the dragoons, who had come before the ladies, said, casting his eyes upon him: "Mlle Guéant, here is one of your most faithful admirers." He had often seen Nicolas at the theater, in a state of overwhelming emotion, always applauding the performance of the beautiful actress. She turned to the young man and said, with the most charming smile and the most penetrating tone: "I am delighted, monsieur, to find you one of us." Nicolas was as startled to hear for the first time this familiar voice addressed to him as he was to see this beloved statue come down from its pedestal, momentarily alive and smiling for him alone. He could only think to reply: "Mademoiselle, I'm but a devotee, charmed to remain here and admire you longer."

There was in him that singular feeling experienced by all who see a woman of the theater up close for the first time; it was having to get acquainted with a person they already knew so well. They are often quick to realize that the difference is great: the maid is without spirit, the coquette is without grace, the lover is heartless, and moreover, the light that rises from the footlights changes one's appearance so much! However, Mlle Guéant triumphed over all these otherwise unfortunate differences. Nicolas stood petrified at seeing her, with her snowy neck and shapely form, climbing the stairs in the arms of the colonel.

"Well, what are you doing there?" said Mlle Prudhomme; "Give me your arm and let's go up."—Nicolas gradually felt reassured. That day, fortunately, his linen was impeccable, his lustring coat was almost new, the rest was suitable, and moreover, he saw passing near him other guests much more negligent in their attire than himself.

"Where are we?" he whispered to Junie (Mlle Prudhomme), and, as he went up the stairs, he told her of his embarrassment. She laughed heartily and said: "My friend, rest easy, here there are only princes and poets, as M. de Voltaire says; it is a mixed company . . . Are you not a bit of a prince?"

"I am descended from the emperor Pertinax," said Nicolas, with a serious air, "and my genealogy is in good standing with my grandfather from Nitry, in the Burgundy region."[8]

"Well, that suffices," said Junie, without too much dwelling on the likelihood of this fact; "I would have preferred your being a poet, because you would have recited something lively for dessert; but what does it matter? A prince is already good, and besides, it is I who will introduce you."

"But where are we?"

"We are," said Junie, "at the Hôtel de Hollande, where the ambassador of Venice is giving a party tonight."

They entered a room (the same where the billiard table of Beaumarchais was; he later occupied this hotel). Nicolas, who had never dined out save at Porcherons the few months he lived in Paris, was astonished by the magnificence of the table where he was invited to sit. Yet his face had such an air of distinction that he could not seem out of place anywhere. They were surprised not to know him, as only representatives of society and literature were present. The women were all actresses from various theaters. Admired was Mlle Hus, so witty, so provocative, but less beautiful than Mlle Guéant; Mlle Halard at that time slim and light-hearted; Mlle Arnould, already famous for her role of Psyche in *Les Fêtes de Paphos*; the young Rosalie Levasseur of the Comedie Italienne, who was accompanied by a stylish abbé; then Mlle Guimard and La Camargo, the first dancer for the French.[9] Mme Favart was seated to the left of Nicolas.[10] Surrounded by such a circle of famous beauties, he nevertheless only had eyes for Mlle Guéant, seated at the other end of the table near the colonel who had introduced her. Junie teased Nicolas mercilessly and got him to tell her the whole story of his beautiful passion for Mlle Guéant. "It's no fun for me!" she said, laughing, "because I have no other partner but you! But no matter, you amuse me very much."

When dinner was finished, Rosalie Levasseur, who had a delightful voice, sang some ballads; Mlle Arnould recited the beautiful song: *Pâles flambeaux*; Mlle Hus played a scene from Molière; Mme Favart sang an aria from *La Servante Maîtresse*; Guimard, Halard, Prudhomme, and Camargo the second executed a dance step from the ballet sequence in *Médée*; Mlle Guéant interpreted the letter in *La Pupille*.[11] The poets were next: each declaimed his verses or sang his song. The night was advancing; the most celebrated authors, the greatest figures of literature, in brief, the *gravity*, had just left. The circle grew more intimate; Grécourt recited one of his tales; an author named Robbé read a poem against the Prince of Conti, who had given him twenty thousand livres not to print it.[12] Piron recited some stanzas marked with the passion of a century that respected nothing; not even love.[13] They were still trembling in the face of such lively poetry when Mme Favart, turning to her neighbor on the right, said to him, "It's your turn!" Nicolas hesitated, especially as the eyes of the beautiful Mlle Guéant were fixed on him. The latter, wanting to reassure him, said with her adorable smile, "Will you give us something, monsieur?"—"He's a little prince," exclaimed Junie, "he's good for nothing, does nothing . . . He's a descendant of the Emperor Per . . . Per . . ." Nicolas blushed up to his ears. "Pertinax, that's it!" Junie said finally.

The Venetian ambassador frowned; he had little faith in the descendants of the Roman emperors, and flattered himself, being a Mocenigo registered in the guestbook of Venice, in knowing all the biggest names in Europe.[14] Nicolas felt that he would make a bad impression if he did not explain himself. So, he arose and began the story of his genealogy; he told how Helvius Pertinax, the son of the successor to Commodus, had escaped the death threatened by Caracalla, and, having taken refuge in the Apennines, had married Didia Juliana, a daughter was also persecuted by the Emperor Julianus.[15] The stylish abbé who accompanied Rosalie Levasseur, and who had pretensions to some learning, shook his head at this allegation; whereupon Nicolas recited in very pure Latin the act of marriage between the two spouses, and cited a multitude of other texts. The abbé admitted defeat and Nicolas then coldly listed the successors of Helvius and Didia, up to Olibrius Pertinax, who had been a captain of the hunt under King Chilpéric, and then an infinite number of Pertinaxes having passed through the most varied states: merchants, prosecutors, or police officers, up to the sixtieth descendant of the Emperor Pertinax, named Nicolas Restif, the latter name being a translation from the Latin, since only the French language was now used in public documents.

The long list would scarcely have been listened to if the remarks with which Nicolas accompanied the principal passages had not persuaded everyone that this was a critique of genealogies in general. The poets and actresses laughed heartily; the grand seigneurs of society accepted the apparent irony of the piece as an exhibition of wit, and the animation and verve of the storyteller earned him all their votes. The drill was so extensive, and Nicolas held up so well against all those minds hanging on the anecdotes with which he accompanied the quoted names, that he was asked for an account of his adventures. He consented to tell the story of his first love. Some pretentious guests, who were starting to get annoyed by the favor Nicolas seemed to enjoy with the ladies, gradually slipped away, so that there only remained an attentive and friendly circle. *The Confessions* were then in vogue. Those of Nicolas were quick, enthusiastic, and had certain features of a naive immorality, which back then charmed vulgar listeners; but getting to the truly human element in his narrative, he showed his true self, which was noble and genuinely passionate; his emotion penetrated deep into this frivolous society, and in all these lost hearts he was able to awaken a spark of pure love for their memories of youth. Mlle Guéant herself, as cold as she was beautiful, and who was also regarded as wise, could not resist a deep sympathy for this young man whose soul was so tender and sensitive. During the final scenes of his story, which Nicolas told in a stifled voice, with tears in his eyes, she exclaimed: "Is it possible? Can we love so intensely?"

"Yes, madame," cried Nicolas, "everything I say is true, like the genealogy of Pertinax . . . As for the person I loved, she resembled you, she had at least some of your features and your smile, and nothing can console me for her loss except to admire you."

Then there was a storm of applause. Some enthusiasts were not afraid to say that they were dealing with a novelist more brilliant than the Prévost of *Exiles*, more tender than Arnaud, more serious than Crebillon fils, with passages of a hitherto unknown realism.[16] And the poor worker was received on the same footing as this company of respected names, great minds, and impure beauties of the time. It was up to him to make his way in the world now.—Yet everything he had said was true; he really considered himself the descendant of the Emperor Pertinax, and he had just related his love for a woman who had died a few months ago.—As his heart could not remain empty, this ideal and poetic love he conceived for Mlle Guéant had gradually consoled him for his loss, the impression of which was still vivid.

There was to be a bizarre conclusion to this dinner, one that occurred often during these kinds of midnight suppers. At a given signal, the lights went out, and a kind of blind man's buff began in the darkness; it is believed that this was the ultimate purpose of the party, at least for the initiates, who were not regular guests. Each one had the right to take home the lady he seized in the darkness during this moment of chaos. These lovers, in name only, contrived to recognize each other; but once done, even if the choice was random, the choice became sacred. Nicolas, who was not expecting it, felt a hand take his own and lead him for a few steps; then another soft and trembling hand was given to him: it was that of Mlle Guéant, who begged him to see her out. As he went down by a private staircase to the corresponding courtyard, he heard Junie, who cried out, "I'm sacrificing myself, I'll console the Colonel."

II. Who Nicolas Was

Thirty years later, this same person, known then by his patronymic *Restif*, to which he had added the name of *Labretone*, which belonged to his father, had occasion to return to the Hôtel de Hollande, located on the old rue du Temple, which at that time belonged to Beaumarchais. The characters from the previous scene had had mixed fortunes. The ambassador of Venice, little esteemed in the world, sometimes treated as a spy and a swindler, had perished, condemned by the order of the Council of Ten;[17] the beautiful Guéant had died of consumption, and Nicolas had mourned her for a long time, although he had only been able to establish a temporary bond with her.—As for himself, he was no longer the poor typesetter of old; he had become a master in this profession, which he thought of as equal to that of a writer and philosopher. If he still deigned to do manual work, it was only after hanging his velvet coat and sword on the wall next to him. Moreover, he only *composed* his own works, and he was so prolific that he no longer took the trouble to write them out: standing in front of his letter case, the fire of enthusiasm in his eyes, he assembled letter by letter on his *composing stick* those inspired pages riddled with errors, the bizarre spelling and calculated eccentricities of which everyone was aware. His system was to use, in the same volume, fonts of different sizes, which he varied according to the presumed importance of a given period. *Cicero* was for passion, for places with the greatest impact, *galliard* for simple narrative or moral observations, *petit-roman* concentrated in little space a thousand tedious but necessary details.[18] Sometimes he liked to try out a new system of spelling; he suddenly warned the reader of it by means of a parenthesis, and then he continued his chapter by deleting some vowels, in the Arabic manner, by throwing consonants into disorder, replacing *c* by *s*, *s* by *t*, the latter by *ç*, etc., always according to the rules he developed at length in his notes. Often, wishing to mark long and short vowels in the Latin manner, he used either capital or lowercase letters in the middle of words; more often he emphasized vowels in a strange way, and especially made excessive use of the acute accent. However, none of these eccentricities discouraged the countless readers of the *Paysan Perverti* [1776, The Corrupted (male) Peasant], *Les Contemporaines* [Contemporary women] or *Nuits de Paris* [Nights of Paris];[19] henceforth, he was the fashionable storyteller, and nothing can give an idea of the popularity that was attached to the deliveries of his works, published in parts, if not the success that some serialized novels obtained in the past. Here was the same method of breathtaking narrative, without dialogues containing dramatic pretensions, this complex web of incidents, this multitude of different characters drawn in broad strokes, of forced but energetic situations, this continual search for the most depraved morals to write about, to create the most licentious portraits, all of which can mean big money in a corrupt time, and all of it elevated amply with humanitarian and philosophical maxims and plans for reform, in which a sort of disordered but undeniable genius shone, which caused this strange author to be called the *Jean-Jacques des Halles.*[20]

This was significant; nevertheless, the man was perhaps better than his books; his intentions were good despite the excesses of a wanton imagination. He often spent the night roaming the streets, penetrating the vilest hovels, the dens of swindlers, either to observe or, in his mind, to prevent evil and do some good. He asserted, he said, the role of Peter the Justicer;[21] not by virtue of the duties of royalty, but of those of the moralist writer. This strange pretension also followed him in his relations with the world, where he was the mediator of quarrels and family divisions or the intermediary between benevolence and misfortune. He also boasts of having, in his nocturnal excursions, comforted or relieved more than one wretch, and snatched a few girls from shame or reproach: this would be enough to forgive his many faults and many errors. Restif is best known as a novelist; however, he has written several volumes of philosophy, morality, and even politics, except he didn't publish them under his own name. *La Philosophie de M. Nicolas* contains an entire pantheistic system, where he attempts, like the philosophers of that time, to explain the existence of the world and of men as the result of a series of creations, or rather, a series of successive and spontaneous outbreaks;[22] his system bears some relation to the cosmogony of Fourier, who was able to borrow from him. In politics and morality, Restif is simply a communist. According to him, *property is the source of all vice, of all crime, of all corruption*; his plans for reform are fully described in the books entitled *L'Anthropographe* [1782, The anthropographer], *Le Gynographe* [1777, The gynographer], *Le Pornographe* [1769, The pornographer], etc., which would prove that modern thinkers have invented nothing on such subjects.[23] Moreover, we find the same ideas put into action in most of his novels. The second volume of *Les Contemporaines* contains a whole banking system of exchange practiced by workers and merchants who, living on the same street, establish between themselves an already *phalansterian* community.[24]

Let us now return to the personal biography of this singular spirit; he planted fragments of it in a multitude of works where he portrayed himself under fictitious names, of which he later gave the key. In a series of plays and individual scenes with dialogue that he called *Le Drame de la vie* [1793, The drama of life], he had the bizarre idea of representing, as in a magic lantern, the principal stages of his existence; it begins with the early games of his youth, and it ends after the massacres of 2 September, which he bitterly deplores.[25]

Another book, *Le Cœur humain dévoilé* [The Human Heart Laid Bare], describes in minute detail all the impressions of this life so laborious and tormented.[26] Before Restif, only five men had formed the bold project of painting a portrait of themselves: St. Augustine, Montaigne, Cardinal de Retz, Jérôme Cardan, and Rosseau. Yet only these last two had completely sacrificed their pride; Restif went perhaps further. "At sixty," he said, "overwhelmed with debt and burdened with infirmities, I am compelled to give up my morals in order to subsist for a few more days, like the Englishman who sells his body."

In reading this first confession, which must not have been one of his least torments, we feel pity for this poor old man who, with one foot in the grave, appears, with the courage and the energy of despair, to exhume the mistakes of his youth and the vices of his maturity, and perhaps exaggerates them to satisfy the depraved taste of an era which had admired Faublas and Valmont.[27] Since then, this realist process of making man himself a sort of anatomical subject has been abused.—We will seek now to turn our teaching toward the study of certain figures whose personality is subject to the saddest illusions and provokes the most inexplicable confessions. We will try to tell the story of this strange existence, without any prejudice and without any sympathy, using the documents provided by the author himself, and by drawing from his own confessions the instructive fact of the misfortunes that befell him as a providential punishment for his faults. Our age is no less eager than the previous century for memoirs and confidences; however, the simplicity and directness of former times are far less in evidence with the writers of today. In any case, this would be an instructive comparison to make, if the truth could have something of the appeal of the novel.

III. Early Years

The village of Sacy, located in the Champagne region on the borders of Burgundy, fifty leagues from Paris and three leagues from Auxerre, is traversed its whole length by a single street composed of a hundred houses on each side. At one end, called *the Door up there*, crossing a stream called La Farge, we find the enclosure of Labretone, whose white walls loom over a horizon of woods and green hills. It was here that Nicolas Restif was born; his grandfather, an educated man and an ally of the magistracy, believed himself to be a descendant of the Emperor Pertinax.[28] It is possible that the genealogy he had established for the purpose of explaining his origin was only a mind game designed to ridicule the pretensions of a few gentlemen, his neighbors, whom he received at his table. In any event, Restif's family was highly regarded in the country as much for its wealth as for its relations: many of its members belonged to the church; they first thought of launching young Nicolas into this career, but his natural independence, and even somewhat wild nature, opposed this for a long time. He only enjoyed himself among the shepherds, in the woods of Sacy and Nitry, and shared in their wandering life and their fatigue. He was about twelve years old when this disposition was favored by an unforeseen circumstance. His father's shepherd, whose name was Jaquot, left suddenly, without a word, for the pilgrimage to *Mont Saint-Michel*, which, for the young men of the countryside was like that of the pilgrimage to the Holy Queen for girls. A boy who had not gone to Mont Saint-Michel was regarded a coward. In the same way, a girl's modesty seemed be lacking something if she had not visited the tomb of the beautiful *Queen Alise*, the Virgin of virgins. When Jaquot left, the herd was without a guardian. Nicolas quickly offered to replace him. His parents were reluctant: the child was so young, and wolves often appeared in the surrounding neighborhood; but in the end there was a shortage of people on the farm, and Jaquot's journey was to last just two weeks: so they appointed Nicolas the temporary shepherd.

What joy! What a feeling of euphoria on that first day of freedom! Here he comes at the crack of dawn, exiting the walled vineyard of Labretone, followed by three large dogs named Pinçard, Robillard, and Friquet. The two strongest sheep carried the day's provisions on their backs with a bottle of red wine and bread for the dogs. Here he is free, free in his solitude! He breathes in the fresh air; for the first time, he feels alive . . . The white clouds gliding in the sky, the wagtail swinging on the molehills, the autumn florets without leaves and without fragrance, the song of the solitary *wheatear*, so monotonous and so sweet, the green meadows bathed in the distance by the mist, all this throws him into a sweet reverie. Passing a bush where Jacquot, two months before, had shown him a linnet's nest, he thinks of the poor shepherd he has replaced and of the dangers he faces in his perilous journey. His eyes are wet with tears, his head exalted, and for the first time he begins to put into verses the song of the pilgrims of Saint Jacques, which he had heard sung to beggars:

Jaquot is on a pilgrimage—to Saint-Michel;
May his journey be watched over—by Raphael!
We'll no longer keep together—the white sheep:
Jaquot crosses the shaking bridge—his soul to keep.

This is the first step taken on a dangerous road; Nicolas was mistaken about his taste for solitude . . . This inclination was more suited to a poet than a shepherd. Woe to the sheep, which he drags to the wildest places and those least rich in pasture. He loves the ruins of the Sainte-Madeleine chapel, and often returns there, under the pretext of picking wild blackberries; the fact is that this place inspires in him gentle and melancholy thoughts. But it wasn't enough. Behind the woods of *Boutparc*, opposite the vineyards of Montgré, there was a dark valley surrounded by tall trees. At first, Nicolas was hesitant to enter the forest; he remembered the stories that Jaquot had often told him, stories of thieves and the excommunicated who changed into beasts. Less frightened than their guardian, the animals jump into the valley. There was the herd: the goats climb the bushes, the sheep graze in the grass, and pigs dig the earth to search there for a kind of wild carrot, which the peasants call *échavie*.[29] As Nicolas followed them to prevent them from going too far, he saw underneath a tree a huge black boar, who, in a boisterous mood, came to mingle with the more civilized band of pigs. The young shepherd trembled with both horror and pleasure, because the sight of the animal increased the wildness of this place, which contained so many charms for him. He was careful not to make a sound among the leaves. A moment later, a deer, then a hare, came to roam on an area of grass; then a hoopoe perched in one of those big pear trees which farmers call the *honeysweet pear tree.* The dreamer thought himself transported to a land of fairies; suddenly, from the bushes, a wolf appeared with its wild hair and its pointed nose and eyes that glowed like coals ... The dogs came to chase it away, and farewell to everything that completed the picture: deer, hare and wild boar, gone! Even the hoopoe, a bird of Solomon, had flown away; except, like a beneficent fairy, it pointed to the tree with the *honeysweet pears,* so sweet and sugary that bees devour them.[30] Nicolas fills his pockets with this delicious fruit and on his return, treats his brothers and sisters to some.

On reflection, Nicolas said to himself: "This valley belongs to no one ... I take it, I seize it; it's my little kingdom! I must erect a monument for it, to serve as a record of my having been here, just as it has always been done according to the Bible my father reads." He worked several days on building a pyramid. When it was finished, it occurred to him, again according to the Bible, to make a sacrifice using the proper rites. A free being like myself, he thought, must be at once king, priest, judge, shepherd, baker, farmer, and hunter. In virtue of these titles, he went in search of a victim, and managed to find one by using his sling to capture a bird of prey, the kind called a *honey buzzard,* which he had just condemned as guilty of disturbing the innocence and safety of the guests of the valley. Perhaps his conscience would have found fault later with this reasoning when the study of universal harmony had taught him the value of harmful beings. For this reason, we speak of these childish remarks only to show the mystical tone of these early ideas of the dreamer.* However, he needed witnesses for this religious act. At noon the draft animals are driven to pasture after the morning work. Nicolas waited for the right hour and then shouted to the shepherds passing by in the distance. Immediately, his companions arrived, those with whom he played games, as well as pretty Marie Fouare and Madeleine Piat. "Come, come," said Nicolas, "I'm going to show you *my* valley, *my* pear tree, and also my wild boar and my hoopoe." (But these animals were careful not to surrender to the wishes of their *owner.*) Nicolas explained to the group his rights as the first occupant of the land, showing them his pyramid and

* It is indeed curious to find in Restif's earliest years this feature of sacrificing to the Eternal, which evokes an analogous account by Goethe, who like Restif became pantheistic in his later life.

his altar as he spoke; they were recognized as sacrosanct. Thus, the ceremony began: the dry wood was lit, and the entrails of the bird were thrown into the fire, according to the patriarchal rite; Nicolas then put the body on a small pyre and improvised a prayer which was accompanied by some verses from the psalms. He stood with a serious expression on his face, convinced of the grandeur of his action; then he distributed the roasted flesh of the bird to his companions, taking the first bite himself, which was terrible. The three dogs alone feasted gladly on the scraps of this priestly cuisine.

Who could have foreseen that this scrupulous proprietor would become one of the most fervent *communists*, whose doctrines ignited the revolutionary era? His pretensions, however, had found jealous persons among the herdsman of Sacy, for the secret was revealed, the sacrifice was treated as an abominable desecration of holy things, and abbé Thomas, Nicolas's brother from the first marriage, who lived a few miles from Sacy, went to La Bretone expressly to whip this young heretic; the abbé was motivated to make this correction a reality since, being the godfather of the culprit, he answered indirectly for his sins.[31] The poor young man had no idea that he had engaged very recklessly in a sacrifice against heaven.

Nicolas had two brothers from the first marriage, who were rarely seen in the family; the eldest was the curé of Courgis; the other, whom we have just encountered, abbé Thomas, was tutor to the Jansenists of Bicêtre, and came to see his family during the holidays. When he returned that year, his younger brother was entrusted to him, and he was responsible for inspiring the boy's mind with some serious ideas. Both embarked for Auxerre by boat. The abbé Thomas was a tall, lanky boy, with a long face, a sallow complexion, shiny skin with freckles, an aquiline nose, and black eyebrows; all this provided by the Restif bloodline. He was focused and very strong, without seeming to be, of a firm disposition and full of passion, which he had managed to subdue by means of an iron will and obstinate struggle. No sooner had he placed Nicolas among the other children of Bicêtre than he regarded him as though he were a stranger. When the latter was alone amidst all these *small curés*, as he put it, lost in the long-vaulted corridors of this monastic prison, he grew homesick for the countryside. The monotony of the religious exercises was not likely to distract him, and the books from the library, the *Provincial Letters* of Pascal, *Les Essais* by Nicole, *La Vie et Les Miracles* of deacon Pâris, *La Vie* by M. Tissard, and other Jansenist works didn't please him either.[32]—The writer, however, later recalled with tenderness the lessons of the Jansenists. According to him, it was to the Jansenist education that Pascal, Racine, and other Port Royalists owed their sagacity, their clarity in reasoning, their precision in the use of words, their depth of detail, and a purity of diction which was all the more surprising since the Jesuits had only produced Annats, Caussins, etc.[33] This is because the Jansenists, serious and reflective, think harder, quicker, and more effectively than the Molinists; they put their energy into the contemplation of the contrary nature of all the passions; they create logicians who become exemplary pious people or resolute philosophers. The Molinist is more agreeable; he does not believe that man is obliged to always have his God before his eyes so as to tremble over every action, over every act of will; but less reflective, tolerant, superficial, his way of being approaches indifference more often than the other approaches impiety.

However, a change was taking place in the situation of the Jansenists at Bicêtre. The Archbishop Gigot de Bellefond, who protected them, died, and was succeeded by Christophe de Beaumont.[34] The latter appointed a new rector who, from the day he was installed, looked down upon the choirmaster and the Jansenist governors. This *intruder* had a fiery temperament and was full of hostility; he asked to see the library and frowned when he saw the controversial books that the abbé Thomas had not sought to conceal, praising their sentiments. The rector exclaimed that such books should not be in a children's library.

"It is never too early to know the truth," said the abbé Thomas.

"Simple tonsured cleric, you want to teach us religion!" said the rector.

The humiliated abbé was silent. The students enjoyed the scene with all the merciless malignancy of childhood. Moving from book to book, the rector fell on the New Testament annotated by Quesnel.[35]

"This one here," he said, "goes against the Final judgment of the Church!" And he threw it to the ground with an expression of horror. The poor abbé Thomas humbly picked it up and kissed it.

"Monsieur, do you think," he said, "that the text of the Gospel is the whole story?"

The rector, even more irritated, wished to remove all the students' copies of the New Testament. The abbé Thomas then raised his voice: "O my God!" he exclaimed, "they're taking away the Word from your children!"

This time, the students took the side of the choirmaster. Nicolas dared to confront the rector and said to him: "I learned from my father, whom I believe more than you, that this is the Testament of Jesus Christ." "Your father was a Huguenot," answered the rector. At that time, this word was synonymous with "atheist." The scene concluded with the intervention of two priests from the house, who endeavored to calm everyone; but the abbé Thomas felt it was necessary he leave the place. Indeed, a few days later, he was warned that an order of expulsion from the Jansenists was going to be dispatched to him. It was prudent to avert it. Students were sent back to their parents and then the abbé set off with his vice-master and Nicolas to return to Sacy.

IV. Jeannette Rousseau

Returning to his village, Nicolas trembled with joy, and when he saw the hills of Côte-Grêle, his heart leapt and his tears flowed in abundance. He soon discovered the *Vendenjean*, the *Farge*, the *Triomfraid*, and finally the *Boutparc*, behind which was his valley. He wanted to share his enthusiasm with the abbé Thomas, and indulged in a picturesque description, to which the latter replied: "I understand that all this is very touching since you are weeping; but as we are approaching Sacy, let us recite the *sexts* before we get there."[36]

The abbé Thomas did not like the paternal home. The next day, he took Nicolas to his older brother, a curé at Courgis, who was to teach him Latin. *The Fables* of Phaedrus and *The Eclogues* of Virgil soon opened the imagination of the young man to new and charming horizons. On Sundays and during festivals, the church was filled with a crowd of young girls on whom he looked furtively. It was on Easter Sunday that his fate was sealed. High Mass was celebrated with deacon and sub-deacon; the sounds of the organ, the smell of incense, the pomp of the ceremony, all at once exalted his soul; he felt a kind of intoxication. During Communion, the communicants were seen parading in their most beautiful attire, followed by their mothers and sisters. A young girl came last, tall, beautiful and modest, her complexion pale, "as if to give more luster to the blush of modesty"; she was dressed more tastefully than her companions; her bearing, her finery, her beauty, her virginal complexion, all realized the ideal figure of which every young soul dreams. When mass was over, the scholar came out behind her. The celestial beauty walked with a harmonious step in a manner we attribute to the ancient Graces. She stopped when she saw the curé's housekeeper, Marguerite Pâris.

The latter approached the girl and said: "Good day, Mademoiselle Rousseau." And she kissed her.

"So, that's her surname," said Nicolas to himself.

"My dear *Jeannette*," added Marguerite, "your face is as angelic as your soul."

"Jeannette Rousseau!" says Nicolas to himself, "what a pretty name!"

And the young girl answered the woman with a few words, in a soft, clear voice, whose tone was enchanting.*

From that moment on, Nicolas was more occupied with Jeannette than with anything else. For the rest of the day he sought her out, and only saw her again on the occasion of the *Magnificat*, when everyone in the choir turned toward the nave. The next day, the impression was even stronger; he was determined to be worthy of her by applying himself to his studies; from that day also, his mind expanded and forever broke with the frivolous preoccupations of childhood. Left alone one day in the presbytery, because the curé and the abbé Thomas had gone to sow the curé's field, Nicolas had a singular idea: it was to look into the parish records for Jeannette's baptismal certificate to find out her exact age; he himself was fifteen, and he sensed that Jeannette was older. He went back to 1730 and was delighted to read the following lines: "On 19 December 1731 was born Jeanne Rousseau, legitimate daughter of Jean and Marguerite Rousseau,

* Many years later, under the Republic, the author had still retained a fond memory of this first love. "Citizen reader," he wrote, "this Jeanette Rousseau, this angel, without knowing it, decided my fate. Think not that I had studied, that I had overcome every difficulty due to strength and courage. No, I've always had a cowardly soul; but I have felt true love: it lifted me higher than myself and allowed me to pass for courageous. I have done everything to make myself worthy of this girl whose name makes me tremble at the age of sixty, after forty-six years apart . . . Oh, Jeanette! If I had seen you every day, I would have been as great as Voltaire, and I would have left Rousseau far behind me! But just the thought of you broadens my soul. It was no longer me, but an active man, ardent, who shared in the genius of God."

etc." Nicolas read this twenty times over, memorizing even the names of the witnesses and officiating priests, and especially the date of *19 December*, which became a sacred day for him. The one sad thought that resulted from this knowledge was that Jeannette was three years older than him, and that perhaps she would be married before he could claim her. Having found out where Jeannette's parents lived, he spent every day in front of the house, situated at the bottom of a valley and surrounded by poplars watered by the stream of the *Fontaine-Froide*; he greeted the trees as his friends, and a sweet melancholy took possession of his soul.

But it was in the church that the apparition returned in all its charm. Nicolas had recited a prayer which he repeated incessantly to reconcile his religion and his love: *Unam petii a Domino*, he whispered, *et hanc requiram omnibus diebus vitæ meæ*? (I have only asked the Lord for one, and I will seek her all the days of my life!) Trusting in this prayer, he felt overjoyed, and no one ever suspected the cause. It so happened that the bell-ringer was also a winemaker and his work in the church was often in conflict with this other occupation. Nicolas offered to take his place; he would then arrive at the church early and finding himself alone, he would run to the place where Jeannette was usually seated, kneel, lean forward in the same place she had and kiss the stone that had touched the feet of the girl, reciting his favorite prayer.

One summer day, during a time of drought, there was no water for watering the garden of the vicarage. The abbé Thomas said to Nicolas and a choir boy named Huet: "Go fetch some water from M. Rousseau's well." But it turned out that the well lacked a rope. What to do? Huet immediately said he saw Mlle Rousseau and was going to ask her for one. Nicolas, trembling, held Huet by his coat. Talk, to *her*? . . . He trembled, not out of jealousy, but at Huet's boldness. However, Jeannette, who had seen their predicament, brought them a rope, and as she was helping Huet install it, her hands sometimes touched those of the young boy. Nicolas did not envy him this happiness; the touch of those delicate hands would have burned him like fire. He could not speak or breathe until Jeannette had withdrawn. But he then reflected that she had not spoken to him or to his companion and had even lowered her eyes when passing near him. Would she have noticed that in the church his gaze was always fixed on her? The fact is that, shortly after this, a churchgoer named Mlle Drouin warned the curé's housekeeper that Nicolas, during the sermon, always had his eyes turned toward Mlle Rousseau. Marguerite kindly repeated this to the young man, assuring him that several people had made the same remark.

V. Marguerite

Marguerite Pâris, the curé of Courgis's housekeeper, was close to forty years old; but she was as fresh as a devotee and like a woman who had always lived above her needs. She wore her hair tastefully and in the same way as Jeannette Rousseau. She ordered her shoes from Paris and chose ones with thin, high heels, emphasizing the finer points of her legs, which were covered with well-cut blue cotton stockings. It was the day of the Assumption; it was hot; after vespers the housekeeper undressed and changed into white clothes. The choir boys were playing in the courtyard, the abbé Thomas was at the church, Nicolas was studying at his little table near the window; Marguerite, in the same room, prepared a salad; from time to time the young man's eyes turned away from his work and followed Marguerite's movements, all while thinking about Jeannette. What united these two ideas in his mind was the memory of Marguerite and Jeannette's encounter some time before, upon leaving the church.

"Sister Marguerite," he asked, "is Mlle Jeannette Rousseau very rich? You know, the daughter of the notary . . ."

Marguerite made a movement of surprise, left her salad, and went over to Nicolas.

"Why do you ask me that, my child?" she said.

"Because you know her . . . and perhaps my parents might be happy if I married a rich young lady . . ."

The delicate nature of this schoolboy, who wanted to reconcile the desire of his parents with his platonic flame, was not lost on the housekeeper; but suddenly a strange thought crossed her mind, and she came to sit down at Nicolas's table, full of tenderness, her breast heaving with sighs. Then she told him effusively, that formerly M. Rousseau, Jeannette's father, had sought her hand in marriage but was unable to obtain it.

"So," she said, "I love this pretty girl very much, telling myself I could have been . . . her mother! And you," she added, "my poor child, your love interests me because of that. If I could do anything about it, I would go and see your parents and her family; but you are too young; and she is two years older than you . . ."[37]

Nicolas began to weep and put his head on Marguerite's shoulder; their tears mingled without either the child or the woman thinking of the different nature of their emotions . . . Marguerite suddenly came to and stood up with a serious expression on her face, red with shame; but Nicolas, who pressed her hands, felt his heart weakening. Then the good woman, who had for a moment wanted to be severe with him, took him in her arms, threw water on his face, and asked him, when he came to: "What's happened?"

"I don't know," said Nicolas; "speaking of Jeannette, looking at you, embracing you, I felt a longing in my heart . . . I could not help contemplating your neck, so white, where your hair falls; your eyes wet with tears drew me, Marguerite, like a viper watching a bird; the bird senses danger but cannot flee . . ."

"But if you love Jeannette . . . ," said Marguerite, in a serious tone.

"Oh, it's true, I love her! . . ." Saying these words, Nicolas was seized with a kind of shiver and felt cold as ice. The sanctus bell rang and he went to church. There, no matter what he tried to do, the sight of Marguerite crying and agitated, her breast heaving with sighs, came before his eyes and pushed away the chaste image of Jeannette. The appearance of the latter in her usual place restored calm to the young man's excited senses: she had never troubled them; her power worked on the noblest sentiments of his soul and inspired in him every virtue.

Marguerite was neither a coquette nor a devout hypocrite; she felt nothing but maternal kindness for Nicolas; her heart was sensitive; she had loved. That is why this very young love, which reminded her of her best years, moved her beyond measure. Poor Nicolas, like her, knew nothing of the danger that exists in these confidences, in these effusions, in which the senses exalt the soul with less purity. One day, as he passed by Mlle Rousseau's house, Nicolas had seen her sitting on a bench, spinning yarn next to her mother, and he was struck by the small size and shape of her foot as it followed the movements of the spinning wheel. Returning to the presbytery, he glanced into Marguerite's room and saw there a Moroccan green leather mule with a thin heal, whose seams had retained their whiteness. "How pretty that mule," he sighed, "would be on Jeannette's foot!" And he carried it off to admire it at his leisure.

The next morning, which was a Sunday, Marguerite looked for her shoe throughout the house; Nicolas trembled lest she discover his fantasy, and when he entered her home, he dropped the mule into a chest as skillfully as possible; the housekeeper was not fooled by this maneuver, but she put on her shoes without saying a word. Nicolas admired how this small object so easily took the shape of the housekeeper's foot. "Admit something to me," she said with a smile, "it was you who had hidden my mule . . ." Nicolas blushed but admitted the truth. The mule had spent the night in his room. "Poor child!" she said, "I forgive you, and I see that you would be able to do as much for Jeannette Rousseau as a certain Louis Denesvre did for . . . another."

"For whom, sister Marguerite?" (That was how she was known at the presbytery.)

Marguerite did not answer. Nicolas dreamed for a long time about this half-confidence. Two days later, the housekeeper had errands in the neighboring town, which is to say in Auxerre. The curé's donkey was a very stubborn nag, which had compromised the safety of his mistress several times already. Nicolas, stronger than the choir boys who usually guided it, was chosen for this service. Marguerite briskly mounted the donkey; she had on a bagnolet hat of fine muslin, her waist was pinched by a soft whalebone corset, over which she wore a white cotton casaquin, as well as a red-checked apron, a dove-colored silk skirt, and her famous Moroccan leather mules decorated with a gemstone on the buckles.[38] Her usual smile was not without an interesting languor, her black eyes were soft and sparkling. During the difficult descent of the Montaleri Valley, Nicolas took her in his arms to help her dismount, and supported her until they reached the bottom of the valley, where she walked for some time on the grass. It was then necessary to raise her back up onto the donkey, as the path was now level for the rest of the way to the city. Nicolas from time to time arranged Marguerite's skirt over her legs, steadying her feet on the basket; she smiled when she saw him touch her green mules, which animated the conversation about Jeannette; then the donkey stumbled, Nicolas supported the sister by her waist, and this made her blush like a rose.

"How you love Jeannette!" she said, "since the mere thought that my green mules might suit her foot is still troubling you now."

"It's true," said Nicolas, removing his hands with embarrassment from her feet on the basket.

"Well," said Marguerite, "I, too, cannot help tenderly loving the daughter of a man who was dear to me, and who never deliberately wronged me. So I support your seeking that pretty girl's hand; but take care to say nothing to your brothers of it, as they do not love you, being children of a first marriage . . . I will undertake to speak to Jeannette on your behalf, and later see her parents."

Nicolas threw himself onto Marguerite's hands and showered with tears her delicate arms, which were much more beautiful than those of Jeannette, who, like all young girls, was not yet fully formed. Sister Marguerite, a bit moved and wanting to bring this exaltation to a close, reminded the young man that it was time to read the *canonical verses*. Nicolas immediately collected himself and began with the man's part, the sister reciting alternately her verse and he the prayer and all that is the responsibility of the celebrant, so that they arrived innocently in the city.

Marguerite carried out the curé's errand, did some shopping, and then took Nicolas to dine with Mme Jeudi, a Jansenist haberdasher from whom she usually bought some trimming and church lace, as well as ribbons and other trinkets for herself. Her daughter was a very pretty girl, newly wed to a young Jansenist from Clamecy through an arranged marriage. The mother's devotion pursued the young couple into their simplest interactions, and they could neither say a word to each other nor be together without her permission. The young wife was still called *Mlle* Jeudi. Moreover, this way of doing things was common among *honest people* (which is what the Jansenists called themselves). There was also a great-niece in the house, twenty-six years old, whom the mother had appointed as supervisor to both spouses, and who was authorized, in cases of abuse, to treat them severely. When Mme Jeudi had to be absent for one reason or another, she had her great-niece keep a record of any breech of propriety of which her son-in-law and daughter might be guilty. Such was the rather austere atmosphere inside this house.

Nicolas, seated between the two young people, cast sidelong glances at the new wife, whose sad fate was of great interest to him, and told himself that in the husband's place, he would have shown more character in asserting his rights; the solemn guimpe worn by the great-niece, seated on his left, made him think twice. However, from the dinner table, located in the back of the shop, he still had the distraction of watching passersby in the street.

"Ah, how pretty the girls are in Auxerre!" he exclaimed suddenly. Mme Jeudi glared at him.

"But the prettiest are still here," Nicolas hastened to say.

The husband lowered his head and blushed to his ears; the great-niece was crimson; Marguerite made every attempt to appear indignant, and Mlle Jeudi looked at Nicolas with gentle compassion.

"Is he the brother of the curé of Courgis?" the Jansenist tradeswoman asked Marguerite sternly.

"Yes, Madame, and the abbé Thomas; but he is not intended for the church."

"No matter, he has bold eyes, and I would advise his brothers to monitor him."

Nicolas and the housekeeper left Auxerre at four o'clock so as to return to Courgis before dark. Arriving beyond Saint-Gervais, they recited together the nones and the vespers, then talked about the family life they had just seen. Marguerite did not scold Nicolas too much for his uncalled-for observation at the dinner table and consented to laugh at the poor husband's melancholy situation. At the entrance to the Montaleri valley, there was an area covered by grass, shaded by willows and poplars, and traversed by a fountain that filtered out between the pebbles. The travelers decided to have their evening meal there; Nicolas took out the provisions from the basket and put the bottle of wine in the fountain to cool. While enjoying their food, Nicolas recounted that after dinner he had seen, at Mme Jeudi's, the husband stop his wife between two doors and kiss her tenderly, while the mother and the great-niece were busy with the dessert.

"That's enough talk about it!" said Marguerite, rising; but Nicolas held her by her dress, and was strong enough to make her sit back down.

"Well, then let us talk a little more," said Marguerite after having resisted in vain.

"I want to show you," he said, "how he kissed his wife . . ."

"Ah, Monsieur Nicolas, that's a sin!" cried Marguerite, who was surprised despite herself. "And what about Jeannette, what would she say if she saw you?"

"Jeannette! Oh, yes, Marguerite . . . you're right; but I don't know why my thoughts are of her, when it is you who agitates my heart so strongly I cannot breathe . . ."

"Let us go, my son," said the housekeeper gently and in a tone so dignified, and with an accent so endearing, that Nicolas thought he heard his mother. As he helped her onto the donkey, he touched her only with a sort of terror, and it was then that Marguerite gave him a chaste kiss on the forehead.

She seemed deep in thought, as if seized by a painful impression, and finally broke the silence. "Take care, Monsieur Nicolas," she said, "this passionate soul of yours pours into everything that surrounds you. You are inclined to sin, as was M. Polvé, my uncle, who raised me. Passions that are poorly repressed lead further than we think; in middle age they grow stronger, and even old age is defenseless against tainted souls; then they assume a brutality that horrifies even the loved one. My uncle was the cause of all my misfortunes, and though he made every effort to fight against this guilty love he had conceived for me, he could not avoid feeling a sterile jealousy that drove him to refuse the request M. Rousseau had made for my hand. He told him that he did not want me to marry, that he intended to make me a nun, and to ensure that this union remained impossible, he arranged for another one, together with M. Rousseau's parents, so that the latter eventually married . . . the one who gave him . . . your Jeannette. The retreat of M. Rousseau encouraged another young man, M. Devesvre, to court me; but I was so timid and ignorant of my uncle's secret motives that I did not wish to unseal the letter that was given to me by M. Devesvre, so that he finally resolved to officially ask for my hand in marriage. M. Polvé replied that "no inhabitant of the countryside was worthy of his niece." So, M. Denesvre arranged to speak to me in secret, and his complaints were so touching that I agreed to listen to him at night from a low window. Then my uncle awoke, saw what was happening and went up to his attic, from where he fired a rifle at M. Denesvre. The unfortunate man did not scream and managed to drag himself, while losing blood, out of the alley across from my window. Because he didn't have the wound dressed . . . which could have compromised me . . . he died a few days later. He had sent me a letter written on his deathbed . . . I still have it . . . and since then I have never thought about marriage!"

Marguerite wept bitterly as as she told Nicolas this story; she passed her hands through Nicolas's hair and could not refrain from looking at him with tenderness, for he reminded her of M. Rousseau because of his love for Jeannette, and poor Denesvre because of his exaltation, his ardent glances, and the very gentleness she felt at seeing herself again the object of a passion which caused Nicolas to turn away from Jeannette. Moreover, if her former pains had made her indulgent toward him, their difference in age gave her some security.

It was nearly nine o'clock when the governess and Nicolas returned to the vicarage. They went to bed at ten. The young man's imagination embellished all that he had heard, and a multitude of incoherent thoughts prevented him from sleeping. He slept in the same room as the abbé Thomas on the ground floor; there were also the two small canopies for the choir boys, Huet and Melin. Marguerite's room, situated at the other wing of the house, gave onto a low window overlooking the garden. Suddenly the image of young Denesvre braving danger to see Marguerite vividly reappears in Nicolas's thoughts. In his mind he imagines that he himself is that young man, that there is something beautiful in shedding his blood to talk of love and, half awake, half subject to a feverish hallucination, he slips out of bed and manages to enter the garden through the kitchen door. There he is in front of Marguerite's window, which she had left open because of the heat. She was asleep, her long hair loose upon her shoulders; the moon cast a reflection that made her regular features stand out, beautiful and youthful, as once before in the favorable twilight. Nicolas made a noise as he stepped over the windowsill. Marguerite, dreaming, murmured: "Let me be, my dear Denesvre, let me be!" What a terrible moment: the double illusion which perhaps would bring a sad morrow! "Death strike me down, if need be!" Nicolas cried, seizing the extended arms of the sleeper . . . The only thing missing was the gunshot of the jealous uncle. Another catastrophe took its place. The abbé Thomas had followed Nicolas in his escapade; with a brutal foot, he removed in an instant all the poetry of the situation. Meanwhile, poor Marguerite, quite frightened, believed she saw a renewal, after twenty years and in another form, of the sinister denouement of the lover's drama she had been dreaming about. The two choir boys, hearing the noise, came to complete the scene. The abbé Thomas, in a rage, chased them away; then taking Nicolas by one ear, he brought him back to his room, made him dress at once, and without waiting for morning, set off with him to his father's house. The scandal was such that the following day a family meeting was held where it was decided that Nicolas would be apprenticed to M. Parangon, a printer at Auxerre. Marguerite herself was suspected of having given rise to the scene through her indulgence and vanity, and she was replaced at the presbytery by a churchgoer with a robust figure whose name was Sister Pilon.

Taken to Auxerre by his father just two days later, Nicolas dined a second time at Mme Jeudi's, the Jansenist tradeswoman, a friend of the family. The tranquility of this house was no less troubled than that of the presbytery at Courgis. The young bride was doing penance and appeared at the table with a large headdress with paper horns. Her crime was to have escaped the double surveillance of Mme Jeudi and her great-niece, in such a way that was made obvious by her shortening her skirt without having asked her mother's permission to do so. The son-in-law was returned to his parents as a libertine and a corrupter of morals. Mme Jeudi, at any given moment, exclaimed: "My daughter was defiled a second time by original sin!" However, the son-in-law, less timid than before, pleaded for his wife and for her dowry.

VI. The Apprenticeship

M. Parangon's printing house in Auxerre was near the fraternity of the Cordeliers.[39] The presses were on the ground floor, the letter cases in a large room above. The first duties entrusted to Nicolas had nothing attractive about them; it was mainly a question of collecting from the sweepings the letters that fell under the feet of his companions, *recomposing* them afterward, and then *recasing* them; he also had to run errands for thirty-two workers, draw water for them, and suffer all their rude whims. The lover of the beautiful Jeannette Rousseau, the student of the Jansenists, accepted these humiliations with difficulty; but his intelligence, his taste for work, and above all his knowledge of Latin soon earned him the respect of his fellow workers. There were a few books in the boss's office; Nicolas, who on holidays preferred reading to the parties of his comrades, developed a great admiration for Mme de Villedieu's novels.[40] The ease with which the lovers write to each other in these sorts of compositions led him naturally want to write a love letter to Jeannette in octosyllabic verses; yet through an astonishing neglect of precaution given the circumstance, he simply threw the letter into the post, so that it fell into the parents' hands, then was sent to the presbytery, where the curé, the abbé Thomas, and Sister Pilon uttered cries of indignation. The family was all the more convinced in their decision to remove from the countryside such a dangerous seducer, and the impossibility of his being able to return to Courgis after this scandal deeply saddened the young lover.

Suddenly, an unexpected appearance completely changed the course of his ideas and was to exert over his life an influence that changed the whole of its destiny. Mme Parangon, the boss's wife, whom Nicolas had not yet seen, returned from a trip of several weeks she had made to Paris. Here is the portrait that the writer would later write when he had reached the peak of his literary life: "Imagine a beautiful woman, admirably proportioned, whose face presented beauty, nobility, and that sharp attractiveness of a Frenchwoman that tempers majesty; an animated whiteness rather than color; fine hair, ashen and silky; arched eyebrows, luxuriant and black; beautiful blue eyes, which, veiled by long lashes, gave her an angelic and modest air, the greatest charm of beauty; a timid voice, pure, sonorous, and coming from the soul; a gait sensual and dignified; a hand soft without being plump, perfect arms, and the most delicate foot that was ever to be seen on a pretty woman. She carried herself with exquisite taste; it seemed that she gave to the simplest adornment that victorious charm of the girdle of Venus[41] which could not be resisted. An affable and engaging tone was the sweetest of her charms; it made her cherished when a difference in sex didn't compel adoration."

Such was Mme Parangon, married a short while, and whose husband seemed unworthy of so amiable a companion. In the early days of his apprenticeship, Nicolas, finding himself alone on a Sunday to guard the workshop, had heard the cries of a woman leaving M. Parangon's study. He rushed over and saw Tiennette, the maid, on her knees before her boss, whom she begged to spare her honor. "You are very bold," shouted the latter, "to enter here! Leave at once." Nicolas's attitude was such that he was determined to make the master yield and give Tiennette time to flee. Afterward, M. Paragon, in fact a bit ashamed, sought to allay his apprentice's well-founded suspicions.

Nicolas was at work when it was announced: "Madame has returned!" He was still working, his nose in the dust, picking up the letters, *spaces*, and *ems*.[42] He only had time to clean himself up in a bucket and go down to the ground floor, where the crowd of workers were gathering. Mme Parangon, who paid attention to everyone and had a look, an obliging word for each, soon noticed Nicolas.

"Is this the new *student*?" she asked the foreman.

"Yes, Madame," replied the latter... "He has a future."

"But where is he?" said Mme Parangon as the young man, after greeting her, was lost again in the crowd.

"Merit is modest," observed one of the workers with some irony.

The apprentice reappeared, blushing.

"Monsieur Nicolas," resumed Mme Parangon, "you are the son of a friend of my father; you also merit our friendship..."

At this moment, the young woman's gracious smile recalled to Nicolas a faded memory. He had seen this woman before, but not as she appeared to him now; her image was half buried in one of those vague childhood impressions which return at times like the memory of a dream.

"What?" said Mme Parangon. "You don't recognize little Colette de Vermanton?"

"Colette? Is it really you?... It is you, Madame!" Nicolas stammered.

The workers returned to their labors; the young apprentice remained alone, dreaming of that scene, the result of so simple a coincidence. Meanwhile, the lady had gone into a back room, where her maid was helping her remove her traveling clothes. She emerged a few minutes later. "Tiennette told me that you are a very honest boy... and very discreet," she added, alluding no doubt to what happened in M. Parangon's study. "Here is an object that you will find useful in your work." And she gave him a silver watch.

After that, Nicolas was highly respected in the workshop and exempted from the most off-putting jobs. His taste for study, his estrangement from dissipation and debauchery, to which several of his comrades fell victim, increased his esteem in Mme Parangon's eyes, who liked talking to the young apprentice and questioned him often about his readings. The novels of Mme de Villedieu, and even the *Princess de Clèves*, did not seem to her very solid teaching. "But I also read Terence," said Nicolas, "and I have even started a translation."—"Ah! read me that!" said Mme Parangon. He fetched his notebook and read part of *Andria*.[43] The passion he put in his delivery, especially in the passages where Pamphile expresses his love for the beautiful slave, gave Mme Paragon the idea of having him read *Zaïre*, which she had seen performed in Paris.[44] Her eyes followed the text and indicated from time to time the intonations used by the actors of the Comédie Française; but soon she began to prefer the young man's natural and relaxed delivery. She had put her arm around the back of the chair on which he was seated, and this arm, whose warmth he felt on his shoulder, conveyed to his voice the sound and quivering timbre of emotion. A visit interrupted this moment, which Nicolas was prolonging with delight. It was Mme Minon, the procurator, a relative of Mme Parangon. "I'm still quite moved," said the latter; "M. Nicolas was reading *Zaïre* to me."—"So he reads well?"—"With soul."—"Oh! so much the better," exclaimed Mme Minon, clapping her hands . . . "He will read us *La Pucelle*, which is also by M. de Voltaire.[45] That will be amusing." Nicolas in his ignorance, and Mme Parangon in her innocence, agreed to this project, which, however, was not realized; it was enough for the lady to open the book and flip through the pages to appreciate its levity.

Nicolas's morality was soon to receive a more serious attack, however. He was alone one night in the room on the ground floor when he saw a man enter furtively, his clothes in disorder, or rather half-dressed, whom he recognized as one of the Cordeliers, whose monastery was near the printing shop. This character, whose name was Gaudet d'Arras, told him he was being pursued, that they had lured him into a trap, and that moreover, he could not return to the convent through the usual door, since they would ask him what he had done with his robe. The door of the printing shop led to the courtyard of the convent; it was the best way to avoid any scandal. Nicolas agreed to save this poor monk, whose escapade remained a mystery to him.

A few days later, the Cordelier returned, wearing his robe this time, and invited Nicolas to come to lunch in his cell. He confessed to him during some effusive moments, after an excellent meal accompanied by an exquisite wine, that the religious life had long been a burden for him, especially as it was not the result of a choice on his part, but a requirement of his family. He was, moreover, in a position to break his vows, which could serve as an excuse for the lightness of his conduct.

Naturally, Nicolas's independent spirit gave him a profound antipathy for these feudal institutions that still survived in the tolerant society of the eighteenth century, and which compelled some of the children of great families to utter, without a vocation, austere vows that they were easily allowed to violate, provided they avoided a scandal. At first, Nicolas did not feel much sympathy for this monk who had forgotten his robe in the wheat field; but the idea that Gaudet d'Arras was only anticipating a future time when he would be free made his behavior relatively excusable. A close bond was thus soon established between Nicolas and the Cordelier. If the actions of the former have been favorably appreciated up to this point, one can still see in him an honest heart carried away only by exalted reveries; as for the other one, he was already a spirit completely in the grip of the materialism of the time. His mother provided him with a large pension, which enabled him to often invite the other monks to dine in his cell, which was cheery and overlooked the garden. Nicolas sometimes attended these parties, where they drank wildly and spoke of doctrines more philosophical than religious. The influence of these ideas later determined the tendencies of the writer; he himself often admits it.

This dangerous intimacy naturally led to confidences. The Cordelier deigned to take an interest in the young man's first love, while at times smiling at his innocence. "In principle," he told him, "you should avoid any romantic attachments. The only way not to be subjugated by women is to make them dependent on you. It is then good to treat them harshly; they'll love you all the more for it. I noticed your attachment to Mme Parangon; be careful of the worship with which you surround her. You are a mouse with which she plays, the humble servant she wants to keep as long as possible in that position. It is up to you to take the dominant role by depriving the beautiful lady of the glory she would gain by resisting you . . ." Nicolas did not understand a doctrine so bold; he even suffered to see his friend profaning the pure feeling he attached to his patroness. "What do you mean?" he finally remarked.—"I mean you have to stop feasting on smoke. Dare to declare yourself, and lead the way, or else occupy yourself with another woman: this one will come to you herself, and you will have at once two triumphs."—"No," said Nicolas, "I will never act in such a manner!"—"I recognize here," said Gaudet d'Arras, "the respectful lover of Jeannette Rousseau."

Nicolas vowed never to see the Cordelier again, but the poison was already in his heart; this sweet existence, this utterly Christian passion he would never have confessed, and which had no other goal but the pure union of souls, this image so chaste and so noble that it repulsed not even the image of Jeanette Rousseau in his heart and accompanied it like a beloved sister, all these charming sensations of a poet's mind that sufficed for the dream would henceforth be exchanged for the ardor of a purely material passion. Full of the new ideas he had drawn from his philosophical readings, he was helpless in avoiding the advice of Gaudet d'Arras; his solitude rang out at him in those mocking and melancholic voices which came from the Latin muses, and which reproduced the sophisms he had just heard: "A woman is like a shadow: follow her, she flees; flee from her, she follows." The Cordelier had said the very same thing.

He wished to enter the church, where the chants of vespers resounded. The Cordeliers Gaudet d'Arras had trained that morning rendered the plainsong with unusual vigor. Nicolas recognized the voices of his table companions, soaked with the most generous wines of Burgundy; he went to the cemetery to escape this memory, and began mechanically deciphering the oldest inscriptions on the tombs. One of them was in Gothic lettering: *Guillain*, 1534. Reflecting on the two centuries that had separated the death of a stranger from the time of his own birth, Nicolas felt the nothingness of death and life, and yielded to this voluptuous sadness the Romans took pleasure in exciting at their feasts; he cried out like Trimalcion: "Since life is so short, we must make haste . . ."[46]

Returning to the printer's shop, he picked up a book so as to change the course of these ideas; but shortly after, he saw Mme Parangon leaving the procurator's home, where she had dined. She was wearing mules with a strap, green trim and heels, fastened with a sparkling rosette. These mules were new and probably bothered her feet, and as Tiennette had not returned, she asked Nicolas to clear off a small crimson armchair so that she could sit down. Nicolas, seeing her seated, rushed to her feet and removed her mules without unbuckling them. The lady just smiled and said: "At least give me other shoes to wear." Nicolas hastened to find some; but Mme

Parangon, on his return, had hidden her feet under her dress and wished to put on her shoes herself. "What are you reading?" she asked.—"*Le Cid*,[47] madame," said Nicolas, and he added: ". . . Ah! How unhappy Chimene was! But how lovely!"—"Yes, she was in a cruel position."—"Oh! So very cruel!"—"I very much believe that these situations . . . augment love."—"Certainly, Madame, they augment it to such a point . . ."—"Well, how do you know that at your age?"—Nicolas was embarrassed; he blushed. A moment later, he dared to say, "I know it as well as Don Rodrigo does."—Mme Parangon rose with a burst of laughter, and then resumed in a more serious tone: "I wish for you the virtues of Rodrigo, and his happiness above all!"

Nicolas felt, through the benevolent irony that ended this conversation, that he had gone a bit too far. Mme Parangon had retired, but her mules with the glittering buckles remained near the armchair. Nicolas seized them with a kind of ecstasy, admired their shape, and dared to write in small letters, inside one of these charming objects: "I adore you!" Then, as Tiennette was returning, he told her to put them back.

VII. The Star of Venus

This strange action, this declaration of love so singularly placed, the audacity, especially as he was only an apprentice, to have addressed the master's wife in a such a manner, was the first step along a dangerous slope on which Nicolas was no longer able to stop. So far, we have seen him easily yielding to his emotions without thinking twice about the drives of his heart; we even had to remain silent on the many adventures with the girls of Sacy and Auxerre, often worshiped, often betrayed . . . Henceforth, this soul, still so young, no longer feels innocent; it was the uncertain moment when one has to choose between good and evil, the point in every man's life at which he decides his whole destiny. Ah, if we could stop the hands of the clock and turn them back! But one would only disturb the visible clock; the eternal hour always marches on.

That same day, M. Parangon and the representative of the printing office attended a banquet of the Freemasons; Nicolas had to dine alone with the printer's wife. He did not dare sit at the table. Mme Parangon said in a slightly altered voice: "Take your seat." Nicolas sat in his usual place. "Set yourself before me," said Mme Parangon, "since we are only two." She served him. He kept silent and slowly carried bits of food to his mouth.—"Eat, you're at the table," said the lady. "What are you dreaming about?"—"Nothing, Madame."—"Were you at High Mass?"—"Yes, Madame."—"Did you receive communion?"—"No, Madame, I was behind the choir, where it isn't distributed."—"Here is a piece."—And she showed it to him on a silver platter, but she did not give it to him.—"You seem deep in thought," she added.—"Yes, Madame . . ." And, suddenly feeling the impropriety of his answer, he regained a little courage; he remembered that this day was that of the birth of Mme Parangon: "I was thinking," he said, "that today is a special day . . . I should like to have a bouquet to present to you; but I only have my heart, and that is already yours." She smiled and said: "The wish is enough for me."—Nicolas had risen and approached the window, looking at the sky. "Madame," he added, "if I were a god, I would not think of offering you flowers, I would give you the most beautiful star, the one I see there. They say it is Venus . . ."—"Oh, Monsieur Nicolas! What are you thinking of?"—"That which we cannot reach, Madame, the sky at least allows us to admire. So now, every time I see this star, I will think: 'Here is the beautiful star under which Mademoiselle Colette was born.'" She seemed touched and replied: "That's nice, Monsieur Nicolas, and very lovely!"

Nicolas congratulated himself on escaping the reproaches he no doubt deserved; but the dignity of his mistress seemed to him cold; Mme Parangon retired. The young man felt so agitated that he could not keep still. The evening was not yet advanced, so he left the house and went for a walk near the rampart of the Benedictines. When he returned, the house was empty; M. Parangon had received a business letter that had obliged him to leave for Vermanton; his wife had gone with him to the carriage and was accompanied by her servant Tiennette. Nicolas was so full of emotion that he was upset at not knowing whom to speak to. As he glanced across the courtyard of the Cordeliers, he saw Gaudet d'Arras, who was walking with long strides, looking at the stars.

As we have said, this philosopher monk had a singular mind. There was in his head a mixture of both spiritual and material ideas that surprised one at first. His enthusiastic speech instilled in all who listened to him the sense of an empire from which it was impossible to escape. Nicolas went on a few walks with him, following as best he could the transcendental reveries of Gaudet d'Arras. His platonic love for Jeannette, and his sensual love for Mme Parangon, excited his head to such a degree that he could not help letting some of it show. The Cordelier replied with apparent distraction. "O young man," he said, "ideal love is the generous drink that beads on the edge of the cup; be not content with admiring its rosy hue; nature opens at this moment its inexhaustible vein, except you have but a moment to quench your thirst with its divine flavors, reserved for others after you!"

These words threw Nicolas into even greater confusion. "What!" he said, "are there not reasons that oppose our delirious ardor? Are there not positions one must respect, deities to worship on our knees, without even daring to ask them for a favor, a smile?" Gaudet d'Arras shook his head and continued his theories that were both abstract and material. Nicolas spoke of eternal justice, of punishments reserved for vice and crime . . . But the Cordelier did not believe in God. "Nature," he said, "is subject to the preconditions of harmony and numbers: physical law governs the universe."—"It would come at a great cost, nevertheless," said Nicolas, "to renounce the hope for immortality."—"I firmly believe in it myself," said Gaudet d'Arras. "When our body has ceased to live, our freed soul, seeing itself free, is overjoyed and wonders how it had ever loved life . . ." and indulging in a kind of inspiration, he continued, as if filled with a prophetic spirit: "Our free existence seems to me to be two hundred and fifty years old . . . for reasons based on the physical calculation of the movement of the stars. We can only revive the material that comprised the generation of which we were a part; perhaps this material is not completely dissolved, enough to be revivable, until after the time of which I speak. For the first hundred years of their spiritual life, our souls are happy and without moral sorrows, as we are in our corporeal youth. They exist then for a hundred years more in the age of strength and happiness, but the last fifty years are cruel because of their terror of returning to earthly life. What souls are most ignorant of is the state in which they will be born; will one be master or servant, rich or poor, beautiful or ugly, intellectual or foolish, good or wicked? This is what terrifies them. In this world, we cannot know how things are in the other life, because the new organs which the soul has received, as it enters a material form, are new and without memory; otherwise, the unblemished soul remembers all that has happened to him, not only in its previous life, but in all his spiritual existences . . ."

During these bizarre sermons, Nicolas was lost in his romantic reveries; Gaudet d'Arras noticed this and put aside the development of his system for another day; except he had cast into the heart of this young man the germ of dangerous ideas which, by their apparent philosophical basis, destroyed the last scruples owed to a Christian education. The conversation ended with some small talk about what was happening in the house. Nicolas learned from his friend, with indifference, that M. Parangon had left for Vermanton: "There you have a beautiful widow . . ." exclaimed the Cordelier, and they parted on these words.

Going back into the house, Nicolas felt like a drunken man coming in from the cold to a heated place. It was late, everyone was asleep, and he carefully opened the doors to return to his room quietly. When he reached the dining room, he began to think of the meal that he had, alone with his mistress, a few hours earlier; the window was open, and he looked for *Mlle Colette's beautiful star*, the star of Venus which had shone in the sky with so serene a light: it was no longer there. Suddenly, a strange thought crossed his mind; he recalled the last words spoken by Gaudet d'Arras, and like a thief, like a traitor, he hurried to the room where the lovely woman was asleep. Thanks to the trusting nature of the people in this province, a simple closed glass door with a latch was the only defense for this modest retreat, and the door wasn't even securely closed. Mme Parangon's steady breathing marked the fleeting moments of that night with a sweet sound. Nicolas dared to open the door halfway; then, falling to his knees, he slowly advanced to the bed, guided by the glow of a nightlight, and then he gradually rose, encouraged by the silence and the stillness of the sleeping woman.

The quick and fearful look Nicolas cast on the bed did not bring his soul all the fire he expected. It was the second time he had had the audacity to penetrate the sanctuary of a sleeping woman; but Mme Parangon had none of the abandon or reckless nonchalance of poor Marguerite Pâris. She slept severely draped like the statue of a Roman matron. Without the gentle breathing and the undulation of her veiled throat, she would have produced the impression of an austere figure carved on a tomb. Nicolas had probably half awakened her with his movement because she reached out her hand and weakly called on her servant Tiennette. Nicolas threw himself to the ground. His fear of being touched by his mistress's extended arm, which would have certainly awakened her, made such an impression on him that he remained motionless for some time, holding his breath, trembling as well at the thought that Tiennette might enter. He waited a few minutes and, now that it was quiet, the apprentice had just enough strength to crawl out of the room. He fled to the dining room and remained standing in the corner by a sideboard; soon after, he heard a bell. Mme Parangon had awakened her maidservant and had her sleep by her.

How dare he appear before the Cordelier after such a ridiculous attempt? This thought preoccupied Nicolas more strongly the next day even than the regret of a lost opportunity. Corruption was thus making rapid progress in this youthful soul, and the pains of pride dominated those of love.

The next day, after dinner, Mme Parangon asked Nicolas to read to her, and she choose the *Lettres du Marquis de Roselle*.[48] Nothing, however, in her tone or in her look, indicated that she knew the cause of the noise that had awakened her the previous night. Nicolas soon felt reassured; he read with charm, with enthusiasm; the lady, seated in an armchair by the fireplace, occasionally closed her eyes; Nicolas, perceiving this, could not help but think of the beloved and chaste image he had glimpsed the night before. His voice trembled, his pronunciation was muffled, and then he stopped reading altogether.

"But I'm not asleep! . . ." Mme Parangon said in a delicious tone of voice; "Moreover, even when I am, I am a very light sleeper."

Nicolas trembled; he tried to resume his reading, but his emotion was too great.

"You are tired," replied the lady, "stop. I was very interested in this Leonora . . ."

"And I," said Nicolas recovering his courage, "still prefer the more angelic character of Mlle Ferval. Ah, now I understand: every woman can be loved, but there are some who are goddesses."

"The most important thing is to always respect them," said Mme Parangon. Then, after a silence Nicolas dared not break, she resumed, with a gentle tone: "Nicolas, it will soon be time for you to establish yourself . . . Have you ever given thought to marriage?"

"No, Madame," said the young man coldly, and he paused, thinking he had uttered a hateful lie: the irritating image of his first love came to mind; Mme Parangon, who knew nothing about it, continued: "Your family is honest and allied with mine, so think carefully on what I'm about to tell you. I have a sister much younger than me . . . who resembles me a little." She added these words with some embarrassment, but with a charming smile . . . "Well, Monsieur Nicolas, if you work hard, then my wish is for my sister to marry you. Let the promise of this future be for you an incentive to educate yourself and preserve your morals. We shall speak of it again, my friend."

The worthy woman stood up and made a gesture of farewell. Nicolas rushed to her and took her hands, which he bathed with tears. "Ah, Madame," he exclaimed in a broken voice, but Mme Parangon would hear no more. She left him entirely to his own thoughts and his admiration for such grace and kindness. It was clear to him now that she knew everything, and that she had delightfully understood and repaired everything.

VIII. The Surprise

We are now going to see events accelerate. Nicolas is no longer that naïve and simple young man, a lover of solitude and the Latin muses, at first a rough and savage peasant, then a studious pupil of the Jansenists, then again an ideal and platonic lover to whom a woman appears as a fairy he dare not touch lest his dream vanish. The air of the city was fatal for this indecisive soul, energized only through his love of nature and pleasure. Thanks to the treacherous advice he was pleased to hear, thanks to those books of suspicious philosophy in which morality offers the attractions of vice and wears the mask of wisdom,* he is now freed from all restraint, enlightened too soon by the cold faculty of analysis such as old age owes to experience, rushing headlong, thus armed, into an atmosphere of vulgar entertainments, the habit of which is usually rationalized by those who often engage in it because of their ignorance of a better way of life. Mme Parangon's indulgence, that gentle pity, that exquisite sympathy for an honest love which goes astray; he had not felt its full delicacy. He understood that the noble woman was not as irritated as he had feared over his nocturnal attempt. However, every time he was alone with her since then, she spoke only of her plan to marry him to her sister, and he himself at times

* He later wrote: "Without my love of work, I would have become a scoundrel."

was beginning to think that he would one day discover in this future child another *Colette*; indeed, she had her charming features, she promised to be her image, but how long he would have to wait! In these returns of virtuous feeling, he became a dreamer, and Mme Parangon could not refuse him her hand, a smile he would hypocritically demand as a mirage of the legitimate happiness reserved for his future. She realized the danger of these conversations, these kindnesses, and told him: "You must distract yourself. Why don't you go to parties, to the promenades, like other boys? Every evening and every Sunday, you stay here to read and write; you'll make yourself sick."

"Well," he thought, "that's it, we must finally live!"—And he thereon plunged, with the rage of melancholy minds, disappointed minds, into all the pleasures that little city of Auxerre had to offer, which at the time was no more virtuous than Paris. He became the hero of the public balls, the driving force in workers' meetings; his astonished comrades invite him to all their parties. He steals their mistresses; he passes from brown-haired Marianne to spicy Aglaé Ferrand. Sweet Edmée Servigné and coquettish Delphine Baron quarrel over him. He writes poetry to both, contemporary verses, in the style of Chaulieu and de Lafare. He sometimes takes pleasure in creating a scandal from these liaisons, rumors of which travel to Mme Parangon; he responds to her criticisms, made with tears in her eyes, and assumes a triumphant air: "A young man has to enjoy himself a bit, you told me so . . . It makes us better husbands later . . . Witness M. Parangon!" And the poor woman leaves him without answering and returns home to burst into tears. Alas, he sometimes has the drunken voice, the bold gesture, the bad taste of a handsome tavern dancer. Mme Parangon observes all this with sorrow.

Suddenly, his conduct changes and he became sedentary again, but sad; one of his ephemeral mistresses, Madelon Baron, had just died, and even though he hadn't loved her deeply, this catastrophe spread a veil of sadness over his life. Mme Parangon felt sincerely sorry for him and took part in his pain, which she no doubt believed was stronger than it was. She had stopped feeling distrustful. One Sunday they were alone in the house; Tiennette had gone on an errand and Mme Parangon, who was tidying up the strands of yarn on a tall cabinet, called to Nicolas to pass her the bundles. She was standing on a double ladder, and as she was doing this,

Nicolas's eye rested on a slender leg, her white droguet shoe, whose thin, high heel gave even more delicacy to the prettiest foot imaginable. We know that Nicolas had never been able to resist such a sight. The charm redoubled when Mme Parangon, having difficulty in coming down since her feet were feeling numb, allowed him to take her in his arms, and he was obliged to place her on a pile of linen that was on the ground. How to express what took place in this moment as fleeting as a dream? Love long held in check, modesty conquered by surprise, everything conspired against the poor woman, so good, so generous, who fell almost immediately into a deep swoon like death. Nicolas, at last frightened, had only the strength to carry her to her room. When Tiennette came home, he told her that her mistress had fainted and called on him. He described his embarrassment and despair, then fled when she seemed to come to life, not daring to bear her first glance . . .

So, it all came to pass. The poor woman, who perhaps had loved in silence, but whose duty it was to keep it in check, does not rise the next morning. Tiennette tells Nicolas only that she is ill and that lunch has been prepared for him alone. So much reserve, so much goodness, that it is a fresh torture for a soul that feels guilty. Nicolas throws himself at the feet of the astonished Tiennette, and he bathes her hands with tears. "Oh, let me, let me see her, let me ask her forgiveness on my knees, so that I can tell her how much I regret my crime."

But Tiennette did not understand.

"What crime are you talking about, Monsieur Nicolas? Madame is unwell; are you also ill? . . . You certainly have a fever."

"No, Tiennette! But let me see her! . . ."

"My God! Monsieur Nicolas, who is preventing you from going to see Madame?"

Nicolas was already in the patient's room. Prostrate beside the bed, he wept without saying a word, and dared not even raise his eyes to look at his mistress. She broke the silence.

"Who would have thought," she said, "that the son of so many honest people would commit such an action . . . or at least would want to commit it . . ."

"Madame, hear me!"

"Ah, you can talk . . . I have not the strength to interrupt you."

Nicolas rushed to take the hand which Mme Parangon withdrew at once; his inflamed face was imprinted on the fresh linen sheets without his being able to find a word to restore his peace of mind. His disorder frightened even the woman he had so gravely offended.

"Heaven punishes me," she said . . . "It is a terrible lesson! I had a dream of this family union that would have brought us closer and made everyone happy, without any crime! No longer . . ."

"Ah, Madame, what are you saying?"

"You did not want to be my brother!" cried Mme Parangon, "Alas! You will be the lover of a dead woman; I will not survive this shame!"

"Ah, your words are too harsh, Madame!" And Nicolas rose to leave with a sinister resolution.

"He still has a soul!" said the ill woman . . . "Where are you going?"

"Where I deserve to be! I outraged the most perfect image of divinity . . . I no longer have the right to live . . ."

"Stay!" she said. "Your presence has become necessary to me . . . Our common position will tend to our remorse . . . My existence, cruel young man, depends on yours: dare abandon me now! . . ."

"I am unworthy of your sister," said Nicolas, bursting into tears; "had I been her husband, it is you I would have always loved. It was to not separate from you that I accepted the idea of this union! I do not want to be unfaithful to you, or to your sister . . ." And uttering these words, he fled. He went to the alleys which at that time skirted the ramparts of the city, seeking to calm the moral exaltation that would have killed him after the sorrow of such a scene.

It was a Monday: the promenade was covered with festive workers playing various games, young girls who were walking about in isolated groups of two or three. Nicolas recognized a few regulars from the dance halls he had recently attended. He tried to distract himself by joining one of these parties which at least left his heart free and calmed his mind through wild agitation. After a meal in the countryside, Nicolas left his friends, and his bitter thoughts crowded back to him when, passing rue Saint-Simon, near the hospital, he heard loud bursts of laughter. Three young girls were laughing at one of their companions, whom they had surprised letting herself be kissed by a worker from the Parangon printing press named Tourangeau, a big, ugly man, usually very rude, and a bit drunk that night. The poor insulted girl had fainted. The press worker, furious, rushed at the beautiful laughing girls and struck one of them very brutally. Young men had rushed over to the commotion and wanted to knock Tourangeau down. Nicolas reached his printing companion first and, taking him by the arm, told him, "You have just done a nasty thing. Without me, they'll tear you to pieces, but the situation has to be resolved. Let us fight at once with swords. You were in the army, you have the heart for it."—"I'm ready," said Tourangeau. The others tried in vain to separate them. One of the young men went to get two swords, and by the light of a streetlamp, the duel began according to the rules. Nicolas barely knew how to hold his sword, but Tourangeau wasn't very steady on his feet that night either. The press worker received a random stroke of the sword and fell from a neck injury which caused a lot of blood to flow. The attack wasn't fatal. Nicolas, however, was obliged to flee the authorities. He saw Mme Parangon, whose husband had returned, but for a moment, and she understood that there had been despair and secret bitterness in the young man's actions. Moreover, this duel had done him great honor in Auxerre, where he was now regarded as the *defender of beautiful women*. This reputation made its way even to his family, to whom he returned for some time.

IX. Epilogue of Nicolas's Youth

It was following these events that Nicolas, after spending a few days with his parents in Sacy, came to Paris to practice the typesetting skills he had learned in Auxerre. We have already seen how every new object exerted influence on this ardent soul, always prey to violent passions and, as he himself said, more impregnated with electricity than anyone else. It was some time before his ephemeral liaison with Mlle Guéant that he suddenly received notice of the death of Mme Parangon. The poor woman had survived only a few months after the painful scenes we have just described. The careless and frivolous life Nicolas had led in Paris had not been hidden from her, and doubtlessly caused her much bitterness in her final moments.

Nicolas, born with good instincts but still driven to evil by the lack of solid principles, later wrote, thinking back to that time in his life: "Morality is a pearl necklace; untie the string, and everything scatters."

However, his habits of dissipation had exhausted both his health and his resources. A simple worker, however clever he might be, earning at most fifty sous a day, cannot continue for long the existence that his new affairs had created for him. A letter came to him suddenly from Auxerre . . . It was M. Parangon. As Fate would have it, Nicolas was out of work and running out of money at the time this letter was handed to him; moreover, he felt a kind of nostalgia and thought of going away for some time to breathe his native air. M. Parangon, after some polite remarks and regret expressed over the death of his wife, complained of the isolation to which he was reduced, and proposed his former apprentice come and take the place of a foreman who had left him. "It is Tourangeau," he added, "who made me think of you . . . You see how far he is from bearing a grudge against you for the sword you planted in his neck."

When the letter arrived in Paris, Nicolas had only twenty-four sous; he was obliged to sell four linen shirts to pay for his seat in the coach to Auxerre. M. Parangon received him very well, and as Nicolas did not wish to lodge in his house, the printer pointed him to the hotel of one named Ruthot.

Fate consists of a series of random events, insignificant in appearance, which, through some unforeseen detail, can change the course of an entire life, either for better or for worse. Such at least was the opinion of Nicolas, who did not believe in Providence. He told himself later: "Oh, if I had not gone to stay at Ruthot's!" Or: "If I only had more than twenty-four sous when I received M. Parangon's letter"; Or again: "What a pity that I had not changed lodging, as I had thought of doing before the letter arrived!"

Near the hotel run by Ruthot lived a Mme Lebègue, the widow of an apothecary, whose daughter, Agnès, endowed with a somewhat masculine beauty, was to receive some fortune from her father's inheritance. Ruthot was a fairly handsome man and courted the widow Mme Lebègue. He invited Nicolas to some suppers, where Agnès Lebègue displayed many graces and kindnesses toward the young printer. He later learned that the expenses for these meetings had been paid by M. Parangon. He was all the more convinced given that the wine was very good, as M. Parangon was a connoisseur. The seduction continued its course, and soon there was talk of marriage. Nicolas wrote to his parents, who, informed by M. Parangon, easily gave their approval. Everything conspired to ruin the unfortunate Nicolas. His old friend, the Cordelier Gaudet d'Arras, who would have been able to enlighten him this time with his experience, had long since departed from Auxerre, having been morally devastated through his impiety. Moreover, M. Parangon gradually exerted a great influence on Nicolas, whom he had released from poverty with a few loans. "Ah, when Jupiter reduces a man to slavery, he takes away half his virtue," as the good Homer said. At the last moment, something strange occurred: Nicolas received an anonymous letter which gave him many details about the former life of his intended wife. Fate continued to pursue him on this occasion: he recognized the writing in this letter to be that of a mistress he had had in Auxerre during his apprenticeship, and he attributed it to the spite of an impotent jealousy. The marriage therefore took place without further difficulty. Upon leaving the church, a mocking smile began to flourish on M. Parangon's blotchy face. Nicolas had married one of the most maligned girls in the city. The property she brought into the marriage was burdened by a number of unpaid debts which reduced the total value to very little. It soon became clear to the poor young man that M. Parangon had been informed of what had happened long ago in his house. Nicolas was not totally convinced until later; but he ended up fleeing the hateful abode at Auxerre. Agnès Lebègue had already run away with one her cousins.[49]

Nicolas returned to Paris, where he joined André Knapen's printshop. "The work paid a lot at that time," and a good typesetter earned twenty-eight livres a week printing factums. This relative prosperity bolstered Nicolas Restif's courage, who soon wrote his first novels, among which we should distinguish *La Femme infidèle* [1786, The unfaithful woman],[50] where he revealed how his wife conducted herself; later, he published *Le Paysan perverti* in which he introduced, in the form of a novel, most of the events of his life.

PART TWO

1. Septimanie

The taste for autobiographies, memoirs, and confessions or confidences—which, like a periodic disease, occurs from time to time in our century—had become all the rage in the last years of the previous century. The example of Rousseau, however, had no more daring imitator than Restif. He didn't hold back in turning his adventures and those of people he had known into a great number of stories and novels; he published a precise and meticulous journal in sixteen volumes entitled *Monsieur Nicolas, or The Human Heart Laid Bare*, and, not content with this narrative, he repeated the main episodes in dramatic form. That produced a dozen plays in three and five acts that filled five volumes, of which he is, under various names, the eternal hero.

As far as our modern authors may push the sentiment of personality, they still lag far behind the self-esteem of such a writer as Restif. We have seen him already reading, in the salons of the great lords and financiers of the time, the scabrous adventures of his life, revealing his loves as well as his depravities, and the secrets of his family as well as those of his own household. A still greater audacity was on display when he wrote the series of plays he called *Le Drame de la Vie*, and to have them performed in various homes, sometimes with actors hired from the Comedie-Italienne, and sometimes with the aid of Chinese shadow puppets that an Italian artist made move while he himself took care of the dialogue. It's impossible to find a better portrait of pathology and moral anatomy. And woe to those who complacently attended this dangerous spectacle! They hardly dreamed they would one day take their place in this illuminated frame of a reflection of real life, with their profile boldly outlined, their absurdities and vices portrayed for all to see; that an entertainer would make them move, make them speak with the very intonation of their voices, using words they had used on such-and-such a day, on such-and-such street, in such-and-such a salon, in some more or less acceptable company, all in the presence of the merciless observer. Who would not have fled the company of such a man had they known that after having publicly debased himself, he would take revenge on those who mocked him, those who admired him, even on those simply curious? To each he will repeat: *Quid rides? . . . De te fabula narratur!*[51] He will enter your princely hotels, your alcoves, he will reveal the secrets of these houses, otherwise so well guarded, whose history he will have learned by seducing your maid, or by meeting at a cabaret with your beadle or your lackey. Such was the man—sustained to the very end, it is true, by this strange illusion in which he saw himself as a moralist in his profession of novelist and sententious spy.

What was always lacking in Restif de la Bretone was moral sense in his conduct, order, and taste in his imagination. His excessive pride prevented him from ever perceiving this. He always attributed his vices either to temperament, to poverty, or to a certain fate which, never letting faults go unpunished, by this very fact guaranteed absolution. It was a sort of religion he had formed, in which the suffering of this life held the expiation of all faults. Such a system led to everything being permitted for the one willing to suffer everything. It is only as episodes between Nicolas's youthful love affair and the one which brought his career to a sad end that we will now cite two adventures whose contrast is remarkable. In order to speak of them, we must refer to this strange depravity of eighteenth-century society, which certain novels, such as *Manon Lescaut* and *Dangerous Liaisons*, paint a picture which seems not too far from reality.

II. Episode

When Nicolas was still working at Knapen's, he would often take evening walks along the banks of the Ile Saint-Louis, a place he loved because of the view one could enjoy back then of the two banks of the Seine, covered by verdant crops and gardens. He usually stayed until sunset. Returning one evening by the Quai Saint-Michel, he noticed in passing a woman shrouded by a black satin hood and accompanied by a mature man wearing a square wig with three marteau loops,[52] who could be her husband or her steward. This lady's foot, wearing green mules, filled him with admiration—we know that this was his weakness—and he could only compare it to that of Mme Parangon or the duchess de Choiseul.[53] Her face was hidden; he had to derive the rest of the person from the foot, according to the system that Buffon has applied to the study of races.[54]

Having decided to follow this mysterious couple, he soon saw the mature man and the lady descend the bridge and go down rue Saint-Jacques to the junction it forms with rue Saint-Séverin. Once there, the man indicated to the lady an alley door, watched her enter, made sure she was received into the house, and then walked away. What intrigued Nicolas most about the separation of this couple he had followed was that he knew the house the lady had entered was a rather suspicious dwelling; it was one of those gambling dens where gamblers and women of all types assembled around a game of pharaon.[55] He entered resolutely, took a seat at the table with an air of indifference, and examined all the mules of the ladies at the table, who occasionally got up and roamed around the room. None wore a green mule; and none had the foot of either Mme Paragon or Mme de Choiseul. What had become of the veiled woman? . . . He finally decided to ask the lady presiding over the gaming table; but as he approached her, Nicolas recognized, beneath her glittering outfit and the daring adjustments to her person, a compatriot, a woman of Nitry—once very beautiful, but since fallen into the class of a Baroness de Lansquenet.[56] The encounter was touching. The *baroness* remembered having made young Nicolas dance on her knees when she was just a peasant.

"What are you doing here?" she asked him; "Despite what I have become, I still can't see the son of honest people in such a place."

Nicolas told her of his sudden love for the green mule and especially for the delicate foot which it supported on its three-inch hollow heel.

"How is it that I saw her enter," he said, "and she is not here?"

"She is here," said the baroness; "she is in the next room, which leads to the drawing-room through a glass door . . . Behave yourself; she may be looking at you."

"Me?" Nicolas said.

"As well as these gentlemen ... She is a great lady, curious to know what takes place in these houses that are forbidden to her, and if..."

"If..."

"Well, as I said, look sharp... be graceful!"

None of this made sense to Nicolas. It was time for supper. The game was interrupted, and everyone took part in this banquet, which in these kinds of houses customarily takes place at around one o'clock in the morning. Yet the lady with the green mule did not appear; suddenly, the lady of the house, who had left the room for a moment, returned to Nicolas and whispered in his ear: "You've been found pleasing... I'm glad to see such good fortune for a boy from our region. Only, resign yourself: there is one condition... You will not see her! It's already enough that you've seen her green mule."

The next morning, Nicolas woke up in one of the rooms of the house. The dream had vanished. It was the story of Cupid and Psyche in reverse: Psyche had left before dawn; Cupid was alone. Nicolas, a bit confused, and all the more charmed, tried to question the hostess; but she was a discreet woman and certainly paid to be so. She even tried to persuade Nicolas that he came into the house a little animated after some generous drinking... and that he had dreamed it all. Nicolas, who drank only water, did not accept this explanation.

"Well!" said Massé (such was her name), "now, tremble. You don't know who this lady of the *green mule* is... You will never know."

"What! Can't I see her again?"

"You never saw her."

"Find her again?..."

"Beware of even trying to track her down. Moreover, she will no longer wear green mules, you can rest assured of that. You will not meet her again on foot, as you did last night. Forget all this."

And to bolster this advice, she handed him a purse full of pistoles, which Nicolas threw to the ground with indignation. It was only some time later, in some literary salons where he related this adventure, that he caught a glimpse of a mystery concerning some great lady; but at that time, one didn't dare encourage such assumptions. It may also be surprising today, given the manners of the heroes of modern novels, that he would not have done everything possible to find the unknown lady; but a poor printer with almost no resources had too much to risk in such an undertaking.* His heart, moreover, had no trouble moving on.

Fifteen years later (1771), Nicolas leaves Paris to fulfill a sad duty. He is on a coach to Sens; sad and pensive, he looks despairingly at a company of elegantly dressed ladies, who chat and laugh in the back of the coach: "How many people," he exclaims, "are less unhappy than myself . . . Wretch! I'm going to see my mother die!"[57]

Two ladies pull away from the crowd and chat in passing, without seeing him, the dark corner where he is huddled. "What name," said one of the two, "shall we give the young lady to conceal hers?"—"Let us call her *Queen*," said the other. "She is in fact almost a queen, but who will know?"—"Queen, yes," replied the first with a laugh, "if she really were the daughter of the Prince of Courtenay,[58] the oldest name in France; but it is her mother alone who says so."—"Was she not right," said the other lady, "to want to revive this ancient branch, the most noble one in Christendom? Just think, my dear, there won't be a Courtenay in England anymore.[59] Who dares now to wear the coat of arms with the five besants of gold, brighter than any fleur-de-lis?"[60]—"After all, she's but a girl," said the other lady, "and therefore *she* was wrong. A boy was needed to not let the hereditary title perish and inherit the positions!"—"She did what she could. Legitimacy is not always a happy affair."—"And was the young man okay?"—"She had seen him without his being able to see her; he was about twenty years old . . ."

At this moment, the ladies perceived the presence of Nicolas who, in the shadows, his head in his hands, seemed not to have heard them.

"Poor man!" said one of the ladies, "he appears to be in great pain: he's been weeping since Paris. He is no longer young, but his eyes have a penetrating liveliness . . . See with what tenderness he looks at Septimanette . . . He's still weeping. He has perhaps lost a daughter her age!"

The young girl had indeed drawn near her two governesses; Nicolas stood up as if he had heard the last few words. "Yes, exactly her age!" he said

* Restif de la Bretone claims in one of the accounts he made of this adventure that a man was stationed to follow him and kill him if he had tried to follow the mysterious lady. He would later be assured of the fact.

with a deep emotion that warmed the hearts of the two ladies and the girl . . . "Allow me to kiss her."

The girl gave herself to him with a childlike grace.

"And . . ." said Nicolas, looking up, "one of you ladies is doubtless her mother?"

"Neither of us . . . Her blood . . ."

One of the ladies signaled to the other to stop speaking.

"Oh, fine blood!" Nicolas said, after waiting in vain for the end of the woman's sentence . . . "Her father must be happy!"

"Her father does not love her because she's a girl . . . and he was hoping . . ."

A second glance from one of the ladies suppressed the other's indiscretion. At this moment, the coach stopped before a meadow at the end of which a castle could be seen. A boat came for the ladies and the girl, for whom a coach decorated with a coat-of-arms was waiting on the bank.

"May I kiss her a second time!" Nicolas said.

They granted this out of pity for his grief, although it appeared, this time, somewhat indiscreet. Kissing the girl, Nicolas drew a flower from the bouquet she was carrying and put it in a book. The coach had resumed its way to Sens.

"What is that castle?" Nicolas asked a sailor.

"It's Courtenay."

So, it was true: the unknown lady was the famous Septimanie, the Countess of Egmont, Richelieu's daughter, the wife of a prince who had not been able to provide an heir.[61] It explained everything, and he regretted the imprudent accounts he had made of this adventure, because to declare himself the hero could not be very honorable or very prudent. It was not until 1793 that Nicolas dared to tell this last episode; the first had appeared in 1746 but was disguised in such a manner that no one could recognize the characters. Such adventures were frequent at that time; they sometimes even took place with the husband's consent, either with the idea of retaining titles or privileges in a family, or to prevent large assets from going to indirect descendants as a result of sterile unions.

III. Zéfire

After the story of this great lady's whim, it will be necessary to descend very low into the crowd, and to rise to very great emotional heights to explain the bizarre circumstances of the narrative we have now to tell. Since the death of Mme Parangon, no episode was more painful in the writer's life, and he has reproduced it in the triple form of novel, play, and memoir. It takes place when he was still working as a typesetter and had not yet published any of his books. He no doubt owed to this adventure the idea for one of his first works.

Nicolas was spending one Sunday near the Opera House, which was then part of the Palais Royal.—He noticed at a window in rue Saint-Honoré a young girl who was singing while plucking a harp. She seemed to be only fourteen years old; her smile was divine, her mood was lively and gentle; the sound of her voice penetrated the heart; she rose, and her *wasp* waist, as it was then called, moved with sweet abandon. For a moment, Mme Parangon was forgotten;—a moment later, her memory, even keener, restored to Nicolas the strength to flee this siren.

Returning home that evening on rue Sainte-Anne, he took the same road as before. The girl was no longer at the window; she was walking along the shops, on the muddy pavement, with pink leather mules and a dress with frills. Nicolas, still young and with his heart full of a dear memory, felt only a sense of pity. He questioned the poor girl, who replied that her name was Zéfire, and that she lived in a house with her mother, her sister, and their friends. There was such apparent innocence in her answers, or rather such ignorance as to what evil or good, vice or virtue, was that Nicolas thought she was playing a role learned in advance. He left and returned quite pensive to his lodging, which he shared with another journeyman printer named Loiseau. The next day, as they were returning home together after work, Nicolas pointed out the girl to his companion, pitying the fate of the poor child—lost without even knowing she was—and wanted to stop to question her further; but Loiseau, a man of severe morals who was about to be married, led Nicolas away, telling him of the danger that existed if he merely leaned over an abyss.

"What if someone is to be saved?" said Nicolas.

Loiseau shook his head and Nicolas began a long philosophical dissertation on the corruption of big cities, the need to moralize the police, and all of it mixed with considerations on the ancient institution of *hetaera*, on regulations to be established regarding the taste of those whom Jeanne de Naples had established in her good city of Avignon. He never ran out of arguments or scientific proofs. The good Loiseau confined himself to saying a few words regarding Mme Parangon. Nicolas kept silent; however, he couldn't help spending the evening on the left side of rue Saint-Honoré, still watching the poor child and addressing a few words to her. Loiseau waged war with him again over it. He thereafter took a different path to get from the Louvre printing shop to rue Sainte-Anne.

For some time, Nicolas had been feeling ill; he was having periodic choking fits that lasted several hours. Work became impossible for him; he had to stay in bed. Loiseau did the work for both of them; but their resources were soon exhausted. The unfortunate lived on the sixth floor, at the lodging of a fruit seller, who was also a billposter. A mean bed, two chairs, a rickety table, an old chest; such was his furniture. He received daylight through a ventilation hole covered with two panes of oil paper. The boards of the partition which separated his nook from that of Loiseau's were covered with theater posters the fruit seller had used to cover the chinks in the wall, and the patient had nothing else to do than read *Mérope*, *Alcyone*, and *La Bohémienne*, in which he had admired Mme Favart, as well as *La Gouvernante*, in which Mlle Hus was so mediocre, but so pretty; and again *Les Dehors Trompeurs*, which reminded him of the beautiful Mlle Guéant, or *Arlequin Sauvage*, a unique drama in which shone a certain Coraline, whose features bore some resemblance to those of . . . Zéfire.[62] Suddenly the door opened, and the fruit seller leaned his head in and said to Nicolas: "Your cousin is asking to see you."

"I have no cousin in Paris," said Nicolas.

"You see very well, Mademoiselle," said the fruit seller turning back, "that it's a pretext . . . We don't receive women like you in this house."

"But I'm telling you, he's my cousin Nicolas," replied a flute-like voice. "I've come from the countryside."

"Oh, but you're all spruced up, and he is hardly so . . ."

The caller finally slipped under the fruit seller's arm and entered the room:—"Oh, what misery! . . . But, Monsieur, he's dying," she quickly said to the fruit seller.

Indeed, for a moment, the choking fits had resumed.

"What is most urgent?" said the girl in a resolute tone. "Here's some money." And she gave him some gold coins.

"Most urgent," said the fruit seller, mollified, "would be broth."

"Bring some of yours right away."

Nicolas, recovering his senses, felt a child's hand lift his head as another hand brought a spoon to his mouth. He could no longer be in doubt; this compassionate beauty was Zéfire. She had seen Loiseau on his way to the printing shop, had followed him, and asked him: "Why do we no longer see your friend pass by here?"—"He is very ill," Loiseau had replied, and he had given her their address indifferently when asked for it.

As Nicolas, feeling better, found the strength to rise partway up from his cot, Zéfire, in a pink taffeta dress, swept the garret and organized the chairs and table; then she returned to his bedside, put some candy infused with *drops of England*[63] in his mouth and, drawing a handkerchief from her pocket, wiped his forehead; she put her headscarf on him, which she tied with a ribbon; then she suddenly said: "I'm not properly dressed to look after a patient, I'll come back in a quarter of an hour." The fruit seller returned in her absence and brought a second helping of broth: "Your cousin," he said, "must be a maid in a great house; she paid me for a month and gave my little girl a gold cross." Nicolas, weakened by illness, saw only a beneficient fairy in this poor girl who had risen from the abyss to help him, the way others come from heaven.

Zéfire soon returned in a calico dress and stayed with Nicolas until nightfall; the fruit seller brought his dinner up to him and, delighted by the alleged cousin's good will and kindness, even wanted to add at his own expense a *little dessert* which Zéfire shared with the patient. However, night had come; she rose with a painful feeling:—"Where are you going?" asked Nicolas.—"Home; this is the time I'm expected," says Zéfire . . . And she fled to hide her tears. Nicolas hardly had any time to think over Zéfire's last words before the sound of Loiseau's footsteps could be heard on the stairs.

Loiseau was not in a good mood; his companions at the printing shop hadn't been able to lend him much: he had only brought sugar for the patient and bread for himself. The smell of beef stew surprised him at first. It was the dinner that the fruit seller had brought up for Zéfire, who had barely touched it. "Excellent," said Loiseau, "this good man has taken pity on us!" And he pulled the table to him to take advantage of this windfall. A bag of écus fell to the ground. "What's that?" said Loiseau. Nicolas was no less surprised than him. Loiseau continued: "Did they send you money from back home?"—"Huh, who gives me a thought? … other than you and … but it's her!"—"Who?"—"Zéfire, whom you met this morning, and who came to look after me in your absence."—"What? *A girl of the world*? …"[64]

Honest Loiseau's ideas were all turned upside down; he went from admiring the young girl's kindness and devotion to wanting to return the unclean money she had left with them. In the end, knowing she was to return the next day, he put the money in the trunk to return to her.

The next morning Zéfire reappeared; she was so pretty, so naive, so touching in her pity that Loiseau was moved. "Does it matter where virtue comes from?" he exclaimed, "I bow down and adore it! … But we cannot accept this money …" Zéfire read his thoughts. "This money comes from my father," she said; "it was my older sister who kept it for me and gave it to me upon learning that there was a poor sick person who needed help." Loiseau went so far as to open the bag and count the écus, shedding tears of emotion. The two friends were overwhelmed with so many pressing debts that the thought of them weakened their scruples. That evening, Zéfire lost track of the time and stayed until nightfall; Loiseau found her still there when he returned home; she asked him to see her out. "Me?" he said, "see you …"—"Otherwise, they'll arrest me."—"Let's go," said Loiseau, "I'll get a good reputation in the neighborhood!" As for Zéfire, she found her position very simple. Her mother had told her that women were divided into two classes, both useful in their own way, both relatively honest; she belonged to the second class, having not been born in the first, that's all.

The next day was a Sunday; she stayed with the two friends and told them, "My mother taught me everything; she lets me come for the whole day. She approves of my feelings; she would rather see me frequent the company of a good worker than an officer who would beat me, or a gambler who would take me for everything I had. She is very good, my mother …" Loiseau kept silent, frowning. Nicolas, regaining his strength, rose suddenly with his former enthusiasm and put on his only coat.—"Let us visit her mother," he told Loiseau.—"Go back to bed," answered the latter …—"No! I'll die writhing in despair on this bed. This crisis is saving me! This young girl must not return to that house tonight … My illness has changed its nature; I no longer feel oppressed, I only feel feverish and agitated every night the moment she leaves us: do you understand why?"

Loiseau tried in vain to understand; Nicolas did not listen in his moments of enthusiasm. They went to rue Saint-Honoré to the mother, whose name was Perci. She was a former clothes dealer and pawnbroker, who had arranged meetings between suitors and great ladies who had been caught by the police; she had been sentenced a heavy fine, less for the crime itself than for not having paid the customary dues to the police; since then, she had taken a license for her peace of mind. When questioned by Nicolas and Loiseau, she swore that her daughter had so far remained honest, but that they were waiting for her to reach a suitable age to bring her *out into the world* with the permission of the police lieutenant. The two workers shuddered at these details, which Perci listed with the greatest complacency. Loiseau could not refrain from expressing his indignation.—"What do you want me to do?" the mother said, "Don't I have a record? Who would marry her? . . . Moreover, raised as she was, and pretty, with her talents, should she resign herself to earning a few sous a day sewing, or doing hard work, become a servant? Who would want her? . . . And in any case, would she be any less lost? We know what happens to pretty girls among the people . . ."

"Well then, I will marry her," Nicolas said, "if she wishes to no longer be dependent on you and learn to work."

Perci threw herself around his neck. "Are you telling the truth, my boy? Well, you have made me weep, and I had lost the habit . . . Listen carefully: don't think my daughter won't have a dowry . . . it will be good money and well-earned at that. I was a retailer, I lent at interest: it's honest, it is!"

"Let us not speak of these things," said Nicolas; "I feel strong now, and I earn a lot when I work . . . So, you agree that your daughter will not return here anymore? You are a good woman at heart."

"My God!" Loiseau said, "is it possible that there is virtue even in such souls . . . I did not know; yet I would have preferred not to know."

Loiseau was right; it is better, in the interest of morals, to assume that vice completely corrupts its victims, except for the chance of atonement and repentance, than to expose oneself to the difficult moral questions that result from a dubious mixture of good and evil. That was the reasoning of a common but wise man. Nicolas was neither one nor the other, unfortunately.

Zéfire delightedly accepted the proposal to live for the man she preferred. Her love for him alone assured Nicolas of her virtue. Good Loiseau still needed to give her a moral education and lessons on decency and modesty. They had her read good books, she who had read only the novels of Crébillon the Younger or Voisenon.[65] They taught her to speak a different language than the one she had heard until then, and it was only when they had nothing to fear anymore from her habitual manners or her reckless chatter that they sought out a profession for her. Loiseau's betrothed, whose name was Mlle Zoé, greatly helped the two friends in Zéfire's preliminary education. She recommended her as a shopgirl to a fashion merchant at the corner of rue des Grands-Augustins. Her *grisette* clothing, her powderless headdress, and her tulle bonnet changed her appearance to such a degree that it would have been impossible to recognize her.[66] Her mother, informed by Nicolas, approved of all these arrangements, and promised never to visit her daughter during her apprenticeship.

Nicolas could only see Zéfire on Sundays; on that day Mlle Zoé would go to fetch her, and they took walks beyond the gate with Loiseau. Nicolas, impatient as always, could not help passing every night in front of the boutique; he looked in the windows, and was regarded as the diligent suitor of one of the girls, without anyone knowing which one. The shopkeepers of Paris are never surprised by these loves from a distance, which are common. One Sunday, Nicolas reached an agreement with Zéfire that he would write to her every evening. As she had been placed near the front window, he took care to fold his letter *into a fan fold* and pass it through one of the *bolt holes*. Zéfire deftly pulled out the paper and was happy until the next day. Sometimes when the ladies were asleep, he came to the deserted street with his friend Loiseau, who played the lute very well, and they performed the newest operatic arias, such as *L'Amour m'a fait la peinture* or even better, *Dans ce charmant asile*, preferring to choose verses with the word "Zéfir" . . . Love tries to be witty when it can.

Their Sunday walks usually took place in the hills of Montmartre. One day, they were followed by three musketeers to a food seller where they were to dine.—One of them recognized Zéfire from having seen her on rue Saint-Honoré. Finding her in the company of simple workers in their Sunday best, they wanted to take her away. Fortunately, the fruit seller had accompanied them, so there was an equal number of men on both sides, apart from the swords, which Nicolas and Loiseau lacked. On the other hand, the fruit seller, anticipating the attack, had seized a long skewer from his kitchen.—"Watch your step, knave," said one of the musketeers threatened by this instrument, "we are gentlemen, and we'll have you thrown into the Châtelet."—"You dishonor your family and the military uniform!" Nicolas shouted . . .—"It's a question of honor! . . . It concerns *Zéfire* who is with you: well, ask her whether she prefers a lord to a simple worker? . . .We have gold, my lovely!" added the musketeer, jingling the coins in his pocket.

The quarrel had turned into a discussion, because of the attitude of the three defenders; but these last words left Loiseau beside himself with anger: "Villain!" he exclaimed, "you've just committed a great crime . . . you have profaned *the return to virtue*!" As for Nicolas, he had seized a chair. "What's this?" said one of the musketeers, drunker than the others, "a virtue that arises out of . . . vice? And that other hussy, is she also a virtue?" He tried to approach Zoé at the same time. Loiseau roughly pushed him away: "Respect the fiancée of a citizen," he shouted (this was in 1758).—"A citizen!!," said the musketeer, laughing, "they only speak like that in Geneva . . . You look to me like a Huguenot!"

Loiseau grabbed a stool and struck the musketeer who had spoken. Everyone joined the fray. Zéfire and Zoé intervened with the combatants in vain; the fruit seller worked wonders with his skewer, and the musketeers had been defeated when the guard arrived, summoned by the food seller; Nicolas, exasperated, still wanted to fight, but Loiseau opposed it, and all he could do was take the unconscious Zéfire from the room. When the police chief arrived, the musketeers, themselves embarrassed by their escapade, made use of their previous conjecture to assert that Loiseau, who looked grave and was dressed in black, was a Protestant minister who was holding a sermon, adding that they had arrived in time to disperse the heretics. The police chief accepted this explanation, and had already handcuffed the three men, promising them that they would be hanged, when one of the musketeers, less drunk than the others, was finally willing to admit that he and his companions were somewhat in the wrong. "This is a generous confession," observed the police chief . . . "We recognize here people of noble birth."—"In truth," said the musketeer to the workers, "the writerly platitude would have me renounce my privileges as a gentleman! . . ." Then, unable to refrain from adopting a superior tone: "Au revoir!" he said as he walked away, "we'll cut your ears off another day!"

The police chief had left, but only after taking down the names and addresses of the fighters. Despite the withdrawal of the musketeers, the adventure could have disastrous consequences for poor devils like Nicolas and Loiseau; moreover, the investigation of the affair, however unimportant it had become, inevitably brought attention to the special position of Zéfire, the innocent cause of the fight. However, the poor girl was less worried about that than about the danger her friends might face; they brought her back to the store in the grip of a fever. Unfortunately, the shop girls had returned; they heard, as did the mistress, what she said in her delirium: "I'll go to my mother! She has powerful guardians . . . But I'd sworn never to set foot in her house again! . . . but I must . . . My mother is a close friend of the police lieutenant: he gave her a license . . . and she's rich . . . and she knows great ladies . . . My mother's so accommodating! . . . All these people have ruined her . . . but she has a good heart deep down! . . . Otherwise Nicolas and Loiseau would be hanged as Huguenots, and it would be my fault . . . Why? Because I'm . . . my mother's daughter! . . ."

Loiseau and Zoé trembled at these interspersed confessions and the astonishment of those in the shop. They had to confess everything; they were deeply affected by their misfortune and their companion's situation. Nicolas was not present at this scene, because he did not go to the fashion boutique, afraid of compromising Zéfire. Moreover, he didn't suspect the gravity of her condition and thought, on returning home alone, that she was only indisposed as a result of having fainted. Loiseau, meeting back up with him that evening, dared not tell him of the scene he had witnessed. The next morning, Nicolas was calmer than the day before, so Loiseau thought he could tell him part of the truth. Nicolas wasted no more time and ran to the fashion merchant. "Come then," the woman told him, "I know who you are . . . Go up and see her: she's been crying out for you."

Zéfire was overwhelmed and in pain, but calm; she pretended to appear tired from the emotions of the preceding day; she told Nicolas that he should go to his printing shop and let her rest, then kissed him twice, saying, "See you tonight." All the workers were astonished at Nicolas's pallor. At eight o'clock, Loiseau said to him, "Let's have something to eat, and then

I will take Zoé to see Zéfire. You will not show yourself at first, so as not to agitate her; your pallor would give her cause for concern." Indeed, he did not show himself, but he heard her speaking from the next room. Loiseau said to him, "Go and get some rest, she's better; it is you I'm worried about . . ."

Nicolas, on waking, was surprised not to find his friend; the fruit seller told him that he had been out all night. He ran to the printing press. Loiseau was working at his letter case: "And Zéfire?"—"Zoé and I spent the night by her side."—"Oh God, without me!"—"The sight of you would have increased her fever."—"How is she?"—"Much better." Loiseau blushed saying these last words. He tried to calm Nicolas's anxiety by speaking of some urgent work to be done; but, after some hesitation, the latter took his coat and ran to the shop. Loiseau followed and caught up with him. Zéfire had a choking fit, yet she took the hand of her lover, tried to smile, and said: "It's nothing." He refused to leave her. That evening, as Zoé was sitting on a couch, Zéfire made a sign to Nicolas that she wanted to put her head on his breast, that she would breathe easier . . . He lay forward in his chair, half leaning over the bed, and supported that blonde head, which had been so fresh just two days earlier. After two hours in this tiring position, a great sigh awoke Zoé. "Go get some rest now," she said to Nicolas. And, lifting Zéfire's head, she set it gently on the pillow. Zéfire had drawn her last breath. Nicolas, deceived by his friends over the seriousness of her illness, only learned about it the next day. "And I am also going to die!" he said calmly. He was—in his own words—consoled by despair.

Yet he only suffered one serious illness, mingled with delirium and lethargy; the first words he uttered were: "I have *finished* losing Mme Parangon." Zéfire's features had reminded him of that adored woman, as she herself had seemed to bear some resemblance to Jeannette Rousseau, his first love.

This theory of resemblances is one of Restif's favorite ideas; he built several of his novels on similar assumptions. This idea is specific to certain minds and indicates a love founded more on the external form than on the soul; it is, so to speak, a pagan idea, and it is difficult to accept, as Restif claims, that he has only loved the same woman . . . in three persons. Resemblances almost always stem from the same region or race, which could be said of Jeannette Rousseau and Mme Parangon. So Restif supposes that

Zéfire, through her mother, originated in the same region as they did. In general, there is an aspect to his philosophical system that is always mingled with the most truthful accounts of his life.—He believed in the division of races as an Indian does, and rejected, according to this system, the doctrine of absolute equality; even the intermixing of foreign families did not seem to change his opinion on the subject, because he showed that, in general, some children were more like the father, others more like the mother, although he admitted that in Europe there also existed the detritus of bastards and mixed natures. These strange problems amused many distinguished men in the eighteenth century; but no man explored, to the extent that he did, this spirit of paradox, sometimes illuminated by a flash of truth.

As touching as the death of Zéfire was and the thought of atonement relating to it, one cannot refrain from lamenting the fatal influence this affair had on the works and morality of the writer. As Loiseau rightly felt, corruption cannot be touched on with impunity. *Le Pornographe*, a work with moral pretensions, but in which the author takes pleasure in exposing arguments of an often questionable morality, was the result of Nicolas's meditations on the fate of a certain class of women whom he wished to raise up in their own eyes as well as in the eyes of the world.

IV. Sara

We now arrive at a fertile time in Nicolas's life, a time of profound teachings and painful memories. Nicolas is no longer the handsome dancer of Auxerre, the beloved apprentice to Mme Parangon, the lover of those eleven thousand virgins, most of them martyrs, whose names were Jeannette Rousseau, Marguerite Pâris, Manon Prudhot, Flipote, Tonton Laclos, Colombe, Edmée Servigné, Delphine Baron, or Rose Lambelin; he is no longer even that lover formed by Mlle Prudhomme and the beautiful Mlle Guéant, or that obscure gallant, whom the blonde Septimanie, Countess of Egmont, had the opportunity to choose to compensate for the coldness of her noble husband.—The year is now 1780; Nicolas is forty-five years old. He is not yet old, but he is no longer young either; his voice is hoarse, his skin is wrinkled, and silver strands mingle with the locks of black hair that can sometimes be seen under his unkempt wig. The rich man can maintain the freshness of his illusions for a long time, like those early crops and rare flowers obtained with difficulty in the middle of winter; but the poor man is forced in the end to submit to the sad reality which the imagination had long concealed. Woe, then, to the middle-aged man mad enough to open his heart to the deceitful promises of young women! Until the age of thirty, the sorrows of love slide over the heart they press against without penetrating it; after forty, every sorrow awakens previous ones; the man who has arrived at the complete development of his being suffers doubly from broken affections and outraged dignity.

At the time of which we speak, Nicolas was living on rue de Bièvre, at Mme Debie-Léeman's. This lady was a Jewess from Antwerp and forty years old, still beautiful, the widow of a problematic husband, and living with a M. Florimond, a worn-out gallant and ruined lover reduced to playing the role of whipping boy. When Nicolas first came to Mme Léeman to find lodging, he hardly noticed a girl of fourteen, who was already reproducing, in a fresher and purer manner, the mother's former attraction. Over the next four years, he only paid attention to this child when he heard her mother scold or beat her. Eventually, however, she became a tall blonde of eighteen years, with white and transparent skin; she had a graceful nonchalance in the movement of her waist, her poses, and her walk, and in her eyes a melancholy so touching that just by looking at her, Nicolas often felt tears in his eyes. This was a warning from his heart, which he had believed dead, but which had only been asleep.

For a long time, Nicolas had been living alone, talking to no one, working during the day, and wandering about the deserted streets at night. His friends were dead or scattered, and he had gradually fallen into that profound slump, that complete indifference, which usually follows too restless a youth. At least he felt at peace in his ruin when, one Sunday morning, a little white hand gently knocked on the door of his room. He opened it. It was Sara.

"Monsieur Nicolas," she said, "I have come to ask you to lend me some book you're not using; you have so many, and I love reading."

"Choose, Mademoiselle," said Nicolas; "you may read them all, one after the other, as you like."

Sara seemed so shy, and she seemed so afraid of being troublesome; her modesty, her blushing, and her discomfort were so natural that Nicolas surrendered entirely to her charm. She didn't stay long and, upon leaving, she presented her forehead to the writer's paternal kiss.

All week long she worked with the Amey girls, a position her mother found for her so that she could learn how to make lace;[67] but on Sundays she didn't leave home, so she renewed her visits, always to borrow books, which Nicolas ended up giving to her. Nothing was as pure and touching as these first meetings. Nicolas had learned of some rumors concerning the young girl, but he regarded them as slander. Perhaps this girl had been compromised by something because of her mother's greed; she appeared so innocent to him that he would have been reluctant to alter by a word, a gesture, even a glance, the purity of her innocence; he showed her respect, held her in high esteem, and felt an enthusiasm for her the nature of which he dared not explain. Sara sensed it, or at least her mother sensed it for her, because at this point the visits became more frequent, the conversations more intimate; at first, she brought him some very well-chosen songs, those called "brunettes," and sang to him the one most relevant to the position she wished to take with regard to him.[68]

If passions are less sudden in one's forties, the heart is nevertheless much more tender: man has less ardor, violence, anger; but instead, he loves selflessly and with devotion. The future terrifies him, and he clings to the past in order not to die; he wants to begin life again, and the younger the beloved woman is, the more vivid and lively the man's emotions are. Let us judge with what rapture Nicolas listened to the following verses sung by the prettiest mouth with an expression so tender:

At dawn my heart will sigh anew.
I blush and blush throughout the day;
At night, my heart still longs for you;
I feel at once both joy and pain!
I dream of you when I'm in bed,
Your name stirs me, takes hold of me;
At morningtime, I lift my head,
I see your face, I cannot flee . . .

"You sing with feeling," said Nicolas. "Is your heart as sensitive as your voice is touching?"

"Ah, Monsieur," said Sara, "if you knew me better, you would not ask me this question; but you will appreciate me one day, and you will discover whether I am consistent with my feelings."

"That is the most pleasant thing your pretty mouth could tell me."

"My God, it's quite natural. When one has loved once, is it not for life? And can one ever forget the person that one has loved?"

"Now that is a very nice moral!"

"It's natural."

"You have wit and philosophy, Mademoiselle."

"I have seen a bit of the world, it's true . . . Someday, I'll tell you about it."

Nicolas frowned, but he quickly reassured himself when he heard the girl add naively that she had been invited with her mother to a very beautiful dinner, noting that it was in a country house a few leagues from Paris, at the home of a magistrate of the court who came from high society. Perhaps he would have thought more about this if the babbling child hadn't suddenly changed the subject.

"You know," she said, "I have been to the convent . . . Well, I received such a fine education that it occurred to me to put on a play. Ah, the theater is what formed me. I would have gone more often, except Mamma doesn't like good shows; she finds comedy boring and only likes Nicolet and Les Grands Danseurs du Roi.[69] Audinot is too serious for her, or, if you like, too . . ."[70]

Sara dared not utter the word she had in mind. Nicolas later thought she had meant to say "too decent."

"Well," he continued after a pause, "since you love the theater, you must try out your abilities, your grace, and your wit."

"No," she said, "I am reserving them for something more important."

"Important how?"

"To earn your respect."

The blow had struck; Nicolas looked at her tenderly and hugged her.

Imperceptibly, the visits multiplied. Mme Léeman displayed the inexplicable blindness and complacency of a mother. Relations were established between the neighbors. When the Day of Kings arrived, Nicolas offered the cake for the family—among whom he had to include M. Florimond.[71] The latter, entirely dependent on Mme Léeman, had a superficial conversational style in which a studied politeness reigned, and which he affected to have retained from his memories of being a man of the world. At dessert, the lucky charm was not found in the cake, and Florimond was suspected by the girl of having done away with it to dispense with paying for his accession to royalty.[72]

"What did it look like?" asked Mme Léeman, "We know very well that it's always my money getting thrown around."

M. Florimond rejected these insinuations with the dignity of outraged honor.

"I rather think," Nicolas said, "that it is I who have inadvertently swallowed the charm; I find myself obliged to offer you some mulled wine."

Florimond's satisfaction and the admiration of the two women for Nicolas's tact was payment with interest for his sacrifice.

The next day, Mme Léeman came to visit Nicolas. "I must speak with you," she said, "about my daughter." And she told him that her intention had been to give Sara's hand to a certain M. Delarbre, a young man who had frequently come to the house, but then suddenly ceased his visits. She asked Nicolas if her daughter had spoken to him about these previous and, moreover, innocent relations. "Yes," he said, "but it was something that I had completely forgotten about." The mother replied that this party was in no way suitable for her daughter; then, softening her voice, she added that a new proposal was made to her. A man named Monsieur de Vesgon, an old friend of the family, offered to assure the fate of this child by means of a donation of twenty thousand livres, and this from a paternal sentiment, resulting from the friendship that this respectable man once had with Sara's father . . . However, Sara had refused the proposal, and Mme Léeman, feeling her authority as a mother powerless to overcome the girl's resistance, came to ask Nicolas to act instead, by using the persuasive powers that his superior mind was sure to produce.

Nicolas could not suppress a movement of surprise. Mme Léeman pointed out the poor state of her health. "If my poor child were to lose me, what would happen then?" the mother added . . . "I've some experience myself, my good Monsieur Nicolas; time passes, beauty fades; Sara would obtain with this amount a small annuity that, along with the little that I leave her, would later allow her to live honorably . . ." Nicolas shook his head; the mother pressed him further because of his friendship with her daughter, and even suggested he have dinner with M. de Vesgon so that he might ascertain the purity of the old man's intentions.

Nicolas felt wounded in his heart and could not sleep that night. The next morning, Sara came upstairs to him as usual. He openly broached the issue of the twenty thousand francs and asked the girl if she thought she could accept it without compromising her reputation. Sara lowered her eyes, blushed deeply, sat on Nicolas's lap and began to cry. Nicolas urged her to reply.

"Ah, if I dared speak!" she exclaimed between two sighs.

"You can confide in me, my lovely child."

"If you only knew how unhappy I am!"

"Unhappy! Why and since when?"

"I've always been . . . I have a mother . . ."

"I know about her."

Sara seemed to make a violent effort to speak.

"My mother," she said at last, "made my sister die of grief. At that time, I was just a wild child, giddy and always laughing . . . I've changed a lot since then! Even today, my mother makes me tremble; just hearing her footsteps makes me shudder with fear!"

And she told him the story of a time when she lived with her mother on a side street in the Marais district, at a carpenter's home. New faces would follow each other in befriending the widow, and the little girl was almost always relegated to an attic, suffering from cold, from hunger, even . . . When she cried too loudly, her mother would come and furiously pinch her, twist her hands, or leave her face bloody. One evening, a man dared to climb up to the attic . . . and . . .

"Poor child!" exclaimed Nicolas.

"Ah, my friend! Ah, my father!" Sara replied, throwing herself into the writer's arms, her face wet with tears: "I swore long ago that I would never consent to marry . . . and in any case, that I would never marry a young man . . ."

Nicolas looked at her tenderly.

"A young man! And yet, this young man Delarbre who came here a few months ago . . . so often?"

"Him," Sara said with a sigh, "Oh, I may as well admit it, I loved him . . . as much as one can love at the age that I was then; but he won't be coming here anymore . . . I told him everything!"

Nicolas put his head in his hands, thought a moment, then exclaimed, filled with pity: "And he left you! He did not understand that the purity of your soul . . . redeemed a thousand times, poor victim, the vile and cowardly act committed against you!" In stopping at this idea, Nicolas involuntarily thought of Mme Parangon. The memory of that fatal event returned, taking on new form, to return an avenging iron into his eternal wound. He stood up and ran around the room, making desperate gestures. Sara, who did not understand the causes of such an acute grief, ran to him, had him sit and, trying to smile through her tears, embraced him and said: "Why pity me so much? Why such despair? This will prevent the tenderest friendship between us from lasting, my protector, my guide! Think on it; alas, I am not guilty, and you will have nothing to forgive me . . . Do you think if Delarbre had not left me, I would be here with you . . . in your arms . . . talking, crying . . . laughing? . . ."

She sat back on his lap and passed her arm around his neck, an already perfect Jewish arm, though she was only fifteen years old,[73] that small slender hand whose pink fingers passed through the curls of Nicolas's hair.

Calm gradually returned to the writer's heart; his nervous agitation subsided; Nicolas rested his eyes, charmed by the smooth features of the poor child; he could not suppress a confession he had long held back: "What is it?" Sara said, seeing that he appeared to be dreaming.

"I'm thinking of you," he said, "delightful child! I must finally tell you that I've loved you for a long time. . . and that I always fled you, afraid of your youth and your beauty!"

"Always, until the morning when I came to see you myself!"

"What could I offer you? A heart withered by pain . . . and regret!"

"What do you regret now? Has your heart not calmed?"

"It beats more than ever. Here: touch my chest."

"Oh! It probably holds . . ."

"Ah! What, then?"

"Love! . . ." Sara said quietly.

Nicolas came to; his philosophy as a writer gave him a moment of strength.

"No," he said gravely; "I have for you, my child, only a sincere and constant friendship.

"And what if I had love?"

"It would end too soon."

Sara looked down.

"A year ago," said Nicolas, "I had once again yielded to someone's charm . . ."

"Whose?" Sara asked, quickly raising her head.

"An image I had created in myself, a chimera, fleeting as a dream, and which I did not even think to realize; one of those impossible loves I have pursued all my life, and which some fate now and then makes possible."

"But what was this image? What was this dream?"

"It was you."

"Me . . . dear God!"

"You whom I saw running here and there in the house, you who passed me on the stairs, in the street . . . and who grew more and more, and who became ever more beautiful, and whom I sometimes surprised in the evening on the doorstep with young Delarbre . . ."

Sara blushed and said: "But I swear to you . . ."

"Oh, what does it matter?" Nicolas said, resolutely; "Was he not young, was he not handsome and no doubt worthy of you? . . . Is it not natural, is it not even a pleasant sight for a man's heart to witness pure love between two young and beautiful beings? . . . I loved you in a different way; I loved you as we love those strange visions we see passing in dreams, such that we wake up enamored of a beautiful passion, a weak memory of the impressions of youth . . . at which one laughs a moment later!"

"Oh, my God! One can see you are a poet!"

"Indeed. We do not live! We analyze life! . . . Other creatures are our eternal toys . . . and they get their revenge too! Friendship, love, what is it? Am I sure myself of having loved? The images of the day are to me like the visions of the night! Woe to the person who enters my eternal dream without being an impalpable image! . . . Like a painter, cold to all that surrounds him, and who traces calmly the spectacle of a battle or a storm, we see everywhere only models to describe, passions to render, and all those who meddle in our lives are the victims of our egotism, as we are of our imagination!"

"You frighten me!" cried Sara.

"No, I am calm," said Nicolas; "It's experience, my dear child; I have come to know others and myself, and if I have bitterness in my heart, at least I have no irony on my lips . . . Do you know what we do, we others, with our loves? . . . We turn them into books to earn our keep. It's what Rousseau the Genevan did . . . it's what I myself did with my *Paysan perverti*. I told the story of my love affair with a poor woman from Auxerre who died; but, as I am more discreet than Rousseau, I did not reveal everything . . . perhaps also because it would have been necessary to tell . . ."

He stopped. "Oh, let me read this book," Sara exclaimed.

"Not yet!. . . But you'll now see how dangerous my friendship is . . . I have already put you in my *Contemporaines*!"

"What joy!" cried the girl, clapping; "But how is this possible?"

"Given you are willing to forgive me, my charming girl, here is the book. You see the name of Adeline: that's the name I gave you."

"Oh, what a pretty name! I prefer it to my own . . . And who does she love?"

"Chavigny."

"Chavigny? . . . So, this is name you have chosen for yourself."

"No, I chose it for young Delarbre, who at that time came here every day. Seeing him so anxious, so in love, so tender, a memory of my youth came back to me . . . I imagined myself in his place, and it was me who loved you. Oh, that I would have been more tender and more enthusiastic . . . He himself represented only the weakened and vague image of my youth, and yet I could not hate him . . . I hoped for nothing. So, I expressed to myself, I expressed in his place the feelings you inspired in me. What was but love for him was for me adoration; I would have been jealous of him, and if necessary . . . I would have killed his rival! . . . I would have married you in his place."

Sara, ashamed, hid herself in Nicolas's arms, then looked up at his face, smiling through her tears.

"Oh, keep talking.," she said, "Let me admire you in your enthusiasm, in your goodness, in your genius . . . Before today, I loved listening to you more than anything . . . Now I look at you and I find you young and handsome; oh, how I envy those you have loved!"

"Only one was worthy of you, my dear Sara! but she had only friendship for me ... She is no more ... Let us talk again of this strange love where I substituted myself in thought for the one who seemed more worthy of you than I did myself; you do not know how far my madness went ... There is a place where I like to walk at night; from there you can see the most beautiful sunsets in the world: it is the Île Saint-Louis ... Well, driven by my thoughts of you, I carved, furtively, there on the gray stones of the quay, the initials of the name I had chosen for you: AD. AD. For me this meant: Adored Adeline ..."

"Oh, we will go together on the next beautiful day, and you will show me these letters," Sara said, "and tell me everything you thought of while carving them!"

"Yes, my friend, if you wish ... But alas! I'm now even older by a year, and I have suffered so much!"

Sara threw herself on his neck, laughing and crying in turn, pouring a divine balm on the wounds of the unfortunate one.

"Your sorrows will also be mine!" she said. "We will speak together of this woman from Auxerre you loved so ..."

"Oh," said Nicolas, "so much joy ... so much sorrow ... this breaks my heart! God bless you, my girl, my child! Yes, I love you ... I am still mad enough to love you; forgive me ..."

At that moment, they heard the voice of the widow Léeman from the stairs, calling her daughter for lunch.

"I must go down," Sara said; "I just have one thing to ask you before I leave, Monsieur."

"You're speaking formally now?"

"No, that was a slip ... I wanted to speak to you about one of my friends you've seen me with, because she works at the same shop for lacemakers ... Mlle Charpentier."

"I've seen her. She's lovely."

"And she is so nice! ... But in truth, I dare not tell you ..."

"What is it? Speak quickly, my lovely child!"

"I'm so afraid of being indiscreet ... My friend lost her mother who, after a long illness, left her only with debts ... How I would like to be rich so I could help her! ... At present, just one louis would be needed to save her from the greatest embarrassment! . . . She would pay it back to you in six weeks."

"A louis! Only a louis?" exclaimed Nicolas. And he went to fetch a large case from which he grabbed two louis, put them in Sara's white hand, and added a kiss.

"Oh, she will be so happy!" said Sara, and she rushed joyfully down the stairs.

From that day on, Nicolas renounced all his lonely projects. The aversion he had conceived for the widow Léeman, as a result of her daughter's confession, soon yielded to the desire to see her more often; he cultivated the friendship of M. Florimond by flattering his aristocratic tastes, and that of the widow by inviting himself to her home for dinners he had delivered from a caterer; he even took care to always add some poultry, which would reappear over the following days on the miserly Mme Léeman's table.

We have said that it was only on Sundays that Sara could come to visit Nicolas. The rest of the week she stayed in the house where she was undertaking her apprenticeship. The next Monday, there was a loud noise in the stairwell. "You are a brazen girl," cried Mme Léeman to her daughter.—"If I am, it's your fault," replied the latter.—"You wait, insolent child, just wait . . . !" And Nicolas came down to Sara's cries. "What a daughter, Monsieur, to answer me so rudely," cried the mother.—"My dear Sara, calm down!" Nicolas said; but the girl greeted him just as badly, though calmed down as she dressed for work. Mme Léeman said to Nicolas, when she had left: "Is it not unfortunate to have but one child and see her go elsewhere?"—"Why not keep her at home with you?"—"Ah, Monsieur, I'm so poor . . . and then I wouldn't want to be in my friends' debt."

At that time, Nicolas was in a rather good position; his first novels, especially *Le Paysan Perverti* and *Les Contemporaines*, earned him much more than what he was paid as a printer:—"Bring your daughter home," he told Mme Léeman, "and we will do what we can for her upbringing."—"In fact," the mother said, "there is a lodging on the second floor that will be free; we will furnish it with common expenses. You will be her father, and we will make a single family."

At the end of that week, Sara stopped going to work with the Amey girls. Soon the arrangement became complete, indissoluble. There were endless talks and delicious dinners, often in the countryside or near the gate, with the mother and Florimond . . . At every meal, Sara's little foot would rest on Nicolas's; they also went to the theater with tickets the writer obtained through his literary connections, and there the girl, indifferent to the admiration excited by her ravishing beauty, always let one of her hands fall into that of her dear friend.

However, Mme Léeman made it so that no one could enjoy themselves without her, and when, during the day, there was an opportunity for Nicolas to go out with the girl, she always had them accompanied by Florimond. The latter, worn out by excesses of all kinds, was rather dull company, but there was nothing hostile in his attachment to the two lovers. He followed them like a sheepdog, without interrupting their tender conversations. One day, Nicolas had undertaken to buy seeds and flower bulbs for the mother. She was, as we have said, from Brabant, and curious about tulips. Sara and Nicolas departed for the Quai aux Fleurs and were so long in choosing their flowers that Florimond, who was very bored, decided to enter a tavern from which he followed them with his eyes. When he returned, he could barely stand up. Sara told him to take charge of the bag of seeds, and as he tried to keep himself up leaning on her shoulders, she penciled a note for her mother in which she told her that Florimond was so tipsy that, wishing to go for a walk, she and Nicolas realized they were just dragging him along. Florimond left with this note, which he did not read.

"Why don't we go to the theater!" Sara said cheerfully. Nicolas glanced at her. She was very nicely dressed, wearing an English-style hat and a casaquin of tafetta with changing highlights. They still had time to spare before the show started, so they didn't rush. Nicolas led the girl along the waterfront to l'Île Saint-Louis, which he was particularly fond of visiting, as we know, in his solitary walks. The view was lovely at that time, because on one side there was the countryside, and on the other, the magnificent sight of both arms of the Seine, the old cathedral, and the Hôtel de Ville; Le Mail and La Râpée extending to the right and left, bordered in the distance by open-air cafés with their green bowers, also presented a very lively spectacle. Nicolas had another thought: to show Sara the stones on the quay on which he had carved the mystical figure: AD. AD. (Adored Adeline), back when he came to these very places to give voice to his complaints over a hopeless love. Everything had changed. The lovers, one after the other, carved under these half-erased figures the real initials of their names, and left l'Île Saint-Louis only after seeing the sun descend behind the enormous towers of the petit Châtelet. They went up through Place Maubert, rue de Séverin, rue de Saint-André-des-Arts and de la Comédie* to arrive at this very theater that was still, for Nicolas, full of memories of the beautiful Mlle Guéant. On the way, he recounted with tears in his eyes this story of his youth, and Sara joined with all her heart in her friend's grief.—"Dead! She is dead!" exclaimed Nicolas. "Dead like this other one, so beautiful and more loving (Mme Paragon), and all whom I have loved are now in the tomb! . . ."

"And me, would I not love you like them?" said Sara tenderly.

"For a time perhaps; but after?"

"My friend, stop talking like that . . . Remember that I am extremely impressionable; never put to the test this sensitivity which has only tortured me."

"Oh, forgive me, dear girl! It is because I have lived so much, suffered so much, and you . . ."

"I myself have only suffered, and I would be more affected by what you say and do than all that has happened to me."

They had taken their seats in the theater. *La Pupille* by Fagan was playing, the very drama in which Mlle Guéant had been so delightful, with such emotion and grace. Nicolas, like all proud souls, always believed in a destiny which, with regard to himself alone, took the place of chance. He could not refrain this time from finding the play detestable and the actress unpleasant, and he didn't notice that in the next box over, a very pretty woman had just sat down, with the most beautiful ashen hair (at this time powder was no longer worn), beautiful eyes beneath dark eyebrows, and distinguished manners. Sara pointed her out to him. "She is pretty," he said, "but you are more beautiful!" This woman, seeing herself the object of Sara's admiration, took an opportunity to say something kind to her. The latter replied coldly. As Nicolas was surprised, she said in his ear: "I'm very jealous. If I engaged in conversation with her, you would have been able to talk to her, and you have too much merit not to please her . . ." Nicolas replied, full of joy, "But who could please me if not Sara?"

* Nicolas Restif retained these minor details to mark more vividly his final day of happiness and illusions.

After this delightful evening, the only challenge was facing the wrath of Mme Léeman, but Nicolas had the triumphant idea for dealing with the matter: it was to buy her a pair of very beautiful pendants at a jewelry shop on rue de Bussy. The precaution was not in vain, for on entering, Nicolas and Sara discovered the unfortunate Florimond at the door, whom the widow had put out after seeing him return home alone. Sobered up by the scene of imprecations he had suffered, he yielded to despair. Nicolas bravely faced the storm, which he succeeded in calming, by allowing his recent acquisition to shine between his fingers. Everything returned to normal.

The mother, however, was determined not to accept the fact that they could enjoy themselves in her absence. "Since Sara needs distraction," she said one day, "I will take her for a stroll on the Grands Boulevards." And so, they went there one beautiful spring evening. Nicolas, retained at his printing shop until seven o'clock, was to join them later. He found them seated on chairs along a sidepath, among two or three rows of very elegant, striking women. A well-dressed man, very dark, who seemed to be a Creole, was sitting beside them and had already established a fairly sustained conversation with the mother. Sara seemed serious; she smiled when she saw Nicolas and made room for him next to her. The cavalier was not long in greeting his new acquaintance and resumed his stroll.

Two or three days later, an important affair prevented Nicolas from going to meet the ladies at the usual hour. Mme Léeman told him mockingly that the dark cavalier had kept them company. The same circumstance was repeated on one of the following days. Sara took Nicolas aside and said: "You are abandoning me to plans of which you are aware . . . Ah, my friend!" A few days later, Mme Léeman spoke of an opportunity that had arisen to marry her daughter to a man of some standing. It was a stab in the heart for the writer who, as we know, was married, although separated for some time from the unworthy Agnès Lebègue. He replied with a sigh that Sara's happiness for him came before anything, but he hoped that the intended would be worthy of her. The next day, as he was indisposed, he saw a letter slip under his door that read:

> *They absolutely intend your daughter to leave today without you, my dear friend! . . . We must suffer what we cannot prevent. Try to cure your cold and take care of yourself . . . If you could find me a situation*

with a lady or just some work, I would have the fortitude to resist, and I would live as satisfied as anyone can be in my position. Always love your friend.

SARA

That very day, Nicolas went to visit a lady of means who lived on l'Île Saint-Louis, and of whom he often spoke in his *Nuits de Paris*.[74] The latter agreed to take on Sara as a female companion. Returning home, he encountered the mother and the daughter in a carriage. Mme Léeman shouted to him that they were going to the Palais-Royal, and that he had only to join them as usual. Reassured as to Sara's feelings through her letter, he was careless enough not to hurry. When he arrived, they were gone.

Nicolas returns home; the light is out . . . The lock on the door has not been removed. He goes up to his room, consumed with impatience, walks about with great strides, and goes out from time to time, anticipating the arrival of the two women. Nobody comes; midnight strikes; on the last ring, he bursts into tears . . . He recalls what Sara told him, what her mother implied. At one o'clock in the morning, unable to stand it any longer, he starts roaming the streets. Chance brings him back to the deserted quays of l'Île Saint-Louis. He searches by the moonlight for the stones on which he had inscribed the loving initials, completed by Sara's hand, and finding them, he moans and utters cries of despair. A man opens his window and asks what's wrong: "I'm a father," he answers, "who has lost his daughter!" He returns to his room in the hope they had been invited to a ball. Still nothing. At five o'clock in the morning, Nicolas dozes off, exhausted; Sara appears in his dream, her beautiful blonde tresses scattered over her chest, crying out: "My friend, save me, save me!" He wakes up . . . it's already late in the day; no one had come back.*

It was only the following day that Nicolas heard a carriage stop at the door. Until then, every passing carriage had caused his heart to leap . . . He rushed down the stairs. Mme Léeman had come home without her daughter, accompanied by a stranger, or rather, a very recent acquaintance, the gallant Creole from the boulevards.

"Where is your daughter?" Nicolas exclaimed brusquely.

* Two weeks later the writer said, recounting this night of anguish: "And at that point I wasn't yet jealous!"

"She stayed in the countryside at the home of M. de la Monette, whom you see, and who was good enough to bring me here."

"And why do you leave your only daughter alone at a man's home?"

"And why do you ask? . . . Besides, Sara is not alone, she is there with the gentleman's family. . . and the gentleman is with me, as you can see!"

M. de la Monette bowed, carefully observing the strange expression on Nicolas's face. Moreover, it was also clear that the widow Léeman was anxious to be tactful: "Had my daughter not told you of our day in the countryside?" she said in a gentler tone.

"I didn't hear a word about it!"

"Ah, that silly goose! . . ." cried Mme Léeman. She used an even sharper term, immediately begging M. de la Montette to excuse the severity of a mother's comment on her child. "The gentleman has become a second father to my daughter," she added, pointing to Nicolas, "and I understand his concern . . . But Sara had put a note under your door," she said to him.

"Yes, it is true, Madame," he replied as he withdrew, "I had forgotten."

Nicolas was confused. If it was a question of marriage to a man of standing, his generosity would prevent him from opposing it, and even his heart would have certainly been less offended; but the letter from Sara, which moreover had not said a word about the day in the countryside, indicated a danger of another kind. As his thoughts tumbled about in their uncertainty, the carriage set off again, for Mme Léeman had come home only to gather up some personal effects. Nicolas had once chased a carriage to find out where it would stop with some success; but what would it look like for a man over forty to try to repeat such a stunt! He had to wait the whole night long and another day.

Two days later, Sara knocked on her friend's door in the usual way; he toppled everything over to open it. Sara said, with an ice-cold air:

"Well, *what is it*? Here I am!"

"What is it? . . . Did I say anything to you, my poor child?"

"No," said Sara, embarrassed, "but you had a bewildered look . . ."

"My look was not a reproach . . . You only *planned* that after disappearing for three days . . ."

"You will have dinner with us, right?" resumed Sara, who had kept near the door; and at that moment her mother called her.

Nicolas saw that it was all over. "Now," he thought, "let us truly be a father and find out if this man is capable of making her happy." He went down for dinner and found M. de la Montette there. He was a man of about forty, and someone who had never been overly troubled by passion . . . Nicolas felt very inferior to his rival, and still he believed it was only a marriage of convenience; it made the young girl's reserve understandable; except he felt sorrow in no longer feeling Sara's little foot pressing against his.

The dinner would have ended peacefully if, toward the end, the mother, in an effusive moment, had not exclaimed, looking at M. de la Montette: "And to think we didn't know this gentleman two weeks ago! If Monsieur Nicolas had joined us before seven o'clock, as we had intended to go to the theater, we would not have had the pleasure of meeting so amiable a cavalier . . . who has become for us a true friend!" O torture! Nicolas said to himself: "And I must admit that I'm to blame!" Sara leaned with a languid air on the Creole's arm and seemed in no way shocked by her mother's trivial exclamation. Nicolas summoned all his philosophy to aid him and displayed no astonishment. After dinner, they went for a walk in the Jardin des Plantes. Politeness dictated that the guest take Sara's arm, which obliged Nicolas to offer his to her mother; but he immediately thought that this was usually a duty that fell to Florimond, who had gone on a trip concerning the widow's affairs. Nicolas, already known as a writer, feared people staring and contented himself with walking next to Mme Léeman instead. The latter, annoyed, told her daughter: "A young person has no need to lean on an arm; I'm doing fine without one!" M. de la Montette had to do as Nicolas; but his conversation with Sara seemed quite lively and even tender. At the end of the evening, M. de la Montette invited the two ladies to dinner the following day and included Nicolas in the invitation. He was a gentleman. Yet the writer felt a mortal pain in his heart; his rival had the advantage of this moment because, according to Sara herself, "M. Nicolas had been very gloomy this evening."

The next day, M. de la Montette, with a great deal of courtesy, did the honors of his villa; his conversation was witty; at least he knew how to compensate through his knowledge of the world what Nicolas had most elevated through his imagination. The day was terrible for the latter; everything demonstrated the superiority of a man of taste and property. Several other guests were gathered in the house, mainly lawyers and men of finance.

Sara felt ill at ease because her mother occasionally indulged in comments that betrayed her lack of education; she felt the need to almost continuously maintain the conversation and did so with a certain spirit of freedom and confidence that proved less naïve than Sara had hitherto allowed one to suppose. When they arose, Nicolas went to a window and wept bitterly, saying to himself, "It's all over!" Sara, passing near him, poked him, and laughing out loud, said, "What are you doing there? You're not coming to the garden?" He did not turn around, daring not to show his contorted face. Sara abruptly exclaimed: "Well, suit yourself ... You are very tiresome!"

Outraged pride dried the wretched man's tears. "It suits you well," he thought, "to be loving again! Remember those you've made miserable and cast away!" He recovered and went down to the garden. Sara was picking some roses with childlike joy and formed bouquets that she passed around to the society ladies. M. de la Montette, seeing Nicolas approaching, led him along a lane and spoke with such affability that he seemed not to have even conceived of the possibility of a rivalry between them. They spoke for a long time about the girl; Nicolas could not help but praise her with enthusiasm. The writer deployed all his imagination in this panegyric; his heart also added to it all the fire which still burned. M. de la Montette, astonished, said to Nicolas: "So you love her?"—"I adore her!" he replied.

"But her mother told me that you only had a paternal friendship for this child ... I would have thought rather, given your age, you had some tender feeling for Mme Léeman, who is still beautiful ..."

"Me! ..." cried Nicolas, deeply offended, and, facing M. de la Montette, he thought: "But this man is almost my age ... How could it be! Five or six years younger and he believes me incapable of being his rival for a young girl!" He restrained himself, however; but the bitterness of jealousy and wounded pride completely changed the tone of his conversation. All his resentment burst out at what he had to say about the mother. He related the story of the daughter's love for the young Delarbre, the proposal of twenty thousand livres made by M. de Vesgon, and which had nearly been accepted ... He did more; he betrayed his own position, the sacrifices he had made; Sara's love, so often sworn, the meetings, the parties at the theater, the letters written ... "Now," he finally cried out, "I see how I was played, deceived ... as you will be!"

"Deceived!" said M. de la Montette, "How so? I have some experience, and I had known all that."

"What! You would allow a mother to sell you her daughter?"

"But no, my friend, I do not buy love."

"You see now that you must renounce her?"

"But why? . . . If she likes me better than anyone else!"

The moment when Nicolas, stunned by this response, was to gather his strength for a provocation, the girl's fresh and smiling face appeared between the trees. Carefree and playful, and unaware of what had just been said, she brought a bundle of roses which she divided into two parts and offered to them. It was already getting dark in that lane and she could not see Nicolas's sad face. He felt all his anger dissipate. Sara told them both kind things, then disappeared as if to leave them to the charms of a serious discussion on politics or philosophy.

"Listen," said de la Montette, "I am no longer at the age where I am ruled by passion, and yours surprises me. It appears to last longer with writers . . . Since you love this girl so much, I will renounce my vows . . . But if she did not love you, you have *spoken to me so well of her* that I would have sought all the more to please her . . ."

A moment ago, Nicolas would have provoked a duel with M. de la Montette, and now he felt ridiculous; his rival's composure had conquered him. With that profound terror of the truth characteristic of betrayed lovers, he dared not take matters any further; he only claimed to have certain business that obliged him to return that same evening to Paris. They seemed to deeply regret his departure, and everyone went out to see him off. Sara walked alongside de la Montette as cheerful as before; the latter said to her, "Take M. Nicolas's arm." This generosity was the deepest blow to a defeated rival. Nicolas tried to hide his grief, but he could not help saying to Sara that he had informed M. de la Montette of Mme Léeman's intentions and of other unedifying peculiarities. Then the girl flew into a rage. "Truly, Monsieur," she said, "I am sorry to have known you and to have been affectionate and good to you. What right have you to meddle in my affairs? What right have you to reveal secrets and dishonor my mother? . . . Besides," she added, raising her voice, "I don't know why we're walking like this together. Probably to make it appear that our relations have not always been so innocent. Dare say so, Monsieur!"

Nicolas did not even want to answer. His face red, with death in his heart, he had not the strength to be generous and support the girl's lies. He bowed awkwardly to the company, and it was only as he continued on his journey that he gave voice in turn to his complaints and his curses. A single thought came to temper his grief; it was to recognize that Providence had rightly struck him down.

V. The Marriages of Nicolas

Nicolas's marriages are the sad aspects to his life: the dark flip side of this dazzling coin from which so many beauties shone with such a graceful profile. Marriage was to make Nicolas expiate the favors so multiplied by love, and, according to his system of Providence in which expiation always followed the fault committed, he had no reason to complain about the moral pains that overwhelmed him until the last days of his life. He even took some comfort from his troubles in the thought that Hell already existed for him on earth, and that death would return him pure and sufficiently tested to the womb of the universal soul. This doctrine, developed at length in his *Morale*, has the disadvantage of not preventing anyone from engaging in evil acts, by braving, in an hour of intoxication, the fatal consequences that are to only manifest later. Is this not a singular application of that superstitious Epicureanism that Cyrano, one of the students of Gassendi, gave to Séjanus, threatened by thunder:

> *Thunder never falls down to the earth in winter:*
> *I've six more months to laugh at the heavens above,*
> *Then shall I make my peace with the gods thereof!*[75]

Nicolas's first marriage occurred at the time of his first visit to Paris, under unique circumstances. He was walking to the Jardin des Plantes, recently recovering from an illness caused by the sad denouement of his adventure with Zéfire. Two English ladies came to sit on a bench where he was resting. One of them was called Macbell—she was the aunt of the other, whose name was Henriette Kircher—a ravishing figure surrounded by admirable clusters of golden hair which escaped from under a large hat in the style of Pamela.[76] A conversation begins. The aunt speaks of a lawsuit involving the entire fortune of the young person, and which they were going to lose, considering their status as foreigners. There is only one way to prevent the misfortune: Henriette Kircher must marry a Frenchman, and within twenty-four hours, because in two days the trial will be decided; but how to find a suitable match in such a short time? Nicolas, the man of quick impressions and sudden resolutions, declares himself madly in love with the young miss; the latter finds him to her liking, and the very next day, in front of four witnesses, domestics of the English embassy, the marriage is celebrated in turn at Nicolas's parish and at the Anglican chapel. The trial was won. From that moment on, Nicolas lived with his new family, loving more and more the charms of the Englishwoman, who appeared to adore him. A lord named Taff was the only vistor received in the house. He had long conversations with the aunt and seemed to be annoyed at the shows of affection exchanged by the couple.

One morning, Nicolas awakens and is surprised to not find his wife beside him; he calls her; he gets up; the apartment is a mess, cabinets are open, everything is empty, even her clothes have vanished. Here is the letter he finds on a table:

> *Dear husband, they're taking me away from your tenderness. I'm being delivered to this lord you've seen . . . But be sure, if I'm able to escape I will once again be in your arms.*
>
> *Your loving wife,*
>
> HENRIETTE

It would be difficult to portray the shame and despair of Nicolas. They had taken from him a large sum he had deposited in the bank. His only consolation was to later see the marriage annulled because, as a Catholic, he could not legally marry a Protestant. His revenge was to write, using elements from this adventure, a comedy entitled *La Prévention Nationale.*

We have seen that he was also duped into marrying Agnès Lebègue. Unfortunately, that was to last longer. Although he had not retained any illusions as to the character and conduct of his wife, he lived for a time with her in relative harmony, philosophically ignoring some of her shortcomings—for which he retaliated by courting Agnès Lebègue's girlfriends or the wives of her suitors. The cynicism of these confessions indicates an utterly systematic moral depravity. An extraordinary episode in the early years of his marriage may well have inspired Goethe with the idea for his novel *Elective Affinities*, in which we find established a kind of *chassez-croisez* of affections between two mismatched households that, isolating themselves from the world, agree to repair the error of their legal situation. It is curious, in any case, to see the poet of pantheism encounter, in this immense paradox, a writer who lacked the genius to clarify certain inspirations in which all the elements of the Hegelian doctrine are to be found.

To conclude all that relates to the love life of Nicolas, it is good now to speak of his final marriage, which took place at the age of sixty.—It is that which concludes that long series of three- and five-act plays he entitled *Le Drame de la Vie*.—Nicolas, tired of the revolutionary scenes taking place in Paris before his very eyes, returns one beautiful autumn day in 1794 to Courgis, the village in which he spent his early years, where he learned Latin with his brother the curé, where he served as an altar boy at Mass, where he had loved Jeannette Rousseau. The church is empty and desolate; but this is not what strikes him: unsympathetic to republican ideas, he nevertheless borrowed their hatred of the Christian principle—or rather, he had always hated it. He walks, bitterly dreaming of the lost days of his youth. He thinks of Jeannette Rousseau, the only woman he ever loved, to whom he never dared say a word. "Perhaps happiness consisted in this: marrying Jeannette, spending his life in Courgis, as a decent laborer—having never had adventures, having never written novels; such could have been my life, such had been that of my father . . . But what became of Jeannette Rousseau? Whom did she marry? Is she still alive?"

He inquires in the village . . . She is still alive; she remains unwed. Her life was spent first working in the fields, then educating the girls in neighboring castles; happy with this life, she refused several proposals for marriage . . . Nicolas goes to the notary's house; an old maid at the door: it's Jeannette; she is the figure of Minerva, with black eyes, smiling through the wrinkles; her form, though slightly bent, retains the finesse and flexible elegance once admired. As for himself, he still has the tender expression of his eyes, the prominent cheekbones protruding from his face, his gracefully cut mouth, still fresh, full of sensuality—as Lavater had indicated in his portrait of 1788—and that hooked nose of the Restif family line, which in

Paris had earned him the nickname *the owl*; above those brown eyebrows, thick and arched, is a bony forehead, broad, on which his hair is receding to make the forehead seem larger. He is no longer the charming little man of former days, as his lovers used to call him; but time has respected, in his appearance at least, ten years of his life.

"Do you recognize me, Mademoiselle," he says, "at sixty years old?"

"Monsieur," said Jeannette, "I remember your name well; . . . But my eyes would not have recognized you, for you were a child when I was nineteen; I am now sixty-three."

"I am little Nicolas Restif, the choirboy of the curé of Courgis . . ."

And the two old people embrace, shedding tears.

There was an outpouring of emotion, full of delight and sadness. His memory suddenly revived, Nicolas recounted his too discreet love, his childish tears, and the immortal memory that followed him amidst his greatest errors; a virginal and pure image he was powerless, alas! to preserve, as it was always fleeing, like Eurydice, whom fate tears away from the arms of the disloyal poet! . . . He thought bitterly that fate had justly punished him for having forgotten his first love for an adulterous passion—for that virtuous and charming Mme Parangon, whose husband had taken revenge by making him marry Agnès Lebègue, who for forty years had overwhelmed him with grief.—Reciprocity! Reciprocity, that fatal doctrine issued from the sophist's brain, had been applied to him very severely, and this man, who had believed only in the ancient fate of the Greeks, found himself now forced to confess that he was an instrument of Providence!

"Oh, what does it matter! There is still time," he said, "I am free now, and I see that you have remained so . . . you were the wife nature had intended for me: although it is late in life, do you wish to become her?"[77]

Jeannette had read, in a castle where she was a governess, several of Restif's writings; she knew what he had always thought of her. Those distraught pages of admiration and regret, to be found in all the writer's books—she had meditated bitterly on them: "I believe," she finally said, "you were in fact the only husband that heaven had destined for me, so I did not want to be anyone else's wife. Since we can no longer marry for happiness, let us marry so we can die together."*

* *Le Drame de la Vie*, volume 5, page 1,251. (The author continued the same pagination throughout all the volumes of the same work.)

If we are to believe the author, who repeated the scene we have just described in three different works, the marriage would have been performed before a priest, and in secret, because of the time—which would indicate either a requirement of his last wife or a late return to Christian ideas.

PART THREE

I. Restif's First Novel

The interest in memoirs, confessions, autobiographies, even travel writing, stems from the fact that the life of every man becomes a mirror in which each person can examine some of their own good qualities or defects. That is why, in this case, personality is not shocking, provided the writer does not wrap himself more than is appropriate in the mantle of glory or in the rags of vice. With St. Augustine, confession is sincere. It resembles that which the ancient Christians offered at the door of a church before their assembled brethren, to obtain the absolution of certain sins which barred them from the entrance to the holy place. With the good Lawrence Sterne, it becomes a kind of benevolent and almost ironic confidence, which seems to say to the reader: "Are you better than me?" Rousseau mixes these two distinct sentiments and fuses them with the flame of passion and genius; but if he lowered himself in public with confidences that belonged only to the ear of God, if he has, on the other hand, spread waves of destructive irony on those who considered themselves better than him, he wanted at least to serve the truth; he believed he was attacking vices, and did not realize that human nature would rely on his example to excuse bad inclinations, without, on the other hand, accepting remorse, privations, and the moral tortures he had imposed upon himself to expiate them. It may be said, above all, that if Rousseau presented seductive scenes in his *Confessions*, he never intended to offend moral sensibilities. He wrote in a depraved time and for a privileged society to which the episode of the Galley girls,[78] or that of the courtesan of Venice and his relationship with Mme de Warens offered only a very bland and weakly spiced stew. He sometimes embellished with a bit of cynicism the edges of the bowl he thought to have filled with a generous drink. As for Restif, his rustic and vulgar competitor, how could we excuse him? It was not the beautiful ladies, the great jaded lords, the financiers, the men of the legal profession, or the coquettes his books were intended for; it was the bourgeois classes, who, though still of the people, differed from them more by education and by their gradual neglect of what were then called prejudices. If Rousseau sometimes said: "Young man, take this and read," other times he exclaimed on the front page of a work, which today is not considered dangerous: "Any girl who reads this book is lost!" Poverty and pride prevented Restif from doing the same.

His books were addressed, in all forms, to anyone who could read. The titles excited the attention of all; numerous prints, attractive even in their mediocrity, seduced the eyes of the crowd. The modern novel, in its most violent combinations, offers nothing to surpass these images of kidnapping, rape, suicide, dueling, nocturnal orgies, and contrasting scenes in which the debauched life of the salons mixes its unhealthy exhalations with the intoxicating perfumes of the boudoirs. For example, here is the old Pont-Neuf, seen at night, and higher up, the Samaritaine; thieves hidden under l'arche Marion avoiding the moonlight; a coach stopped on the bridge; a woman gets out, throws herself into the black water, a gentleman leans over the railing, another rushes from the open door.—Who has not seen this illustration? Who has not asked "What does it mean?" What more does one need for success? Restif's novels did not owe their popularity to these effects alone, which his contemporaries, moreover, also provided. He portrayed with great passion, sometimes with grace and wit, the manners of the bourgeoisie and the working classes. The little he knew of the world came to him from his associations with Beaumarchais, La Reynière and the Countess de Beauharnais, as well as from certain salons that mixed men of the robe with the nobility, where he was sometimes received out of curiosity;[79] but it is the morals of the bourgeoisie and the working classes that he mainly portrays in his novels, his stories, and his long series of tales known as *Contemporaines* [Contemporary women], *Parisiennes* [Parisian women], *Provinciales* [Provincial women], which delighted the provincial and the foreigner long after Paris had forgotten them.

So far, we have separated, so to speak, Restif the writer from the man himself. We must now show this strange nature under one last aspect, to tell of this literary life which, in its errors and its quirks, reflects the cynicism of the eighteenth century and foreshadows the eccentricities of the nineteenth. What we know of the man will help us better appreciate the method of the storyteller. We will easily show that all the novels Restif wrote, with some modifications and names changed, are but different versions of the adventures of his own life. If he is to be believed, all his heroines would have been his mistresses; the number itself is such that he composed a calendar, and the three hundred and sixty-five notes dedicated to the principal women fill an entire volume. What a power of attraction this man had, who presented himself as the most highly *electrified* of his age! We must believe that in the final years of his life, he mingled a great deal of infatuation with a somewhat manic erethism in these lists: preoccupied with the number of good fortunes of his youth, he believed he encountered everywhere one of his offspring. Legally, he had only the children with Agnès Lebègue: two girls,[80] whose existence became the subject of a long trial, at first with his wife, and then with his son-in-law, whose name was Augé, and who seems to have been the cause of the greatest sorrows in the writer's old age.

Les Mémoires de M. Nicolas, *Le Drame de la Vie*, and *Les Nuits de Paris* in turn reveal to us, in all their aspects, the literary life of Restif. He himself tells us how he was led to write his first novel.

As we know, Restif's marriage with Agnès Lebègue was not a happy one. After several reciprocal infidelities, they agreed to bear their common life together. The hard work of a simple laborer was not sufficient to dispel the habits of a coquettish woman. Restif, discouraged, worked little at the royal printing house, where he had just begun working, and often allowed himself to get caught reading the masterpieces of the great minds of the time; it then happened that the director, Anisson Duperron, reduced his schedule to a half-day for 25 sols.[81] His misery and humiliation became such that were it not for the fear of dishonoring his father, he would have, he admits, taken some *vile and downward course*. This inner struggle constantly reminded him of the thoughts and virtues of Edme Restif who, in his region, had been nicknamed "the honest man,"[82] and who made him conceive the idea of writing the book entitled *La Vie de mon père* [My father's life], which appeared a few years later, and is of his writings perhaps the only one that is irreproachable.

However, to write a lengthy work, Restif needed more moral strength and leisure than he had at that time. A more favorable opportunity opened up for him in 1764; one of his friends gave him a position as the foreman in a printing shop under Guillau, on rue du Fouarre.[83] It was a job that paid 18 livres per week and, in addition, he would receive a *copy* of every book, which amounted to an extra 300 livres. This good luck lasted three years. His taste for work returned with this improvement to his life, and it was thanks to the leisure of this position that Restif wrote his first book, *La Famille vertueuse* [The virtuous family]. With a frankness that not all writers possess, he admits he has never been able to imagine anything, that his novels were never, according to him, but the implementation of events that had happened to him personally or that he had heard recounted; this is what he called the *basis* of his narrative. When he lacked subjects, or when he was embarrassed by some episode, he created for himself a romantic adventure, the various vicissitudes of which, occasioned by circumstances, furnished him with fairly good motivation. It was as far as literary *realism* could be taken.

Thus, passing one Sunday through rue Contrescarpe, Restif noticed a lady accompanied by her two daughters going to the Palais Royal. The beauty of one of them struck him with admiration; he follows this family on their walk and draws their attention by sitting on the bench near them, and various other such actions. He then follows the ladies as they return home; they live on rue Traversière, in a silk shop. From that day forward, Restif comes every night to admire through the window the beautiful Rose Bourgeois, as he used to do with Zéfire. The cherished memory of that poor girl gives him the idea of writing love letters, which he will slide through a bolthole into the shop. He manages to introduce a new letter through it every evening and after doing so, he walks by the shop again indifferently; the father and mother are in possession of the letter which they read aloud as a joke, especially since they don't know to which sister the declaration is addressed. This lasts twelve days; such insistence seems more serious; but they pursue the guilty party in vain. Finally, one night, neighbors point him out; he is stopped, and the shop boys prepare to take him to the police commissioner. The street is full of people. The father, fearing a scandal, brings Restif into the backroom. "Don't hurt him!" the two sisters exclaim. The door is shut. "You wrote these letters?" says the father; ". . . to which of my daughters?"—"To the eldest."—"It should have been stated . . . And now, by what right do you seek to trouble the heart of a young woman, let alone two?"—"I do not know, an overwhelming feeling . . ." He defends himself with passion; the father softens and finally says: "There is soul in your letters . . . Make yourself known; take advantage of your talents, and we will see."

Restif dared not say he was married and kept this scene to utilize in his novel, where he conscientiously used the letters written for two purposes, the innocent jealousy of the two sisters, the arrest, the scene with the father, whom he made an Englishman because Richardson was in vogue at the time;[84] he added a few episodes from his own adventures, and strengthened the whole with a Jesuit character who, having become the father of a daughter, marries her in California, "a country," says the author, "where one is at least as stupid as in Paraguay." When the manuscript was finished, Restif wanted to consult an *Aristarchus*.[85] He chose a certain Progrès, a novelist and critic, whose masterpiece was *La Poétique de l'opéra bouffon*.[86] Progrès had him cut out half the book. A censor was still required; choosing one was up to the author. Restif *obtained* M. Albaret, who gave him a flattering approval.[87] "This approval," said Restif, "lifted my spirit." He hastened to send it to M. Bourgeois, the silk merchant, asking him to allow the book to be dedicated to Mlle Rose; the merchant replied by declining this honor with a very polite letter. "How," says the author, "could I have imagined that he would allow me to dedicate a novel to such a beautiful young person and to a class of citizen who must remain in honorable obscurity! . . ." The book was sold to the widow Duchesne at 15 livres per page, which made more than 700 francs.[88] Never had Restif had such a large sum in his hands. With that, he recklessly left his position as supervisor at the printing press: the axis of his life had now shifted.

As for Rose Bourgeois, he never saw her again; but he would have overlooked something about this adventure if chance had not added to it a final novelistic detail to crown those that Restif had himself created. Both sisters were the daughters of a Rose Pombelins, with whom Restif's father had been in love. Suppose this father had been less virtuous than he in fact was, and an entire family drama arises with a potentially terrible denouement . . . One could not ask for a stranger plot, even today.

II. Restif's Philosophical Novels

Restif's literary life doesn't really begin until 1766. We have seen that the focus of his youth had been divided between love and the unprofitable work of a typesetter. As he began to recount this new phase of his existence in his *Memoirs*, he exclaimed: "I here conclude the shameful period of my life, that of my failure, my misery, and my degradation." He attributes the lack of success of *La Famille vertueuse* to the audacity of the orthography, which was entirely in accordance with pronunciation and regulated by a system that he modified several times after.

Lucile ou les Progrès de la vertu [Lucile or the progress of virtue], which appeared shortly afterward, narrates the escapades of Mlle Cadette Forterre, the daughter of a wine broker and one of the most charming girls in Auxerre that Nicolas had ever dreamed of. He signed this book *a musketeer*, and wished to dedicate it to Mlle Hus of the Comédie-Française, who refused the honor with a very polite letter in which she expressed her fear that the levity of the book might harm her reputation. Perhaps Restif hoped then, but in vain, to be admitted to the financier Bouret's famous table, open to literature through the taste and good grace of Mlle Hus, and of whom Diderot gave a piquant description in *Rameau's Nephew*.[89]

Le Pied de Fanchette [Fanchette's foot, also known as The shoe] contains this curious preface: "If I had only aimed to please, the fabric of this book would have been different. Fanchette, her maid, an uncle and his son, as well as a hypocrite, were enough for the intrigue; if Fanchette's first lover had been this uncle's son, the plot would have been more natural and the denouement more lively; but it was necessary to tell the truth." This novel is nothing other than the story of a pretty woman loved by an old man who is seduced by her foot, the most charming in the world, but which leads to the most risqué madness. One finds in the book, and in the notes that accompany it, this constant preoccupation with women's feet and their footwear, something to be noted in all the author's writings. This monomania was present every single day. As soon as he had found a pretty foot on his walks, he hastened to fetch Binet, his draftsman, so that he could make a sketch.[90] According to him, "women who wear flat shoes, like the infamous little teachers with *pointy* shoes, are *clumsy* and *mannish* in a most horrifying way, while, on the contrary, high heels *refine* the shape of the leg and *sylpherize* the whole body."[91] The strange, albeit expressive words that punctuate this sentence give an idea of the unique phraseology that, together with the boldness of the orthography, make Restif's first books difficult to read. However, his reputation begins with *Le Pied de Fanchette.* There is originality and even style in this novel, which earned him very little owing to the large number of forgeries, a result precisely due to its success.

Le Pornographe followed *Le Pied de Fanchette*, and consists of a novel in letters whose purpose was to prove the usefulness of reforming certain police regulations; a thesis supported by appendices and relevant documents. The author admits that it is necessary, in large population centers, for some women to devote themselves to guaranteeing and protecting the morality of others. In India, they were the women of lower castes; in Greece, slaves were assigned this social function. The modern age would find similar classifications in the study of temperaments or in the innate misery of certain situations.—There is something in the doctrine of Fourier that advances this hypothesis; the *butterfly passion*, according to Restif, is the dominant law of certain organizations.[92] In these lower natures, however, changes take place, brought about by the times or by moral ideas, or by some unexpected feeling that purifies the mind and heart. In this case, all aid and encouragement must be given to those who wish to return to the general order of regular society. The main trend that should prevail in the peculiar institution of the *parthénions* Restif wanted to create, following the example of the Greeks, would be to bring even these minds to the desired result.[93] Restif supposed that the most depraved natures do not deteriorate entirely because they are weighed down by contempt for their past, because of a situation resulting from the misfortune of birth, the consequences of a single mistake, or from a complication of poverty difficult to assess. The greatest merit of the regulations he had conceived was, he said, to shield young people from external temptations, to keep families from viewing the spectacle of vice insolently parading its luxury before them day after day, to ultimately cancel out, for a man, that moment he goes astray and encounters the possibility of committing the sort of evil known to every race.

This book was a success in Europe and the ideas it contains deeply affected the philosophical spirit of Joseph II,* who applied in his states the draft of regulations contained in the second part of the book. *Le Pornographe* was followed by several books in the same genre, which the author collects under the title *D'Idées singulières*. The second volume is titled *Le Mimographe ou le Théâtre réformé* [The mimographer or the reformed theater]. In this book, Restif insists on the need to admit the absolute truth in the theater and renounce the conventional system of tragedy and comedy, whose academic rules have oppressed even such geniuses as Corneille and Molière. One would think one was reading the prefaces of Diderot and Beaumarchais—who, luckier or more skilled, managed to realize their theories—whereas Restif's theater was always rejected by the stage. The excessive reality he sought to introduce is demonstrated by the fact that he proposed, in order to increase the unity, morality, and sensual delight of the theater experience, that love scenes be played by actual lovers on their wedding day.

Until his book *La Paysan perverti*, Restif had earned almost nothing apart from his work as a printer, which represented a livelihood for him the way copying music did for Jean-Jacques Rousseau. Booksellers rarely paid their bills, counterfeiting reduced much of the potential profits, and censors often censored works already printed or burdened them with huge fees by barring out dangerous passages. "On 18 August 1790," says the author, "I was even poorer than during my *foremanship*. I quickly ate up the profit from my *Famille vertueuse*; my *École de la jeunesse* [School of youth] was refused by the bookseller, my *Pornographe* by the censor . . . I didn't get discouraged, however. I wrote *Lucile* in five days. I was only able to sell it for three louis to a bookseller, who printed fifteen hundred copies instead of a thousand, and who gave the proofs to counterfeiters.[94] This man, a police informer, made a fortune and died the moment he began to enjoy it." This passage shows the state of French bookselling at the time. *Le Pornographe* and *Le Mimeographe* had earned Restif little owing to a rather unproductive partnership the writer established with a worker who advanced him some funds. *La Fille naturelle* [The natural girl] and *Les Lettres d'une fille*

* Some years later, Restif, now with more of a reputation, received from Joseph II a certification as a baron, enclosed in a snuffbox decorated with a portrait of the emperor. He returned the certificate and maintained the image of the sovereign philosopher.

à son père [Letters from a girl to her father], published by Lejay, didn't earn much more.[95] A novel adapted from Quevedo, entitled *Le Fin Matois*, had paid him banknotes that were worthless.[96] In this novel, Restif oscillates between various foreign trends that influenced the writers of his time, before achieving a definitive self-assurance in *Le Paysan perverti*.

Restif, having received some money from his father's estate, was able to pay the expenses for *Le Paysan perverti*, which the bookseller Delalain had refused to buy.[97] The first print run sold out in six weeks, and the second in twenty days. The third sold more slowly because of forgeries; but its success outside of France was such that there were up to forty-two printings in England alone. Historically, the portrait of French manners has interested foreigners more than France itself. At first, the book was attributed to Diderot, which gave rise to a host of complaints. It was withdrawn from the market; however, by means of a present to the censor, Demaroles, Restif won restitution on the condition that he print some *cards* for the places indicated as being dangerous.

La Paysanne pervertie [The perverted (female) peasant] appeared three years after *Le Paysan*, and the two works were collected under the title *Paysan-Paysanne* [The male-female peasant]. Here the ideas of the reformer, mixed with the dramatic ploys of the novelist, are clearly developing. On this matter, we must speak of the general system of philosophy and morals the author had conceived, and which he would later develop in some peculiar books. He attributes its initial conception to the talks he had with the Cordelier Gaudet d'Arras in the time of his apprenticeship. The latter's knowledge made up for what the young man's adventurous thoughts lacked, and the system was thus formed, like the ancient chimera of two natures strangely coupled.

It seems evident from the life of Restif de la Bretone that he followed in his philosophical ideas a sort of traced-out pattern, which his whimsical imagination took pleasure in embroidering. The logic of his system is completely lacking with regard to his personal conduct, and he can only exclaim at every moment: "Ah, how mistaken I was, how weak I have been!"—Here is the reformer.—For Gaudet d'Arras, on the contrary, whose character he detailed at length in *Le Paysan perverti*, there is neither virtue nor vice, cowardice nor weakness. All that man does is good, insofar as he acts according to his interest or his pleasure and never exposes himself to the vengeance of laws or that of men. If evil ensues, it is society's fault for not foreseeing it. Yet Gaudet d'Arras is not cruel; he is even affectionate to those he loves because he needs companionship; sensitive to the misfortunes of others because of a sort of nervous tension that makes him experience the spectacle of suffering; but he could be hard, selfish, insensitive, have a high opinion of himself, and would only see it as a coincidence of his makeup, or rather the mysterious goal of that immortal nature which made the vulture and the dove, the wolf and the lamb, the fly and the spider. Nothing is good, nothing is evil, but nothing is indifferent. The vulture rids the land of putrefied flesh, the wolf prevents the proliferation of countless races of rodents, the spider reduces the number of harmful insects; such is the case for everything: the stinking manure is a fertilizer, poisons are medicines . . . Man, who governs the earth, must know how to regulate the relations of beings and things with respect to his interests and to that of his race. There, and not in religions or forms of government, lies the principle of future generations. With good social organization there will be no need for virtue,—benevolence and mercy will be the business of magistrates;—with a solid philosophy, even moral punishment will be annuled, being the result of either religious education or reading novels.

Nothing is very new today in this doctrine of 1750, which dates back directly to the illustrious Epicureans of the age of Louis XIV, where we find the whole of it in *The System of Nature*.[98] We have wanted only to underline the foundation underlying the whole system of the author of *Le Pornographe*. As for himself, he only came to accept the ideas of Gaudet d'Arras by exploring them in greater depth. This absolute materialism disgusted him, and he congratulated himself for having found in another friend, his comrade at the printing shop, the good Loiseau, an entirely spiritual nature to oppose the Epicurean feelings of the Cordelier. But between Gaudet and Loiseau, there was an average to be taken. Loiseau, though a philosopher, believed in a remunerative God, and even in angels or spirits, *divine acolytes*, whose existence the famous Dupont de Nemours has since sought to prove outside of any religious tradition.[99] The aridity of primitive naturalism was in this way corrected by certain mystical tendencies to which Pernetty, d'Argens, Delille de Salles, d'Espréménil, and Saint Martin later succumbed.[100] However strange these variations of the philosophical spirit may seem today, they follow the exact same path as in ancient Rome, where the Neoplatonism of Alexandria succeeded the school of the Epicureans and Stoics of the age of Augustus.

However weak the value of *Monsieur Nicolas*'s philosophical ideas may be, it was impossible not to mention them in this assessment of his literary work, for Restif is one of those authors who do not write a line, be it verse or prose, novel or drama, without tying it by some thread to a universal synthesis. This pretension to the analysis of characters and the criticism of morals had already manifested itself in the three or four obscure novels that preceded *Le Pornographe*; after that book, the author's reformist tendencies multiplied, thanks to the success he had obtained; after *Le Mimographe* comes *L'Anthropographe* and *Le Gynographe*, man and woman reformed, followed by *Le Thesmographe* [The thesmographer] and *Le Glossographe* [The glossographer], concerning laws and language.[101] The first two do not stray far from Rousseau's ideas. Following the example of the philosopher of Geneva, Restif sees no other remedy for corruption than to visit the fields and work the land, but he abstains from casting blame on the theater and the arts. But where is the merit of philosophy, if it finds no other means of raising social and moral standards than the destruction of cities? Must we suppress all the wonders of industry, arts, and the sciences, and limit the role of man to the production and consumption of the fruits of the earth? It would doubtless be better to seek to establish principles of morality for all states and for all situations.

III. Restif's Confidential Works

In addition to the novels with a philosophical claim, Restif's collection includes other novels we have already described, and which are only chapters of the same confession: these stories might be called the *confidential* works of Restif. It is to this group that belongs the *Mémoires de M. Nicolas* in which he frankly relates his strange life straightforwardly and hiding nothing; it is to this group that we must also attach certain sections from a voluminous collection of narratives and sketches on manners and customs, *Les Contemporaines*.

Les Mémoires de M. Nicolas, which is the very life of the author, offers nearly all the elements of the subject already treated in *Le Paysan perverti*.

The analysis of the novel will clarify the *Mémoires*. In the novel, he represented himself under the name of Edmond, and his adventures in Auxerre form the first part: we see that there is no great expense of the imagination; the art shows through in the arrangement of details and the portrait of characters. That of Gaudet d'Arras is especially striking and can count as the prototype for those dark characters who hover over the novel's plot and inevitably direct its threads. These satanic and mocking heroes have since been overused, but Restif has the advantage of having portrayed a true character, unfortunately offset by the misfortune of having known him. Seeing reality thus serve the dramatic tale, one thinks of those groups of sculptures that certain sculptors compose not from study or the imagination, but which are molded from life. Through this method, we thus see the adorable character of Mme Parangon and, in opposition, Zéfire. There is no point in repeating the whole story; but one can see that Mme Parangon and Gaudet d'Arras meet with the author in Paris, representing his good and his evil genius. It is this portion that constitutes the strength and merit of this book, which would otherwise merely be a sketch of personal memories. Gaudet d'Arras becomes the *disastrous* Mentor of Edmond; he leads him through all the disorder, all the corruption, all the crimes of the capital, and this without interest, without hatred, and even with a sort of compassionate friendship for a young man whose company pleases him. According to his philosophy, developed at length, if one is to be happy, one must know everything, make use of everything, and satisfy one's passions straightforwardly and without enthusiasm, then gradually dry up the heart to arrive at the contemplative insensitivity of the sage, which becomes one's true crown and prepares one for the future sweetness of death, one's only reward. By following this system, Edmond, after having lived a joyful life, dishonored his benefactress, and attempted the most shameful refinement of vice, ends up marrying a sixty-year-old woman for her fortune; she dies after three months and Gaudet d'Arras is accused of having poisoned her. This ultraphilosophical action leads him to the scaffold, but Gaudet kills himself instead. Edmond is sentenced to the galleys. After long years of pain and remorse, he manages to escape and returns to his village; he is so changed, so wracked by suffering, that no one recognizes him. His parents have died of grief: he goes wandering in the cemetery, searching for their graves; he meets his brother Pierrot, who had not left the village, and who has led a quiet life cultivating his field; it is a very touching scene and a nice contrast in the work. The author has somewhat fallen back into a banal romance by having Edmond then find his benefactress, Mme Parangon, who forgives him, consoles him, and even consents to marry him; but on the very same day of the wedding, he is hit by a carriage that runs him over.

We can see that the author has not spared himself by portraying himself in the character of Edmond. It is certain that he himself exaggerated the character's traits to make him more striking, and that he did not in reality consider himself worthy of the required punishment. In Edmond, however, the very essence of the character betrayed in *M. Nicolas* is clearly recognized; that is to say, there is a sort of presumptuous weakness in him which singularly invalidates the philosophical pretensions of this disciple of Gaudet d'Arras. Edmond can never find the moral strength needed to resist evil or abjection; forced at every moment to confess his weakness, he only addresses pity or that feeling that makes him repeat a thousand times: "I wanted to portray the events of a natural life and leave it to posterity as an anatomy of morals"; he makes a merit of his daring to "name everything, to compromise others, to sacrifice them, with himself, like himself, to the public interest." Jean-Jacques Rousseau, according to him, told the truth, but he wrote too much like *an author*. He praises him only for having rescued Mme de Warens from oblivion and making her live forever; he notes, in this respect, the relationship between her and Mme Parangon, congratulating himself for having celebrated the latter and reported, under fictitious names, his adventures with her in *Le Paysan perverti*, published in 1775, before Rousseau's *Confessions*. "Do not be angry with me," he adds, "because I am human and weak; it is why I should be praised, for if I only appeared virtuous in your eyes, where would the work on myself be? I had the courage to *strip myself* before you, exposing all my weakness, all my imperfections, my depravity, to allow you to compare your peers with yourselves . . . It is believed," he adds, "that one educates oneself with fables: Well, I am a great fabulist who instructs others at his own expense; I am a multiple animal, sometimes cunning as a fox; sometimes dumb, slow, and stupid as a donkey, often proud and brave as a lion, sometimes elusive and hungry like the wolf . . ." The eagle, goat, or hare still provide him with relatively modest assimilations; but what, then, is this singular philosophy that, on the pretext of living according to nature, lowers man to the level of a beast, or rather elevates him only to the level of a *multiple animal*?

We now come to *Les Contemporaines*, one of Restif's best-known works. Many of his early novels were reproduced in this immense collection, which comprises forty-two volumes from 1781 to 1785. *Les Contemporaines*, illustrated with five hundred engravings, carefully executed for the most part, will remain a curious but exaggerated portrait of the costumes and customs of the late eighteenth century. This collection was very successful, especially in the provinces but also abroad. It was this enormous compilation, for which he was paid forty-eight livres a page, which enabled the author to have a hundred and twenty figures engraved for the *Paysan-Paysanne pervertis*. Like Dorat, he spent a fortune to have them illustrated.[102] The success of this collection led to a great many sequels, such as *Les Françaises, Les Parisiennes, Les Provinciales*, up to a final series of scabrous descriptions entitled *Le Palais-Royal*.

At that time, Agnès Lebègue no longer lived with him. Having retired to the countryside, she had devoted herself to the education of some youths. Restif charmed his isolation through a close relationship with the daughter of a baker, Virginie, which cost him some money and caused him great sorrow, as she would spend the proceeds from the sales of his masterpieces with students. Moreover, she called him a miser and eventually left him for a bank teller. The author's only vengeance was to write *Le Quadragénaire* [The forty-year-old], in order to earn back from this sad adventure at least the money she had cost him. This title indicates the age at which the seducer's decline begins, even more pronounced five years later when he had the misfortune of knowing Sara. The sadness he felt gave him the idea to undertake *Le Hibou ou Spectateur Nocturne* [The owl or Night spectator], designating himself as this bird of night that had bequeathed him the formerly graceful dark eye and aquiline nose that was now already turning into a caricature. This book is at the origin of *Les Nuits de Paris*.

When Restif wrote *Le Nouvel Abailard* [The new Abelard], he was in love with a pretty butcher named Mlle Londo, because he always needed a model for each of his works. We find in this book the germ of his *Physics*. The butcher, unenlightened, was no less curious about astronomy than the beautiful marchioness to whom Fontenelle addressed his scholarly discussions. From this comes an entire cosmological system within reach ... of pretty butchers! By dint of exploring these otherworldly ideas, Restif was led to write *L'Homme Volant* [The flying man], a very compelling argument for the aerostation.[103] The machine that transports Victorin through the air is described with scrupulous care. He was probably inspired here by Cyrano de Bergerac's *Voyage*, which predicted, so far in advance, the discoveries of the Montgolfier brothers.[104]

Finally appeared the work entitled *La Vie de mon père*, which, without obtaining the material success of *Le Paysan perverti*, added to Restif de la Bretone's reputation among a more serious readership. He describes with simplicity and charm the peaceful existence and modest virtues of an honest man, whose example he admits he should have followed. Two portraits of his father Edme Restif and his mother Barbe Bertrô illustrate this book, in which the author shows, for the sake of virtue and the purity of morals, the regrets that the fallen angel experienced after leaving Paradise.

A bitter, painful book, full of rage and despair, followed this domestic idyll: *La Malédiction paternelle* [The paternal curse]; it is a book in which perhaps is revealed the sad memory of a family drama, and contains the story of Zéfire, which charts the first stage in the writer's moral decline.[105] *La Découverte australe* [The discovery of the austral continent] and *L'Andrographe* [The andrographer], philosophical works in which utopia plays a major part, belong to this last period of Restif's literary life, in which he ended up writing eighty-five volumes in six years.[106] At this time, Restif had the misfortune of losing a precious friend who had often helped him financially, and who, as head censor, protected him in the publication of his works. This man, whose name was Mairobert, was bored with life.[107] Determined to die, he had the good idea to *initial* in advance several of Restif's works. The latter came to take them and told him of the sorrows of his household and of his fortune. At the same time, Nicolas envied the lot of Mairobert, who was young, rich, and in great credit.—"So many people," replied the latter, "are considered happy and are in a state of despair!" The following day, Restif learned that his protector had cut his veins in a bath and concluded with a pistol shot. "I am alone!" exclaims Restif in *Le Drame de la Vie*, after having recorded the painful end of this man. "O God, how fate pursues me! This man was going to give me a means of living... Let us fall back into the void!"

However, another wealthy friend named Bultel-Dumont took Mairobert's place.[108] Restif was introduced by this latter patron to a kind of intermediate society in which the upper middle class, those of the legal profession, literary people, and some nobility gathered. Robé, Rivarol, Goldoni, Caraccioli—actors, artists—the Duke of Gèvres, Préval, and Pelletier de Mortefontaine:[109] such was the brilliance of this society, eager for readings, philosophy, paradoxes, witticisms, and spicy anecdotes. The salons of Dumont, Préval, and Pelletier in turn opened their doors to this intimate audience. Someone who made the greatest impression on Restif, still a bit of a newcomer to this world, was Mme Montalembert, who received him with sympathy.[110]—"To be thirty years younger!" he cried, and he was so inspired by the character of this amiable woman that he made her the *marchioness* in *Les Nuits de Paris*, a kind of occult Providence that he charged with determining the fate of the unhappy and suffering individuals he encountered on his nocturnal expeditions.

Around the same time, Restif made the acquaintance of Beaumarchais who, appreciating his talent both as a writer and a printer, wished to place him at the head of the printing office of Kehl, where the great edition of Voltaire was being published; he refused and later regretted it.[111]

Another home whose doors opened to this writer now growing increasingly famous was that of Grimod de la Reynière's son, a young witty man, with an ardent soul and a rather weak mind, who at the time hosted literary gatherings with such choice guests as Chénier, the Trudaine brothers, Mercier, Fontanes, Count Narbonne, Chevalier de Castellane, Larive, Saint-Prix, etc.[112] The amphitryon's eccentricity was always on display in his scheduling of his parties. All of Paris took notice of two major philosophical parties that La Reynière gave, in which he established ceremonies according to the taste of the Ancients. The modern element was represented by an extraordinary abundance of coffee. To be admitted, you had to commit to drinking twenty-two cups of coffee at lunch. The afternoon was taken up with electricity seances. They then dined at a large round table in a room lit by three hundred and sixty-six Chinese lanterns. A herald, dressed in a Bayard costume, preceded, spear in hand, the fourteen courses, led by La Reynière himself in black dress.[113] A procession of cooks and pages accompanied the dishes, served in enormous silver dishes, with pretty *servants* in Roman costumes, placed near the dinner guests, offering their long hair for the guests to wipe their fingers.

IV. Restif the Communist: His Life during the Revolution

We now know enough of Restif's strange life to classify him among those writers the English people call *eccentric*. To the characteristic details indicated here and there in our account, it is worth adding a few special features. Restif was not tall, but sturdy and somewhat stout. In his later years, he was spoken of as a gruff man who dressed carelessly and was unapproachable. One day, the chevalier de Cubières was leaving the Comédie-Française;[114] he stopped at the widow Duchesne's shop to buy a fashionable item. A man was standing in the middle of the boutique with a large folded-down hat that covered half of his face; a very large black coat came down to his knee, the belt tied tightly around his waist, with some pretension, undoubtedly to make him appear thinner. The chevalier examined him curiously. This man drew from his pocket a small candle, lit it at the counter, put it in a lantern, and went out without looking at or greeting anyone. At the time, he lived at the shop. "Who is that character?" Cubières asked—"What, you don't know him? That's Restif de la Bretone," was the answer. Amazed at hearing this famous name, the chevalier returned the following day, eager to strike up a conversation with a writer he loved to read. The latter did not reply to the compliments paid by this affected writer, so cherished in the salons of the time. Cubières was content to laugh at this rudeness. Having later had the opportunity to meet Restif among some mutual friends, he saw him in a different light, full of eloquence and cordiality. He reminded him of their first meeting.—"What do you expect?" Restif said, "I am a man of momentary impressions; I was then writing *Le Hibou nocturne* and wishing to be a real owl, I vowed not to speak to anyone."

There was indeed some affectation in this role of the gruff man, adopted from Jean-Jacques. It excited the curiosity of society people, and women of the highest rank prided themselves in being able to tame the bear. Then he became friendly again; but his out-of-the-blue gallantries, his audacity, renewed from the time when he played the role of a second-rate Faublas, sometimes frightened imprudent people forced to suddenly listen to some cynical joke.

One day, he received an invitation to lunch at with M. Senac de Meillan, intendant of Valenciennes, along with some provincial bourgeois who wished to see the author of *Le Paysan perverti*.[115] There were also academicians from Amiens and the editor of the *Feuille de Picardie*. Restif found himself placed between Mme Denys, a merchant of striped muslin, and another modestly dressed lady he took to be the maid of a great house. Facing him was a pleasant provincial youth called *Nicodemus*, as well as a deaf man who amused the company by speaking now and then of things that had nothing to do with the conversation. A tidy little man, wearing a coat of white camlet, acted as though he was important, and called the political and philosophical ideas the novelist put forward complete nonsense.[116] A Mme Laval, a lace merchant from Malines, defended him and *found depth to him*. This was in 1789, so there was talk during the meal of the new constitution of the clergy, the extinction of aristocratic privileges, and legislative reforms. Restif, finding himself amidst good, well-rounded people who were listening to him with general favor, developed a host of eccentric systems. The deaf man interrupted them with different topics in a very uncomfortable way, the man in the white camlet pierced them with a sharp line or a quote full of seriousness. They finished, as was customary at the time, with readings. Mercier read a political fragment, Legrand d'Aussy a dissertation on the mountains of Auvergne.[117] Restif developed his system of physics, which he proclaimed more reasonable than that of Buffon, and more likely than that of Newton. He was embraced and the whole of what he said was proclaimed to be sublime. Two days later, the abbé Fontenai, who had also been at that lunch, informed him that he had been the victim of a hoax, the result of which, however, had turned out in his favor.[118] The muslin merchant was the Duchesse de Luynes, the lace merchant was the Countess de Laval, and the chambermaid was the Duchesse de Mailly; *Nicodemus* was Matthieu de Montmorency; the deaf man was the Bishop d'Autun; the man with the camlet coat, the abbé Sieyes, who, to repair the severity of his observations, sent Restif a collection of his writings.[119] They had wished to see the Jean-Jacques of les Halles in all his ardor and all his cynical indifference. They instead found him to be an amusing storyteller, a somewhat reckless Utopian, a dinner guest so unacquainted with the customs of the world to exclaim that it was the first time he had eaten oysters, but attentive to the ladies and caring for them almost exclusively. If indeed anything can mitigate the writer's many wrongs, his incredible personality, and the continual inconsistency of his conduct, it is that he has always loved women for themselves and with devotion, with enthusiasm, with madness. His books would otherwise be unreadable.

But we are soon in the midst of the Revolution. The philosopher who claimed to obliterate Newton, the Socialist bold enough to astonish the formal mind of de Sieyès, was not a Republican. As with the principal creators of utopias, from Fénelon and Saint Pierre to Saint-Simon and Fourier, he was utterly indifferent to the political form of the state.[120] Communism itself, which formed the basis of his doctrine, seemed to him possible under the authority of a monarch, just as all the reforms of *Le Pornographe* and *Le Gynographe* seemed to him feasible under the paternal authority of a good lieutenant of the police. For him, as for the Muslims, the prince personified the State's universal proprietor. In thundering against *infamous* property (that is the name he gave to it a thousand times over), he tolerated personal possessions, transmissible to heirs under certain conditions, and even to the nobility as a reward for good deeds, but which was to be canceled for their children if they did not renew their family line with traits of courage or virtue.

In the second volume of *Les Contemporaines*, Restif offers a plan for an association of workers and merchants that reduces capital to nothing:—this is the Exchange Bank in all its purity.—Here's an example: twenty merchants, workers themselves, live on a street in the Saint-Martin district. Each of them is the representative of a useful industry. Money is lacking because of political anxiety, and this street, once so prosperous, is saddened by the forced idleness of its inhabitants. A jeweler-goldsmith who has traveled to Germany, and who saw the *hernutes* there,[121] conceives the idea of a similar association for the inhabitants of the street:—they will undertake not to use any currency and to buy or sell everything by exchange, so that the baker gets his meat from the butcher, gets dressed at the tailor, and puts his shoes at the shoemaker's; all associates must do the same. Everyone can acquire or spend more or less, but inheritance returns to the masses, and children are born with an equal share in the assets of this company; they are raised at common expense, in the profession of their father, but with the option to choose another profession should they show an aptitude for a different line of work; they will all receive a similar education as well. The associates will regard themselves as equal, even though some may be of liberal professions, because their education will put them at the same level. Marriages will preferably be between persons of the association, save in extraordinary cases. Trials will be supported for the benefit of all; acquisitions will benefit the masses, and the money that will accrue to the company as a result of sales made outside of it will be spent on buying raw materials according to the needs of each state.—Such is the plan, yet the author did not intend on applying it to the whole of society, since he left the choice open between different forms of associations, allowing experience to determine the conditions for the success of the more useful one, which would naturally absorb the others. As for the old society, it would not be stripped, it would only inevitably suffer the fortunes of a struggle that would be impossible for it to sustain for very long.

However, the writer was getting older, growing increasingly morose, overwhelmed by debt, by the sorrows within himself. His only contact with the world was to go at night to the Café Manoury, where he sometimes argued political and philosophical matters. A few old regulars of this café, located on the Quai de l'Ecole, still remember his old blue greatcoat and the muddy cloak in which he wrapped himself in all seasons. Most often he sat in a corner and played chess until eleven at night. At that point, whether the game was finished or not, he would rise quietly and leave. Where did he go? *Les Nuits de Paris* tells us: he went to wander, whatever the weather, along the quays, especially around la Cité and l'Île Saint-Louis; he would plunge into the muddy streets of the crowded districts and returned only after obtaining a good collection of observations about the chaotic and bloody scenes he had witnessed. He often intervened in these dark dramas and became the Don Quixote of persecuted innocence or vanquished weakness. Sometimes he acted through persuasion; sometimes his authority was due to the suspicion that he had been charged with a mission by the police.

He even dared make inquiries with the porters or valets as to what was happening in each house, gaining entrance to the families under such and such a disguise, penetrating secret alcoves, surprising the wife's infidelities, the daughter's nascent secrets, which he divulged in his writings under transparent fictions. From this came lawsuits and divorces. One day, he was nearly murdered by a certain E. . . whose wife had appeared in *Les Contemporaines*. It was usually in the morning that he wrote down his observations of the day before. He wrote no less than one story before lunch. In the final days of his life, during the winter, he worked in bed for lack of wood, his breeches over his cap, for fear of drafts. He also had certain peculiarities that varied with each of his works, but which in no way resembled the peculiarities of Haydn's and Buffon's cuffs.[122] Sometimes he was condemned to silence as at the time of his encounter with Cubières; sometimes he let his beard grow and told anyone who made fun of it, "I will not shave until I have finished my next novel."—"And if it ends up being several volumes?"—"It will have fifteen."—"So you won't shave for fifteen years?"—"Don't worry, young man, I write half a volume a day."

What an immense fortune he would have acquired in our time by racing against our most fearless runners of the feuilleton and the trivial passions, those fearless explorers of second-rate miseries! His writing was affected by the disorder of his imagination; it is irregular, wandering, illegible; ideas appear like a mob, pushing the pen, and preventing him from forming the letters. This is what made him the enemy of double letters and long syllables, which he replaced with abbreviations. Most often, as we know, he just composed straight from the printer's case. He finally acquired a small printing office where he *set down* his works himself, aided only by an apprentice.

The revolution could not be dear to him in any way, because it brought to light politicians who were not very sensitive to his philanthropic plans, who were more concerned with Greek and Roman formulas than with fundamental reforms. Babeuf alone could have realized his dream;[123] but, discouraged by his own plans at that time, Restif showed no sympathy for the platform of the Communist Party. The assignats had swallowed up all his savings,[124] which amounted to less than seventy-four thousand francs, and the nation had scarcely thought of renewing, for his works, the subscriptions of the court and of the nobility, which he had used profusely. Nevertheless, Mercier, who had not ceased to be his friend, was able to obtain for Restif a reward of two thousand francs for a work useful for morals, and even proposed him as a candidate for the National Institute. The president replied dismissively: "Restif de la Bretone is a man of genius, but he has no taste."—"Well, I ask you gentlemen," replied Mercier, "who among us can call himself a genius!"

Several accounts of the revolution are to be found in Restif's final books. He reports a few scenes with dialogue in the fifth volume of *Le*

Drame de la Vie. It is regrettable that this practice had not been carried out more fully. Nothing is as gripping as this reality caught in the act. Here, for example, is a scene taking place on 12 July in front of the Café Manoury:

> A MAN, WOMEN—"Lambesc! Lambesc! . . . There's a slaughter at the Tuileries!"
> A TRADER OF LOTTERY TICKETS.—"Where are you running to?"
> A FUGITIVE.—"We're getting our wives back."
> THE MERCHANT.—"Let them escape on their own, and turn back."
> HIS WIFE-TO-BE.—"Come on! Let's go, get back."

There's no more than these five lines; one can sense the brutal truth: Lambesc's dragoons charging from the distance;[125] the doors closing; one of those riot scenes so common in Paris.

Later, Restif showcases Collot d'Herbois, and congratulates him on his *Paysan Magistrat* [The peasant judge]; but Collot is only concerned with politics.[126] "I have become a Jacobin," he says, "why are you not one?"—"Because of three very troublesome infirmities . . ."—"That's a reason. I'm giving myself entirely over to public affairs, and I won't waste my time or my efforts. First I want to join Robespierre; he is a great man."—"Yes, invariable." Collot continues: "I have the power of speech, I have the gesture, grace in representation . . . I have a motion to make Kings tremble. I have just completed *L'Almanach du père Gérard*—an excellent title.[127] I will try to receive a prize for the instruction of the campaign; my name will spread throughout the départements; someone will appoint me . . ."[128]

Is not Collot d'Herbois's silhouette entirely present? But the author did not always limit himself to these rapid portraits, and alongside these fleeting sketches are pages that almost rise to the interest of history, such as those that he devotes to Mirabeau, and which this great figure seems to have illuminated with his immense reflection.[129]

V. A Visit to Mirabeau

The conversation between Restif and Mirabeau constitutes of the most curious chapters in *Mémoires de Nicolas*. The author, who had a rage for pseudonyms, disguises himself here under the name of Pierre, which he had previously used in other works. "Approaching Mirabeau," he said, "I saw a man overcome with anxiety who needed to unburden himself." Restif expressed to him doubts as to the purity of this revolution that had begun with murders:

> "Thoughtful by nature," he added, "and brave through reflection, the heads frightened me; when I witnessed the body of Bertier[130] dragged by twenty-four little devils, I shuddered—I pinched myself *to make sure it was not me* . . . However, at the sight of the Bastille, seized and demolished, I felt a thrill of joy . . . I had feared that terrible Bastille!"
>
> At that moment, Mirabeau shook my hand, overcome with emotion: "Look at me," he said; "all the energy of the assembled French together has no equal to that which was in this head; but, unfortunately, it has weakened! . . . It was I who seized the Bastille, killed Delaunay, Flesselles[131] . . . It was I who wanted the king to come to Paris on 17 July: it was I who made him stay, receive friends, applaud; it was I who, seeing the spirits return to their seats, had Berthier arrested in Compiègne by one of my own, who sent for him in Paris, and who, the day before his arrival, sought an old scapegoat in Foulon,[132] his father-in-law, whom I caused to be brought to the spirits of ministerial despotism: it was I who brought his mounted head before his son-in-law, not to increase the horror of that unfortunate man's last moments, but to *energize* the soft and vain soul of the Parisians with this atrocity . . . You know that I succeeded, that I scared off the Count of Artois, Condé,[133] and all the dull courtiers and the brazen courtesans; it was I who did everything, and if the revolution succeeds to some extent, I shall one day have a temple and altars. Forget not what I tell you here . . . Continue your questions; I will answer them as needed."
>
> "And Versailles, on the 5th and 6th of October?"[134]

"Versailles!" exclaimed Mirabeau. (He was silent at first and walked quickly . . .) "Versailles! It is my masterpiece . . . But go on, go on!"

"I am listening, and I swear to you an inviolable silence!"

"I do not know what you mean by your *inviolable* silence because you have your own terms: we don't violate silence, but grammar! . . . Know that it was I who brought the National Assembly here, and the king, and the court. D'Orleans was not even consulted, although he paid a price[135] . . . Judge how ridiculous the information from this vile Châtelet was, whom I had appointed to be the judge of the crimes of lèse-nation, and who, if there had not been those wigged heads, could have become something! . . . But the horrible and necessary spectacle of Foulon, of Bertier (this is what *created dread*; the Bastille, Delaunay, Flesselles, had frightened only the court), had upset the whole infamous oligarchy of priests, gownsmen, and even the officials, at the head of which my brother wanted to place himself: unfortunately for him, when our parents made him, my father was a writer and my mother a drunk, so that he only had a thirst for power of any kind . . . I had always felt that as long as we were at Versailles we would do nothing worthwhile, surrounded as we were by gardes-du-corps and Swiss guards; a smile, a caress, could land you in the court; I managed to arrange it all. I bore no grudge; I wanted, after having intoxicated the people with anarchy, as during the five-day interregnum of the ancient Persians, to restore the king, and be made . . . mayor of the palace . . . But, busy with all the rabble, including the loose women of rue Jean-Saint-Denis, there came some disturbance which I brought to a halt with my emissaries. Some of those poor wretches had threatened the queen; I learned of it and had them quickly shot. The excitement was such that all of Paris was shaken, everyone: honest, dishonest, improper, prostitutes, wives, young girls, men of courage and cowards alike; we saw, in the fray, even little Rochelois Nougaret, who was closing in on the hunter Josse, recently become a bookseller[136]. . . I laughed wholeheartedly; I felt I was at the Grande-Pinte, and they were putting on the tragedy of *Peccata*;[137] allow me this farcical notion, perhaps the last I'll have; it was suggested to me when I saw a crowd of journalists in the troupe, Camille Desmoulins alongside Durosoi,

> Royou as a tailor's assistant, Geoffroi as a shoemaker, abbé Poncelin as a chimney sweep, Mallet du Pan as a writer of the mass graves, Sautereau and Dussieux as pork butchers, abbé Noël and Rivarol as wigmakers . . ."[138]

Here, the list grows satirical and attacks most of the authors of the time; a certain *authoress* is even cited, mounted on a cannon, shouting: "My rose to the first hero!"—"Have you a million of them?" replied an enthusiast. Mirabeau compares himself to Brother Jean des Enthomures[139] and, after the farcical narrative of this terrible expedition, complains of his enemies, who by means of gold have won a little Jewess, his mistress, whose name was Esther Nomit . . . "But I know all about it," he adds, "and I deceive both Delilah and the Philistines."

Then the conversation turns to the abolition of the nobility, the new constitution of the clergy, with interruptions and bizarre asides that evoke the dialogues of *Rameau's Nephew*. Mirabeau indulges in lengthy tirades, which he occasionally interrupts to take a breath, telling his interlocutor: "Come on, speak, continue . . . ; because I know you love to hold forth . . ." Then, at the first objection, he shouts: "You buzzard! . . . Poor man! I've seen you more eloquent in the past." Then he begins a dissertation on the property of the clergy and complains of the little talent Maury displayed on this subject.[140] "This is what I would have said in his place," he exclaims and, walking about his room like a lion in a cage, he delivers the entire speech the abbé Maury ought to have presented. Occasionally he pauses, surprised at not hearing the applause of the Assembly, so much has he assumed his role. He claps his hands, weeps over the arguments he tears from the supposed eloquence of his opponent; then, when the emotion to which he has given rise has dissipated, he wipes the sweat from his brow, lifts his black hair, and says: "And if Maury had had the nerve to speak like that, here's how I would have responded . . ." A new speech that lasts an hour and leads to a peroration that begins: "In summary, gentlemen . . ." Finally, he bursts out laughing, realizing he has just exhausted his lungs for a single listener.

He returns to the simple discussion, and offers a portrait of Necker:

> ". . . A great man, because he happened to have a great position . . . Moreover, smaller than he appeared on the outside, like all mediocre

men . . . He was modeled to be a senior clerk; he would not have dishonored himself in that position, where one is never seen but in twilight. Today he is a poor seigneur, incapable of a solid resolution, and who cowardly returns to the nobility who hate and despise him. Like fools and petty scoundrels, he is astonished at what he has done . . . Judge how many such men inspire me with contempt, I, who would walk alone against a million! Think about it! How many in our Assembly are like Mirabeau in appearance, but who would have been Neckers if they had not been supported by an assembly! . . . No, my friend, I see not one, not one, who would have done alone what I did alone . . . When I held the ministerial despotism in my nervous hands, I squeezed its throat; I told it: *A fight to the death! I'll suffocate you, or you'll suffocate me!* I almost choked it to death . . . But it keeps tripping me up . . ."

"In truth, I believe," I then said, "my dear Riquetti, that you would make a great minister! . . . May you manag to earn in this position the only true glory, that of contributing to the happiness of the people! . . ."

"So, you too are under the influence of the trivial virtue of our philosophes! The people! The people! The people are made for men of merit, who form the brain of the human race: it is only through us and for us that they should be happy. Moses was the Jewish brain, Muhammad the Arab brain; Louis XIV, small as he was, was the French brain for forty years . . . It is I who am it now."

Here, Restif raises the question of whether liberty is good for individuals.

"Liberty," says Mirabeau, "is not a real advantage for children, imbeciles, madmen . . . or for certain men who are not mad, but whose judgement is false—like all villains, troublemakers, and those wicked by nature—the *overly passionate*, as we have been on occasion," he adds, "gamblers, fornicators, drunkards, in a word, three-quarters of mankind! . . .

"*Republicanism*," he adds, "as Robespierre and some others conceive of it, is anarchism, an unstable government; but the leaders in the National Assembly are supported by subordinates, to whom they do not pay enough attention: Camille Desmoulins, who shouts, complains, is obstinate, speaks badly, writes well; a more obscure man, Danton, is deceitful, a rogue, selfish, a villain in every sense of the word, as some people say I am; another schemer who stirs up trouble, and is immensely active, is the ex-Capuchin, Chabot;[141] Grangeneuve is an honest man, but too fanatical[142] . . . Oh! I pity the nation if these fools are put in positions of power! I pity the nation if one puts *non-entities* in power, as we have too many already in our present Assembly! A crowd of prosecutors, lawyers, Chapeliers,[143] Sumacs,[144] . . . the Assembly stinks of trickery and chicanery . . . My friend, if I cease to exist, these plumassiers will do harm![145] . . . If a despised man, like this scoundrel Robespierre, were to obtain a high position in government, you would see him get serious, covert, atrocious . . . I alone could stop him . . ."

A few days after this conversation, Mirabeau died. "I could not be present," says the writer, "during his last illness, because his people did not know me, especially Monsieur Cabanis[146] . . . Ah, if Préval had lived, Mirabeau would still be alive!" Préval was a doctor who had saved Restif from several dangerous illnesses.

Restif attributes the death of Mirabeau to the total collapse of the monarchy. It was seeing themselves deprived of this last support, a self-interested support no doubt, since Mirabeau intended to become a sort of *mayor of the palace*, that Louis XVI and Marie Antoinette decided on the flight to Varennes[147] . . . "This man was," he says elsewhere, "the last hope for the motherland, which his very vices would have saved . . . whereas the virtues of such fools as Chamillard and d'Ormesson have led to her ruin."[148] And, returning to his own poverty, caused by the depreciation of assignats which caused him to lose his seventy-four thousand francs in savings, he remembers with bitterness what Mirabeau had told him: "We must punish any money trader with a bullwhip, and burn alive or pulverize in a mortar all those who caused the depreciation of assignats."

VI. The Novelist's Old Age

At that time, Restif de la Bretone spent part of his days at the Palais Royal, where he established a sort of trading venue which became a measure of the value of assignats. Every day he saw his fortune melt and hoped in vain for a favorable return:—the final volumes of *Les Nuits de Paris* are full of imprecations against speculators who raised the price of gold to incredible heights and destroyed the paper wealth of the Republic;—then he would spend his evenings at the Caveau, because his resources no longer allowed him to go to the Café Manoury.[149] When on the rare chance the assignat had risen one day, he would take a few women of average virtue to have dinner at La Grotte Flamande, where they still allowed a few cheap orgies.[150] His sorrows sometimes weakened his spirit, which had always been passionate, and in every attractive person with an elegant shoe he believed he found one of his daughters, the product of one of the numerous affairs of his youth. It is likely that this fatherly monomania was often abused to obtain gifts or dinners from him.

Uncommunicative or very cautious about political matters, he was in no danger during the Reign of Terror. Men mattered little to him, and he found the ambition of political parties to be repugnant. What he saw happen at that time in no way corresponded to his dreams. Nobody thought of Communism; the Jacobins, at most, wanted goods to be shared, which is just another form of property—a fragmented property, that of the people. As for *pantheism*, who thought of it, save for a small number of *illuminés*? . . . People were generally atheistic. The festival given by Robespierre for the Supreme Being seemed to him a feeble trend toward a philosophical renewal;[151] yet he felt some regret in seeing Robespierre overthrown by people *who were not his equal*. From that moment on, his man was Bonaparte.[152] In the mystical writings of his final days, he represents him as a mediating spirit, coming from the planet Syrius, whose mission was to save France. To understand this strange assumption, one must have an idea of Restif's book entitled *Lettres du Tombeau ou les Posthumes* [Letters from the tomb or the posthumous], which appeared under the name of Cazotte.

The first two volumes of this work were inspired by a charming idea from the Countess de Beauharnais and created partly by Cazotte, as Restif acknowledges in his *Memoirs*.—A young man named Fontlèthe is in love with the wife of a magistrate; the latter is very old, and the woman, the victim of a marriage of convenience, promises Fontlèthe that he will eventually become her second husband. The young man grows tired of waiting; in a moment of discouragement, he renounces life and takes some opium. At this moment, they bring him a note to inform him of the news of the death of the magistrate. Doubly desperate, he runs to his doctor, who gives him an antidote. He thinks he is saved: he soon marries the woman he loved; but, a few days after the wedding, an unknown languor seizes him: he consults the doctors. It is the poison the antidote couldn't fight against that is causing him harm. They inform him, after his repeated requests, that he has little more than a year to live. It is true, death frightens him less than the thought of leaving a young, honest woman, even though she would ultimately remarry after him. He then designs a unique project: it is to leave his wife and to ensure she does not know when he will die. He asks the minister for a mission to Italy and leaves for Florence, under the pretext of important services to be rendered to the state. He prolongs his stay under various pretexts, and in the year that is left to him, writes a series of letters that will be sent to his wife from different parts of the world and at various times, as if the State had sent him from country to country without his being able to refuse his services. Indeed, these letters, confided to friends he trusted, follow one another for several years, bringing solace to the widow *without her knowing it*. The posthumous correspondent's only thought is to prove to his wife, a little addicted to the materialistic ideas of the time, that the soul survives the body and finds in other realms all of one's loved ones. This framework is certainly very beautiful; except Restif, who in reality was a sort of pagan spiritualist, derives most of his arguments from the doctrine of the Hindus and the Egyptians. Sometimes the soul passes into another body after a thousand years, as it was with the ancients; sometimes it rises to the stars and discovers there countless paradises, as in Swedenborg;[153] sometimes it becomes ethereal and passes into the state of a winged angel, as in Dupont de Nemours; but after all these hypotheses, the real system unmasks itself, and we arrive at a complete cosmogony, which presents most of the suppositions of Fourier's system. A character named Multipliandre has discovered the secret of isolating his soul from his body and of visiting the stars without losing the possibility of returning at will to his human *rag*. He settles on the summit of the Alps, in a cave covered with snow, and, having coated himself in materials to keep warm and having hidden himself in a safe place well defended against bears, he reaches this state of ecstasy and detachment to which some Indian saints are reduced, they say, for entire months. Here begins the description of the planets, the suns, and the cometary planets, with bold hypotheses we have not been spared since. It is very curious to enter this universe, formulated, after all, according to some scientific basis, where we find the moon without an atmosphere, Mars inhabited by fish with proboscises, and the sun by men of such size that the traveler finds himself conversing with a tiny insect walking on the outfit of a *solar* individual: this insect is only one league tall, and its intelligence, although far superior, approaches that of men. It explains that the Supreme Being is only an immense central sun, the brain of the world, from which emanate all the suns; each of them living and reasoning and giving birth to cometary planets, that is, shaking them in space, somewhat in the way the *aster* shakes its seeds in our gardens. When the cometary planets become what are now called *nebulae,* they swim in the ether like fish in water, mate, and produce smaller asteroids. In dying, they settle and become planets or satellites. They only exist for a few billion years in this state, and it is from their successive decomposition that plants, animals, and men are born. Species degenerate as corruption advances; the planet rots altogether or dries up, eventually the victim of a sun that consumes it to reproduce the elements in new forms. The solar insect knows no more, and the author admits that he may have been mistaken on many points; but how superior this data already is to human intelligence! Multipliandre eventually finds the secret to creating a race of winged men and repopulating the earth. Moreover, most of the hypotheses of this book are presented in the caustic form of *Micromegas* and *Gulliver's Travels*:[154] this is what makes the reading bearable.

Never had a writer possessed the precious qualities of the imagination to a greater degree than Restif. Yet his life was one long battle against indifference. A warm heart, a picturesque quill, an iron will; none of this was enough to form a good writer.—He lived with the strength of several men; he wrote with the patience and resolution of several authors. Diderot himself was more correct, Beaumarchais more clever; but did either have half of this reckless and intense enthusiasm, which does not always produce masterpieces, but without which masterpieces cannot exist?—Everyone knows his style through one of these works, which one rarely admits to having read, but on which we sometimes cast our eyes. A line worthy of the classics suddenly appears in the manure like the jewels of Ennius.[155] We already knew this one: "Morality is a pearl necklace; untie the string, and everything scatters." Here he paints the portrait of a man with a single stroke: "Mirabeau served the patriots the way Santeuil praised the Saints, with a bad heart."[156] When he lacks a word, he creates it, and sometimes skilfully; he speaks of a *cythéréique* smile, of the *mignonnesse* of a woman ... "I *chimérais*," he said, "while waiting for happiness."[157]

To find a counterpart to Restif de la Bretone in the past, one would have to go back to Cyrano de Bergerac for the extravagance of his hypotheses, to Furetière for those comical analyses of language and human character in which he delights, to Aubigné for that audacity of Gallic immorality, which he could not endure—because, being very often capable of refinement and pretentious research, he at other times elaborated, in his own words, details which it would have been better to conceal.—Like Voltaire, at whose school he was honored to belong, he hated the critics, the journalists, and often attacked them using strong language. He calls them either dishonest or *cruel little street urchins*; for him, La Harpe is a *stupid animal* that should be dragged *into a river*; Fréron, a scoundrel; Geoffroi, a pedant.[158] De Marsy, editor of *l'Almanach des Muses*, is a simple *brute* who read *Le Paysan Perverti* without being affected.—This does not even approach the *literary amenities* of the old man from Ferney, but Restif did not have the credit needed to speak up at this point. However, his criticism of even those who were sympathetic to some of his writings eventually brought against him a *conspiracy of silence*. He remained the only one to advertise his books, as he had for a long time been the only one to print them, and as he ended up being the only one to sell them. Booksellers did not like him very much, because once introduced into their homes, he told the romantic story of their wives, fell in love with their daughters, was meticulous in his portraits of them, and talked about their adventures. Obscuring their real names by creating anagrams was not always sufficient to prevent the curiosity that arose about them. Mérigot became Torigém; Vente, Etnev; Costard, Dratsoc,[159] and so on ... so that it is not surprising to find in his last books this simple description: "Printed at home, and sold at Marion Restif's, rue Bucherie n. 27." This partly explains the lack of success of his final works, and the decision to publish the most remarkable of them, *Les Lettres du Tombeau*, under the name of Cazotte, who, moreover, had cooperated in the plan of this work heavily influenced by *illuminism*.

It has been wrongly said that Restif died in poverty. The collapse of the assignats had led him to lose his savings; the little he earned from his books during the Revolution often reduced him to a discomfort made more painful by his familial responsibilities; but a few friends, Mercier, Carnot, and Mme de Beauharnais, supported him in his most critical moments, and when the state became more peaceful, he was given a position that earned 4,000 francs, which he held until his death in 1806.

In 1811, Cubières-Palmezeaux published a posthumous work of Restif's entitled *Histoire des Compagnes de Maria* [The story of Maria's companions]. The first volume is devoted entirely to an evaluation of literature which, in many respects, is witty and heartfelt. Cubières quotes a line which will prove that Restif, although a Communist, was not an enemy of the monarchy. He had at the National Convention a friend that he liked and believed in for a long time. On the day of Louis XVI's condemnation, Restif went, with a pistol in his pocket, to wait for his friend under the portico, and said when he saw him leave the Assembly: "Did you vote for the king's death?"—"No, I did not vote."—"Good for you," said the writer, "because I would have blown your brains out."

The complete works of Restif de la Bretone amount to more than two hundred volumes. We have not included in our list several novel-pamphlets such as *La Femme infidèle* [The unfaithful woman] and *Ingénue Saxancourt*, the former directed against his wife, Agnès Lebègue, the latter against his son-in-law, Augé. This mania for wanting to constantly use the public as arbitrator and judge in his domestic dissensions had grown, in the last days of the novelist's life, into a vertible illness, one of those which doctors rank among the varieties of hypochondria. It is conceivable that a blind injustice may have resulted from this disposition. However, his wife herself understood him well, because, in a letter to Palmezeaux, who asked her for information on the character of her husband, we found nothing but praise for his charity and his sympathy for humanity in general, which, as in the case of most reformers, did not always extend to his close friends and relatives.

We have given, with perhaps too much development, the story of an existence whose interest doubtless lies only in the evaluation of the moral causes which brought about our revolutions. The great upheavals of nature bring to the surface unknown materials, obscure residues, monstrous or aborted combinations. Reason wonders at it, curiosity avidly feeds on it, the bold hypothesis finds in it the seeds of a new world. It would be foolish to build on what is only an efflorescent and unhealthy division of substances, or a sterile combination of heterogeneous substances, a deceptive foundation, on which generations once believed they could establish a strong foothold. Otherwise, intelligence would just resemble those lights that flutter over swamps and illuminate what appears to be the green surface of a vast meadow, yet which only covers an infested and stagnant sludge. True genius likes to rely on more solid ground, and momentarily gazes at the vague images of the mist only to illuminate them and gradually dispel the dark beams with its radiance.

Our age has not met a man with an intellect and a passion superior to his, and he, grasping the true relations of things, would have restored peace to the contending forces and restored harmony to troubled imaginations. We are always prey to vulgar sophists, who only develop ideas, under a thousand forms, the basic principles of which they have not even invented. The same is true of this school, so numerous today, of subordinate observers and analysts who study the human mind only in its insignificant or suffering aspects and indulge in the search for a suspicious pathology in which hideous abnormalities of decomposition and disease are cultivated with the same love and admiration that a naturalist devotes to the most attractive varieties of regular creations.

The example that Restif's private life and literary career would demonstrate, if need be, is that genius can no more exist without taste than character without morality. The confessions he made of his constant regrets and the misfortunes that followed his mistakes seem to us to offset the thoughtlessness of certain details. There was a lesson he had to give in its entirety, and a greater reserve might have weakened its significance.

CAZOTTE

I

The author of *The Devil in Love* belongs to that class of writers we call humorous,[1] in the same way that the Germans and the English do, and which our literature has seldom produced save as under the veneer of a foreign imitation. The clear and rational mind of the French reader takes to the whims of a dreamy imagination with difficulty, unless the latter acts within the traditional limits and conventions of the fairy tale and the opera pantomime.[2] Allegory pleases us, the fable amuses us; our libraries are full of these witty compositions, initially intended for children, then for women, and which men of leisure do not despise. There were many in the eighteenth century, and fictions and fables were never more successful than at that time. The most serious writers, Montesquieu, Diderot, Voltaire, were rocked and put to sleep by these charming tales, this collection of works which their principles were to destroy in their entirety. The author of *The Spirit of the Laws* also wrote *The Temple of Gnide*; the founder of the *Encyclopedia* charmed the lady and her friends in the bedroom[3] with *The White Bird* and *The Indiscreet Jewels*; the author of the *Philosophical Dictionary* embellished the characters of the *Princess of Babylon* and *Zadig*[4] with marvelous fantasies from the East. All this was invention and nothing more, though of the finest and most charming kind.

But the poet who believes in his fable, the narrator who believes in his legend, the inventor who takes seriously the dreams hatched in his mind, this is what was unexpected in the eighteenth century, when poetic abbés were inspired by mythology and certain secular poets created fables using the Christian mysteries.

One would have astonished an audience back then by showing them that there was in France a spiritual and naive storyteller who continued *The*

Thousand and One Nights, that great unfinished work that M. Galland had grown weary of translating as if the Arab storytellers themselves had dictated the work to him;[5] it was not just a clever pastiche, but a serious and original work written by a man totally imbued with the spirit and belief systems of the East. Most of these stories, it is true, Cazotte had dreamed at the foot of palm trees among the dreary hills of Saint-Pierre—far from Asia, no doubt, yet under its brilliant sun. The majority of this unique writer's works found success without adding to his glory, and it is to *The Devil in Love* alone and a few poems and songs that he owed his reputation that accompanied the misfortunes of his old age. The end of his life revealed the secret to the mysterious ideas that presided over the invention of nearly all his works and added to them a singular value which we will undertake to appreciate.

A certain vagueness reigns over Jacques Cazotte's early years. Born in Dijon in 1720, he had studied with the Jesuits, like most of the fine minds of that time. One of his brothers, grand vicar of M. de Choiseul, bishop of Châlons,[6] summoned him to Paris and placed him in the administration of the Navy, where he obtained the rank of Commissioner General by 1747.[7] At this point he had already taken a bit of interest in literature, especially poetry. The salon of Raucourt, his countryman, brought together writers and artists, and he made himself known by reading some fables and songs, preliminary drafts of a talent that was to contribute more to prose than to poetry.

At this time, he was required to spend part of his life in Martinique, where he obtained the position of chief inspector of the Leeward Islands.[8] He lived there in obscurity for several years, but was highly regarded and liked by everyone, and married Mlle Élisabeth Roignan, the daughter of the chief judge of Martinique.[9] When he was on leave, he sometimes returned to Paris, and there published a few poems.[10] Two songs, which soon became famous, date from this period, and seem to have been influenced by the fashion that had spread for reviving the old French Romance or ballad, in imitation of Sir Monnoye.[11] It was one of the first attempts to evoke a fantastical or Romantic atmosphere, which our literature was to later wear out and abuse, and it is remarkable to see it already taking shape, with some impropriety, through the adventurous talent of Cazotte.

The first is titled the "Vigil of the Good Woman," and begins:

In the heart of the Ardennes,
Sits a castle upon stone,
With ghosts by the hundreds.
Travelers leave it alone:
Upon its tower
Rests the vultures' bower,
They watch all fortune fade.
Alas, my dear, alas! I am afraid!

Here we can already recognize the genre of the ballad as the poets of the North conceived it,[12] and we can see its fantastical seriousness; we are far from the musky poetry of Bernis and Dorat.[13] The simplicity of Cazotte's style is not without a firm and vivid tone that shows through in some of the verses:

All around its walls
We can hear the werewolves howl,
We hear metal drag through their calls,
We see blood flow, fire prowl,
All at once,
Very sinister cries
Your chilled heart invade.
Alas, my dear, alas! I am afraid!

Lord Enguerrand, a brave knight returning from Spain, wishes to lodge within this terrible castle. He is told great stories of the spirits that inhabit the place; but he laughs, has his boots removed, his dinner served, and new sheets put on his bed. At midnight, the uproar the good people foretold begins. Terrible noises make the walls tremble, a thick infernal cloud blazes on the paneled walls; at the same time, a gust of wind blows opens the doors and *the sound of voices* is heard.

A damned soul, in the grip of demons, crosses the room, uttering cries of despair.

His mouth was foaming,
Melted lead flowed from his eyes . . .

A disheveled shade
Pierced his heart with a dagger blade;
With thick smoke
The horrifyingly dark blood sprayed.
Alas, my dear, alas! I am afraid!

Enguerrand asks these sad figures the reason for their torments.

"Seigneur," responds a woman armed with a dagger, "I was born in this castle; I was the daughter of Count Anselm. This monster you see, whom the heavens compel me to torture, was my father's chaplain, who fell in love with me, to my misfortune. He forgot the duties of his position and, unable to seduce me, he invoked the devil and offered his soul to obtain a favor from him.

"Every morning I went to the woods to breathe in the fresh air and bathe in the pure water of a stream."

There, by the water flume,
A certain rose pleased my eye;
Fresh, bright, barely in bloom,
To be plucked is what it seems to cry
Alas! It seemed
That from it streamed
The sweetest odor to pervade.
Alas, my dear, alas! I am afraid!

I want to decorate my hair
To add more radiance to my complexion,
I know not what uncanny air
Repulsed my hand on my inspection.
My heart did quake
And beating spake:
This flower is of the devil made! . . .
Alas, my dear, alas! I am afraid!

This rose on which the devil cast a spell delivers the lady over to the evil intentions of the chaplain. But soon, having recovered her senses, she threatens to denounce him to her father and the wretch silences her by stabbing her with a dagger.

Meanwhile, in the distance, one hears the voice of the count looking for his daughter. The devil then approaches the guilty chaplain in the form of a goat and says to him, "Mount, my dear friend; fear nothing, my faithful servant."

He mounts and with no dismay,
Feels the devil move, the earth below churn;
The air is poisonous along the way,
And the ground beneath him seems to burn.
In an instant they dive
And he is plunged alive
Into a realm of pain and shade!
Alas, my dear, alas! I am afraid!

The conclusion of the adventure is that Lord Enguerrand, witness to this infernal scene, by chance makes the sign of the cross, which causes the apparition to vanish. As for the moral: women should distrust their vanity, and men should distrust the devil.

This imitation of old Catholic legends, which would be looked down on today, was a fairly new effect in literature then; our writers had long obeyed the rule of Boileau, which says that Christians, because of their Faith, must not borrow any of Romantic poetry's decorative elements; and, in fact, any religion that slips into the domain of poets is soon adulterated and loses its power over souls. But Cazotte, who was more superstitious than a believer, cared little for orthodoxy. Furthermore, the minor poem of which we have just spoken was unpretentious and indicates to us the early tendencies of the author of *The Devil in Love* for a kind of fantastical poetry, which became vulgar after him.

It is said that Cazotte composed this ballad for Mme Poissonnier, his childhood friend and nurse to the Duke of Burgundy, who had asked him for songs she could sing to lull the royal child to sleep. He probably could have chosen a topic less melancholy and filled with visions of death; but we will see that this writer's sad fate was to foresee every misfortune.

Another ballad from the same period, "The Inimitable Feats of Ollivier, Marquis of Edessa," was also very popular.[14] Its subject is taken from old chivalric legends, but treated more in the popular style.

The daughter of the Count of Tours,
Is now beset by labor pains;
The count, who knows of her amours,
Feels fury he cannot restrain:
"Seek out my page, Ollivier,
Have him drawn and quartered this very day . . ."
"Warm the bed and turn down the light;
Hear you not the stroke of midnight?"

More than thirty couplets are then devoted to the exploits of the page Ollivier, who, pursued by the count over land and sea, saves his life numerous times, telling him at each meeting:

"It is I, your page; and now will you have me quartered?"

"Get out of my sight!" the stubborn old man replies each time; nothing can persuade him to change his mind, and Ollivier eventually decides to go into exile from France and wage war in the Holy Land.

One day, having lost all hope, he wishes to put an end to his woes; a Lebanese hermit takes him into his home, consoles him, and shows him, in a glass of water, a sort of magic mirror, everything taking place in the castle of Tours; how his mistress languishes in a dungeon, "in the mud among the toads"; how her child was lost in the woods and nursed by a doe,[15] and even how Richard, the Duke of the Bretons, has declared war on the Count of Tours and is besieging him in his castle. Ollivier generously returns to Europe to save his mistress's father and arrives just as the castle is about to surrender.

See the blows that they deliver
With fury so animated,
Besieged attacking besieger,
The attacks reciprocated;
Famine is here, the people cry,
The time to surrender is nigh.

"Warm the bed and turn down the light;
Hear you not the stroke of midnight?"

But like a whirlwind passing through,
My Ollivier then arrives;
He breaks apart his spear in two
So as to strike from both his sides.
With these blows, my dear Bretons,
You'll be forced to retreat!...
"Warm the bed and turn down the light;
Hear you not the stroke of midnight?"

We see that this simple poetry has a certain brilliance to it; but what struck connoisseurs most back then was the Romantic subject, in which Moncrif, the famous historiographer of Cats, thought he saw the makings of a poem.

Cazotte was still only the modest author of a few fables and songs; the academician Moncrif's support inspired him, and, on his return to Martinique, he treated the subject of Ollivier as a prose poem, interweaving his chivalric tales with comical episodes and fairy-tale adventures in the Italian style. This work does not have much literary merit, but it makes for an amusing read and its style is strong.

At the same time, he translated *Le Lord Impromptu*, an English novel written in the intimate style, which offers interesting details.[16]

It must not be supposed, however, that the author of these fantasies ignored his administrative duties; we have before us a handwritten note he addressed to the Duke of Choiseul during his ministry, in which he nobly draws upon his duties as a Commissioner of the Navy and proposes certain improvements to the department, with a solicitude that was undoubtedly appreciated. In addition, when the British attacked the colony in 1749, Cazotte was very active and even exhibited strategic knowledge in the arming of Fort St. Pierre. The attack was repelled, despite the descent of the British.[17]

However, the death of Cazotte's brother called him back to France a second time, this time as an heir to all of his property, and he soon began to seek retirement: it was granted him with the most honorable terms and with the title of Commissioner General of the Navy.

II

He brought his wife Elisabeth back to France and settled in his brother's house at Pierry, near Epernay. Determined not to return to Martinique, Cazotte and his wife sold most of their property to Father Lavalette, Superior of the Jesuit mission, an educated man with whom Cazotte had maintained pleasant relations during his stay in the colonies. Cazotte accepted, in exchange for his assets, a promissory note from the Society of Jesuits in Paris.

At issue were fifty thousand écus; Cazotte presented his case and the Society of Jesus protested.[18] The Superiors said that father Lavalette had engaged in dangerous speculation they were unable to credit. Cazotte, who had sold most of his possessions in the transaction, was reduced to pleading against his former teachers, and this trial, from which his religious and monarchical heart suffered, was the origin of all those that would later swoop down upon the Society of Jesus and bring it to ruin.

So began the misfortunes of this unique existence. There is no doubt that, from this moment on, his religious beliefs began to turn in a certain direction. The success of the *Ollivier* poem encouraged him to continue writing; he published *The Devil in Love*.

This book is famous for several reasons; it not only holds a unique position among the works of Cazotte owing to its charm and its precision of detail, but it surpasses them all through the originality of its concept. In France, and especially abroad, this book gained widespread acceptance and inspired many works in the same vein.

The phenomenon of such a literary work is not independent of the social milieu that produces it; in antiquity, Apuleius's *The Golden Ass*, also a book full of mysticism and poetry, served as a model for these kinds of works. Apuleius, an initiate of the cult of Isis and a visionary pagan, half skeptical and half credulous, seeking beneath the remnants of mythologies destined for oblivion the traces of previous or persistent superstitions, explaining the fable through the use of symbols and miracles by a vague definition of occult forces in nature, and then, a moment later, mocking himself over his credulity, casting here and there some ironic opinion that disconcerts the reader who is ready to take him seriously—this Apuleius is at the forefront of this family of writers, among whom we can also include the glorious author of *Smarra*, that dream of antiquity, that poetic realization of the most striking phenomena regarding the nightmare.[19]

Many people have only seen in *The Devil in Love* a kind of fairy tale, similar to many others of the same period and worthy of a place alongside *Le Cabinet des Fées*.[20] At most, they would have placed it in the same class as the allegorical tales of Voltaire; it is as if one were comparing the mystical work of Apuleius to the mythological antics of Lucien. The Alexandrian philosophers long used *The Golden Ass* as a source for the theory of symbols; Christians themselves respected this book, and St. Augustine cites it with deference as the poetic expression of a religious symbol: *The Devil in Love* is entitled to the same praise and marks a singular advance in the talent and style of its author.

So here was this man, initially a graceful poet of the school of Marot and La Fontaine, then a naive storyteller, sometimes in love with the flavor of old French fables, other times with the iridescent shimmer of Oriental legends made fashionable by the success of *The Thousand and One Nights*; after all, he followed the spirit of his century more than his own disposition, and he succumbed to the most terrible danger of a literary life: that of taking one's own inventions seriously.[21] Indeed, this resulted in the misfortune and glory of the greatest authors of that time; they wrote with their blood, with their tears; they betrayed without mercy, for the benefit of a vulgar public, the mysteries of their minds and their hearts; they played their role seriously, like those ancient comedians who stained the stage with real blood for the pleasures of the sovereign people. But who would have expected, in that century of disbelief, when the clergy themselves had so little defended their beliefs, to encounter a poet whose love of the supernatural, in a purely allegorical sense, gradually led him to a sincere and ardent mysticism?

Books dealing with the Cabala and the occult sciences inundated libraries at this time; the most bizarre speculations of the Middle Ages were revived in a form that made for light reading and dealt with spiritual matters in such a way as to win the favor of a frivolous public, half impious, half naive, like those of the final ages of Greece and Rome. The abbé de Villars, Dom Pernetty, and the Marquis d'Argens popularized the mysteries of the *Oedipus Ægypiacus*[22] and the esoteric dreams of the Neoplatonists of Florence. Pico della Mirandola and Marsilio Ficino were born again, permeated with the musky spirit of the eighteenth century, in *The Comte de Gabalis*, *Lettres cabalistiques*, and other works of transcendental philosophy that made their way into the salons.[23] One spoke only of elemental spirits, occult interests, charms, possessions, the migration of souls, alchemy, and mesmerism above all. The heroine of *The Devil in Love* is just one of those weird sprites that can be seen described in the article "Incubus or Succubus" in Bekker's *The World Bewitched*.[24]

The somewhat sinister role that the author ultimately gives to the charming Biondetta would suffice to show that he was not yet initiated into the mysteries of the Cabalists or the Illuminati, who have always carefully distinguished elementary spirits, sylphs, gnomes, undines, and salamanders from those dark minions of Beelzebub. Yet it was said that shortly after the publication of *The Devil in Love*, Cazotte was visited by a mysterious figure with a grave demeanor and the emaciated features that result from long hours of study, whose brown cloak draped over an imposing stature.[25]

He asked to speak with him privately, and when they were alone, the stranger began to make some strange signs at Cazotte, such as those initiates use to recognize each other.

Cazotte, astonished, asked him if he was mute and to explain more clearly what he had to say. But the latter only changed the order of his signs and indulged in even more enigmatic demonstrations.

Cazotte was unable to conceal his impatience.

"Forgive me, Monsieur," said the stranger, "but I thought you were one of us and belonged to the highest grades."

"I know not what you mean," replied Cazotte.

"Otherwise, where would you have gotten the ideas that dominate your *Devil in Love*?

"Why, from my imagination."

"What! Those evocations in the ruins, those mysteries of the Cabala, the occult power of a man over the spirits of the air, those striking theories on the power of numbers, on the will, on the fate of existence, you imagined all these things?

"I read a lot, but without following a doctrine or any particular method."

"And you are not even a Freemason?"

"Not even that."

"Well, Monsieur, either by wisdom or by chance, you have penetrated into secrets only available to initiates of the highest orders, and perhaps from now on it would be prudent for you to refrain from revealing such things."

"What! I did that?" exclaimed Cazotte, frightened. "I only thought of entertaining readers and demonstrating that one must be wary of the devil."

"And who told you that our science has any ties to that spirit of darkness? Such is the conclusion to be drawn from your dangerous work. I took you for an unfaithful brother who had betrayed our secrets, and I was curious to know your motive . . . Since you are indeed a layman, ignorant of our supreme goal, I will instruct you, and show you how to penetrate further into the mysteries of this world of spirits that presses upon us from every side, and which through your intuition alone has already revealed itself to you."

This conversation lasted a long time; biographers differ as to the words that were exchanged, but all agree on signaling the sudden revolution that took place thereafter in the ideas of Cazotte, who was an adept without knowing it, unaware that the secret doctrine still had representatives in the world. He confessed that he had been too severe in *The Devil in Love* toward the Cabalists, of whom he had but a very vague idea, and that their practices were perhaps not as reprehensible as he had assumed. He even accused himself of having slandered those innocent spirits that inhabit and animate the middle region of the air by likening them to the dubious personality of a female sprite who answers to the name of Beelzebub.

"Remember," said the initiate, "that father Kircher, the abbé de Villars, and many other casuists[26] have long demonstrated the perfect innocence of these spirits from a Christian point of view. Charlemagne's capitularies referred to them as beings belonging to the celestial hierarchy; Plato and Socrates, the wisest of the Greeks, Origen, Eusebius, and Saint Augustine, those lamps of the church, agreed to distinguish the power of the elemental spirits from that of the descendants of the abyss . . ." This was more than enough to convince Cazotte who, as we will see, would later apply these ideas, not to his books, but to his life, and who remained convinced of their truth until his last moments.

Cazotte must have been very inclined to repair the fault reported to him, for it was not a minor thing to incur the hatred of the Illuminati, who were numerous, powerful, and divided into many sects, societies, and

Masonic lodges that corresponded with each other from one end of the kingdom to the other. Cazotte, for allegedly having revealed these mysteries of initiation to the profane, exposed himself to the same fate as had befallen the abbé de Villars, who in *The Comte de Gabalis* had delivered to the curious public, under a half serious disguise, the whole doctrine of the Rosicrucians concerning the spirit world. This cleric was found murdered one day on the road to Lyon, and sylphs or gnomes could not be accused of the matter.[27] Cazotte also chose not to ignore the advice of the initiates concerning the vow of silence because he was naturally very attracted to these kinds of ideas. The turbulence that resulted from his unmethodical studies had spread throughout his thoughts and exhausted him as he strove to find the connection to a comprehensive doctrine. That of the Martinists, in whose company he was received, had been introduced into France by Martinez Pasqualis,[28] and it simply revived the institution of the cabalistic rites from the eleventh century, that last echo of the formula of the Gnostics, in which aspects of Jewish metaphysics mix with the obscure theories of Alexandrian philosophers.

The School of Lyon, to which Cazotte belonged at that time, professed, according to Martinez, that the Intelligence and the Will are the only active forces of nature, from which it follows that to modify phenomena, it is enough to channel the energy of what you desire to your Will. It added that by the contemplation of one's own ideas and the abstraction of the All, corresponding to the outside world and the body, man could rise to the perfect concept of the universal essence and the control of those *spirits*, the secret of which was contained in *The Triple Constraint of Hell*, an all-powerful conjuration used by the medieval Cabalists.[29]

Martinez, who had covered France with Masonic lodges that followed his rite, had gone to die in Santo Domingo; the doctrine could not be kept pure, and was soon modified by adding the ideas of Swedenborg and Jacob Boehm; it was difficult to combine these separate ideas under the same symbol. The famous Saint-Martin, one of the youngest and most ardent of the neophytes, was particularly attached to the principles of Boehm. At that time, the school of Lyon had already merged with the Society of the Philalèthes,[30] which Saint-Martin refused to be associated with, saying that he cared more for the science of the *soul*, according to the doctrine of Swedenberg, than that of the *mind*, according to the doctrine of Martinez.

Later, speaking of his stay among the Illuminati at Lyon, this illustrious theosophist said: "In the school where I spent twenty-five years, *communications* of all kinds were frequent; I played my part as so many others did. The manifestations of the sign of the *Reparator* were visible there:[31] I had been prepared for it with initiations. But," he adds, "the danger of these initiations is that they expose you to *violent spirits*; and I can only say that the forms that communicated with me were not borrowed forms."

The danger Saint-Martin feared was precisely the one Cazotte engaged in, and which perhaps caused the greatest misfortunes of his life. For a long time, his beliefs were gentle and tolerant, his visions clear and pleasant; this was during the time when he composed the *New Arabian Tales*, which—long confused with *The Thousand and One Nights*, of which they formed a sequel—did not earn the author all the glory he deserved. The principal tales were "La Dame inconnue," "Le Chevalier," "L'Ingrat puni," "Le Pouvoir du Destin," "Simoustapha," "Le Calife voleur," which provided the subject of "Le Calife de Bagdad," "L'Amant des étoiles," and "Le Magicien or Maugraby," a work full of descriptive charm and of interest.[32]

What dominates in these compositions is Cazotte's attention to detail and his charm; as for the richness of invention, this cannot be attributed solely to what is contained in the Oriental tales themselves, which is explained by the fact that several original subjects had been communicated to the author by an Arab monk named Dom Chavis.

The theory of the elemental spirits, so dear to all mystical imaginations, is also found, as we know, in the beliefs of the Orient, and the pale ghosts seen in the Northern mists at the cost of hallucination and vertigo there seem to take on the hue of the lights and colors of a splendid atmosphere and an enchanted nature. In his "Tale of the Knight," which is a true poem, Cazotte is particularly successful in his blending of romantic themes with the distinction he draws between good and evil spirits, an idea that was skillfully revived by the Cabalists of the Orient. The luminous genii, subject to Solomon, give the followers of *Eblis* the strength to fight;[33] talismans, incantations, star-studded rings, magic mirrors, all these marvelous complexities of the fatalistic Arabs are tied together and revealed in this tale with order and clarity. The hero exhibits some traits of the Egyptian initiate in the novel *Sethos*, which at that time was extraordinarily popular.[34] The passage where he crosses, through a thousand dangers, the mountain of Caf, the eternal palace of Solomon, king of the genii, is the Asian version of the tests of Isis; the preoccupation with the same ideas appear under the most diverse forms.

This is not to say that a great number of Cazotte's works don't belong to ordinary literature. He had some reputation as a fabulist, and in the dedication of his volume of fables to the Academy of Dijon, he took care to remember one of his ancestors who, being a contemporary of Marot and Ronsard, had contributed to the progress of French poetry.[35] At the time when Voltaire published his poem entitled *The Civil War of Geneva*, Cazotte had the amusing idea of adding to the first cantos of the unfinished poem a seventh canto written in the same style, which was believed to be by Voltaire himself.

We have not spoken of his songs, which bear the mark of a unique spirit. Let us remember the best known among them, entitled "O May! Lovely Month of May":

It is the first of May,
A new day awaits!
I bring to you a bouquet,
Carnations in an array;
I picked them along the way,
A dew-filled display.

The rest continues on in this way. It is a delightful fan painting, which unfolds with the naive and affected grace of olden times.

Why not also cite the charming ronde: "I'll Always Love You"; and especially the cheerful villanelle that includes these verses:

What troubles and pains,
Living in your chains, Thérèse!
What troubles and pains,
Living in your chains!

If these stockings you see
Have holes on each knee, Thérèse,
I made them all at your feet,

You have power over me!
If these stockings you see, etc.

My five hundred francs:
What's left in my bank, Thérèse?
Not even six blancs,[36]
And it's you I've to thank!
My five hundred francs etc.

Your years are twenty,
And you've pleasures aplenty, Thérèse,
But your lovers, if any,
Won't say, after many,
Your years are twenty, etc.

We have said that the Opera-Comique owed the subject of the *Caliph of Baghdad* to Cazotte; his *Devil in Love* was also represented in this genre with the title *The Infante of Zamora*.[37] It was undoubtedly on this subject that one of his brothers-in-law, who had come to spend a few days at Cazotte's country home in Pierry, reproached him for not trying the theater, and praised comical operas as being works of great difficulty. "Give me a word," said Cazotte, "and tomorrow I will have finished a play in the comic genre that will lack for nothing."

This brother-in-law saw a peasant come in wearing clogs. "Well then, *clogs*," he exclaimed, "make a play with that word!" Cazotte asked to be left alone; but a unique character, who had joined the gathering that evening, offered to provide the music as Cazotte wrote the opera. It was Rameau, the nephew of the great musician whose wayward life Diderot recounted in that masterpiece of a dialogue, the only modern satire that can hold up to Petronius.[38]

The opera was created that night, sent to Paris, and soon staged at the Comedie-Italienne, with some alterations by Marsollier and Duni, who deigned to put their own names on it.[39] Cazotte's only royalties were free admission, and Rameau's nephew, that misunderstood genius, remained as unknown as ever. It was good that there existed such a musician for Cazotte, who doubtless had many strange ideas concerning his bizarre companion.

The portrait he created in his preface to *La Nouvelle Ramêide*, a mock-heroic poem composed in honor of his friend, deserves to be preserved as much for its style as for its being a useful note to complement Diderot's thorny moral and literary analysis:[40]

> He was by nature the most pleasant man I have ever known; his name was Rameau, the nephew of the famous musician, and a classmate in middle school; it was a friendship that never waned for either of us. This person, the most extraordinary man of our time, was born with a natural talent for many things, which some defect of his mind never allowed him to cultivate. I can only compare the uncanny effect of his jokes to those Dr. Sterne displays in his *Sentimental Journey*. Rameau's witticisms were so instinctive that only a painting could render them. They were not clever remarks, but strokes that seemed to come from a deep knowledge of the human heart. His physiognomy, which was quite ludicrous, added an extraordinary piquancy to his witticisms, which was all the more surprising since he usually just talked nonsense. This man was a born musician, as much or perhaps even more so than his uncle, though he never could plunge into the depths of art; but he was adept at creating songs and had the strange ability to find, spontaneously, pleasant and expressive music to go along with whatever words one gave him; only a true artist was needed to arrange and correct his phrases and compose his scores. His face was both horribly and pleasantly ugly, and often very boring, because his genius rarely inspired him; but if his eloquence served him, he would make you cry laughing. He was poor, being unable to work any profession. But his absolute poverty made him honorable in my mind. He was not penniless; but to repair his financial situation, he would have had to rob his father of his mother's estate, and he refused to consider reducing to misery the author of his days, who had remarried and had children. He showed, on several occasions, proof of the goodness of his heart. This singular man lived passionately for glory, which he could not achieve in any respect . . . He died in a religious home his family had placed him in, which after four years of retirement he had taken a liking to, having won the hearts of all those whom he at first thought were just his jailers.

Cazotte's letters on music, several of which are replies to J.-J. Rousseau's letter on the Opera, come from his brief involvement with lyrical drama. Most of his writings are anonymous and have since been collected as diplomatic statements in *The War of the Opera.*[41] Some are certainly by him, others are of doubtful authenticity. It would be surprising if the latter were to include *The Little Prophet of Boehmischbroda*, a fairy tale attributed to Grimm,[42] since it would show, if need be, the strong similarity between Cazotte and Hoffmann.

These were still the good days in Cazotte's life; here is the portrait Charles Nodier gave of this famous man, whom he had encountered in his youth:

> To an extreme kindness, which was reflected in his handsome and happy appearance, to a tenderness, which his blue eyes, still lively, expressed in the most seductive way, M. Cazotte added his invaluable talent at telling stories better than anyone in the world, stories that were at once strange and naïve, and which expressed both the most common reality through the exact descriptions of circumstances, and the world of enchantment through his use of the supernatural. He had received from nature a special gift which allowed him to see things in a fantastical light, and I was of such a disposition as to delight in this kind of fantasy. So, when a heavy step was heard in equal intervals on the floor of the adjacent room, and when his door opened with a methodical slowness, exposing the light of a lantern, carried by an old servant who was less nimble than his master, and whom M. Cazotte cheerfully called his *pays*,[43] and when he himself appeared with his tricorn,[44] his long frock coat of green Camelot embroidered with a little stripe, and his shoes with the square tips that firmly supported the foot, fastened with a strong silver buckle, and with his tall golden-knobbed cane, I never failed to run to him with displays of wild joy, which were further increased by his caresses.

Charles Nodier then put into his mouth one of those mysterious stories he liked to tell everyone, and which were eagerly listened to. It concerned the long life of Marion Delorme, whom he claimed to have seen a few days before her death, aged almost a century and a half, as was confirmed, moreover, by her baptismal certificate and her death certificate preserved in Besançon. Admitting the very controversial question of Marion Delorme's age, Cazotte had been able to see her when she was twenty-one years old. In this manner he said he could relate unknown details regarding the death of Henry IV, which she had been able to witness.

But the world back then was full of these conversational friends of the supernatural; the Count Saint-Germain and Cagliostro turned heads everywhere, and Cazotte, by comparison, had perhaps no more than his literary genius and a reserve of honest sincerity. Yet if we are to believe the famous prophecy recorded in the memoirs of La Harpe,[45] he played the fatal role of Cassandra, and was not wrong, as he was sometimes accused, *for always being on the tripod.*[46]

III

"It seems to me," says La Harpe,

> it was only yesterday, and yet it was at the beginning of 1788. We were having dinner at the home of one of our colleagues at the Academy, a nobleman and a man of culture; many people were in attendance and of every profession: men of the robe, men of the court, men of letters, academicians, etc. They were cheerful as usual. At dessert, there were wines from Malvasia and Constance,[47] which added to the gaiety of this good company the kind of freedom that does not always guard its tone: we had come to a point in our conversation where anything was permitted to get a laugh.
>
> Chamfort had read to us his impious and licentious tales and the *grandes dames* listened to them without even having to resort to their fans.[48] Subsequently, there were a deluge of jokes about religion—and applause. A dinner guest stood up, and holding up his full glass, exclaimed, "Yes, I am as sure that *there is no God* as I am that Homer is a fool."[49] Indeed, he was as sure of one as of the other; we had discussed Homer and God, and there were guests present who had spoken well of both.

Then the conversation grew more serious; we were admiring the *revolution that Voltaire had wrought*, and we agreed that it was his main claim to glory: "He set the tone for his time, and he was read in the antechamber as in the salon."

One of the dinner guests, laughing, told us that his hairdresser, while powdering his wig, said "*You see, Monsieur, I may be just a miserable old saw-bones, but I'm no more religious than anybody else.*"

It was concluded that the revolution was not long in coming; it was imperative that *superstition and fanaticism gave way to philosophy*, and that we could calculate the probability of it happening in our time and who among us would see the *reign of reason*. The older guests lament over not being able to enjoy it; the younger take some pleasure in being able to realistically hope for it; and above all, the Academy was praised for having prepared this great work, and with having been the seat of power, the center, the *motivation for the freedom of thought*.

The only guest who had not taken part in all the joy of this conversation, and had even dropped a few jokes, guardedly, about our great enthusiasm, was *Cazotte*, an amiable and unique man, but unfortunately infatuated with the dreams of the *Illuminati*. His heroism has since rendered him forever illustrious.

He spoke in a more serious tone. "Gentlemen," he said, "take some satisfaction; you will all see this *great and sublime revolution* you so desire come to pass. You know that I am a bit of a prophet; I repeat, *you will see it come to pass*."

We reply with the usual refrain: *You don't need to be a wizard to know that*!

"So be it, but perhaps it takes a bit of a one for what I have left to tell you. Do you know what will come of this *revolution*, what will happen to all of you here, and what will immediately come to be, its well-proven effect, its well-recognized consequence?"

"Well, do tell us," says Condorcet, with his sly and stupid air; "a philosopher is always happy to meet a prophet."

"*You, Monsieur Condorcet, you will meet your end on a prison floor*; you will die from the poison you will have taken to escape the executioner; the poison which the 'joys' of that time shall compel you to always keep on you."

At first, great astonishment; but we remembered that the good Cazotte often daydreamed, and so we laughed even more loudly.

"M. Cazotte, the tale you are telling here is not as pleasing as your *Devil in Love*; but what devil put in your mind this *prison*, this *poison*, and these *executioners*? What does all this have in common with *philosophy and the reign of reason*?"

"That is precisely what I am telling you: it is in the name of philosophy, humanity, liberty, and under the reign of reason that you will come to an end, and it will indeed be the reign of reason, for *it will have temples*, and throughout all of France in these days to come, there shall only be *temples of Reason*."

"By my faith," says Chamfort with a sarcastic laugh, "you won't be one of the priests of these temples."

"I should hope not; but you, *Monsieur Chamfort*, who will be, and very deserving of the title, *you will cut your own veins* with twenty-two slashes of a razor, and yet you'll only die of it a few months later."[50]

We look at each other and laugh again. "*You, Monsieur Vicq-d'Azir*, you won't open your veins yourself, but, after they have been opened six times following an attack of gout, you will die at night. You, *Monsieur de Nicolaï*, you will die on the scaffold.[51] You, *Monsieur Bailly*, on the scaffold . . ."[52]

"Ah, thank God!" said Roucher,[53] "it seems that the gentleman is only after the Academy; he's just performed a terrible execution on it; and I, thank heaven . . ."

"You! You will also die on the scaffold."

"Oh, this is a bit much," everyone exclaimed, "he has sworn to exterminate everyone."

"No, I'm not the one who has sworn it."

"So, we're to be subjugated by the Turks and Tartars? Or others? . . ."

"Not at all, as I've told you: you're to be governed by *philosophy* alone, by *reason* alone. Those who will treat you this way will all be *philosophers*, will be uttering all the same phrases you've been producing this past hour, will be repeating all your maxims, will quote, as you do, the verses of Diderot and *The Maid of Orleans* . . ."

We whispered to each other: "You can see *he's mad* (for he was so serious). Can't you see that he's joking? And you know there's always something fantastical about his jokes."

"Yes," Chamfort resumed, "but his fantasy isn't cheery; it's too sinister. And when will all this take place?"

"*Six years shall not have passed before all I say to you takes place . . .*"

"That's a fair number of miracles (and this time it was I myself who spoke); and you see nothing for me?"

"You will encounter a miracle just as extraordinary: you'll become Christian."

Great exclamations. "Ah!" Chamfort resumed, "I am reassured; if we are to perish when La Harpe becomes Christian, then we're immortal."

"Well," said the Duchesse of Grammont,[54] "we women are lucky to have nothing to do with these *revolutions*. When I say nothing, it's not that we don't take some part; but it's accepted that we won't be held responsible, and our sex . . ."

"*Your sex, Mesdames, will not protect you this time*; and even if you take pains not to take part, you will be treated just like men, without any difference whatsoever."

"But what are you saying, Monsieur Cazotte? You are preaching the end of the world."

"I know nothing of that; but what I do know is that you, Madame la Duchesse, *will be led to the scaffold*, you along with many other ladies like yourself, in the executioner's tumbrel, with your hands behind your back."

"Ah! I hope, in that case, that I will at least have a coach draped in black."

"No, Madame, greater ladies than yourself will go like you in a tumbrel, with their hands bound just like you."

"Greater ladies! What are you saying! *Princesses of the blood*?"

"*Even greater ladies still . . .*"

At this point a distinct movement overtook everyone there, and the master of the house's face darkened. We began to find that the joke had gone too far.

Madame de Grammont, to dispel this cloud, didn't insist on this last response, and merely said, in the lightest of tones: "*Just wait and see, he won't even grant me confession!*"

"*No, madame, you'll have none, nor will anyone else. The last victim to have one out of mercy will be . . .*"

He paused for a moment.

"Well, so who is the happy mortal to be granted this perogative?"

"It will be the only one left to him: *the King of France.*"

The master of the house arose abruptly, and everybody else along with him. He went over to Monsieur Cazotte and said, in a very serious tone: "My dear Monsieur Cazotte, it is one thing to prolong this dismal joke; but you take it too far and compromise this company, and yourself as well."

Cazotte did not answer and was about to leave, when Madame de Grammont, who always wanted to avoid a serious conversation and to maintain a cheerful mood, approached him:

"Monsieur Prophet, you tell us about our future, but you say nothing about your own."

He was silent for a few moments, with downcast eyes.

"Madame, have you read the siege of Jerusalem in *Josephus*?"

"Oh, probably; who hasn't read that? But pretend I haven't."

"Well, Madame, during the siege, a man spent seven straight days circling the ramparts, in view of the besiegers and the besieged, incessantly shouting with a sinister and thundering voice, '*Woe, woe to Jerusalem and to myself!*' And in an instant a huge stone was launched by enemy machines; it hit him and tore him to pieces."

After this response, Monsieur Cazotte bowed and left.

While we can only invest relative confidence in this document and recall the wise opinion of Charles Nodier, who said that when this scene took place it was perhaps not difficult to predict that the revolution to come would choose its victims from the highest society of the time and then devour the very people who had created it, let us also recall a singular passage in the poem *Ollivier*, published exactly thirty years before '93, in which we note a preoccupation with severed heads which can well pass, if somewhat vaguely, for a prophetic hallucination.

About four years ago we were both drawn by enchantments into the palace of the fairy Bagasse. This dangerous witch, saddened by the progress of Christian arms in Asia, wanted to stop them by laying traps for the Knights defending the faith. She built a magnificent palace not far from here. Unfortunately, we set foot along its avenues: then, lured by a charm, thinking that it was only the beauty of the grounds that captivated us, we reached a peristyle which was at the entrance to the palace; but no sooner had we come to it than the marble on which we walked, which appeared solid, started to weaken and gave way beneath our feet: we unexpectedly plummeted down under a moving wheel fitted with sharp iron spikes, which in the blink of an eye separated every part of our bodies; and what was most astonishing was that death did not follow such a strange dissolution.

Driven by their own weight, our body parts fell into a deep pit and formed a large pile of limbs. Our heads rolled like balls. This extraordinary movement completely did away with the little reason this supernatural adventure had left me; after some time, I opened my eyes and saw that my head was placed up on one of the tiers by me, facing eight hundred other heads of both sexes and every age and color. They still retained movement of the eyes and tongue, and especially the movement of the jaw, which allowed them to yawn almost continuously. I heard only these words, rather poorly articulated: "Ah, how boring! It's hopeless."

I could not resist the impression this general condition made on me and began to yawn like the others.

"Another yawner," said a big woman's head across from mine. "It's hard to take; it shall be the death of me." And she began to yawn even more.

"At least this mouth is fresh," said another head, "and look, enamel teeth." Then, addressing me: "Madame, can one know the name of the amiable companion of misfortune the fairy Bagasse has given us?"

I saw the head that addressed me: it was that of a man. He had no distinguishing features, but a lively air of confidence and was somewhat affected in his pronunciation of words.

I began to reply: 'Sir, I have a brother . . ." I didn't have the chance to say more.

"Ah, heavens!" exclaimed the female head that had addressed me first, "another storyteller with a story; we've had enough tales already. Yawn, Madame, and never mind your brother. Anyway, who doesn't have a brother? If not for mine, I would have reigned peacefully and not be where I am now."

"Sir," said the big head, "you've already made yourself known for what you are: the most wicked head of them all . . ."

"Ah!" interrupted the other, "if I only had my limbs . . ."

"And me," said the adversary, "if I only had my hands . . . And furthermore," he told me, "you can see that he's got a lump in his throat."

"But," I said, "these disputes go too far . . ."

"What? No, let us be; isn't it better to quarrel than to yawn? What else can people do who have only ears and eyes, who have lived face to face for a century, who have no relationships and can't form pleasant ones, to whom even slander is forbidden since we don't know whom to speak of to make ourselves heard, who . . ."

He would have said more, but we were suddenly overcome with a violent urge to sneeze all together; a moment later, a hoarse voice, coming from no one knew where, commands us to seek out our scattered limbs; at the same time our heads roll to the spot where they were piled up.

Is it not remarkable to find in a mock-heroic poem of the author's youth this bloody dream of severed heads and separated limbs, this strange association of ideas that bring together courtiers, warriors, women, and dandies, all discoursing and joking about the details of torture as will later in the Conciergerie[55] those lords, those women, those poets, those contemporaries of Cazotte, who, like them, will come bring his head in turn, trying to smile and joke like the others over the whims of that bloody fairy who, unbeknownst to them, would one day be called the Revolution!

IV

We have gotten ahead of ourselves: having reached barely two-thirds in this life of our writer, we have revealed a scene from his last days; following the example of the illuminated one himself, we have with one stroke united the future and the past.

Our plan, moreover, was to appreciate Cazotte's life in turn as a literary man and as a mystical philosopher; but if most of his books bear witness to his interest in the science of the Cabalists, it must be said that he is generally not dogmatic about it; Cazotte seems not to have taken part in the collective labors of the Martinist *illuminés*, but to have derived from their ideas only a particular and personal rule of conduct. Indeed, it would be wrong to confuse this sect with the Masonic institutions of the time, although they had a certain rapport on the surface; Martinists admitted the fall of the angels, original sin, the Restorative Word, and did not depart from any essential point in the dogmas of the Church.

Saint-Martin, the most illustrious of them, was a Christian spiritualist in the style of Malebranche.[56] We said earlier that he deplored the intervention of *violent spirits* in the bosom of the Lyon sect. However we are to understand this expression, it is clear that this group veered toward a political trend that alienated several of its members. Perhaps the influence of the Illuminati both in Germany and France has been exaggerated, but there is no denying that they had a great effect on the French Revolution and the direction of its movement. Cazotte's monarchical sympathies pushed him away from this direction and prevented him from supporting with his talent a doctrine that deviated from his own thinking.

It is sad to see this man, so gifted as a writer and as a philosopher, spend the final years of his life disgusted with literary life and sensing political storms in the air he felt powerless to avert. The flowers of his imagination had withered; that turn of mind, so clear and so French, which imparted such a wonderful style to his unique creations, appears only rarely in his political correspondence, which was the cause of his trial and his death. If it is true that some souls can predict sinister events, it is also true that this faculty is more a cursed ability than a heavenly gift since, like ancient Cassandra, they can neither persuade others nor protect themselves.

Yet Cazotte's final years on his land in Pierry in the Champagne region still offer some images of happiness and tranquility in his family life. Retired from the literary world, which he frequented only during short trips to Paris, having escaped the whirlwind that animated, with increasing furor, philosophical and mystical sects of every sort, father of a lovely daughter and two sons as full of enthusiasm and as generous as him, good Cazotte seemed to have gathered around him all the conditions for a peaceful future; but the stories of those who knew him at that time always show him darkened by the clouds he had anticipated beyond the peaceful horizon.

A gentleman named Plas had asked him for the hand of his daughter Elisabeth; these two young people had long loved each other, but Cazotte delayed his definite answer and allowed them only to hope. A graceful and charming author, Anna-Marie, has related some of the details of a visit made to Pierry by Mme d'Argèle, a friend of the family. She portrays an elegant living room on the ground floor, fragrant with the scents of a plant from the colonies Mme Cazotte brought back, and which received a particular atmosphere of elegance and strangeness from the time spent with this excellent person. A woman of color working for her, birds from America, curiosities arranged upon the furniture: all this, along with her bearing and her hairstyle, testified to a fond memory of her homeland. "She had been perfectly lovely and still was, although by then she had grown children. She exhibited the untidy and somewhat nonchalant grace of the Creole, and a slight accent to her speech gave it a tone that was both childlike and sensual, which made her very attractive. A small bichon dog was lying on a tiled floor by her; they called it *Biondetta* after the little spaniel in *The Devil in Love*."

There was also an elderly woman, tall and majestic, the Marquise de la Croix,[57] the widow of a great Spanish nobleman; she was part of the family and exercised a certain influence in it owing to the rapport of her ideas and beliefs with those of Cazotte. She had been one of Saint-Martin's followers for many years, and her interest in Illuminism also bound her to Cazotte through those intellectual ties the doctrine regarded as a kind of anticipation of a future life. Because of their difference in age, this second mystic marriage ruled out any idea of impropriety, yet it caused Mme Cazotte more a sense of disquiet than sorrow, and for very human reasons, having to do with the restlessness she witnessed in these two noble minds. The three children, on the contrary, sincerely shared the ideas of their father and his old friend.

We have already spoken on this issue; but, nevertheless, must we always accept the lessons of the vulgar common sense that operates in life without ever taking concern in the dark mysteries of the future and death? Does the happiest destiny stem from this lack of foresight that remains surprised and disarmed in the face of the fatal event, and which has nothing but tears and cries to oppose the late blows of misfortune? Mme Cazotte, of all these people, was the one who had to suffer the most; for the others, life was just a fight and nothing more, perhaps against considerable odds, yet with a reward that was assured.

To complete the analysis of the theories we will find later in some of the fragments of correspondence that were the subject of Cazotte's trial, it is useful to consider some of the latter's opinions in the narrative of Anna-Marie:

> We all live, he said, among the spirits of our fathers, and the invisible world presses upon us from all sides ... there are friends of our thoughts there who ceaselessly approach us with familiarity. My daughter has her guardian angels; we all have ours. Each of our ideas, good or bad, sets in motion a spirit which corresponds to them, the way each movement of our body shakes the column of air we support. Everything is full, everything is alive in this world where, since original sin, veils have obscured matter ... And I, through an initiation I did not seek and which I often regret, I lifted them the way the wind lifts a thick fog. I see the good ones, the evil, the right ones and the wrong; sometimes the confusion of beings is such to my eyes that I don't always know how to distinguish at first those who live in their flesh from those who have stripped away all coarse appearance ...
>
> Yes, he added, there are souls that have remained material, their form so dear, so adherent to them that they bore into the other world a kind of opacity. For a long time, they resemble living beings.
>
> In the end, what can I tell you? Whether it is a problem with my eyes, or I am seeing clearly, there are moments when I cannot tell the difference. This morning, during prayer, when we were all gathered

> under the eyes of the Almighty, the room was so full of the living and of the dead, from all ages and from all countries, that I could no longer distinguish between life and death; it was a strange confusion, and yet a magnificent spectacle!

Mme d'Argèle witnessed the departure of the young Scévole Cazotte,[58] who went to join the King's guards; difficult times were approaching, and his father was not unaware that his son was devoting his life to danger.

The Marquise de la Croix met with Scévole Cazotte to give him what they called *their mystical powers*, and later we will see how he realized the mission entrusted to him. The enthusiastic woman made on the young man's forehead, lips, and heart three mysterious signs accompanied by a secret invocation, and thus consecrated the future of the one she called *the son of her intelligence*.

Scévole Cazotte, no less passionate about his monarchical convictions than his mysticism, was among those who, on the return from Varennes, was able to protect the life of the royal family against the fury of the Republicans. For a moment, in the middle of the crowd, the dauphin was taken from his parents, and Scévole Cazotte managed to bring him back to the queen, who thanked him with tears in her eyes. The following letter, which he wrote to his father, was after this event:

> My dear father, 14 July has passed and the king has returned home safe and sound. I fulfilled to the best of my abilities the mission you had charged me with. Perhaps you will know whether it has had the effect you expected. On Friday, I approached the holy table; and, upon leaving the church, I went to the altar of the homeland where, to each corner, I spoke the commands necessary for putting the whole Champ de Mars under the protection of the angels of the Lord.
>
> I reached the coach, against which I was leaning when the king got back in; Mme Elisabeth even glanced at me, which lifted all my thoughts to heaven; under the protection of one of my companions, I accompanied the coach along the road and the king called to me and said: Cazotte, was that you I noticed in Epernay, and to whom I spoke? and I replied: Yes, Your Majesty; when he descended from the

coach, I was there . . . And I withdrew when I saw them into their apartments.

The Champ de Mars was covered with men. If I were worthy enough for my commands and my prayers to be fulfilled, they would produce furiously adverse binds for the enemy.[59] On the way back everyone shouted Long live the king! as he passed. The national guards gave it everything they had and the march was a triumph. The day was beautiful, and the commander said that for the last day that God left to the devil, he had left him the color of the rose.[60] Farewell, join your prayers to make mine more effective. Let us keep in touch. I embrace my mother, Zabeth (Elisabeth). My respect to the Marquise (the Marquise de la Croix).

Whatever opinion one may have of them, one cannot fail to be touched by the devotion of that family to each other, even if one smiles at the feeble means on which such ardent convictions rested. The illusions of beautiful souls are respectable whatever form they take; but who would dare say that this thought that the world is governed by superior and mysterious influences, upon which the faith of man can act, is pure illusion? Philosophy has a right to disregard this hypothesis, but every religion is forced to admit it, and political sects have made of it a weapon for every party. This explains Cazotte's isolation from his former brothers of Illuminism. We know how often the Republican spirit had used mysticism during the English Revolution; the tendency of the Martinists was the same; but, drawn into the movement of the philosophers of reason, they carefully concealed the religious side of their doctrine, which at that time had no chance of popularity.

Everyone knows the reason why the *illuminés* became involved in the revolutionary movements. Their sects in France, Germany, and Italy were organized under the law of secrecy, and particularly influenced great men more or less informed as to their real purpose. Joseph II and Frederick William II of Prussia often acted under their influence. We know that the latter, having put himself at the head of the coalition of sovereigns, had entered France and was only thirty leagues from Paris when the *illuminés*, in one of their secret meetings, evoked the spirit of Frederick the Great's uncle, who forbade him to go farther.[61] It is said that because of an apparition (which was accounted for in numerous ways), the monarch suddenly withdrew from French territory, and later concluded a peace treaty with the Republic;[62] in any case, the monarch also owed his safety to the cooperation between the French *illuminés* and those of Germany.

V

Cazotte's correspondence shows us both his regret over the path his former brethren had followed, and his isolated attempts against a political era in which he believed he saw the fatal reign of the *Antichrist*, whereas the *illuminés* greeted the arrival of the invisible *Reparator*. The demons of the former were divine spirits and avengers for the latter. Understanding this will allow one to better understand certain passages in Cazotte's letters, and the unique circumstance that would lead to his sentence being pronounced by a Martinist *illuminé*.

The letter from which we will quote short fragments was addressed in 1791 to his friend Pouteau, secretary of the civil list:[63]

> If God does not raise a man who can marvelously put an end to all this, then we will be exposed to the greatest misfortunes. You know my system: "*Good and evil have always been the work of men in the world, for whom this globe has been abandoned by the eternal laws.*" We will thus only have ourselves to blame for all the evil that will have been done. The sun continually hurls its rays, more or less obliquely, onto the earth; for us this is the Image of Providence; from time to time, we accuse this star of lacking heat when our location, the mass of vapors, or the effect of winds make it so that we cannot feel the continual influence of its rays. Now if some thaumaturge does not come to our aid, then there is nothing more to hope for.
>
> I would like you to read my comments on the grimoire of Cagliostro.[64] You can also ask me for clarifications; I will send you the least obscure explanation possible.

The doctrine of the theosophists appears in the highlighted passage; here is another passage that refers to his former relations with the *illuminés*.

> I've received two letters from close friends among my colleagues, the Martinists; they are demagogues like Bret;[65] people of good name, fine fellows up to this point; but the devil is their master. With regard to Bret's fierce magnetism, I brought this illness upon him; the Jansenists affiliated with the Convulsionaries are in the same situation;[66] this phrase applies to them all: Outside the Church there is no *salvation*, nor even common sense.
>
> I told you that there were eight of us in France, absolutely unknown to each other, who constantly raised, as Moses did, our eyes, our voices, our arms to the sky, calling for a decisive outcome to the fighting in which the elements themselves are at stake. We believe we are seeing the brink of an event in the Apocalypse that will usher in a new era. Calm yourself, this is not the end of the world: that has been put off for another thousand years. It is not yet time to say to the mountains: *fall upon us*; but as we do our best to wait, this will be the cry of the Jacobins, for the guilty will come in many robes.[67]

His system on the necessity of human action for establishing communication between heaven and earth is clearly stated here. He also often refers in his correspondence to the courage of Louis XVI, who still seemed to him to rely too much on Providence. His recommendations on this matter often have something of the sectarian Protestant about them rather than the pure Catholic:

> We need the king to come to the aid of the national guard; he must show himself and say: I want, I order, and in a firm tone. Then he can be sure that he will be obeyed and not be taken for the weakling the democrats depict him as, which makes me suffer in every part of my body.
>
> May he go quickly, with twenty-five guards on horseback like himself, to where there is unrest: everyone will be forced to bend and prostrate themselves before him. The hard part will be done, my friend; the king has resigned himself and put himself in the hands of his Creator; judge to what degree His power will sustain him; remember Ahab, rotten with vices, having humbled himself before God with a single act, obtained victory over his enemies. Ahab had a false heart, a depraved soul; but my king has the most honest soul that has come

> from the hands of God; and the august, celestial Elizabeth bears on her forehead the aegis which relies on the strong arm of true wisdom . . . Fear not Lafayette: he is as bound as his accomplices. He, like his cabal, is delivered to the spirits of terror and confusion; he doesn't know how to take a course of action that will be successful, *and it is best for him to be put at the mercy of his enemies by those in whom he believes he can place his trust*. Let us not cease raising our arms to the sky; let us think upon the attitude of the prophet when Israel was at war.
>
> Man must act here, since it is the place for his action; good and evil can only be carried out through him. Since almost every church is closed, whether by ban or profanation, may all our houses serve as oratories. The moment is crucial: either Satan will continue to reign on earth as he does now, until men come forth who can face him as David did Goliath; or the reign of Jesus Christ, so beneficial for us, as predicted by the prophets, will be established on earth. This is the crisis in which we find ourselves, my friend, and of which I have spoken to you rather confusedly. We may, for lack of faith, for lack of love and zeal, miss our opportunity, but we must stand firm. Moreover, God does nothing without us, we who are the kings of the earth; it is for us to seize the moment prescribed by God's decrees. Let us not allow our enemy, who without us can do nothing, continue to do everything, and through us.

In general, he had few illusions as to the triumph of his cause; his letters are filled with advice that might have been good to follow; but his discouragement eventually ends up dominating in the face of so much weakness, and he comes to doubt himself and his science:

> I am glad my last letter was able to give you some pleasure. You are not an *initiate*! Be thankful for that. Remember the words: *Et scientia eorum perdet eos*.[68] If I am in any danger, I whom the divine grace of God removed from the trap, imagine the risk of those who remain . . . Knowledge of the occult is a stormy sea from which one cannot see the shore.

Does this mean that he had abandoned those practices that seemed able to act on baneful spirits? We saw only that he had hoped to defeat them with their own weapons. In a passage from his correspondence, he speaks of a prophetess, Broussole,[69] who, like the famous Catherine Théot, obtained communications from the rebel powers for the Jacobins; he hopes to have successfully acted against her. Among these priestesses of propaganda, he also mentions elsewhere the Marquise Durfé,[70] "the doyenne of the French Medeas, whose salon was full of empiricists and people who galloped after the occult sciences . . ." He particularly criticizes her for having elevated the Minister Duchatelet and put him on a bad path.[71]

It is hard to believe that these letters, found unexpectedly in the Tuileries Palace on the bloody day of 10 August,[72] would have been sufficient to condemn an old man in the grip of innocent mystical reveries, if certain passages hadn't suggested more substantial conspiracies. Fouquier-Tinville, in his indictment, reported that some of the expressions in the letters indicate Cazotte's cooperation in the plot of the *Knights of the Dagger*,[73] who were caught off guard on the 10th and 12th of August; a more explicit letter indicated an escape plan for the king, a prisoner since his return from Varennes, and traced the route for his flight; Cazotte had offered his own house as a temporary asylum:

> The king will advance as far as the plain of Ay; there he will be twenty-eight leagues from Givet; forty leagues from Metz.[74] He can find himself accommodation in Ay, where there are thirty houses for his guards and company. I would prefer he chose Pierry, where he would also find twenty-five to thirty houses, one of which holds twenty master beds, with room enough at my home alone for a guard of two hundred men, stables for thirty to forty horses, and a space for setting up a small camp behind the walls. But we need more skilled and more disinterested men than myself to calculate the real advantage of these two positions.

Why must partisanship prevent us from appreciating in this passage the touching solicitude of an almost octogenarian man who was *less disinterested* in offering the exiled King the blood of his family, his house for asylum, and his garden for battlefield? Shouldn't such conspiracies in these letters simply be filed away among the other delusions of a mind weakened by age? The letter he wrote to his father-in-law, M. Roignan, the council clerk of Martinique, to induce him to organize resistance against the six thousand Republican envoys sent to seize the colony evokes the great enthusiasm he displayed in his youth for defending the island against the English: he indicates measures to be taken, areas to fortify, and the resources his former maritime experience inspired in him. It is easy to understand how such a letter would have been judged guilty by the revolutionary government; but it's unfortunate that they didn't examine the writing that followed more closely, which dates from the same period and would have shown that it was more a matter of *reveries* than the dreams of the unfortunate old man.

MY DREAM OF THE NIGHT FROM SATURDAY TO SUNDAY ON MIDSUMMER'S EVE 1791

I had been in a storage attic for some time without realizing it, although a small dog I saw run across a roof and jump from one slate-covered beam to another should have given me a clue.

I enter an apartment; I find there a young lady, alone; something in me tells me she's a relative of the comte de Dampierre;[75] she seems to recognize me and greets me. I soon realize that she's dizzy; she seems to say sweet things to an object facing her; I see that she's having a vision of a spirit, and suddenly I order the spirit to appear by making the sign of the cross on her forehead.

I see a person, fourteen or fifteen years old, not at all ugly, but with the dress, appearance, and attitude of a beggar; I bind him, and he protests. Another woman appears, possessed in the same way. I do the same to her. Both spirits abandon their forms, face me, and are being insolent when a door opens, and out comes a short, stout man, dressed as a turnkey: he takes from his pocket two small handcuffs that attach themselves to the wrists of the two spirits I had captured. I put them under the power of Jesus Christ. I don't know what leads me to pass for a moment from this room to another, but I quickly return to ask for my prisoners; they are sitting on a bench in a sort of alcove; they rise at my approach, and six figures dressed like archers of the poor seize them.[76] I go after them; some sort of chaplain walks beside me. I am going, he said, to the home of M. le Marquis so-and-so, he's a good man; when I have some free time, I go to visit him. I believe I had decided to follow him, when I realized that my shoes were slippers; I wanted to stop and set my feet somewhere so that I could pull up the quarters of my shoes, when a big man came to attack me in the middle of a large courtyard filled with people; I put my hand on his forehead and bound him in the name of the Holy Trinity and Jesus, under whose support I put him.

In the name of Jesus Christ! exclaimed the crowd around me. "Yes, I said, and I will put you all under after I've bound you. There was a great murmur about this.

A carriage resembling a coach arrives; from the door a man calls me by my name: But, Lord Cazotte, you speak of Jesus Christ; are we all able to fall under the power of Jesus Christ? Then I spoke again, and at length, about Jesus Christ and His mercy to sinners. Be happy! I added: You shall change your shackles. Shackles! cried a man locked in the carriage on which I had climbed; Can anyone give me a moment of rest?

Come, someone said, you're lucky, you are about to change masters, and what a master! The first man who had spoken to me said: I was thinking the same thing.

I turned my back to the carriage and walked into this expansive courtyard lit only by the stars. I observed the sky; it was a beautiful pale blue with many stars: as I compared it in my mind to other skies I had seen from the storage attic, it was troubled by a terrible storm; a dreadful thunderbolt set it all aflame; a tile fell a hundred feet away and came rolling toward me; a spirit emerged from it in the form of a bird the size of a white cock, its body more elongated, with shorter legs and a blunter beak. I ran at the bird making signs of the cross; and, feeling myself filled with a more than ordinary strength, it fell at my feet. I wanted to put it on my head . . . A man as tall as the Baron de Loi,[77] as handsome as he was young, dressed in gray and silver, confronted me and told me not to trample upon the bird. He pulled out a pair of scissors from a diamond-studded bag and made me understand that I had to use it to cut the beast's neck. As I grabbed the scissors, I was awakened by the sound of the crowd singing in chorus in the storage attic: it was a plainsong, out of tune, whose unrhymed lyric was:

Let us sing of our happy deliverance.

I awoke and began to pray; but, defiant against this dream, as against so many others in which I can imagine Satan wanting to fill me with pride, I continued my prayers to God through the intercession of the Blessed Virgin, and relentlessly, to obtain from her the knowledge of His will upon me; thus I will bind on earth what seems to me fit to be bound for the greater glory of God and the needs of His creatures.

Whatever judgment serious minds may bring to bear on this overly faithful portrait of certain dream hallucinations, and however unconnected the impressions of such an account may be, there is, in this series of bizarre visions, something terrible and mysterious. We must not see, in the care taken to record a dream partly lacking in sense, just the concerns of a mystic who draws a connection between the actions of the outside world and the phenomena of sleep. Nothing in the mass of writings preserved from this period in Cazotte's life indicates any diminution of his intellectual abilities. His revelations, always imprinted with his monarchical opinions, tend to present in all that takes place at that time a relationship to the vague predictions of the Apocalypse. This is what the school of Swedenborg called the science of correspondences. A few sentences from the introduction are worth noting:[78]

> I wanted, in offering this faithful picture, to provide a great lesson to those thousands of individuals whose pusilanimity always leads to doubt because of the effort it would take to believe. In the circle of life, they mark but a few relatively quick moments, like a clock that does not know what mechanism leads it to indicate the space of the hours or the movement of the planets."
>
> What man, in the throes of painful anxiety, tired of questioning all the beings who live or vegetate around him, and unable to find anyone to respond and give him, if not happiness, at least rest, has not raised his tearful eyes to the vault of the heavens?

It seems then that sweet hope comes to fill for him the immense distance separating this sublunar world in which he resides from the unwavering foundation on which rests the throne of the Eternal. The fires strewn about the azure veil that embraces the horizon from one pole to another shine not in his eyes alone: these heavenly lights pass into his soul; the gift of thought becomes that of genius. He communicates with the Eternal itself; Nature seems to be silent so as not to disturb this sublime conversation.

That God reveals to man the secrets of His supreme wisdom and the mysteries to which He subjects His all too often ungrateful creatures, so as to force them to fall back onto His paternal breast: what a majestic Idea, how comforting! Because, for the truly sensitive man, tender affection is worth more than any flight of genius; for him, the joy of glory, even of pride, always ends where the suffering of those he loves begins.

The day of 10 August put an end to any of the illusions the friends of the monarchy may have had. The people entered the Tuileries, having slain the Swiss Guard and a fair number of noblemen devoted to the king; one of Cazotte's sons fought among the latter, the other served in the armies of the emigration.[79] They looked everywhere for evidence of the so-called royalist conspiracy known as the *Knights of the Dagger*; seizing the papers of Laporte,[80] intendant of the civil list, they discovered all the correspondence between Cazotte and his friend Pouteau; an indictment was immediately issued against him and he was arrested at his house in Pierry.

"Do you recognize these letters?" asked the Commissioner of the Legislative Assembly.

"Indeed, they are mine."

"My father dictated the letters to me," cried his daughter, Elisabeth, who wanted to face the same danger and imprisonment.

She was arrested with her father, and both were taken to Paris in Cazotte's coach and confined at the Abbey in the final days of August. Mme Cazotte begged in vain to accompany her husband and daughter.

The unfortunates gathered in this prison still enjoyed some freedom inside. They were allowed to meet at certain times, and often the old chapel where the prisoners were gathered presented a scene of brilliant gatherings of high society. These revived illusions made them reckless; they gave speeches, sang, and appeared in the windows, and popular rumors claimed that these prisoners of 10 August were rejoicing in the progress of the Duke of Brunswick's army and awaiting their release.[81] Complaints arose over the slowness of the special court, which the Legislative Assembly reluctantly created in the wake of threats from the Commune; it was believed that a conspiracy had formed in the prison to force open the city's gates at the approach of foreigners, and then to disperse throughout the city and create another Saint-Barthélemy's day for the Republicans.[82]

The news of the capture of Longwy and the premature rumor over that of Verdun managed to exasperate the masses.[83] A state of emergency was declared and the divisions met at the Champ de Mars. However, furious groups went to the prisons and established a sort of tribunal of blood to replace the other one.

At the Abbey, the prisoners were gathered in the chapel, engaged in their usual conversation, when the turnkeys unexpectedly cried out: "Send up the women!" Three gunshots and a drum roll added to the terror, and the men were separated from the women; two priests, walking between the prisoners who had parted to let them pass, appeared in an upper gallery of the chapel and announced to all the fate that awaited them.

A mournful silence reigned over this sad assembly; ten men of the people, preceded by the turnkeys, entered the chapel, lined the prisoners up against the wall, and counted fifty-three of them.

After that, names were called out every quarter hour: about the time needed for the improvised tribunal stationed at the prison entrance to pass judgment.

Some were spared, including the venerable abbé Sicard;[84] most of them were beaten as they emerged by the fanatical murderers who had taken on this sad task. Around midnight, they shouted the name of Jacques Cazotte.

The fearless old man presented himself before the members of this bloody-thirsty tribunal, who sat in a small room guarded by a turnkey, and over which the terrible Maillard presided.[85] At that moment, some madmen demanded that the women should also be summoned, and they were forced to come down into the chapel one by one; but the tribunal members rejected this horrible demand, and Maillard, having given the order to the turnkey Lavaquerie[86] to send them back up, shut the bolt of the prison door and called out Cazotte's name. At the mention of his name, the prisoner's daughter, who was going back up with the other women, rushed back down the stairs and pushed through the crowd as Maillard pronounced the terrible words: Be strong! Which meant: Death!

The outer door opened: the long courtyard, surrounded by cloisters, where they continued to slaughter, was full of people and still echoed with the cries of the dying; Elizabeth courageously darted between the two killers who had already laid their hands on her father, who were apparently called Michel and Sauvage, and asked them, as well as the people, to show mercy for her father.

Her unexpected appearance, her touching words, the age of the sentenced man, who was almost eighty, and whose political crime was not easy to define and state, the sublime effect of these two noble figures, a touching image of filial heroism, roused the tender emotions of part of the crowd. Cries for mercy came from all sides. Maillard still hesitated. Michel poured a glass of wine and said to Elizabeth: "Listen, citizen, to prove to citizen Maillard that you are not an aristocrat, drink this to the health of the nation and the triumph of the Republic."

The brave girl drank without hesitation; the people from Marseille made room for her and the applauding crowd parted to allow the father and daughter to pass together, and they were escorted back home.

Connections, however remote, have been sought in Cazotte's dream quoted above and the happy deliverance chanted by the crowd at the conclusion of the scene, with the locations and details from the scene we have just described; it would be childish to bring them up again; a more obvious premonition told him that his daughter's beautiful devotion would not shield him from his fate.

The day after he had been escorted home in triumph by the people, several of his friends came to congratulate him. One of them, M. de Saint-Charles, approached him and said: "You're saved!" "Not for long," answered Cazotte, smiling sadly . . . A moment before you arrived, I had a vision. I thought I saw a gendarme who came for me on behalf of Pétion;[87] I was forced to follow him; I appeared before the mayor of Paris, who had me taken to the Conciergerie, and from there to the revolutionary court. My time has come."

M. de Saint-Charles left him, believing that his reason had suffered from the terrible trials through which he had passed. A lawyer named Julien offered Cazotte asylum at his home and means for escaping the search; but the old man was determined not to fight against destiny. On 11 September he saw the man from his vision enter his house: a gendarme bearing an order signed by Pétion, Pâris, and Sergent;[88] they took him to the town hall, and from there, to the Conciergerie, where his friends were not allowed to see him. Elisabeth obtained, by means of her entreaties, permission to serve her father, and remained in the prison with him until the final day. But her efforts to sway the judges did not have the same success as with the people, and Cazotte, on the indictment of Fouquier-Tinville, was sentenced to death after twenty-seven hours of interrogation.

Before pronouncing the sentence, they confined his daughter to a solitary chamber, fearing her making a final effort and influencing the audience; the defense speech of citizen Julienne[89] attempted in vain to express what was sacred about this victim who had escaped the justice of the people; the tribunal seemed to obey an unshakable conviction.

The strangest incident in this trial was the speech made by President Lavau, a former member, like Cazotte, of the society of the Illuminati.[90]

"Fragile plaything of old age," he said,

> you whose heart was not big enough to sense the price of holy freedom, but who proved, by your safety during the debates, that you knew how to sacrifice your very existence to support your opinion, listen to the final words of your judges! May they pour into your soul the precious balm of consolation! May they, in causing you to pity the lot of those who have just sentenced you, inspire in you the stoicism that must preside over your final moments, and instill in you the respect for the law that we impose upon ourselves! . . . Your peers have heard you, your peers have condemned you; but at least their judgment was as pure as their conscience; at least no personal interest interfered with their decision. Go, take courage, gather your strength; envision this death without fear; realize that it should not shock you:

it is not a moment that should frighten a man such as yourself. But before you depart from this life, witness the impressive attitude of France, from whose bosom you feared not to call out to the enemy; witness your old country as it opposes the attacks from her vile adversaries with as much courage as you had attributed cowardice. If the Law could have foreseen that she would have had to deliver a verdict against a guilty party such as yourself, taking your old age into consideration, she would not have sentenced you otherwise; but take comfort: though she is severe when she is in pursuit, after she passes sentence, the sword soon falls from her hands; she bemoans the loss of even those who wanted to tear her apart. Witness her shedding tears upon your white hair, which she respected until the moment of your condemnation; may this vision instill repentance in you; let her impel you, wretched old man, to take advantage of this moment that still separates you from death, to efface every trace of your conspiracies with a sincere feeling of regret! One word more: you were a man, a Christian, a philosopher, an *initiate*; learn how to die as a man and as a Christian; this is all your country can still ask of you.

The unusual and mysterious premise of this speech bewildered the Assembly, and made no impression on Cazotte who, during the passage where the president was trying to be persuasive, looked up to heaven and made a sign of unwavering faith in his convictions. He then said to those around him "that he knew he deserved to die; that the Law was strict but that he found it just."* When they cut his hair, he advised them to cut it as short as possible and asked his confessor to give it to his daughter, who was still confined in one of the prison chambers.

Before walking to his execution, he wrote a few words to his wife and children; then, having mounted the scaffold, he cried out in a very loud voice: "I die as I have lived, faithful to God and to my king." The execution took place on 25 September, at seven o'clock in the evening, on the Place du Carrousel.

Elisabeth Cazotte, long promised by her father to the Chevalier de Plas, officer in the regiment of Poitou, eight years later married this young

* M. Scévole Cazotte has written us to protest this phrase which played a part in the account at the time. He claims that his father could not have uttered such words.

man, who had followed those emigrating. The fate of this heroine was to be no happier than before: she perished giving birth to a child through a Caesarean section, crying out for them to tear her into pieces if necessary to save the child. The child lived only a few moments. There remain, however, several people of the Cazotte family. His son Scévole, who miraculously escaped the massacre of 10 August, lives in Paris, and piously preserves the tradition of his father's beliefs and virtues.

CAGLIOSTRO

(Eighteenth Century)

I. On Revolutionary Mysticism

When Catholicism decisively triumphed over paganism throughout Europe and constructed thereafter the feudal edifice that survived until the fifteenth century—that is to say, for the space of a thousand years—it could not suppress and destroy everywhere the spirit of ancient customs, nor those philosophical ideas that had transformed the pagan principle at the time of Emperor Julian's polytheistic response.[1]

It was not enough to have overthrown the last refuge of Greek philosophy and those earlier beliefs by destroying the Alexandrian *Serapeum*,[2] and dispersing and persecuting the Neoplatonists[3] who had replaced the external worship of the gods with a spiritualist doctrine derived from the mysteries of Eleusis and the Egyptian initiations; the Church still had to pursue its victory throughout all localities immersed in ancient superstitions, and persecution was not as powerful as time and oblivion for this difficult outcome.

But if we concern ourselves with France alone, we recognize that pagan worship has long survived the official conversions effected by the change of religion of the Merovingian kings.[4] The people's respect for certain consecrated places, for the ruins of temples and even the debris of old statues, forced the Christian priests to build most of the churches on the site of ancient pagan shrines. Wherever this precaution was neglected, particularly in solitary places, the old worship continued—as at the abbey of Mount Saint Bernard, where in the last century, the god *Jou* was still honored at the site of the ancient temple of *Jupiter*.[5] Although the ancient goddess of the Parisians, Isis, had been replaced by Saint Geneviève as protector and patroness, there was still, in the eleventh century, an image of Isis, inadvertently preserved under the porch of Saint-Germain des Prés, devoutly honored by the wives of sailors, which forced the Archbishop of Paris to reduce it to dust and cast it into the Seine.[6] A statue of the same deity could still be seen at Quinipily, in Brittany, a few years ago, where it received the tributes of the population.[7] In an area of Alsace and Franche-Comté, a cult of *Mothers* has been preserved, whose faces on bas-reliefs can be found on several monuments, and who are none other than the *great goddesses* Cybele, Ceres, and Vesta.

It would take too long to review the various superstitions that have assumed a thousand forms, depending on the time. In the eighteenth century there were clerics, such as the abbé de Villars, Father Bougeant, Dom Pernetty,[8] and others who argued that the gods of antiquity were not demons, as the overly severe casuists had claimed, and were not even damned. They relegated them to the class of *elemental spirits* who, having taken no part in the great struggle that originally took place between angels and demons, had not needed to be cursed or destroyed by Divine Justice, and had been able to enjoy a certain power over the elements and over men until the arrival of Christ. The abbé de Villars gave as evidence the miracles that the Bible itself acknowledges as having been produced by the god of the Ammonites, the Philistines, or others for the benefit of their people, and that often fulfilled the prophecies of the *spirits of Typhon*.[9] Among the latter he placed the oracles of the Sibyls favorable to Christ, and the last oracles of Apollo at Delphi, which were cited by the Church Fathers as proof of the mission of the Son of Man.

According to this system, the entire ancient hierarchy of pagan gods would have found its place among the thousand attributes Catholicism assigned to the lower offices, to be carried out in matter and space, and would have become what have been called the spirits or genii, which are divided into four classes, in accordance with the number of elements: Sylphs for air, Salamanders for fire, Ondines for water, and Gnomes for earth.

Regarding this one detail, there arose between the abbé de Villars and Father Bougeant, a Jesuit, a split that long occupied the fine minds of the last century. The latter strongly opposed the transformation of the ancient gods into elemental genii, and claimed that as they could not be destroyed, being pure spirits, they were destined to provide animals with souls, which were reborn from one body to the other, according to their affinities. In this system, the gods animated useful and beneficial beasts, and demons, ferocious and impure beasts. On this point the good Father Bougeant cited the opinion of the Egyptians concerning the gods and that of the Gospel concerning the demons. These arguments could be put forward in the middle of the eighteenth century without giving rise to accusations of heresy.

It is quite clear that these were only lower deities such as fauns, Zephyrs, Nereids, Oreads,[10] Satyrs, Cyclops, etc. As for the gods and demigods, they had supposedly left the earth, it being too dangerous after the absolute reign of Christ had been established, and been relegated to the stars, which have always been dedicated to them, just as in the Middle Ages when a rebellious king was relegated, after his submission, either to the city or to a place of exile.

This view prevailed, particularly during the Middle Ages, among the most celebrated Cabalists, and especially among astrologers, alchemists, and physicians. This explains most of the conjurations based on astral invocations, horoscopes, talismans, and medications, be they of consecrated substances or operations tied to the movement or conjunction of planets. One has only to open a book on the occult sciences for clear evidence of this.

II. Precursors

If the doctrines outlined above have been sufficiently explained, then one will be able to understand the reasons why, alongside the Orthodox Church, a half-religious and half-philosophical school, no doubt fertile in heresies yet often accepted or tolerated by the Catholic clergy, developed without interruption and maintained a certain mystical and supernatural spirit dreamy and delicate imaginations need, as do some populations more disposed than others to spiritualist ideas.

Converted Israelistes were the first who attempted, around the eleventh century, to infuse Catholicism with some hypotheses based on the interpretation of the Bible going back to the doctrines of the Essenes and the Gnostics.

It is then that the word *cabal* starts coming up frequently in theological discussions. It brings in naturally something of the Platonic expressions of the Alexandrian school, many of which were already reproduced in the doctrines of the Church Fathers.

Christianity's prolonged contact with the Orient during the Crusades brought over another large number of similar ideas which, moreover, were easily supported by the local traditions and superstitions of the European nations.

The Templars were among those Crusaders who endeavored to achieve the broadest possible alliance between these Eastern ideas and those of Roman Christianity.

In the desire to establish a link between their order and the Syrian people they were responsible for governing, they laid the foundations for a new kind of doctrine that was engaged with all the religions practiced by the Levantines, without abandoning in essence the Catholic synthesis, but by often making it bend to the requirements of their position.

These were the foundations of Freemasonry, which were connected to analagous institutions established by various Muslim sects and which still survive persecution, especially in the Hauran, Lebanon, and Kurdistan.

The strangest and most exaggerated phenomenon of these Oriental associations was the famous Order of the *Assassins*. The nation of the Druze and that of the Ansarians are today the ones who have retained its last remnants.[11]

The Knights Templar were soon accused of having established one of the most formidable heresies Christianity had ever witnessed. Persecuted and finally destroyed in all the European countries through the combined efforts of the papacy and the monarchies, they had on their side the intelligent classes and a good number of distinguished minds who were against the abuses of the feudal lords; they were what today we would call the *Opposition*.

From their ashes scattered to the wind was born a mystical and philosophical institution which greatly influenced this first moral and religious revolution, which for the people of the North was called the *Reform*, and for those of the South *La Philosophie*.[12]

These reforms were still, all things considered, concerned with the salvation of Christianity as a religion; *Philosophie*, however, gradually became its enemy and, aiming especially at people who remained Catholic, soon established clear divisions between unbelievers and believers.

However, there are many who are not satisfied with pure materialism, but who, without rejecting the religious tradition, prefer maintaining toward it a certain freedom of discussion and interpretation. It was they who founded the first Masonic societies, which soon gave shape to the popular corporations and what are today still called *trade guilds*.

The Masonic order established its highest institutions in Scotland, and it was because of the relations of France with this country, from the time of Mary Stuart to Louis XIV, that strong footholds were established in our own mystical institutions which prepared us for the *Rosicrucians*.

Meanwhile, Italy had seen the establishment in the sixteenth century of a long series of fearless thinkers, including Ficino, Pico della Mirandola, Meursius,[13] Nicolas of Cusa, Giordano Bruno, and other great minds favored by the tolerance of the Medici, and who are sometimes called the *Neoplatonists of Florence*.

The capture of Constantinople, by exiling many illustrious scholars who were then welcomed into Italy, also exerted a great influence on that philosophical movement which revived the ideas of the Alexandrians and led to the renewal of the study of Plotinus, Proclus, Porphyry, and Ptolemy, those first opponents of nascent Catholicism.[14]

It should be noted here that the most learned physicians and naturalists of the Middle Ages, such as Paracelsus, Albert the Great, Jérôme Cardan,[15] Roger Bacon, and others, were somewhat attached to these doctrines, which gave a new formula to what one called the occult sciences: astrology, Cabala, palmistry, alchemy, physiognomy, etc.

It was from these various elements and partly from the Hebrew science, which started spreading more freely in the Renaissance, that the various mystical schools developed in the late seventeenth century. The Rosicrucians first, whose indiscreet disciple, and later its alleged victim, was the abbé de Villars.

Then the *Convulsionaries* and certain sects of Jansenism; by 1770, the *Martinists*, *Swedenborgians*, and finally the Order of the Illuminati, whose doctrine, first established in Germany by Weisshaupt, soon spread to France, where it merged with the Masonic institution.

III. Saint-Germain—Cagliostro

These two figures were the most famous Cabalists of the late eighteenth century. The former, who appeared at the court of Louis XV where he had a certain esteem through the protection of Mme Pompadour, had, say memoirs of the time, neither the impudence that suits a charlatan nor the eloquence necessary for a fanatic, nor the seductive quality that drives superficial scholars. He dealt mainly with alchemy but did not neglect the various other parts of science. He showed Louis XV the fate of his children in a magic mirror, and the king drew back in terror at seeing the image of the dauphin appear to him decapitated.

Saint-Germain and Cagliostro had met in Germany in Holstein, and it was said that the former initiated the latter and gave him his mystical rank. At the time he was initiated, he himself noted the famous mirror that was used for the evocation of souls.

The Count of Saint-Germain claimed to have remembered a host of past lives and related his various adventures since the beginning of the world. One day his servant was questioned on a fact the count had told some dinner guests to do with the time of Caesar. He responded to their curiosity: "Forgive me, messieurs, I have only been in the service of the count for three hundred years."

It is on rue Plâtrière in Paris, and also in Ermenonville, that the sessions were held at which this individual developed his theories.

Cagliostro, after being initiated by the Count of Saint-Germain, went to St. Petersburg, where he had a lot of success. Later he came to Strasbourg, where he acquired, it is said, great influence over the Archbishop Prince de Rohan.[16]

Everyone knows about the affair of the necklace[17] in which this famous Cabalist was implicated, but he emerged from it to his advantage, brought back to his hotel in triumph by the people of Paris.

His wife, who was very beautiful and highly intelligent, had followed him on all his travels.[18] She presided over the famous dinner attended by most of the philosophers of the time, where several people who had recently died were conjured up: according to the system of Cagliostro, *there are no deaths*. So, the table was set for twelve, although there were only six guests: d'Alembert, Diderot, Voltaire, the Duke of Choiseul, the abbé Voisenon,[19] and an unknown sixth party came to sit, though dead, in the seats reserved for them and talked with the invited guests, *de omni re scibili et quibusdam aliis.*[20]

Around this time, Cagliostro founded the famous *Egyptian Lodge*, leaving his wife the task of establishing another for her sex, which was put under the invocation of Isis.

IV. Madame Cagliostro

Women, excessively curious and excluded from the secrets of men, asked Mme de Cagliostro to initiate them. She replied coolly to the duchess of T***, who had been tasked with making the initial overtures, that once thirty-six followers were found, she would begin her course on magic; that same day the list was filled.

The preliminary conditions were as such: 1. Each had to put a hundred louis into a box. As the women of Paris never have a penny, this clause was difficult to fulfill; but the pawnshhop and some favors made it possible; 2. that for nine days, they would refrain from any human interaction; 3. that they would swear to submit to any order, however outlandish it seemed.

7 August was the big day. The scene took place in a large house on rue Verte-Saint-Honoré. They arrived at eleven o'clock. Upon entering the first room, each woman was obliged to remove her basket, her brassiere, her corset, her false chignon, and to don a white Levite robe with a color girdle. There were six in black, six in blue, six in poppy red, six in purple, six in pink, six multicolored. Each was given a large veil which they wore from left to right on a chain.

When they were ready, they were led two by two into a lit temple, in which thirty-six bergères were placed, covered in black satin. Mme de Cagliostro, dressed in white, was on a sort of throne, escorted by two impressive figures dressed in such a manner that it was uncertain if they were specters, men, or women. The light that lit this room gradually dimmed and when objects could barely be made out, the high priestess ordered the women to uncover their left leg up to their knee. After this exercise, she ordered them again to raise their right arm and support it on a nearby column. Then two women holding a broadsword entered, and having received silk bands from Mme de Cagliostro, bound the legs and arms of the thirty-six ladies.

This ceremony now finished, Mme de Cagliostro began a speech as follows:

"The state in which you find yourself is the symbol of your state in society. If men remove you from their mysteries, from their projects, it is because they wish to keep you forever dependent. Throughout the world, woman is man's first slave, from the time of the seraglio when a despot imprisoned five hundred of us, to those savage climes where we dare not sit next to a hunter husband! . . . We are victims, sacrificed at childhood to cruel gods. If, breaking these shameful chains, we were to also develop our own projects together, you would soon see that proud sex crawling and begging for your favors. Let them carry out their murderous wars or untangle the chaos of their laws, but let us take care to govern public opinion, purify morals, cultivate the mind, nurture sensitivity, and reduce the number of misfortunes in the world. These efforts are well worth those of training automatons or delivering verdicts on ridiculous quarrels. If any of you have anything to say in opposition to this, speak freely."

A general cheer followed this speech. Then the Grand Mistress loosened the bands and continued as follows:

"Doubtless, your fiery soul eagerly seized this project to recover your freedom, which is every creature's first right; but more than one trial must teach you to what degree you can rely on yourself, and it is these trials that embolden me to confide certain secrets to you on which the happiness of your life forever depends.

"You will divide yourselves into six groups; each color must come together and go to one of the six apartments that communicate with that temple. Those who succumb must never enter it; the palm of victory awaits those who triumph."

Each group entered a properly furnished room where a crowd of cavaliers soon arrived. Some began mocking the women, asking how reasonable women could trust the words of an adventurer, and they strongly emphasized the danger of public ridicule . . . Others bemoaned seeing love and friendship sacrificed to ancient excesses for no discernible reason or advantage.

The women barely deigned to listen to these heartless jokes. In a neighboring room they could see paintings of the greatest masters: Hercules spinning wool at Omphale's feet, Renaud lying by Armida, Mark Antony serving Cleopatra, beautiful Agnès[21] holding forth at the Court of Charles VII, Catherine the Great whom men wore on trophies.[22] One of the men accompanying them said: "So this is the sex that treats yours like a slave! For whom are the pleasures and attention of society? Does it cause you any harm to spare you trouble? If we build palaces, is it not to devote the best part to you? Do we not love to adorn our idols? Should we adopt the manners of Orientals? Does a jealous veil hide your charms? And far from having repulsive eunuchs close your chamber door, how many times have we not tactfully withdrawn to give way to coquetry?"

It was an amiable and modest man who gave this speech.

"All your eloquence," answered one of the women, "will not destroy the humiliating bars of the convents, the companions you have given us, the powerlessness attributed to our own writings, your patronizing airs, and the orders you give under the guise of advice."

Not far from this apartment another more interesting scene took place. Here, the ladies with the lilac ribbons were with their normal suitors. Their debut was to notify them of their most absolute withdrawal. This room had three doors that opened onto gardens lit by the soft moonlight. The ladies invited the men to walk down into them. They granted this last favor to the disconsolate men. One of these women, whom we shall name Léonore, failed to disguise the disorder of her soul and followed Count Gédéon, whom she had loved until then. "Please, deign to tell me my crimes?" he said. "Is it an act of treachery that you are abandoning? What have I been doing for two days? My feelings, my thoughts, my existence, my blood, do they not all belong to you? You cannot be that fickle! What kind of fanaticism comes to rob me of a heart that has caused me so much pain?"

"It is not you I hate," she answered, "it is your sex; it is your laws which are tyrannical and cruel!"

"Alas! But of this sex that is banished today, you have known only me. Where, then, is my tyranny? When had I the misfortune to aggrieve the one I love?"

Léonore sighed and did not know how to accuse the one she adored. He wants to take one of her hands.

"If you love me," she tells him, "take care not to soil my hand with a profane kiss. I don't believe I will ever be able to leave you. But to prove this obedience in which you want me to believe, stay nine days without seeing me, and know that this sacrifice will not be lost on my heart." Gédéon withdrew; and unable to doubt her and not daring to complain, he went to reflect on the causes of his sorrow.

It would take too long to tell of everything that took place during those two hours of trials. It is certain that neither reasoning nor sarcasm, nor tears, nor despair, nor promises, nor ultimately any of seduction's ploys could do anything against the women's powerful curiosity and secret hope to dominate. Everyone returned to the temple as the high priestess had commanded.

It was three o'clock in the morning. Each took her place. Various liquors were presented to them to give them strength. Then they were ordered to remove their veils and cover their faces. After fifteen minutes of silence, a sort of dome opened and, on a large golden ball, a man descended dressed as a genie, holding a snake in his hand and bearing a bright flame on his head.

"This is the Genius of Truth," said the grand mistress, "whom I wish to teach you the secrets so long concealed from your sex. The one you are to hear is the famous, immortal, divine Cagliostro, born of Abraham's breast without having been conceived, in whom is entrusted all that was, all that is, and all that will be known on earth."

"Daughters of the earth," Cagliostro exclaimed, "if men did not hold you in error, you would eventually join together in an invincible union. Your gentleness, your indulgence would have you adore this people, whom must be commanded if their respect is to be earned. You know neither those vices that disturb reason, nor the frenzy that burns a whole kingdom to the ground. Nature has done everything for you. They jealously debase its work in the hope it will never be known. If in rejecting a deceitful sex you seek true sympathy in your own, you will never blush over those shameful rivalries, those jealousies that are beneath you. Cast your gaze upon yourselves, learn how to appreciate yourselves, open your souls to pure tenderness, and may the kiss of friendship announce what takes place in your hearts."

Here the speaker stopped. All the women embrace each other. The darkness replaces the light, and the Genius of Truth ascends back up through the dome. The grand mistress quickly goes from one to the other; here she instructs; there she comments; everywhere she fires the imagination. Only Léonore shed some tears. "I can guess," she whispered in her ear; "is the memory of what we love not sufficient?"

Then she ordered the profane music to start up again. Gradually the light returned, and after a few moments of quiet, they heard a sound as if the floor was sinking. It lowered almost completely and was soon replaced by a sumptuously laid table. The ladies took their places. Then came thirty-six Geniuses of Truth, dressed in white satin: a mask hid their faces. But given the air of ease and eagerness with which they served, one could imagine that spiritual beings are well above coarse humans. In the middle of dinner, the grand mistress gave a sign to unmask, and the ladies then recognized their lovers. Some, faithful to their vows, were about to stand. She advises them to moderate their zeal by observing that meals were to be devoted to joy and pleasure. They are asked how they happened to be reunited. It was then explained to them that they in turn were initiated into certain mysteries; that if they wore the clothing of genius, it was to show that equality is the basis of everything; that it was not extraordinary to see thirty-six cavaliers with thirty-six ladies; that the essential goal of the great Cagliostro was to repair the wrongs caused by society, and that the state of nature made everyone equal.

The Geniuses dined. Twenty times the sparkling foam of the Sillery wine spurted up to the ceiling. The gaiety increases, witticisms are uttered; one clever remark follows another, the conversation grows giddy, the intoxication of happiness shines in everyone's eyes, theater songs are sung, innocent caresses are permitted; clothing gets a bit rumpled; dancing is suggested, they waltz more than jump; the punch gives way to repeated contredanse; Love, exiled for some time, shakes its torch; the oaths, the Genius of Truth, the wrongs of men are forgotten, the errors of the imagination are recanted.

Yet they avoided the looks of the grand priestess; she retired and smiled to see herself so disobeyed. "Love conquers all," she said, "but think upon our agreements, and gradually your souls will purify. This is but one session; it is up to you to renew it."

Over the following days, they were not allowed to speak of the details, but the enthusiasm for Count Cagliostro was brought to a level of intoxication that was astonishing even in Paris. He seized this moment to develop all the principles of Egyptian Freemasonry. He announced to the lights of the great Orient that they could only work under the Triple Arch, that there could be no more and no fewer than thirteen adepts; that they should be as pure as the rays of the sun, and even respected by those who spread lies, have neither women, mistresses, or undisciplined tendencies, possess a fortune of over fifty-three thousand livres; and above all, the sort of knowledge so rarely found among those with many incomes.

V. The Pagans of the Republic

The episode we have just collected gives us an idea of the movement then taking place in minds that were gradually freeing themselves from Catholic dogma. Already the Illuminati of Germany had shown themselves to be nearly pagan; those of France, as we have said, were called *Martinists*, after Martinez, who had founded several associations in Bordeaux and Lyon; they separated into two sects, one of which continued to follow the theories of Jacob Boehm, wonderfully developed by the famous Saint-Martin, called the *Unknown Philosopher*, and the other came to settle in Paris and founded the lodge of the *Philaléthes*, which soon resolutely entered the revolutionary movement.[23]

We have already cited the various authors who joined forces to establish in France a philosophical and religious doctrine marked by these ideas. They include primarily the Marquis d'Argens, author of *Lettres Cabalistiques*; Dom Pernetty, author of the *Dictionnaire Mytho-Hermetique*; Esprémenil, Lavater, Delille de Salle; the abbé Terrasson, author of *Sethos*, Bergasse, Clootz, Court de Gébelin, Fabre d'Olivet, etc.[24]

One must read Barruel's *History of Jacobinism*, and the *Proofs of a Conspiracy by the Illuminati* by Robinson, as well as Mounier's observations on these two works,[25] to form an idea of how many famous people of that time were suspected of being members of the mystical associations whose influence prepared the Revolution. Most historians of our time have neglected to delve deeper into these details, out of either ignorance or fear of mixing high politics with something they assumed was less serious.*

Robespierre's father, as is known, founded a Masonic lodge in Arras according to the Scottish Rite.[26] It may be supposed that Robespierre's own

* M. Louis Blanc and M. Michelet have addressed these matters, however.

first impressions had some influence on several actions in his life. He was often accused of mysticism, especially because of his relation to the famous Catherine Théot.[27] The materialists were not pleased to hear the opinions he expressed at the Convention on the need for public worship.

"You will do well," he said, "to avoid breaking the sacred link that unites men to the author of their being: it is enough for this opinion to have prevailed over a people for it to be dangerous to destroy it; for the motives for one's duties and the foundations of morality are necessarily bound to this idea; to erase it is to demoralize the people. It follows from this same principle that one must never attack an established practice of worship save with caution and a certain delicacy, lest a sudden and violent change should arise against morality and a dispensation of probity itself. Moreover, anyone who can replace the Divinity in the system of social life is in my eyes a prodigy of genius, but the one who without having replaced it, thinks only to banish it from the minds of men, seems to me a prodigy of stupidity or perversity."

We must also recognize that among the details of the ceremony he instituted in honor of the Supreme Being, there is an echo of the practices of Illuminism in that statue covered with a veil which he set on fire, and which represented either Nature or Isis.[28]

Once Robespierre was overthrown, many philosophers still sought to establish a religious formula outside of Catholic ideas. It was then that Dupont de Nemours, the famous economist and friend of Lavoisier, published his *Philosophy of the Universe*, which contains a complete system on the hierarchy of *celestial spirits* and obviously goes back to illuminism and the doctrines of Swedenborg. Aucler, of whom we shall speak, went still further by suggesting the restoration of paganism and the worship of the stars.

Restif de la Bretone also published, as we have seen, a pantheistic system that did away with the immortality of the soul, but which replaced it with a kind of metempsychosis.[29]—The Father had to be reborn in his race after a certain number of years. The author's moral code was based on *reversibility*, that is, on a destiny that inevitably brought into this life the reward for virtues or the punishment of faults. There is in this system something of the primitive doctrine of the Hebrews.

QUINTUS AUCLER

French Republic

The Thracian

"I thought," said Candide, "that there were no more Manicheans." "There's me," said Martin.
VOLTAIRE

I. Saint-Denis

A visit to Saint-Denis on a foggy autumn day is like reentering the forgotten circle of those austere walks once made by the dreamers of the school of J. J. Rousseau.

Rousseau is the only one of the eighteenth-century masters of philosophy who took a serious interest in the great mysteries of the human soul, and who expressed a positive religious sentiment—which he understood in his own way, but which sharply contrasted with the resolute atheism of La Mettrie, d'Holbach, Helvétius, and d'Alembert, as with the moderate deism of Boulanger, Diderot, and Voltaire.[1]—"Let us crush the infamous!" was the common phrase of this philosophical coalition, but not everyone struck the same harsh blows against religious feeling in general. This hesitation in certain minds more disposed than others to exaltation and reverie is not that surprising.

There is certainly something more frightening in history than the fall of empires: it is the death of religion. Volney himself experienced this feeling when visiting the ruins of once sacred buildings.[2] The true believer can avoid this impression, but given the skepticism of our time, we sometimes shudder to see so many dark doors opening onto nothing.

The last one that still seems to lead to something—this ogival door, whose ribs and worn or broken figurines are devotedly restored—still reveals a glimpse of its graceful nave, illuminated by the magic rosettes of the stained-glass windows; believers crowd upon the marble slabs and along the whitened pillars on which the colorful reflection of saints and angels is cast. The incense smokes, voices resound, the Latin hymn soars to the vaulted ceilings to the grandiose sound of the instruments. Only beware the unhealthy breath issuing from the feudal tombs where so many kings are piled up! An unbelieving century has disturbed their eternal rest—which our own has piously restored to them.

What matter the broken tombs and violated remains of Saint-Denis! Hatred paid homage to them; the indifferent man of today has restored them out of love for art and symmetry, as he would have arranged the mummies in an Egyptian museum.[3]

But is it a faith that, triumphing over the efforts of the impious, has still to fear indifference?

What Catholic could not bear the wild bacchanal of Newstead Abbey, and the Christmas orgy companions of Byron, parodying the plainsong with drinking songs—decked out in monastic robes, drinking *claret* from skulls[4]—rather than see the ancient abbey become a factory or a theater?—Byron's sneering still belongs to religious sentiment, as does Shelley's materialistic impiety. But who today would deign to be impious? No one dreams of it!

Another look into this freshly restored Basilica, the appearance of which gave rise to these reflections. One never tires of admiring the monuments of the Medici under the Gothic arches of the aisles.—Angels and saints! Did you not shudder in the stiff folds of your robes and your dalmatics[5] when you saw those pageantries of pagan art, decorated with the name of the Renaissance, grow and flourish under your tutelary ogives?[6] Look! The Romanesque arch, the marble column with its bronze acanthus, the bas-relief displaying its voluptuous nudes and precise drawings—at the foot of your long hieratic faces now welcomed by irony! Nothing is truer than what was said by a prophet monk of the time: "I see you, unchaste Venus, entering the holy house naked and setting your triumphant foot on the altar!"[7]

These three Virtues are undoubtedly the three Graces, these angels the two lovers Eros and Anteros.[8] This beautiful woman, who rests half naked on a raised bed whose veils she has thrown back, is she not Cytherea herself? And this young man who seems to sleep deeply beside her, is he not Adonis of the Syrian mysteries?

She lies, slumped in her grief, her waist arched with that voluptuousness that comes naturally, her breasts rise proudly, she smiles still, and yet beside her the battered hunter sleeps the sleep of marble, his limbs stiff.

Let us listen to the legend the man of the Church repeats to all: "Here is the tomb of Catherine de Medici. When she was alive, she wished to have herself depicted in the same bed as her husband, Henri II, who died from the thrust of Montgommery's lance."[9]

How noble and seductive this queen is with her disheveled hair, beautiful as Venus and faithful as Artemisia,[10] and she did well not to wake up from this graceful sleep! She was still so young, so loving, and so pure. But she was already striking a blow against religion without meaning to—as later, on St. Bartholomew's day.

Yes, the art of the Renaissance had dealt a mortal blow to the old dogma and the holy austerity of the Church before the French Revolution swept away its remains. Allegory succeeding primitive myth had once done the same thing to the ancient religions . . . It always ends up with a Lucian who writes *The Dialogues of the Gods*[11]—and later, a Voltaire who mocks the gods and even God himself.

If it were true, according to the words of a modern philosopher, that the Christian religion had scarcely more than a century to live,[12] should one not attach oneself with tears and prayers to the bloody feet of that Christ detached from the mystic tree, to the immaculate robe of his Virgin Mother, the supreme expression of the ancient covenant between heaven and earth—a final kiss of the divine spirit that weeps and then flies away!

More than half a century has passed already since this situation was created by men of great intelligence and ended up resolved in different ways. Those of our ancestors who had devoted themselves with sincerity and courage to the emancipation of the human mind were compelled perhaps to confuse religion itself with the institutions whose ruins it adorned. They put the axe to the trunk of the tree, and the heart, rotten like old bark, like thick branches, refuge of birds and bees, like the stubborn wild vine, all were cut down at the same time—and the whole was cast into darkness like a useless fig tree; but though the object be destroyed, the spot remains, still sacred for many. This was what the victorious Church understood long ago when it built its basilicas and chapels on the locations of abolished temples.

II. The Festival of the Supreme Being

These questions were of great concern, at the most burning moment of the French Revolution, for citizen Quintus Aucler. He was not a soul to be content with the allegorical mysticism invented by Chaumette, Hérault de Séchelles, and Larevellière-Lépeaux.[13]—The mountain raised in the nave of Notre Dame,[14] where the beautiful Mme Momoro[15] as the Goddess of Reason was enthroned, had no more impact on his imagination than did the later altar of the Theophilanthropists,[16] loaded with fruits and greenery. He certainly had no respect for the ecstatic Catherine Théot, or for her friend, Dom Gerle, whose practices Robespierre favored.[17] And when the latter himself, carefully powdered, with his iron-ax profile and wearing Werther's blue tail-coat,[18] on the back of which his newly beribboned pony-tail undulated, with his quilted waistcoat, his pants and antique stockings, began to offer a large bouquet to the Supreme Being, like a timid child celebrating his father's birthday, the old Jacobins shook their heads, and the crowd laughed heartily at the fire which, by burning the veil of the statue of the goddess, had made her as black as an Ethiopian;—but Quintus Aucler was indignant; he cursed this ignorant tribune who had not consulted him; he would have told him: "What folly led you to address heaven in these clothes without having carried out beforehand any of the sacred rites? It would even be easy to hide your ridiculous costume under the robes of the flamines;[19] but have you consulted the omens, prepared the victims, fed the sacred chickens barley; did anyone at least indicate with the *lituus* the place where you were to perform the sacrifice? That is how we address the gods, who are not averse to answering with their thunder; whereas you threaten by invoking, as if to say: 'Supreme Being, the nation is willing to offer you some flowers for your feast. We have fired the cannon: answer with a thunderbolt, or else watch out!'"

But certainly, the Supreme Being praised by Robespierre, and in favor of which Delille de Salle had written a memoir,[20] was just an empty allegory like the others in the eyes of Quintus Aucler. He suspected even Robespierre of having guarded, at the bottom of his heart, an old leaven for this Christianity in which he only saw a wicked seed of the Bible. His deepest conviction was that Christians were only the degraded successors of an expelled Jewish sect, made up of slaves and bandits.

How many times he cursed the tolerance of Julian, who had despised them too much to fear them. The result of which, he said, was the fall of the great Greek and Roman civilization which had covered the world with marvels.—Hence, the triumph of the barbarians and the darkness of ignorance that spread over the land for fifteen hundred years! Could there be any doubt that a doctrine derived from the *divine negation*, formulated by a small group of usurers and thieves, would be received with transport by these hordes of distant barbarians whose robberies it favored? Long maintained by the Roman glory within the borders of the civilized world, it took an emperor, guilty of nameless crimes, to rupture this moral dam that had maintained for the Roman world the favor of the almighty gods! The response from the hierophants of Constantine—*Sacrum commissum quod neque expiare poterit, impie commissum est!*[21]—was the fatal judgment of paganism. The law of the gods knew no atonement for the crimes of the emperor, and he was excluded from the celebration of the Mysteries, as Nero had been.—The new Church was less severe, and from then on its triumph was assured. It became clear that all the plunderers and all the barbarians would embrace in their turn a religion that stood ready to pardon those who could pay in wealth and power.

Here are some pages from *The Thracian* published by Auculer:[22]

> . . . And these religions whose leaders were men of bad morals, these atrocious religions that used such horrible means to sustain themselves, claim to have brought to men new virtues unknown to them, those of universal charity and forgiveness of abuses. We are not born for ourselves alone, said Plato, we are born for the fatherland, for our parents, for our friends, and for all the rest of mankind. Nature herself has ordained, said Cicero, that one man shall take an interest in another man, whoever he may be, simply because he is a man. We are all members of one body, said Seneca; did Nature not make us all allies? It is she who gives us this mutual love we have for one another; and this maxim was even spoken in the theaters: I am a man, said the old man in Terence, and nothing concerning a man is alien to me. Had not the Persians their famous law against ingratitude, according to which they punished any lack of love toward the gods, parents,

country, friends; had the Egyptians not confined themselves to simple precepts, they would also have had a law to this effect.

But is it not known, or could it be that we do not want to know, that this universal charity was the first point of the morality of the Mysteries? What good man, asks Juvenal, worthy of the mysterious torch and is such as the hierophant of Ceres wants him to be, thinks that the troubles of others are foreign to him?

It is upon us alone, says a chorus in Aristophanes, that the star of day shines, we who are initiates, and who exercise, to citizen and foreigner alike, every act of justice and piety.

Have they taught men the forgiveness of abuse? Yet the same books of the Jews, despite their horrible zelotypia, have precepts: Seek not vengeance, says Leviticus; if thou meet thine enemy's ox or his ass going astray, thou shalt surely bring it back to him again. Even should you have suffered injury, said Plato, you must not seek vengeance, because vengeance would be an injury, which must not be carried out. This word *revenge*, said Seneca, is not the word of a man, it is that of a wild beast. It is a beast and not a man, said Musonius, that seeks to bite back the one who bites. I would rather receive wrong from you than do you wrong, Phocion told the Athenians. All that I ask of the gods, said Aristides, about to leave Athens to go into exile, is that the Athenians never find that they are in need of Aristides.

Others have highly regarded the morality of these particular religions, and did not know that all that is good in this morality, the renunciation of oneself, the corruption of the flesh, the return of man to his essence, the contempt for earthly things, the victory over his passions, universal charity, are to be found in all nations; but this morality, especially in the Christian religion, brought to the point at which the disciples of Jesus developed it, produced all the errors, crimes, lies, and slander I have just described.

Your morality is now just the doctrine of Jesus. But Jesus, like those who had instructed him, wanted only a small number of disciples: he knew that the sublime and extraordinary things of men can only be enjoyed by a few; he had even given his disciples the precept: Cast not your pearls before swine, he told them, lest they not knowing their worth trample them underfoot and turn and tear you to pieces; but his disciples, longing to be leaders of a sect, wished to have disciples to promote their doctrine: and they wanted them outraged and furious, and they made them such. There is so much difference between some things and others recorded in the speeches of Jesus that it is impossible that the same person uttered them all. For example, Jesus begins his first important speech by saying: Blessed are the poor in spirit: he does not mean by this those who are lacking, nor fools, but those who embrace voluntary poverty and contempt for earthly things, because, he says, the reign of heaven is theirs, and in this was his prediction of the recreation of the Earth. Blessed are the meek, for they shall inherit the earth (that is to say, the earth that was to be recreated). Blessed are those who mourn, for they shall be comforted (in the recreation of all things). Blessed are those who hunger and thirst for righteousness, for they shall be satisfied (in the judgment that is to take place).

But they added: Blessed are those that suffer persecution for justice, because the kingdom of heaven is theirs. Note that the result here is like that of the first proposed Beatitude, and therefore must have been added; but here the maxim is exaggerated. A good man must bravely suffer persecution for righteousness, and never retreat; but why should he rejoice at this persecution? Whatever the reason for it, it is always an evil. It would be much better to be able to practice virtue without suffering persecution.

They also added: Rejoice and be glad when you are persecuted, when you are cursed, when calumnies are invented against you: only a madman can rejoice and be glad that one persecutes him, that one curses him, that one invents calumnies against him; but the leaders of Christianity needed such men.

Jesus had said that a good man would suffer contradictions, but he who perseveres to the end would be saved: this is true; with perseverance we overcome everything, even the difficult ascent up to the summit of the steep rock where the temple of virtue stands. They had him say that he had come to set fire to the earth, divide father from son, daughter from mother, daughter-in-law from mother-in-law, brothers from brothers; that he had come to bring the sword and war to earth and not peace; that if there were five people in a house, three would be divided against two, two against three; that fathers would deliver their children to death, that children would deliver their fathers; but they needed such men. O treachery! O deception! O abominable fanaticism which brought misfortune to the world!

As for the precept of not resisting evil, to offer your left cheek to receive a slap when you have received it on the right is a mad, foolish, preposterous, unjust precept that puts the weak at the mercy of the violent and the unjust, which submits good men to a low and unworthy servitude before an audacious bandit. It perverts every idea of morality and justice.

The dogmatic part follows this passionate demolition of Catholicism:

I will now speak to you of the religion that cannot be otherwise; I am undertaking a great task. How shall I make myself understood? This religion is quite sublime, very different from the religion of the Jews; it is celestial, and you have but terrestrial ideas. So, elevate your minds and hearts; think of spiritual ideas, and rid yourselves of the prejudices of education and childhood that ensnare you, whoever you are, and I speak even of the greatest philosophers of today.

The first lesson you must be given is to ask yourself who you are; and when you see that everything has a purpose, do you think you have come to earth without purpose? The sun is made for the moon, it shoots its rays on her, stimulating what light there is in her by them, and in this way she shines on us: the moon is made for the sun, she opens her womb to receive its rays and its influences which she pours down on us: all the stars are made for each other, all receive each other, and in a clash of movements that form a universal harmony, they maintain movement and life everywhere. When everything has a purpose in nature, is it not preposterous to think that man's place on Earth is without purpose?

Since evil is not the work of the Principle, it is not inherent in any being, and since we feel the enthusiasm of the good, our whole task on earth must be toward our regeneration, and if evil has distanced us from the Principle which cannot embrace it, our whole purpose has to be, through this regeneration, our union with our Principle: such is the whole religious task we are to fulfill on earth. I already said earlier how beasts, not allowing for evil, feel the effects of evil. There are other beings who feel the effects of evil; but for me to speak to you of this would require my speaking the language of the gods, which I cannot, and which you would not understand.

So, let us seek the means for this regeneration; they are universal and the same in all nations. The unanimous consent of all nations was clear evidence of truth for the greatest philosophers of antiquity; indeed, a general idea held by all men cannot be an error, or their Principle would have created them for the error, which cannot be assumed; from which it follows that the means of this regeneration, being universal and the same in all nations, was either taught to all nations by the Deity, or is a natural production of the human mind, and in either case compels all men to employ these means, and an individual who rejects this universal education, or this natural design, isolates themselves and digs out a precipice and an abyss of perdition.

It is not through the mind that we admitted evil; the mind is not mistaken as to the nature of evil, even in its greatest deviations, or when it tries to prove that evil is not evil so as to be able to engage in it; it is through the heart: so the first means of this regeneration must be through a virtue of the heart, which is piety. My opinion is that the Gods taught men the means of regeneration: my wretched century, which can only choose between this opinion and that which says these means of regeneration are a materialistic conception, will choose this latter opinion: it matters little to me for what I have to prove and propose. Piety is thus the first virtue that can regenerate us; but you must know to whom to address it; we must know the beings we are to address.

What language can I use now; how can I make myself heard; what convincing arguments can I use to destroy the effect of terrestrial ideas and the prejudices in which you have enveloped your particular religions that have emerged from these universal documents of the gods or from this natural conception? And yet, of these ineffable mysteries, I can only produce for you a part of what I know and what I see. Open the eyes of your hearts; clarify your understanding; may it be like a smooth surface that receives and retains the forms of what I am to tell you. Silence for a moment the voice of those prejudices of your childhood and your religions and realize there is nothing true except the general, and that there is no truth in the particular: that divinity who doubtless wanted men to regenerate themselves, to be reunited with it, had to have given all men the same means for this regeneration.

Since all beings that we know do not create their fate themselves, there must be a unique, universal being that holds the fates of all beings in his hands, and which is its Principle. I will not say this being had produced first, but produced eternally beings into which it can pour all its productions, or rather, the ideas of its productions. This being is Prothyræa of the hymns of Orpheus: O Venerable Mother and receptacle of all the ideas of things, who hold under your protection all begotten beings, because you were the first born; Great Goddess, ineffable mother; wife of the great god, who, by analogy, if there can be any, alleviates the labor of all women who give birth, hear me; look with favor upon my work; guide my quill, that I may speak things worthy of you; but how? At least things that do not contradict your nature would be enough; may I remain victorious in this work, and may the torch I carry to the people dispel the error in which they are plunged: the torch that the great Pallas has shown me; and may the palladium,[23] which she has dressed before me in her colors and with her helmet and spear, defend me against envy and against ignorance, and produce in my work fruits which are pleasing to you! But this being could not receive within her womb the productions of the Principle save by a certain order and a certain arrangement, and a force was necessary to produce them: Logos, the ineffable Verb; it is the goddess Pallas; in another aspect, Iacchus,[24] dismembered by the giants; it is the *νους*; it is the *mens*, the Primogenitor of the hymns of Orpheus; it is the force of nature and the production of all beings; and this order and this arrangement are the light that illuminates every man who comes into this world.

Qui crederam extersti caecis caliginem ocellis.[25]

This is the first link in the chain; all the others must be similar to it, apart from its position; the closer a link is to the first link, to this principle link, the more similar it is to it, and the nature of the first link is continued throughout the whole series of the chain, and a link acquires more of this first link's nature the closer or the more like it it is. From there arise all the gods and the different orders of spirits, intelligences that all nations, that the universal world honored before an individual took it into his head to cut the chain and propose that only the first link reduces to its ineffable expression. Who are you to deny this universal education? You who have been educated by men in error, one of whom told you that his religion was not celestial, that it was terrestrial, that it was at your feet, that it had its origin in the coarseness of his people.

Can we join diverse beings in nature without a means; the way the earth joins water through its frigidity, water to air through its humidity, air to fire through its heat, fire to the ether through its subtlety and tenuousness; the order of the elements can be no other way. The second link is similar to the first; the third to the second: so on to infinity; all creation resembles the producer. All that the producer produces is already in him in power and in idea. O the beautiful analogy between us miserable mortals and the producer of everything, this first link of the chain! So that we can join him without any intermediary! O beautiful physics that, when everything is full, when everything is filled with inhabitants, opens an immense desert between this first link of the chain and us! Could all survive with such a gap in the universe? O how unhappy you are! Constricted and constrained in your ideas! Broaden yourself, discard the swaddling clothes of your religions which are not celestial; rise up to it, see there an uncountable, infinite, ineffable host of beings, gods, intermediate spirits between you and the first link in the chain, who all have their lives, their activities, their occupations, their affections, their natures, their own manners of existing, all more or less distant from the universal center of all beings.

As I said, we find here in the center of beings, three hypostases, Being, the Word, and the Great Goddess, the great Prothyræa who receives, through the ideas transmitted to her by the Word, the seeds of all the others, these persons are different from the first link in the chain: so we do not attribute to them the being that is the incommunicable privilege of Being which exists by itself. So, in the hymns attributed to Orpheus, which contain this whole doctrine, according to Prothyræa and the Primogeniter we find Saturn and Rhea, then Jupiter and Juno, Janus and the Earth, and so on up to the last link in the chain of spiritual beings, which is the Man whose wife is drawn from his substance.

These hymns, says Pausanias, are the most religious and the holiest of all; they were used in the Mysteries, and they are even more than that, and you shall find there the whole doctrine I wish to show you. Jupiter is also sometimes taken, as you have seen, as the father of gods and men, because he then is the Sacred Quaternary[26] through whom everything exists and by which all of nature is in movement. Thus spoke the intelligent and invisible gods.

Your ideas are rather crude: you think these luminous globes which always keep their place in a fluid that cannot support them, who in opposition and in their various aspects always have regular motions, were placed above your heads to amuse your eyes and the astronomers with their calculations! There is in nature only the dead or the living; all that is dead is not alive, all that is alive is not dead. There is a universal ferment which is the spirit that joins the soul to the world: its action is constant, it changes everything; it is the great Proteus; it dissolves all dead beings and prepares them by dissolving them to be the place where new beings, in a way that you cannot even imagine now, rise from the great abyss of the night to become corporeal. If you know how to interpret Orpheus's Hymn to the Night, you will have one of the first points of this doctrine, you will know how everything takes form, you will see your eyes without a mirror, and shake the bull by the horns. This ferment no longer acts on living bodies because the *animus* that informs them, that maintains them, is stronger than the ferment which tends to dissolve them, being of a superior nature. If the ferment could take any action on beings, it would dispose them to receive a new *animus*, which, in the abyss of the night, would come to assume a bodily form, and in doing so, dissolve them. They must have something in them, then, that repels the attacks of the ferment, and is superior to that spirit; they must each have in them an *animus* that informs them, which maintains their shape and repels the action of the ferment; and in this manner they live. If the earth was not animated, the ferment would dissolve it as well, and would dispose it to receive new beings that would eat away at the harvests, would torment the primitive species, would damage them, destroy them, and they would no longer be a mere alteration; but would no longer resemble the archetypal ideas.

It is in the cadaver's nature to fall: this is the original etymology of the word; it is in the living being's nature to raise and support itself because it has the principle of its movement and its life. In this manner I support my arm, I raise my head: if stars were mere cadavers, they would fall, that is, they would collect in the same place according to the laws of gravity.

Now let us see if they are intelligent. There are in the universe only two kinds of beings; those who are left to themselves, and those who are inherent in another being: of the latter are plants, trees, minerals, which follow the fate of the soil to which they are attached; those left to themselves are animals, men, gods; they have a particular self they must preserve: to implement the means, to choose them, to keep them, they need a ratiocination; thus, stars have this ratiocination. Beasts are their own rule because they are directed only by instinct; man can neglect his rule, because he has his conduct and can choose his actions; stars always follow their rule through the excellence of their intelligence, because pure beings cannot deviate from it: there is nothing heterogeneous in them that can vary their actions; they are always all that they are, apart from their own thoughts they can conceive of bad ones; which does not happen, because they are in unity, because they read in the universality of beings; because they see in the Word all that is beautiful and all that is good; so that, even if it were possible that some of them deteriorated at a time we can barely imagine, they can no longer do so now since by habit they are of the beautiful and the good, according to the identity they have in some way with it: thus, the regularity of the motion of the stars among their opposing forces, their different aspects attest to the excellence of their intelligence; that they are in unity; that they see the beautiful and the good; that they are initiated into the causes of the destiny they create; in short, that they are gods.

This is what Orpheus expressed in two words in his indigitation to Ouranos:[27] *calice terrestris*, O celestial and earthly sky; and, in his indigitation to the stars: *cœlica terrestris gens*; and the hymn to all the Gods begins, *maje Jovi, tellus* . . . great Jupiter, and you, earth. Indeed, what do you see? You see in the sky the greatest objects of nature, and in the well-spoken words of Proclus, we also have a terrestrial sun and moon, according to their earthly natures; we have in the sky all the plants, all the stones, all the animals, but according to the celestial nature, and with intelligent life.

Doubtless the gods taught this doctrine to men; but I say that if they had not taught it to them, the latter would have been able to conceive it themselves. Seeing that the moon received its light from the sun, they would have been able to see how all beings had been created, and seeing these two principal means of creation were not alone in the sky, that there were a multitude of other beings similar to them, they could see that they were also means of creation; that all are divided in these ways according to the consciousness they had; *numina conscia veri*;[28] of the unity of the work they were to complete. If Mars poured over the earth everything scorching and fiery, he would burn everything; if Saturn poured everything cold, he would freeze everything. It is not their distance from the sun that gives stars their different qualities. Mars is more scorching and fierier than Mercury or Venus, which are closer to this burning center. Saturn is much closer to this home, to this heart of the world, than the sun burning with heat. But the temperature of these different influences, emitted with intelligence, forms a general influence, which the sky pours down on the earth. Thus, in the sensible world, the sky is the first agent of the gods; but if the earth emitted influences contrary to those it receives, nothing would happen in Nature; thus, the upper world continually creates the lower world; and the lower world is the reflection of the upper world, and it cannot be otherwise. All production must present the idea of its producer; every being gives what it has; and beings receive the influences of each star according to the receptivity proper to their natures. So gold, by its color, its splendor, its solidity, belongs to the sun; silver, by its gentle color, its less brilliant splendor, its softness and ductility, belongs to the moon; thus, the first two metals in beauty belong to the two lamps of this world. Because, as Ptolemy correctly said, in the presence of other brighter celestial bodies, these two stars would nevertheless, through their influence and by their beauty, be the two lamps of the earth. It is in this manner that the plant named the heliotrope by its figure, by its disk composed of four sides, from which globules emanate, from which five-pointed flowers emerge, which all express the different generations of fire and emanations of light; which by the diverse tints of its golden color, by the tips of its corolla, which blaze from its disk, or in twisted pyramids, forms known to be those of fire, by its heart-shaped leaves, and by the ability of this plant to turn toward its star in such a way that its stalk is often bent, by its numbers four and five, which are the numbers of all generations in the diverse worlds, makes itself known to be solar; and this plant is the terrestrial sun on earth; it is the same for many other trees and plants.

Today we doubtless must, to support such reasoning, always consider the era in which these ideas were established. At the time when Quintus Aucler was writing, there was a clean sweep of religion, and attacking Christianity had become commonplace; this is only a historical introduction to the thesis he wants to support. For Aucler, there are two kinds of religions: those organizing civilization and progress and those that, born of hatred, of cruelty, or of the selfishness of a race, for a fairly long time disrupt the constant and beneficial efforts of others.—It is Typhon, it is Ahriman, it is Shiva,[29] it is all the cursed and titanic spirits that inspire these religions of nothingness: Whom do you worship? he asked the believers in the unitarian sects.[30] You worship Death! Where are the regular civilizations? . . . Among all the polytheistic peoples: India, China, Egypt, Greece, and Rome. Monotheistic peoples are barbaric and destructive; they have the power to destroy, but cannot establish anything durable for themselves . . . What became of the Hebrews? Dispersed. What became of the empire of Constantine when he converted? . . . What did the Turks, conquerors of half the world, found? And what happened to the large feudal edifice! Ruins everywhere. And if civilization began to radiate in Europe in the fifteenth century, it is because the faith in monotheism was almost nonexistent. Do you want proof? Compare the believers in Spain and Italy to heretical Germany and England, and to indifferent France.

III. The Months

Quintus Aucler's paradox concludes as such:

> French people and Belgians, Gallic and Celtic races, you have finally rid yourselves of the cult to which the barbarians adhered; however, all people need a positive religion. What were you before the apostasy of Clovis? You belonged to this great Roman Empire of which you are the branches and which had come to spread among you the civilization and the illumination of thought and the arts, which had given you communal organization and made you citizens of the great Roman unity. Your language, your education, and your manners still give evidence of it even today: therefore, free from the obstacle henceforth, you must think of regenerating yourself to be worthy of reminding your provinces of the favor of the twelve great Gods. This eternal chain that binds our world to the foot of Jupiter is not broken, but your eyes are obscured by the clouds of ignorance. The Gods remain enthroned in their glittering stars, they preside over your destiny and have made fatal what they will bless, when your prayers have reestablished the accord between the heavens and the earth. First address the Gods, as did Codrus and Decius, using the formula of devotion.[31] Poets have written the sacred hymn:
>
> *Cui dabit partes scelus expiandi*
> *Jupiter? Tandem venias precamur*
> *Nube candentes humeros amictus*
> *Augur Apollo.* [32]*

* Whom will Jupiter assign to
purge our sins? We pray you,
come, clouds veiling your bright shoulders,
far-sighted Apollo.

Apollo forgives your having misunderstood his spiritual light, for it has not ceased to pour on your soil its beneficent rays . . . But what will you do to disarm the Star-Gods whom you see only at night, and whose influences preside over your destinies as well as the development and health of the animals and plants useful to you? How appease Mars, a violent and terrible god, "marked with the seal of double reason, *insane and furious*, as expressed in the invocation of Orpheus[33]—by which all species devour each other?" It is Mars who dominates the first month of the sacred year. Like Janus, he has the key to the temple of peace and war that opens one door and closes the other . . . and you see clearly that it is he who reigns at this moment.

Fortunately, your calendar has already made a place for him;—but what will you do for the great Vesta, a deity no less terrible, yet better; the beginning and principle of things, who produces and animates everything, always pure, ever chaste, mingling with earthly things without incurring their filth, presiding over doors and hallways of homes, protecting household gods and the guardian spirits of families?

It is in this month, dedicated to Mars and Vesta, that we must renew the laurels of the flamens and address a new invocation to Mars so that he does not impair the fertility of women. Then we think of Saturn, whose happy reign once followed that of Mars and Janus, and who will bless you more than at the *Saturnalia* on seeing the return of true and genuine equality.

Then, and only on the eve of Nones,[34] will you make the sacrifice to Vesta. Then comes the festival of Liber,[35] which teaches men worship and the laws: to him libations and first fruits. It is under his auspices that your children will don the vesture. Two days after the eleventh day of the Kalends comes the festival for Minerva, to whom all the arts owe their homage. Then the *Hilaria*, celebrations of joy dedicated to the Great Mother of the gods; after that the days grow longer than the nights, and the sky gives to the earth the signal for this feast.

April is dedicated to Venus, but it is still the Mother of the gods who presides over the festivities celebrated on the day before the Nones. One walks among the pageantry of its procession, amid dances formed by the Curetes and the Corybantes,[36] accompanied by flutes, cymbals, and drums.—It is on the day of the Kalends that we sacrifice to Venus, who is invoked under the name of *Verticordia*, so that she diverts our minds from illegitimate loves: "Beautiful Urania, rule out of our hearts the earthly loves that burn and consume without animating!" The month ends with celebrations to Ceres and through the *Floralies* which will crown the sweet month of Floréal.[37]

The Kalends in May are dedicated to the Lares.[38] It is then that women will celebrate at home the holidays of the good goddess, from which all males are excluded, even animals; even their portraits are covered. Every man must leave his home, even the great pontiff. The next day the Lares are honored at crossroads; the heads of poppies are offered to them, as well as to their mother Amanie. Their holidays are followed by the Lemurales, which last three nights.[39] The happy shades are invoked, and beans thrown at others—beans whose flower expresses the gates of hell—repeating nine times: "With these beans I redeem my soul." Souls like the number nine, which is that of generation, because they always hope to return to the world.*

Then come the Argei and the Agonales.[40] This month is dedicated to *Corybante*, genius of the earth.

Then comes the month dedicated to Mercury. Sacrifices are made to Mars and the goddess Carna[41] who presides over the vital parts of the body. Beans and bacon are consumed. On the third of the Ides, the arrival of the Matralia,[42] or the festivals of Leucothea, goddess of the sea—special mysteries for women, who celebrate them in secret. The fifth, the vestalies,[43] is the day of purification. Families dine together and a portion of the food is sent to the temple of Vesta.

The month of Jupiter comes next. On the day of the Nones, women sacrifice to Juno under wild fig trees in the name of fertility.

The month of Ceres brings sacrifices to Hercules and Diana. For the latter, ladies emerge in white robes with lighted torches and make processions in the woods.

* The number 9 is a particularly productive and mystical number; multiply it by itself, you will always obtain 9: for example (1 + 8 = 9), 3 × 9 = 27 (2 + 7 = 9), 4 × 9 = 36 (3 + 6 = 9); 5 × 9 = 45; and so on. The number 9 is the number of matter.

The seventh month is dedicated to Vulcan. It is on the Ides of this month that the First Consul must plant a sacred nail in the temple of Minerva.

Other months present fewer obligatory feasts. Sacrifices are made to furious Mars; a horse is sacrificed to him, then the wells and the fountains are crowned with flowers. Next comes the month of Diana, conqueror of the giants. On the Ides, the *Lectisternium* is celebrated,[44] the day Jupiter invites the gods and heroes to his table . . . ("Whom of us," Quintus Aucler here exclaims, "will be worthy of a seat at this table?")

The tenth month belongs to Vesta; it contains the holidays of the Faunae, the Agonales, and then the Saturnalia, which lasts for seven days. On the day of the sigillarias[45] friends send lighted wax candles.

The eleventh month, dedicated to Janus, witnesses the festival of *Carmentales*,[46] holidays on which people pray for the health of children, and which can only be celebrated by chaste women. ("With what expression on their face," cries Quintus Aucler, "would adulterers and the debauched dare, on this day, appear at the temples of the gods and pray for illegitimate children!")

The last month, which corresponds in part to February, is dedicated to Neptune. On the fifteenth of the Kalends, the *Lupercalia* are celebrated, dedicated to Pan. This is when young people spread out through the city and whip women with straps drawn from the skin of sacrificial victims, to make them fertile. *The Terminales* conclude the year. The borders of the fields are visited, and neighbors call upon Hermes to attest to their good intelligence.

We see that in the pagan year, whose restoration Quintus Aucler proposed, holidays were not lacking. To these obligatory *feria* he added others; he spoke of *conceptives*, the *points* of which had to vary depending on how early the seasons were. Such were the *Ambarvalia*, the *Amburbiales*, the *great Lustre*,[47] which returns only every five years as a general purification festival at which one prepares for the celebration of the Dionysia—the holiday Semailles, the Paganales,[48] the birth of Iacchus, the delivery of the births of Minerva, as well as the celebrations of the solstice and the equinox.

Families also needed their holidays. Everyone, on the anniversary of their birth, had to sacrifice a pig to his genius. The poor could make do with offering wine and flowers. There were also sacrifices at the end of the year for the souls of dead relatives and the Manes, then the novembdiales when believed themselves to be threatened by some misfortune, and the lectisternes during which one is reconciled with one's enemies.[49] Fasting days were to be held the day before the great solemnities and throughout the month corresponding to February. With the Ides of November came the holiday of the dead. This is the day when the Manes spread over the earth.—On that day, *the world is open*; shades emerge to judge the actions of the living and see to the memory we kept of them.

In examining this entire system of pagan restoration, we won't be surprised to see it overlapping with the major Church holidays, which, in principle, were adapted in many ways from the Roman calendar.

The observation of fasting and abstinence from certain foods are of great concern to the new hierophant. He launches an attack against the unholy who eat the meat of solipeds, birds of prey, and carnivorous animals.—To eat horse meat seemed to him an abomination for which no excuse was possible: "Libertines, through bravado," he said, "glory in their vice for eating cat *flesh*, and the people sometimes go so far as to put a raven into their soup ... From these excesses result a deplorable stupor and the most atrocious crimes. Thus, people should avoid eating solipeds, ungulates, and polysulcates ..." But the hierophants and true initiates must do even more to prepare for contemplation. They will not use the pig, though it be bisulcate and completely defenseless, nor fish without fins or scales: "Certainly there is no sight more hideous than a bestial soul aged inside the body of a pig;—as for the aforementioned fish, they are deprived of the *shield of Mars*, and share this with man who has neither natural weapon or clothing."—With plants, it is good to abstain from beans, which are devoted to the dead.

"It has always been so," adds Quintus Aucler, "in our family, whose origin dates back to the *hierophantic* race." He does not doubt the purity of his Roman genealogy, whose offspring have survived the centuries without mixing with profane families, because the gods in their designs watch over him since he is to renew a worship so long oppressed. He takes advantage of this digression to praise his wife for her fidelity to the observances of worship, and even his son, who must one day transmit to the world the repository of knowledge entrusted to his ancestors from the time before the Gallo-Roman civilization gave in to the weapons of Clovis.

It is at this moment that we begin to understand the existence of this hierophantic family, preserved throughout the centuries. "The secrets of Astrology," says Quintus Aucler, "are the same as those of religion; thus, the gods who preside over the months of the year also correspond to the signs of the zodiac. The Celtic gods, translated from the language of our Gallic ancestors, in reality happen to be the same as those of the Roman calendar. The week is composed from it: *Moontag* (Monday) is the day of the moon; *Tues-Tag* (Tuesday) is the day of Mars; *Wednes-Tag*, the day of Mercury; *Theuus-Tag*, the day of Jupiter; *Frey-Tag*, the day of Venus; *Saders-Tag*, that of Saturn, and *Sun-Tag* is the day of the Sun.—This in Indian language, specific to the primitive Celtic tribes that emigrated from the high plateaus of Asia, translates as: *Tinguel*, *Ghervai*, *Boudda*, *Viagam*, *Velli*, *Sani*, and *Nair*,[50] each referring to the corresponding gods."

It is therefore a religion as old as the world that the apostasy of Clovis came to overthrow for a miserable fifteen centuries.—"And again," he exclaims, "if only the barbarians had understood that the new god they imposed by the sword was none other than *Chris-na*, the Indian Bacchus—that is to say, the third Bacchus of the Mysteries of Eleusis, called Iacchus, to distinguish him from Dionysius and from Zagreus, his brothers! But they could not recognize in their god the favorite of Ceres, Ιησοῦς[51] crowned with vine leaves—and regardless of the symbol, they have only preserved the rite of consecration with bread and wine; all ignorant—barbarians, like the Fathers of the Church, those other barbarians, whose naïve works have been redone by pledged sophists!"

It is from this perspective that Quintus Aucler advises Neopagans to have some tolerance for the special believers of Iacchus-Iesus, better known in France under the name of Christ. Imbued with the principles of Rome, he closed his pantheon to no god. Indeed, according to him, it is not because it was Christian that the former Church had been persecuted, but because it was intolerant and dismissive of other religions as sacriligious.

IV. The Rites

We may well wonder today as to the retrospective novelty of these ideas, but such a book certainly had to appear in the course of the old revolution. Moreover, we should perhaps be grateful to Quintus Aucler for having, at a time when materialism dominated, brought minds back to a religious feeling, and also to those special practices of worship that he considered necessary to combat evil instincts or soften the ignorant coarseness of certain natures.

The fasts, vigils, abstinence from certain foods, the customs of the family and the generative acts, subject to instructions for which paganism was no less provident than the Bible, were certainly not anything to please the skeptics and atheists of the time, and some courage was needed to propose the restoration of these practices.

As for the choice of pagan religion, it was dictated by the situation; the civic festivals, the private ceremonies, the worship of goddesses, though allegorical, as in the last days of Rome, were by no means unaffected by the assimilation of a mystical doctrine, which was after all a revival of the purified doctrine of the Neoplatonists. It was simply a question of reconnecting the eighteenth century to the fifth century and reminding the good Parisians of the fanaticism of their fathers for that Emperor Julian, whom they accompanied to the center of Asia. "You have conquered me, Nazarene!" cried Julian, struck by the Parthian arrow.[52] And Paris would have again proclaimed, in the restored Palace of Julian and in the Pantheon that borders it, the cyclical return of those Fates that rendered victory to the divine emperor.—The Sibylline verses had foretold a thousand times those evolutionary developments, from the *redeunt Saturnia regna*[53] to the last Delphic oracle, which, observing the millennial reign of Iacchus-Iesus, announced to later centuries the victorious return of Apollo.

The Roman reform of the calendar, the numeration, the political ideas, the costumes, did all this mean something else? And had this new aspiration to the gods, after a thousand-year interruption of their worship, not begun to appear in the fifteenth century, or even earlier, under the name of the Renaissance, art, science, and philosophy having been renewed by the inspired breath of the exiles of Byzantium? The *mystical palladium*,[54] which had hitherto protected the city of Constantine, was about to break, and already the new seed brought the imprisoned spirits of the old world out of the earth. Did the Medici, welcoming the philosophers accused of Platonism by the Inquisition in Rome, not make Florence a new Alexandria?

The movement already extended to Europe, sowing in Germany the seeds of pantheism through the transitions of the Reformation; England, in turn, stood apart from the pope, and in France, where heresy triumphs less than indifference and impiety, there is a whole school of scholars, artists, and poets who, with their eyes, as with their mind, revive the splendor of the Olympians in every form.—It had perhaps been a joyful caprice that those poets of the *Pléiade* sacrificed a goat to Bacchus,[55] but are they not going to transmit their soul and their intimate thoughts to the Epicureans of the great century, the Spinozists and Gassendists,[56] who will also have their poets, until one sees above all those layers impregnated by the old spirit, the *Encyclopédie* fully armed, completing in less than a century the demolition of the political and religious Middle Ages?

And even in education, as in the books available to these new generations, did mythology not occupy more space than the Gospel? In his thinking, Quintus Aucler thus only complements and regulates an irresistible movement. This is how we can explain a thought that now seems to touch on madness, and which can only be fully grasped in its entirety through the meticulous deductions of a Book that commands respect because of the honesty of its intentions and the sincerity of its beliefs; it is like a final treatise on the Platonic apologies of Porphyry or Plotinus, lost through the centuries—which, at the time when it resurfaced, was unable to meet the last father of the Church to answer him from the womb of the abandoned ruins of the Christian edifice.

Nor should we think that the doctrine of Quintus Aucler was the isolated demonstration of an exalted spirit who sought his faith in the dark. Those who were then called the Theosophists were not far from a similar formula.[57]—The Martinists, the Philalèthes, the Illuminati, and many others affiliated with Masonic societies professed a similar philosophy, whose definitions and practices varied only by their names.[58] Aucler's Neopaganism can thus be regarded as an expression of the pantheistic idea that developed through the progress of the natural sciences.—The old believers in alchemy, astrology, and other occult sciences of the Middle Ages had left their mark on the societies of that time, whose many adepts were strengthened in their beliefs by the astounding developments that Mesmer, Lavater, Saint-Germain, and Cagliostro had just announced to the world with varying degrees of sincerity.—Paracelsus, Cardan, Bacon, Agrippa, those old masters of the cabalistic and spagyric sciences,[59] were still fervently studied.

If we had believed in the influence of the planets—indicated by the names and attributes of the ancient gods, even during the reign of Christianity—it would be natural that, in the absence of a positive religion, we should return to their worship. Aucler thus devotes many pages to the description of the material power of the stars. He is no less afraid of furious Mars than of cold Saturn. Mercury worries him sometimes. Venus does not have a very good influence on the globe since her altars are neglected . . . As for Jupiter, he is too great to remember outrages. It is enough to devote to him the plants and stones that belong to him: the oak and poplar, the lily and henbane, the hyacinth and beryl. Saturn likes lead and the magnet, and among herbs, the asphodel. Venus the violet, verbena, and polithricon;[60] her metal is copper; her animals are the hare, the pigeon, and the sparrow.—As for Apollo, he always had, as we know, a special influence on the cock, the heliotrope, and gold.—Everything thus follows; there is nothing in the three kingdoms of nature[61] that escapes the influence of the gods;—libations, sacrifices, and consecrations therefore consist of elements analogous to the influence of each divinity.

The divinities enthroned in the stars not only act on the diverse series of creation, they also preside over destinies through the conjunctions of their stars, which influence the fate of men and nations.—It would take too long to follow the author in his explanation of the triplicities and the thousand-year cycles that undermine the great revolutions of empires. This Platonic doctrine has long been known, in any case.

Several philosophers of that period followed Quintus Aucler in this renovation of the ideas of the school of Alexandria. It was around this same time that Dupont de Nemours published his *Philosophy of the Universe*, based on the same elements of adoration for the planetary intelligences.

He establishes in the same manner between man and God a chain of immortal spirits he calls *Optimates*, with which every *illuminé* can communicate. It is still the doctrine of the *Ammonean Gods*, the *Eons*, or the *Elohims* of antiquity.[62] Man, beast, and plant have an immortal *monad*, animating relatively perfected bodies according to an ascending and descending scale, which materializes or deifies beings according to their merits. Haller, Bonnet, Leibnitz, and Lavater had preceded the author in these vague hypotheses.[63] They seemed, moreover, so natural that Dupont de Nemours, president of the Council of Ancients, sometimes spoke of them to the Assembly, or made them the subject of sessions at the Institute.

The book by Senancourt,[64] who subsequently took refuge in the skepticism of Lucretius, contained just such a system, which he carefully removed from later editions.

We have only Devisme left to name among those deserving of some attention.[65] His ideas are much closer to Christianity and almost completely reproduce the doctrine of Swedenborg, which is preserved in France by his followers; they form a small church at the head of which Casimir Broussais was seen for a time.[66]

Quintus Aucler's private school still survived in the year 1821, if we are to believe a work entitled *Doctrine Céleste*, by one named Lenain,[67] who seems to have obscurely continued the worship of the gods in the city of Amiens.

As for the Hierophant himself, he published his only book, entitled *The Thracian*, a title he had borrowed from the nickname given by Virgil to Orpheus: *Threicius vates*.[68] It is, in fact, the doctrine of the Thracian mysteries that Quintus Aucler offers to initiates. This Theosophist was born in Argenton (Indre); he died in Bourges in 1814, repenting of his errors, if one is to believe the very weak verses of a pamphlet entitled *L'Ascendant de la religion, ou récit des crimes et fureurs d'un grand coupable*, which he published in 1813.[69]

Thus concludes the life of the last pagan. He renounced those gods who, doubtless, had not brought the awaited consolation to his deathbed.— The Nazarene still triumphed over his resuscitated enemies after thirteen centuries. *The Thracian* is nonetheless a curious appendix to the *Misopogon* of the Emperor Julian.[70]

IMAGE SOURCES

1 Line drawing of old leather-bound books taken from *Historic Byways and Highways of Old England* (1900) by William Andrews.

5 Engraving of Henry II by Emanuel van Meteren (1535–1612) and Simeon Ruytinck (d. 1621).

23 Detail of frontispiece to *L'Histoire du sieur abbé-comte de Bucquoy, singulièrement son évasion du For-l'Évêque et de la Bastille* by Madame du Noyer (Anne Marguerite Petit) (Paris: R. Pincebourde, 1866).

65 Portrait of Nicolas-Edme Restif de la Bretonne by Louis Berthet, after Louis Binet (1785).

185 Portrait of Jacques Cazotte by an anonymous artist.

229 Portrait of Guiseppe Balsamo Cagliostro by Christophe Guérin, 1781.

245 *Maximilien de Robespierre on the Day of the Festival of the Supreme Being* by Étienne Antoine Eugène Ronjat (circa nineteenth century).

TRANSLATOR'S NOTES

MY UNCLE'S LIBRARY

1. Charles de Marguetel de Saint-Denis, seigneur de Saint-Évremond (1613–1703), was a French soldier, hedonist, essayist, and literary critic. After 1661, he lived in exile, mainly in England, following his attack on French policy at the time of the Peace of the Pyrenees (1659). He did not intend his work to be published but the first full collection of his writings was published after his death in London in 1705. He is buried in Poets' Corner, Westminster.
2. The reference here is to the French Revolution of 1789.
3. "Deism" rejects religious knowledge as a source of authority and concludes that reason and observation of the natural world suffice to determine the existence of a Creator of the universe. Unlike pure deism, a "moderate deism," close to Socinianism (a doctrine that denies the Trinity as being contrary to the simplicity of God's unity), does not completely deny the divine character of Christ but makes him a mediator sent by God rather than the second person of the Catholic Trinity.

THE KING OF BICÊTRE

1. Raoul Spifame (1487–1563) was indeed an actual person: a scholar of the occult and a barrister. He eventually went mad after various legal problems dealing with his relatives and a fateful encounter with King Henry II.
2. The historical Raul Spifame in fact had four brothers.
3. Henry II (1519–1559) was a monarch of the House of Valois who ruled as the King of France from 1547 until his death in 1559. He was crowned at Reims on 26 July 1547; the Parliament of Paris returned on 22 November, but there is no evidence that the king was present.
4. According to Arab tradition, to see one's double is to see one's own death.
5. Raoul Spifame is known to have had three daughters from his first marriage with Marie Parent.
6. Noel Brulart, Baron de Crosne (1486–1557), was the Attorney General of the King, in the Parliament of Paris under Francis I and Henry II, from 1541 to 1557.
7. Pierre Lizet (1482–1554) was chief justice of the Parliament of Paris from 1529 to 1550.

His opposition to the Cardinal of Lorraine led to his dismissal. François de Saint-André (?–1571) held the position of chief justice of the Parliament of Paris in 1554 and presided over the passionate chamber established against the Reformists. He then retired to the country, weary of civil dissensions. Antoine Minard, seigneur of La Tour-Grollier (1505–1559), and chief justice of the Parliament of Paris, was the principal adviser to Mary Stuart. Intensely opposed to the Reformation, he was assassinated by the Calvinists. Jacques-Remi Dahan, editor of the critical edition of *Les Illuminés* published by Classiques Garnier (*Œuvres completes*, Tome IX: *Les Illuminés*, Paris, 2015) notes that though Lizet, an ignorant and fanatical man, was the only one who was certainly dismissed, all three were unpleasant figures.

8. An allusion to the hero of Cervantes's *Don Quixote*.

9. Mellin de Saint-Gelais (1491–1558) was a poet and the son of the bishop of Angoulême, Octavian de Saint-Gelais. He was master and guard of the library of Fontainebleau under Francis I and Henry II and nicknamed the French Ovid.

10. The *Sophonisbe* was Mellin de Saint-Gelais's translation of the *Sofonisba* of Gian Giorgio Trissino (1478–1550). Saint-Gelais's popularity was overshadowed by the appearance of Joachim du Bellay's *Défense et illustration de la langue française*, a book in which du Bellay defends the French language and asserts its equal dignity with Latin and Greek. It was an important book for the Pléiade, a group of sixteenth-century French poets, which included Ronsard and du Bellay.

    The *Franciade* is an unfinished epic poem about the history of France by Pierre de Ronsard (1524–1585). He began writing the poem in the 1540s for Henry II, but it was not published until 1572, for Charles IX.

11. The quote is from Seneca's *Hercules furens*: "fluctuque magis mobile vulgus" (the common people are more changeable than the tide).

12. Charles VI (1368–1422) was the Fourth King of France from the House of Valois, and ruled from 1380 to 1422. He suffered from an intermittent madness from 1392 on, entrusting the actual power to his uncles, Louis II of Bourbon, Louis I of Anjou, Jean I of Berry, and Philip II of Burgundy, known as "the Bold."

13. Mary of Scotland (Mary Stuart) married, on 24 April 1558, the Dauphin, François de France, who in 1559 became King Francis II. It was through the Porte Saint-Denis that the kings of France made their solemn entry into Paris; the tradition continued until 1814 during the time of Louis XVII.

14. Maréchal François de Bassompierre, familiar with the court of Henry IV, was born in 1579; neither his father, Christophe de Bassompierre (~1550–1596), nor his grandfather, François de Bassompierre (?–~1543), was physically able to figure in 1558 in the entourage of Henry II.

15. This is pure fantasy on the part of Nerval.

HISTORY OF THE ABBÉ DE BUCQUOY

1. Prince Eugene of Savoy (1663–1736) was one of the greatest generals in the service of the Habsburg emperors. A hero in the fight against the Turks, he brilliantly led a campaign against the French during the War of the Spanish Succession.

2. "Marlbrough s'en va-t-en guerre" (Marlborough has gone to war) is a popular folk song in French. This lament wrongly suggests that John Churchill, Duke of Marlborough (1650–1722), died at the Battle of Malplaquet (11 September 1709), the bloodiest battle of the War of the Spanish Succession. It tells how Marlborough's wife, while waiting for him to return from battle, is given the news that her husband has died. It also tells that he was buried and that a nightingale sang over his grave.

3. The lines are from Boileau: *Louis, les animant du feu de son courage, / Se plaint de sa grandeur qui l'attache au ravage* ("Louis, animating them with the fire of his courage, / Complains of his grandeur that binds him to the shore). In the poem, Boileau is speaking of Louis IV's famous crossing of the Rhine in 1688.

4. The *Fronde* was a series of civil wars in France between 1648 and 1653 during the Franco-Spanish War, which had begun in 1635. The king ultimately overcame the combined opposition of the princes, the nobility, the law courts, and most of the French people.

5. From the *Fables* of Fontaine: "Le bon homme disait: ce sont là jeux de Prince" (The good man said: Such are the games of princes).

6. Michel Chamillart (1652–1721), Controller General of Finance in 1699, was also Minister and Secretary of State for the War of Louis XIV from 1701. Chamillart caused the financial crisis of 1708–1709 by attempting to introduce a kind of paper money, with disastrous results because of the state of credit. Thus, it can be said that his brilliant ascension proceeded from the royal favor more than from his mediocre skills.

7. On 13 August 1704, at the Second Battle of Höchstädt (Höchstädt an der Donau, Bavaria), Prince Eugene and the Duke of Marlborough defeated the French and the Bavarians in the War of the Spanish Succession.

8. Jean-Albert d'Archambaud (1650–1740), known as the abbé du Bucquoy, was an adventurer who had been falsely accused of crimes on the basis of circumstantial evidence. He was constantly imprisoned throughout France, but each time he miraculously escaped. He roamed through France when he was not in prison and adopted many philosophical and ideological ideas during his travels. He even belonged to a Trappist order for a short time. Eventually, he founded a seminary in Rouen that he called "The Dead."

9. After reviewing the conjectures, often fanciful, on the origin of this nickname, the bibliographer Gabriel Peignot, in his book *Les Bourguignons salés* (Dijon: V. Lagier, 1835), concluded that, far from being insulting, "this phrase was only given to the inhabitants of Burgundy in the Middle Ages because of the salt mines that enriched part of their territory."

10. Jeanne-Marie Bouvier de la Motte, Madame Guyon (1648–1717): this quietist mystic counted among her proselytes Madame de Maintenon, the dukes and duchesses of Chevreuse and Beauvilliers, and Fénelon, and was the object of the latter's quarrel with Bossuet.

11. François Michel Le Tellier, Marquis de Louvois (1641–1691), was the French Secretary of State for War during a significant part of Louis XIV's reign. Louvois bore much of responsibility for the destruction of the Palatinate (1688); during the War of the Grand Alliance (1689–1697), the troops of the French monarch Louis XIV ravaged the Rhenish Palatinate, causing many Germans to emigrate.

12. Antoine de Guiscard (1658–1711), known as the abbé de la Bourlie, or the abbé de Bonnecombe, fought to unite the Catholic and Protestant oppositions under the absolute rule of a monarchy and caused many troubles in Rouergue and the Cévennes region

between 1703 and 1706. Having failed to launch a rebellion against the French Crown, he took to wandering around Europe, offering his services to any foreign court that was hostile to France.

13. A presidial court was one that ruled as a last resort in certain cases and for certain sums of money.

14. The circumstance, which he explains in his first interrogation by d'Argenson (22 June 1707), had nothing to do with love: attacked by "scoundrels" while hunting around Strasbourg, Bucquoy owed his salvation to his flight; he also failed to drown while swimming across the Rhine. This misadventure made him promise "to examine the truth of religion in order to be more convinced about it than he was."

15. For-l'Évêque was the name of a prison in Paris that was in operation from 1674 to 1780. It was demolished at the beginning of the nineteenth century.

16. It has been suggested that these "little caps" are small bags that can be sewn into the lining of the clothes to hide secret documents.

17. The normal entrance for prisoners was on rue Saint-Germain-l'Auxerrois.

18. The word "misery" refers to the flooding of the Seine in January 1496.

19. The liaison of Mme de Sévigné's son, the young marquis Charles de Sévigné (1648–1713), with Ninon Lenclos, then about fifty years old, aroused the disapproval of the famous epistolary: see in particular the letter of 1 April 1671 to Madame de Grignon. The legend of the gallant adventures of Ninon de Lenclos, in her old age, with the abbé Gedoyn or the abbé Chateauneuf was discredited by Voltaire, however.

20. Dating back to 1690, the Café Laurent, on rue Dauphine, was in the eighteenth century an important place for the literary life, frequented by Fontonelle, Montesquieu, Houdar La Motte, J.-B. Rousseau, Voltaire, and others. Note that rue Dauphine, at the mouth of the Pont-Neuf on the left bank of the Seine, cannot be placed on the Île Saint-Louis.

21. One of the forms of the libertine current, the "cabal" is the name for a secret society which, from 1615, was a gathering of poets and free thinkers like Maynard, Boisrobert, Tristan L'Hermite, Saint-Amant, and Theophile de Viau. It was dispersed by the arrest and trial of Theophile de Viau in 1629: at the point in time considered here, the "cabal" had not existed for nearly a century.

22. Charles-Auguste de La Fare (1644–1712) was an officer and a minor poet. He was Chaulieu's friend. Guillaume Amfrye de Chaulieu (~1639–1720) was an ecclesiastic and an epicurean poet, protected by the great prior Philip de Vendome and the prince of Conde, and nicknamed the "Anacreon of the Temple."

23. Jacques-Louis de Beringhen (1651–1723), Count of Chateauneuf and Plessis-Bettrand and first squire to the king, was kidnapped on 7 March 1707 between Sèvres and Passy by a party of dragoons in the service of Holland and led by the colonel of Guethen, who thought he was seizing the person of the dauphin; well treated by his captors, Beringhen was delivered to Ham, in Picardy, by the garrison of the fort, without a shot being fired. Saint-Simon and Voltaire recount in detail this incredible affair, in which Bucquoy took no part, but whose consequences would impact him.

24. Pierre Laporte, known as Roland (1680–1704), was a famous French prophet and captain of the Camisards, a group of French Protestants (Huguenots) from the Cévennes region of France. At the time of the events reported here, he had been dead for almost three years.

Jean Cavalier (1681–1740) was the son of Protestants who abjured the revocation of the Edict of Nantes but raised him in the horror of "papism." Originally a baker's apprentice, he was, among the warlords of Camisards, the undisputed master of the countryside. After his brilliant military success, judging the cause of the rebels lost, he negotiated with the maréchal de Villars on 19 May 1704; later, he reached Switzerland, then England, where he was entrusted with the command of a regiment of refugees, and died at Chelsea on 17 May 1740.

25. Marc-Rene de Voyer de Paulmy, first marquis d'Argenson (1652–1721), was the lieutenant general of the Paris police (1697–1718), Minister of State, and member of the Academie francaise (1718). He interrogated Bucquoy on 22 June 1707.

26. Charles le Fournier of Bernaville (~1644–1718) left the lieutenance of the dungeon of Vincennes on 18 October 1706 to carry out the same duties at the Bastille, then became governor of this fortress on 26 September 1708 at the death of Bénigne Dauvergne de Saint-Mars. Bernaville was not a lackey but a valet de chambre and the secretary of the maréchal de Bellefonds (1630–1694); the testimony of the prisoners of the Bastille is unanimous regarding his greed and his ferocity.

27. In the Apocalypse of the Bible, this sentence "bearing the word Mystery" is inscribed on the forehead of the Whore of Babylon.

28. A violently blasphemous image that equates Christ with the Great Beast, scarlet in color, full of names and blasphemies, and who had seven heads and ten horns, and rides on top of the Great Prostitute, the Whore of Babylon.

29. Guillaume de Formanoir, known as Corbé (1649–1740), was one of the three nephews and heirs of Bénigne Dauvergne de Saint-Mars. First a sublieutenant in a company of purveyors of munitions, he joined his uncle in the Bastille when he became governor (1698), as the lieutenant of a company in charge of the custody of prisoners.

Bénigne Dauvergne de Saint-Mars (1626–1708) was the officer of a company of musketeers, and successively the governor of several state prisons: Pignerol (1665–1681), Exilles (1681–1687), Sainte-Marquerite (1687–1698), and finally the Bastille (1698–1708). He had under his care Fouquet (Pignerol, 1665–1680), Lauzun (Pignerol, 1671–1680), and the mysterious Masque de fer (Iron Mask) (Pignerol in 1669, and in the Bastille where he died in 1703).

30. This was the Protestant writer, René-Auguste-Constantin de Renneville (1677–1732), who entered the Bastille on 16 May 1702 and was released on 16 June 1713. Charged with secret missions in foreign countries, Renneville was accused of betraying France to the Dutch. Nerval borrows a lot of information on the Bastille from the work of Renneville, *L'Inquisition françoise ou l'histoire de la Bastille* (1715–1719).

31. The mandille is a kind of vest or coat, which lackeys once wore. It was peculiar to lackeys and distinguished them from the other valets.

32. Madeleine Fouquet de Chalain (1639–1716), who married Bernardin Gigault de Bellefonds in 1655, gave him nine children, and survived him for more than twenty years.

33. Jean-Baptiste Colbert de Torcy (1665–1746) was the nephew of the great Colbert, Secretary of State for Foreign Affairs in 1696, and Minister of State in 1700.

34. In the game of piquet, this is the name given to the player who scores thirty points without his opponent marking one.

35. The College of Clermont of the society of Jesus.

36. The College of Louis the Great.

37. Marguerite Louise de Béthune (1642–1726), widow of the Count de Guiche, had married for the second time in 1681 Henry de Daillon (~1622–1685), marquis d'Illiers and since 1675 duke du Lude, peer of France and grand master of the artillery of France, himself a widower of Éléonore de Bouille. In 1697, the duchess du Lude, widowed for the second time, was chosen to exercise the prestigious function of the lady-in-waiting for Marie-Adélaïde de Savoie, Duchess of Burgundy, wife (at eleven years old) of the grandson of the king.

38. The terror of monsters.

39. A forcemeat made with veal, beef kidney suet, and eggs.

40. Jean-Baptiste de L'Ormeau, Sieur de Falourdet, a Norman gentleman accused of making false titles of nobility, was transferred from Vincennes to the Bastille on 11 September 1702. According to the nineteenth-century historian Frantz Funck-Brentano, he was sentenced on 16 September 1702 to five years imprisonment by the royal chamber of the Arsenal and only left the Bastille on 28 September to be taken to the galleys; nevertheless, if we are to believe Nougaret and the eighteenth-century historian, F. de Fossa, he was declared innocent and released. Be that as it may, Bucquoy could not have met him.

41. The principal complaint against the Poitevin Jacob le Berthon, son of a doctor, was his belonging to the reformed church which adopted reformed confessions; his arrest at Versailles was in fact a consequence of a tavern scene in which he and other soldiers indeed sang "saucy songs," and one in particular "in which Madame de Maintenon was not spared."

42. Antoine de Bourbon (1518–1572) was king of Navarre from 1555 to 1562.

43. René-August-Constantin de Renneville (1677–1732) writes: "This priest who sometimes calls himself Sicilian, sometimes Neapolitan, is called the abbé Papasaredo. He is the most corrupt of all men, the most dissolute, uses the filthiest words, the most mischievous, the most hideous, the sloppiest dressed, the sloppiest in his character, and with the sloppiest way of eating that I have even seen" (*L'Inquisition françoise ou l'histoire de la Bastille* [Amsterdam: Chez Étienne Roger, 1715], 406–407, my translation). This figure, otherwise known as Antoine (Antonio?) Papasodero (~1670–?), was a priest of the diocese of Squillace in Calabria, entered the Bastille on 4 November 1702, for sorcery and the suspicious correspondence with a foreigner. He was released on 20 November 1714 and was exiled from France.

44. A lady by the name of Fleury was detained in the Bastille from 1685 to 1704: she left three years before the arrival of Bucquoy. The names of the other three women (Marton, Bondy, Dubois) are not found for the relevant periods, either on the registers of the Bastille, or even on those of Vincennes.

45. Marie Anne Mancini (1649–1714) was the youngest of the Mancini sisters, nieces of Mazarin. She became through marriage in 1662 Duchess of Bouillon, and in 1680 she was involved in the Affair of the Poisons (a major scandal in Europe from 1677 to 1682 involving murder and charges of practicing witchcraft and poisoning) and suspected of wanting to poison her husband. Although she had not been properly detained in the Bastille (Mazarin had spared her a sentence), she was exiled from the court for fifteen months.

The Academy of Humorists (Accademia degli Umoristi) was a society of intellectuals; it came before the Académie-Française and was instituted in Rome in 1603 by Paolo Mancini (?–1635), grandfather of Mary Anne.

The imprisonment of Mme Guyon was lengthier than Nerval suggests; after being imprisoned in a dungeon at Vincennes from December 1695 to October 1696, she entered the Bastille on 4 June 1698 and was released on 24 March 1703, with orders to go to her son's domain near Blois.

The Barnabite monk François de La Combe (~1640–1715) was Mme Guyon's spiritual director and entered the Bastille on 29 November 1687; he was then transferred to the Île d'Oléron on 29 February 1688. Detained at Vincennes from 16 April to 30 September 1698, he was incarcerated again on 9 December 1698 at Vincennes, where he was to die. La Combe, who spent very little time in the Bastille, did not live there, according to Renneville, at the same time as the abbé Bucqouy.

46. Hugues Aubriot (~1320–1382), was the provost of Paris under Charles V from 1367 to 1381 and laid the foundation stone of the Bastille on 22 April 1370. After the death of the king in 1380, he arrested a number of people who were harassing the Jews in Paris. As a result, such trumped-up charges as heresy, sodomy, and extortion were brought against him, and he was sentenced to life in prison. He was liberated on 1 March 1382 by the popular riot of the "Maillotins" (a group of insurgents who led a riot in Paris in 1382 against King Charles VI's imposition of a new tax on trade) and returned to his native Burgundy, where he died shortly after.

47. Pierre Joyeux, known as Frolich (*sic* for Fröhlich), was a native of Cologne, son of a captain in the Fürstenberg regiment, and a pilot and gunner aboard a Dutch ship; he entered the Bastille on 7 April 1707, accused of attempting to flee and espionage; he was released 20 November 1714, and was banished from France.

48. Nicolas Fouquet (1615–1680) was, from 1653 to 1661, the last holder of the office of superintendent of finances.

49. Jean-Baptiste Colbert (1619–1711) was General Controller of Finance from 1665 to 1683, and Secretary of State of the House of the King and Secretary of State of the Navy from 1669 to 1683.

50. Claude Le Peletier (1613–1711) was the General Controller of finance after the death of Colbert (1683); he held this position until 1689.

51. Louis Phélypeaux de Pontchartrain (1643–1727) was General Controller of Finance (1689), Secretary of State of the Navy (1690), and Secretary of State of the King's House, and Chancellor of France from 1699 to 1714.

52. The Capuchin Father, Henry Florent of Brandenburg, known as Brandenburg (~1663–?), was originally from the region of Liège (Spanish Netherlands) and entered the Bastille on 9 September 1702 on suspicion of spying for profit: this adventurer, who flattered himself that he had received the favors of the Queen Dowager of Spain, left the Bastille on 9 June 1713 and was transferred to the fortress of Lille.

53. Charles le Lorrain, also known as Champre, Du Preuil, and the Count of Soulange (~1678–?), was the former captain of the infantry for the regiment of Orleanais; he entered the Bastille on 21 October 1705, accused of espionage; he was released on 28 November 1714 and banished to the city of Metz. Having violated this injunction, he was imprisoned a second time in the Bastille on 14 May 1716 and transferred on 22 May to the Conciergerie prison to await his judgment; he was ultimately sent to the gallows.

54. Samuel or Germain Gringalet, known as Dupré (~1669–?), was originally from the region of Gex rather than Geneva; he entered the Bastille on 29 November 1702 for espionage for the benefit of Holland and England; he was released on 9 June 1713.

55. "Odricot" refers to the Irishman Cornelius O'Driscol, who entered the Bastille on

25 September 1701; he was accused of seizing a merchant vessel after throwing the crew into the sea. Reported as an accomplice of his compatriots Guillaume Burck and Marc Linch, he was transferred on 22 September 1711 to the Charenton asylum.

56. The "O'Driscol woman" entered the Bastille on 25 September 1701 and was released on 3 September 1703. Renneville assures us that the lady "Odricot" was pregnant twice with the children of both the abbé Giraut and Corbé, without it being known in the case of the first child who the father was; as a result, Corbé wanted to give her another child so as to be sure of being the father (*L'Inquisition françoise ou l'histoire de la Bastille*, lxiii–lxiv).

57. Paul Cardel, Sieur Du Noyer (~1655–1694), was a native of Rouen; he entered the Bastille on 2 March and was transferred the following 18 April to Sainte-Marguerite prison where he died 23 May 1694. Nerval seems to confuse the two namesakes: Paul Cardel, who was a good pastor but only passed through the Bastille (and so Bucquoy could not have known him); and another Protestant, Jean Cardel (~1635–1715), who was a cloth merchant from Tours, was kidnapped in 1685 between Frankfurt and Manheim by a detachment of French troops, accused of a conspiracy against the the king, and first detained at Vincennes, then transferred to the Bastille on 4 August 1690; he died suddenly on 13 June 1715.

58. René Jordan de Launay (1673–1749) was the governor of the Bastille from 1719 to his death. He was the father of the unfortunate Bernard-Rene Jordan de Launay (1740–1789), who was born in the Bastille, and who succeeded Antoine-Joseph de Jumilhac in 1776 as governor of the Bastille; he was killed by the rioters on 14 July 1789.

59. Louis Francois Armand of Vignerot du Plessis (1696–1788), Duke of Fronsac since his birth and then Duke of Richelieu (1715), was the great-nephew of the cardinal, godson of Louis XIV and the Duchess of Burgundy. At the age of fifteen he was imprisoned in the Bastille, on 20 May 1711, at the request of his father, when he still held only the title of Duke of Fronsac, and he was released on 19 June 1712. The reason, Jean-Louis Cara writes in his book, *Mémoires historiques et authentiques sur la Bastille* (Paris, 1789), "for his imprisonment in 1711 was his having slept with a great Princess, mother of a great Prince. He had been caught by de Cavoi, who told this to Madame de Maintenon. At this surprise, M. de Richelieu had jumped out of bed, completely naked, and had hidden himself under it. It was M. his father who brought him to the Bastille." The duke was such a notorious womanizer, it is said Choderlos de Laclos had based the character Valmont in *Les Liaisons dangereuses* on him.

Marie Adélaïde of Savoy (1685–1712) was the duchess of Burgundy through her marriage with the grandson of Louis XIV in 1697. The lover of feasts and pleasures, this endearing princess influenced the king and Madame de Maintenon. She died along with her husband during a measles epidemic in 1712.

60. Louis de France, Duke of Burgundy (1682–1712), was the grandson of Louis XIV, son of the "Grand Dauphin," and father of the future king, Louis XV. Fénelon was his tutor and composed for him his *Fables* and *Adventures of Telemachus* (1699). Whatever may be implied by Nerval, the military laurels of the Duke of Burgundy were scarce, because he showed little skill in the war and suffered a setback during the campaign of Flanders from 1708 to 1709.

61. Anthonie Heinsius (1640–1720) was a Dutch statesman who served as the grand pensionary of Holland (prime minister of the states of Holland) from 1689 to 1720 and was a fierce opponent of France and its king. Like all advanced minds open to science and modernity, Heinsius is supposed to have belonged to the community of the *philosophes*, and was known to have studied philosophy, from 1658 onward, at the prestigious University of Leiden.

62. In the Hebrew Bible, Gehenna was initially the place where some of the kings of Judah sacrificed their children by fire; therefore, it was deemed a wicked place, and the word is sometimes translated as "hell."

63. "To the immortal one" or "to the creation of a royal god."

64. "M. de Cambray" was the nickname of Fénelon, who was removed from the court through his appointment to the archbishopric of Cambrai (1695) and then fell into disgrace after the secret publication of the *Adventures of Telemachus* (1699).

65. The "mother of the Regent" is the princess palatine Charlotte-Elisabeth de Bavaria (1652–1722), who was the second wife of Philippe I, Duke of Orléans, younger brother of Louis XIV.

66. Quintus Curce (in Latin Quintus Curtius Rufus) was a Roman historian who probably lived during the first century CE. He wrote a history of Alexander the Great.

67. In 1700, King Karl II of Sweden won a brilliant victory over the Russian army that besieged the city of Narva (Estonia). The word "Nerva" is the one adopted by many editions of Voltaire's *History of Charles XII*; however, Jacques-Remi Dahan notes that the possibility that the deliberate choice of this form of the word would come back to Nerval cannot be ruled out, since it was intended, according to the testimony of the nineteenth-century historian, Alexander Weill, to refer to the descendant of the Roman emperor Nerva (30–98), to whom Nerval refers to in the fantastic genealogy that he used to justify the choice of his name (Dahan, *Les Illuminés*, 118).

68. In the Greek tradition, Sleep (Hypnos) and Death (Thanatos) are twin brothers, children of the Night (Nyx); however, we sometimes encounter Death as the daughter of Night and Sleep.

69. The translation of the title is *The main incidents of a journey of sixteen years in India* and it is the work of the Dutch hydrographer and cartographer, Jacob de Bucquoy, who worked from 1720 for the Dutch East India Company, and had recorded from 1735 many of his adventures, which he included in his book; he traveled between the Cape of Good Hope and Goa, Madagascar, and the African and Malabar coastlines; then returned home to the Netherlands, where he taught geography.

THE CONFIDENCES OF NICOLAS

1. This hotel, known as the Ambassadeurs de Holland, is in the Marais district, 47 rue Vielle-du-Temple.

2. Victoire Melone Geayant, known as Mlle Guéant (1733–1758), started as a child actress on the stage of the Theatre-Français and made her debut on 25 September 1749 as Junie in Racine's *Britannicus* and Julie in Fagan de Lugny's *La Pupille*. *La Pupille* was a one-act comedy in prose with music by Jean-Joseph Mourer; it premiered on 18 February 1734 at the Théâtre de la rue des Fossés Saint-Germain.

   Les Dehors Trompeurs was a five-act comedy in verse by Louis de Boissy that premiered on 18 February 1740 at the Théâtre de la rue des Fossés Saint-Germain.

3. The meeting point of the streets Mazarine, Bussy (today Buci), Fossés Saint-Germain des Prés, Saint-Andre des Arts, and Dauphine, the crossroads of Bussy was considered a dangerous neighborhood.

4. The Procope café was opened in 1689 by the Sicilian Francesco Procopio dei Coltelli on

la rue des Fossés Saint-Germain des Prés. In the eighteenth century it was an important literary place, frequented by Voltaire, Jean-Baptiste Rousseau, Piron, and Diderot.

5. In the eighteenth century, magistrates and men of the law were sometimes called gentleman of the robe.

6. Literally, "small house." But here a *petit maison* signifies a kind of brothel, a place where nobles or the well-respected bourgeoise relaxed and held parties in which actresses would take part.

7. In other words, if the play was about deception rather than innocence.

8. Publius Helvius Pertinax (126–193 CE), son of a freedman, and close collaborator of Marcus Aurelius, was brought to power by the Senate on 1 January 193 after the assassination of Commodus and was himself murdered on 28 March. This fantastic genealogy is based solely on the semantic equivalence of the Latin adjective *pertinax* ("opinionated, obstinate, stubborn") and the Restif surname.

9. Adélaïde Louise Pauline Hus, known as Mlle Hus (1734–1805), was admitted to the Members of the Theater-Français on 21 May 1753 after performing the role of Hermione in *Andromache*. More beautiful than talented, she retired in 1780 to devote herself to charitable works.

Marie Allard, known as Mlle Allard (1742–1802), began at the Theater-Français as a dancer on 22 July 1756, in an entertainment provided after the comedy *Le Muet* (David Augustin de Brueys and Jean Palaprat, 1691).

Madeleine Sophie Arnould, known as Mlle Arnould (1740–1802), was a famous opera singer and woman of wit and learning, and reigning mistress of the Count of Lauraguais to whom she gave four children. She debuted at the Académie Royale de Musique on 15 December 1757 and was admitted in the following year; she retired in 1778.

Les Fêtes de Paphos was a heroic ballet in three parts: *Vénus et Adonis*, by Collet de Messine; *Bacchus and Érigone*, by Le Clerc de Bruere; and *L'Amour et Psyché*, by Voisenon; all with music by Mondonville. It premiered on 9 May 1758 at the Palais-Royal Theater.

Marie Rose Claude Josephe Levasseur, known as Mlle Rosalie (1749–1826), was an opera singer.

Marie-Madeleine Guimard, known as Mlle Guimard (1743–1816), was a dancer in the opera.

Marie Anne de Cupis de Camargo (1710–1770), sometimes known simply as La Camargo, was a French dancer. The first woman to execute the *entrechat quatre*, she was also allegedly responsible for an innovation in ballet, as she was one of the first dancers to wear slippers instead of heeled shoes.

10. Marie Justine Benoîte Duroncery (1727–1772) was an actress, singer, and woman of letters. She was the wife of Charles-Simon Favart (1710–1792). She started at the Opéra-Comique in 1745 in *Les fêtes publiques* under the name of Miss Chantilly. Respected for her private life as well as for her varied talent, she introduced to the stage a simplicity in terms of costume, which Talma, an actor who was influential in imposing changes to the theater, especially in terms of costumes, established as definitive.

11. "Tristes apprêts, pales flambeaux" [Mournful apparitions, pale flames] is a song sung by Télaire in Rameau's *Castor et Pollux*, act 1, scene 3, a role in which Sophie Arnould garnered great success.

Serva padrona, intermezzo per musica (1733), by Giovanni Battista Pergolèse (Giovanni Battista Pergolesi, 1710–1736), was a great triumph. A performance at the

Royal Academy of Music, on 1 August 1752, triggered the famous "Querelle des Bouffons" [Quarrel of the Comic Actors], a controversy over the relative merits of French and Italian opera.

The ballet-pantomime, *Médée et Jason*, is an interlude in the operatic tragedy by La Borde and Laujon, *Isméne et Isménias ou la fête de Jupiter*, which premiered on 13 June 1763 at the castle of Choisy before the king and the queen and reprised its performance at the Royal Academy of Music on 11 December 1770.

In scene XIV of *La Pupille*, Julie dictates to Ariste, whom she secretly loves and is loved by in return, a letter intended for the marquis, where she expresses her desire for her improvised secretary. When a lackey steals the letter, the lovers are both mortified at not having been able to better express their feelings for each other.

12. Jean-Baptiste Willart of Grécourt (1684–1743) was a libertine poet.

Pierre Honoré Robbé de Beauveset (~1712–1794) was a cynical and licentious poet, mentioned by Diderot in *Rameau's nephew*.

13. Alexis Piron (1689–1773) was a poet, playwright, and man of wit and learning. Nerval slightly glosses over Restif's reference to the famous *Ode to Priapus*, a youthful work by Piron, whose triumphal obscenity attached itself to the author throughout his life, although it was not very representative of the brilliant eloquence of this rival of Voltaire.

14. The Mocenigo family was a Venetian family whose members included doges, statesmen, and soldiers.

15. Emperor Caracalla (188–217 CE), born Lucius Septimius Bassianus, was the son and successor to Septimius Severus, and reigned from 211 to 217 CE.

Didia Clara Juliana was the daughter and only child of the Roman emperor Didius Julianus and empress Manlia Scantilla. She was reputedly one of the most beautiful women in Rome, but virtually nothing is known about her life or her personality. In her younger years, she married a paternal cousin; but in 193 CE she married Sextus Cornelius Repentinus, who served as prefect of Rome.

16. Antoine François Prévost (1697–1763) was a man of the Church, a translator and novelist, and author of the *Histoire du chevalier Des Grieux et de Manon Lescaut* (1733).

François-Thomas-Marie of Baculard d'Arnaud (1718–1805) was a poet, novelist, playwright, and the author of, among other works, the *Épreuves du sentiment* (1775–1778, 5 volumes) and *Délassemens de l'homme sensible* (1783–1787, 12 volumes).

Claude-Prosper Jolyot de Crébillon, known as "Crébillon fils," was the author of such fairy tales and novels as *Le Sylphe* (1730), *Le dialogue des morts* (1745), and *La Nuit et le Moment* (1755).

17. The Council of Ten was, from 1310 to 1797, one of the major governing bodies of the Republic of Venice. Despite its romantic reputation, exploited by Byron in *Marino Faliero* (1820), later adapted by Casimir Delavigne (1829), the Council of Ten was probably not responsible for the premature death of the cavalier Mocenigo; however, the Council of Ten had previously sentenced Mocenigo to seven years in the fortress of Brescia for wanting to leave Venice without having received official authorization.

18. Cicero, galliard, and roman are the names of fonts. Cicero corresponds to a 12-point font, galliard to a 9-point font, and Petit-roman to a 10-point font.

19. *Les Contemporaines, ou Aventures des plus jolies femmes de l'âge présent recueillies* [Contemporary women, or the collected adventures of the most beautiful women of the present age] (1780–1784).

Les Nuits de Paris, ou le Spectateur nocturne [Nights of Paris or The Nocturnal

Spectator] (1788, 1789, 1794). There is an abridged English translation by Nicholas Deakin and another by Linda Asher and Ellen Fertig.

20. Les Halles is a central market in Paris. The phrase Nerval uses is "Jean-Jacques des halles." Although the nickname "Rousseau of the gutter [ruisseau]" was confirmed by the journalist and art critic Friedrich Melchior Grimm, in the notice on the writer Michel de Cubières-Palmézeaux, the equivalent nickname to "Jean Jacques des halles" is mentioned in 1811: "He was called, during his lifetime, 'the Voltaire for chambermaids and seamstresses,' and the 'Rousseau des Halles' and these names, very honorable in my opinion, will never be taken from him" (*Histoire des compagnes de Maria, ou Épisodes de la vie d'une jolie femme: ouvrage posthume de Restif de la Bretonne* [Paris: Guillaume, 1811], Book I, 191).

21. Peter the Justicer was the nickname of the kings Peter I of Portugal (1320–1367) and Peter I of Castile (1334–1360). The first took for a mistress, and then secretly married, Inès de Castro (1320–1355), the "dead queen," assassinated by the king's advisers. Houdar de La Motte popularized the legend in his tragedy *Inès de Castro* (1723). Nerval uses the word *Justicier*, which I have translated as Justicer, i.e., a kind of Robin Hood figure, a righter of wrongs.

22. *Philosophie de M. Nicolas, par l'auteur du Coeur humain dévoilé* [The philosophy of M. Nicolas by the author of *The Human Heart Laid Bare*] (1796, 3 volumes). These three volumes contain his *Physics*, the first part of his *Philosophy*.

23. Anthropography is the study of the physical characteristics of human groups; gynography is defined as radiography of the female genital organs for medical examination.

In his essay "Restif de la Bretonne's State Brothel: Sperm, Sovereignty, and Debt in the Eighteenth-Century Utopian Construction of Europe," Paul B. Preciado writes, "In Restif's essay, *pornograph* refers not to a writer or consumer of representations of sexual, antireligious, or antimonarchic pamphlets but rather to an expert in legal and medical techniques of public hygiene within the modern city. For Restif, pornography is the branch of urban planning and hygiene dealing with the management of prostitution within the modern city and the preservation and maximization of the nation's health. The *pornographer* was for Restif not only a spectator but also a new agent of technical urban management dedicated to map places of prostitution and to make political propositions to improve urban health and pleasure" (https://www.documenta14.de/en/south/45_restif_de_la_bretonne_s_state_brothel_sperm_sovereignty_and_debt_in_the_eighteenth_century_utopian_construction_of_europe).

The following treatises of reformation are arranged by Restif in a general framework entitled *Idées singulières* [Singular ideas]: volume 1: *Le Pornographe* [1769, The pornographer], volume 2: *Le Mimographe ou le Théâtre Réformé* [The mimographer or the reformed theater], volume 3: *Le Gynographe* [1777, The gynographer], volume 4: *L'Anthropographe* [1782, The anthropographer], volume 5: *Le Thesmographe* [1789, The thesmographer].

24. *Phalanstery* is a term created by Charles Fourier, combining the words "phalanx" and "monastery"; it refers to both a group of people living together in a community, free of external regulations and holding property in common, and the building designed for such a community.

25. The wave of killings in Paris and other cities, known as the September Massacres, took place in 1792, from the 2nd to the 4th of September, during the French Revolution. There existed at the time a real fear that the royalist armies would attack Paris and that inmates would be freed from prison in order to join them in the attack.

26. The book Nerval is referring to is Restif's memoirs, *Monsieur Nicolas; ou le Cœur-humain dévoilé. Publie par lui-même. Avec figures* [Monsieur Nicolas; or the Human Heart Laid Bare. Self-published. With figures] (1794–1797). The abridged English translation is by Robert Baldick.

27. The chevalier de Faublas is the hero of the cycle of novels by Jean-Baptiste Louvet de Couvray (1760–1797) that began in 1787 with *Les Amours du chevalier de Faublas* and concluded, in 1790, with *La Fin des amours du chevalier de Faublas.*

The Viscount of Valmont is the cynical and manipulative hero of the epistolary novel, *Dangerous Liasons*, by Choderlos de Laclos.

28. Pierre Restif (1665–1713), of Nitry, is portrayed in Restif's *La Vie de mon père* [My father's life] as a strong personality, who was considered charming on the outside but quite tyrannical in his family.

29. A perennial, hardy herbaceous plant, formerly grown as a vegetable because of its edible roots.

30. The reference to Solomon, absent from the text of Restif, is specific to Nerval: in chapter 27 of the Koran, the hoopoe, a bird of legend, is the messenger sent by Solomon to the Queen of Sheba.

31. Abbé Thomas (1720–1786) was the son of Edme Restif and Marie Dondaine. After his departure from Bicêtre, he was employed by his elder brother to run a school for boys in Courgis. It was not him, but Edme Nicolas, who was the godfather of their half-brother Nicolas.

32. Pierre Nicole (1625–1695) was a distinguished French Jansenist. *Essais de morale* was his most well-known work and consisted of a series of short discussions on practical Christianity. The first volume was published in 1671; other volumes followed, eventually amounting to fourteen volumes.

François de Pâris (1690–1727) was a French Catholic deacon and theologian, and a supporter of Jansenism. He was deacon of the Oratory of St. Magloire and gave his earnings to the poor. In his retirement he lived in a state of extreme poverty. After his death, his place of burial gained a reputation for supernatural events.

Maurice Tissart, deacon of the Oratory of Saint-Jose, and close friend of the deacon of Pâris, died in the odor of sanctity (a specific scent that emanates from saints) on 28 December 1745; he had taught catechism at Bicetre and Saint-Jose.

33. François Annat (1590–1670) was a Jesuit theologian. Nicolas Caussin (1583–1651) was a Jesuit preacher, and confessor of Louis XIII.

34. Jacques Bonne Gigault de Bellefonds (1698–1746), Bishop of Bayonne (1735), then Archbishop of Arles (1741), took possession of the Archbishop of Paris on 2 June 1746 and died on 20 July, at the age of forty-eight, which left him little time to protect the "Jansenists of Bicêtre," assuming he had wished to do so.

Christophe de Beaumont du Repaire (1703–1781), Bishop of Bayonne (1741) and Archbishop of Vienne (1744), took possession of the Archbishop of Paris on 20 November 1746. Private tutor to the dauphin and great chaplain to the dauphin's wife, this fierce opponent of the Jansenists and the *philosophes* took out a mandate, in August 1762, against *Émile or On Education*, to which Rousseau replied on 18 November with his famous *Letter to Christophe de Beaumont.*

35. Pasquier Quesnel (1634–1719), Jansenist theologian and polemicist. His first important publication, *Réflexions morales sur chaque verset, pour en rendre la lecture plus utile, et la méditation plus aisée* (1692, 5 volumes), in which the Jansenist doctrine is exposed in the commentary of the Gospel text, was the subject of a severe papal condemnation in the bull *Unigenitus* (1733).

36. One of the canonical hours, i.e., 12 noon.

37. *Sic.* Previously, Nerval wrote that she was three years older than Restif.

38. The bagnolet is a type of headdress worn by peasant women.

39. The Cordeliers Club, also known as the Society of the Friends of the Rights of Man and of the Citizen, was a populist club during the French Revolution.

40. Marie-Catherine-Hortense Desjardins, Lady of Villedieu (~1640–1683), was a poetess, playwright, and successful novelist. Her relatively short novels display her interest in love, psychological analysis, moral dilemmas, and social constraints.

41. Theocritus mentions this item in his lament for Adonis: "Love's girdle perished with you." The girdle of Venus is a belt with magic powers of magnetism and enchantment, with which she is said to have seduced Mars.

42. In traditional typography, the *space* is a block of lead of variable thickness, intended to be placed between the characters or the words of a line. The *em* is a block of cubic lead often placed at the beginning of paragraph to mark the paragraphs.

43. A Roman comedy by Terence (~190–~159 BCE). Pamphilus, a citizen of Athens, raped Glycerium, a girl from the island of Andros. When she becomes pregnant, Pamphilus, although betrothed to a daughter of Chremes, makes an oath to Glycerium to marry her. Through a reversal, the situation is solved when one discovers that Glycerium is herself the daughter of Chremes. Here the rapist decides to repair the damage of his act through marriage.

44. *Zaïre* is a five-act tragedy in verse by Voltaire. It premiered on 13 August 1732 at the Comédie-Française in Paris.

45. *La Pucelle, or The Maid of Orleans* is Voltaire's satirical poem about Joan of Arc, a complete version of which was eventually published in 1899 even though Voltaire had started writing the text in 1730. As a result of a large amount of negative criticism of the poem for its sexual undertones and supposedly perverted nature, Voltaire grew ashamed of the work, even going so far as to say that the transcript had been somehow corrupted and that it was therefore inauthentic. He published an edited edition of the text over thirty years later, omitting many sections that had been criticized.

46. The quote is from the *Satyricon* of Petronius, book XXXIV.

47. *The Cid* is a five-act French tragicomedy written by Pierre Corneille (1606–1684). It was first performed in December 1636 at the Théâtre du Marais in Paris and published the same year. The following exchange between Restif and Mme Parangon alludes to the plot: Don Rodrigue (The Cid) is in love with Chimène, daughter of one of the kings of Castile's most accomplished warriors. After Rodrigo distinguishes himself in his fight against the Moors, the Moors dub him The Cid, which is Arabic for Lord. Chimène becomes estranged from Don Rodrigue after he kills her father in a duel.

48. A novel by Anne-Louise Morin-Dumesnil, dame Élie de Beaumont (1729–1783). This novel, according to Girault de Saint-Fargeau (1799–1855), a French man of letters, is one of "the small number of those that can be safely placed in the hands of young ladies" (Saint-Fargeau, *Revue des romans* [Paris: Firmin Didot frères, 1839], Book 1, 220, my translation).

49. *La Femme infidèle par Maribert-Courteney* [The unfaithful woman by Maribert-Courtney (Restif de la Bretonne)] (1786). Agnès Lebègue (1738–1808), born in Auxerre, was the daughter of René Lebègue and Agnès Couillard.

50. *La Femme infidèle par Maribert-Courtenay* bears, in the list that Restif made of his works, the number XXVII: therefore, it is not at all one of "his first novels."

51. "Why are you laughing! . . . The story is about you." The quote is from Horace's *Satires.*

52. A square wig was a type of wig worn by judges in the eighteenth century. The Marteau loops refer to a style of the weave and number of curls.

53. Louise Honorine Crozat du Châtel, Duchess of Choiseul (1737–1801), married the future duke and prime minister of Louis XV in 1750, to whom she remained faithful in her disgrace: he was a fickle seducer who deceived her publicly.

54. Buffon was interested in human feet only in the case of Chinese and Japanese women, and the custom of "making the feet of women so small that they can hardly support each other" (Buffon, *Natural History: General and Particular*, ed. and trans. William Smellie [London: T. Cadell and W. Davies; R. C. and J. Rivington; et al., 1812], 320). Nerval's assertion would seem to refer to Georges Cuvier, the father of comparative anatomy, known since 1804 for his ability to deduce the species and the appearance of a fossil animal from a found bone.

55. The game, played with fifty-two cards, would come to be known as "Faro" by the time it spread to the United States in the nineteenth century.

56. The "Baroness of Lansquenet" is a professional cardplayer: lansquenet is a gambling game of German origin that involves betting on cards turned up by the dealer; the word "baron" (accomplice) is, in this context, synonymous with rogue or cheater.

57. Barbe Ferlet died in Sacy on 6 July 1771 at the age of sixty-eight.

58. The last members of the French branch of the House of Courtenay were Roger de Courtenay (1647–1733), abbé de Saint-Pierre d'Auxerre (1659) and abbé des Eschalis (1669), and his niece Hélène de Courtenay (1689–1768), who married Louis Bénigne de Bauffremont (1685–1755). The extinction of the family's paternal line was noted in 1723 by Saint-Simon, who held that "the old prince of Courtenay" Louis-Charles (1640–1723) was the last of his name, although the princely title had been carried after him by his brother Roger and his daughter Hélène.

59. A collateral branch of the House of Courtenay is said to have come from Robert de Courtney and was established in England in the thirteenth century.

60. Besants are heraldic pieces in the form of a solid disc made of metal. A disc of any color is called a torteau. The Courtenay coat of arms, dating from the start of the age of heraldry, display three gold torteaux. In any case, there is no justification for three to five symbolic representations on the Courtenay coat of arms.

61. Jeanne Louise Armande Elizabeth Sophie Septimanie de Vignerot du Plessis (1740–1773). In 1756 she married Casimir de Pignatelli, Count of Egmont (1727–1801). She was the hostess of a famous salon, which included Voltaire and Rousseau among its guests. Although he belonged to the high nobility of Europe, Casimir de Pignatelli could not be related to the House of Courtenay. It is true, however, that no male heir is known to him, since he had three daughters from his first marriage to Blanche Alphonsine de Saint-Séverin d'Aragon (1736–1753), and his second and third unions remained sterile. According to

Restif, without his new "Septimania," the "foreign prince" would have turned away with horror from his last wife, and from his wedding, after he discovered the incestuous proposal made to the very young wife by her own brother. Restif, who dedicated to him *Lucile, ou le Progrès de la vertu* (1768), commemorated there his brief adventure on 26 May 1756 with the supposed Countess of Egmont, from which would be born Septimanette.

62. *Mérope*: a tragedy in five acts by Voltaire.

Alcyone: a lyric tragedy by Houdar de La Motte (1672–1731), with music by Marin Marais. It premiered on 18 February 1706 at the Théâtre du Palais-Royal.

La Bohémienne: a two-act comedy in verse, mixed with ariettes, adapted by Charles-Simon Favart (1710–1792) from Rinaldo di Capua's *La Zingara*.

La Gouvernante: a five-act comedy in verse by Nivelle de La Chaussée. It premiered on 18 January 1747 at the Théâtre de la rue des Fossés Saint-Germain.

Arlequin Sauvage: a three-act comedy in prose by Louis-François Delisle de La Drevetière. It premiered on 5 January 1746 at the Théâtre de l'Hôtel de Bourgogne.

Coraline: Anna Maria Veronese (1730–1782), actress, daughter of comedian and playwright Carlo Antonio Veronese (1702–1762), who wrote, from 1744 on, for the Comédia-Italienne many plays inspired by the *commedia dell'arte* in which Anna Maria played the part of Coraline (Columbine, Harlequin's mistress), under whose name she became known. She debuted at the Comédie-Italienne in 1744 and retired in 1759; she was the mistress of Prince Louis François II of Bourbon-Conti (1734–1814), with whom she had two sons.

63. The French chemist, Nicolas Lémery (1645–1715), in his *A Course of Chymistry* (1675), wrote: "place it in a glass bottle, cap it exactly, and keep it for use as needed; it is the anti-epileptic Elixir called drops of England. It is fit for epilepsy, for apoplexy, for delirium, and other diseases of the brain" (*A Course of Chymistry* [London: A. Bell, 1720], 509).

64. *Fille du monde* (girl of the world) signifies a prostitute.

65. In other words, depraved novels: like Crébillon the Younger, the novelist and playwright Claude-Henri de Fusée de Voisenon (1708–1775), who was a friend of Voltaire and a member of the French Academy, is well known for his licentious tales such as *Zulmis et Zelmaide* (1745) or *Sultan Misapouf et Princess Grisemine* (1746).

66. *Grisette* referred to a French working-class woman from the late seventeenth century; the word remained in common use well into the nineteenth and early twentieth century.

67. The reference, from Restif's *Monsieur Nicolas*, is to Mme Amey, a ruined noble, and her two daughters, who were lacemakers.

68. A *brunette* was a seventeenth- and eighteenth-century type of French popular song with or without accompaniment, with idyllic, pastoral, or amorous subjects.

69. Jean-Baptiste Nicolet (1728–1796) in 1759 brought to the Boulevard du Temple the spectacle he had created earlier at the fairs of Saint-Germain and Saint-Laurent, and which presented acrobatics and tightrope walkers, but also dances, pantomimes, and dramas. In 1772, he obtained the favor of Louis XV, who allowed him to give his company the name Les Grands Danseurs du Roi.

70. Nicolas-Médard Audinot (1732–1801) was a comedian, playwright, and director who in 1770 founded the theater of Ambigu-Comique on boulevard Saint-Martin, where he was the first to put on a show using pantomimes.

71. The Epiphany or Three King's Day is celebrated on 6 January.

72. The French celebrate the Epiphany with the "galette des rois" (Kings' cake), which includes a lucky charm. The person who finds the charm in their slice of the cake becomes the king (or queen) of the day and must choose his or her companion. That person is also responsible for purchasing the next year's cake.

73. *Sic.* (At the beginning of the chapter, Nerval writes, ". . . she had become a tall blonde of eighteen years . . .")

74. Marie-Joséphine de Comarieu, marchioness de Montalembert. Nerval mentions her by name in Part Three.

75. The lines are from Cyrano de Bergerac's play *La Mort d'Agrippine* (1654). Séjanus is one of characters.

76. The story of Henriette Kircher, and the first marriage of Restif, are considered fictitious by biographers. Pamela, the prototype of the virtuous girl, is the heroine of the epistolary novel by Samuel Richardson, *Pamela or Virtue Rewarded* (1740).

77. Agnès Lebègue separated from her husband in 1785 and officially divorced him on 11 January 1794; she died 29 August 1808.

78. In the "episode of the cherries" in Rousseau's *Confessions* (Book IV), only one Galley girl plays a role; the other young girl is Mlle de Graffenried.

79. Alexandre Balthazar Laurent Grimod de La Reynière (1758–1838) was a lawyer, journalist, critic, and gourmet who became friends with Restif in 1782.

Fanny de Beauharnais (1737–1813) was a woman of letters who hosted salons. Restif was introduced to her by Mercier on 8 June 1787. She was the sister-in-law of Francois de Beauharnais (1714–1800), father-in-law of the future empress Josephine.

80. Agnès (1761–1812) married Charles-Marie Augé on 1 May 1781 in Paris, where she had a son, Jean-Nicolas Augé (1781–1855), who became a printer at the Royal Printing Office; she divorced on 11 January 1794 and then remarried, in November 1798 in Paris, Louis-Claude-Victor Vignon, with whom she had another son, Frédéric-Victor Vignon (1794–1856), who became known in literature under the name Vignon Retif de la Bretonne. Marie-Anne, known as Marion (1764–1836), married, on 21 May 1791 in Paris, her cousin Edme-Étienne Restif (1769–1794), king's printer and a collaborator of her father; she settled in 1797 at her father's house in Paris as a widow with three daughters (who died before her). Restif and Lebègue had two other daughters, Marie (1761–1763) and Elisabeth (1763–1770), who died in their infancy.

81. Jacques-Louis-Laurent Anisson-Duperon (?–1788) was the director of the Royal Printing Office. He succeeded his elder brother Louis-Laurent as deputy in 1733 and officially obtained his estate when he died in 1761.

82. Edme Restif (1690–1763) was a laborer and lieutenant of the bailiwick of Sacy.

83. Francois-Augustin Quillau (1743–1804), younger son of the Parisian printer-librarian Gabriel-François Quillau, was a printer-librarian in Paris, and began as a bookseller on 30 April 1763 and a printer on 3 July 1764; he was the printer of the *Journal de Paris*. Restif worked for him from July 1764 to May 1767.

84. A reference to the English novelist Samuel Richardson (1689–1761), best known for his three epistolary novels: *Pamela: Or, Virtue Rewarded*, *Clarissa: Or the History of a Young Lady*, and *The History of Sir Charles Grandison*.

85. *Aristarchus* literally means "good prince," but it usually refers to a grammarian named Aristarchus, who was believed to be an enlightened and severe critic, responsible for sensible criticisms of the best poets, including Homer.

86. Author of over one hundred and forty volumes on numerous subjects, Pierre-Jean-Baptiste Nougaret (1742–1823) appears in Restif's novels under numerous names. In *Monsieur Nicolas*, his nickname is Progrès (Progress).

87. D'Albaret was the librettist of the opera *Scylla and Glaucus* (1746, music by Jean-Marie Leclair), and a royal censor from 1762 to 1776.

88. Marie-Antoinette Cailleau (?–1793) was the daughter of the Parisian bookseller André Cailleau, and wife of Nicolas-Bonaventure Duchesne, bookseller on rue Saint-Jacques at the Temple du Goût. She started working as a bookseller on 4 July 1765, taking over from her deceased husband, and was known as the Widow Duchesne until her death in 1793; she continued the activities of her husband, who was already the publisher of Jean-Jacques Rousseau and Voltaire, and published, from 1774 on, most of Restif's books.

89. In *Rameau's Nephew*, Diderot relates how the lavish financier Etienne-Michel Bouret (1709–1777) opened the way to a fortune by managing to make his dog love the Minister of Justice, Machault d'Arnouville. At the time when Nerval wrote, Diderot's satire was known in France in its original version, though it was redacted later in the Naigeon edition of 1823, after having been published two years earlier in the form of a retranslation by Goethe.

90. Louis Binet (1744–1800) was a history painter, draftsman, engraver, and student of the celebrated painter Jacques Firmin Beauvarlet. He was Restif's favorite artist and illustrated many of his books.

91. *Sylpherize*, i.e., make the whole body appear like a spirit of the air (sylph). In the passage, Nerval shows how Restif equates the erotic with the spirtitual.

92. In Charles Fourier's thought, the *butterfly passion* (the *papillone*) is one of the three "distributive" passions. It refers to the human love of variety, but far from being limited to sexual activity, the *butterfly passion* is the expression of the desire for change proper to humanity.

93. *Parthénions* is the name given to the official brothel in Restif's *Le Pornographe*, which includes a classification of prostitutes according to a complex set of prices and arrangements. The criteria for a prostitute's placement in the hierarchical structure of the "parthénion" is based on age and beauty. *Le Pornographe* is a significant early manifesto for the regulation of prostitution.

94. This bookseller Jacques-François Valade (?–1784) was originally from Toulouse and established himself on rue des Noyers in Paris; he was accepted as a librarian on 6 April 1773 and a printer on 11 December 1778.

95. Edme-Jean Le Jay (?–~1797) set up shop in Paris on rue Saint-Jacques, then rue Neuve-de-Petits-Champs (1788); he was accepted as a bookseller on 5 December 1767 and owned a reading room.

96. This picaresque narrative by Francisco de Quevedo was translated and published by Réstif in 1776. But he added eight chapters to the original text.

97. Nicolas-Augustin Delalain the Elder (~1735–1806) was the son of a notary of Vitry-le-Francois. He set up shop on rue Saint-Jacques in Paris, was accepted as a bookseller on 7 August 1764, and was elected deputy of his corporation on 11 September 1786. He published *Dorat* and the *Almanac of the Muses* by Sautreau de Marsy.

98. *The System of Nature* was published under the name Jean-Baptiste de Mirabuad (1675–1760), but was in fact written by Paul-Henri Thiry, Baron d'Holbach (1723–1789), a French-German author, philosopher, and encyclopedist. He was a major figure in the French Enlightenment, known for being an athiest and for his writings in opposition to religion.

99. The economist Pierre Samuel Dupont de Nemours (1739–1817) was a representative of Nemours to the States General of 1789 and then to the Constituent Assembly (1789–1791). As a member of the Loiret Council of the Ancients, he worked to lay the foundations of a new religion in his *Philosophy of the Universe* (1793), in which he admits the existence of created beings who must surpass us in perfection, in their faculties and in their power, just as we surpass animals and plants. Furthermore, he concludes that they remain invisible to us because we do not have the organs and senses we would need to communicate with them.

100. Antoine-Joseph Pernety, known as Dom Pernety (1716–1796), was a French writer. At various times he was a Benedictine and librarian of Frederic the Great of Prussia. Together with the Polish Count Tadeusz Grabianka, who was also influenced by the Christian mysticism of Swedenborg, he founded in 1760 the secret society of the "Rite hermétique" or Illuminati of Avignon.

Jean-Baptiste de Boyer, Marquis d'Argens (1704–1771), was a French philosopher and writer. An opponent of the Catholic Church, intolerance, and religious oppression, he had to flee his native France and his books were often denounced by the Inquisition. In 1724 he accompanied the French ambassador on a journey to Constantinople, where he lived for a year. After an adventurous youth he was disinherited by his father. He then settled for a time in Amsterdam, where he wrote his famous *Lettres juives* (The Hague, 6 vols., 1738–1742), *Lettres chinoises* (The Hague, 6 vols., 1739–1742), and *Lettres cabalistiques* (2nd ed., 7 vols., 1769).

Jean-Jacques Duval Espréménil (1745–1794) was a magistrate and pamphleteer, a representative in the States-General and the Constituent Assembly, a supporter of mesmerism, and friend and zelator of Cagliostro.

Louis-Claude de Saint-Martin, referred to as the Unknown Philosopher (1743–1803), was a writer of great talent and a theosophist. He was the disciple and secretary of Martinez de Pasqually. He detached himself, after the death of the master, from the other disciples, to preach his work based on an entirely internal path.

101. *Le Thesmographe* addresses a reformation of laws and society. Thesmography is the comparative study of the law.

Le Glossographe: a glossograph is an instrument for recording the movements of the tongue during speech; a glossographer here refers to what would be later termed a linguist. This book was not published by Restif, but he gives an overview of it at the end of his autobiography, *Monsieur Nicolas*, in the appendix.

102. The editions of the works of Claude-Joseph Dorat (1734–1780) were luxuriously adorned with gravure-printed etchings and vignettes.

103. The book Nerval is referring to is *La Découverte Australe par un homme volant, ou Le Dédale francais* [1781, available in an English translation by Brian Stableford as *The Discovery of the Austral Continent by a Flying Man, or the French Daedalus*].

104. The Montgolfier brothers pioneered the use of the hot air balloon, first presented in public on 4 June 1783.

105. Some confusion on Nerval's part: *La Malédiction paternelle* tells not the story of Zéfire but the probably fictional story of Henriette Kircher.

106. *L'Andrographe* is a book on the reformation of man in relation to society.

107. Mathieu-François Pidansat de Mairobert (1727–1779) held the position of royal censor, secretary of the king and of the commands of the Duke of Chartres and was a journalist and man of letters. Mairobert was compromised in the financial disaster of the Marquis de Brunoy; Parliament issued a public reprimand and, feeling himself dishonored, he committed suicide in Paris on 29 March 1779. Restif, who had known Mairobert since 1777, annually commemorated the disappearance of his friend.

108. George-Marie Butel-Dumont (1725–1788) was a royal censor, economist, and historian.

109. The poet Robbé de Beauveset was mentioned in Part One. Antoine de Rivarol (1753–1801) was a Royalist journalist, essayist, and satirist, and author of *De l'Universalité de la langue française* (1784). Restif would have had lunch at Guilbert de Preval's on 22 April 1786 with the Italian playwright, Carlo Goldini (1707–1793), who since 1762 had been the head of the Théâtre-Italien in Paris. In *Monsieur Nicolas*, Restif spoke of Goldini as "the Moliere of Italy." Louis-Antoine Caraccioli (1719–1803) was a prolific writer, and author of a pamphlet against the abbé Maury, *L'abbé Maury frappant sa poitrine, ou La Passion de notre bon et humain clergé* (1790).

Louis-Joachim-Paris Potier, duke of Gesvres (1733–1794), was a Peer of France, the Governor General of the Île-de-France and Monceaux (1758), Lieutenant General of the region of Caux and the Bailiwick of Rouen (1766). He was executed at Vincennes on 7 July 1794. The dinner at the Duke of Gesvres, which took place on 30 January 1785, is reported in detail in Restif's *Monsieur Nicolas*. Claude-Thomas-Guillaume Guilbert de Préval (1716–1788), was a doctor, who became known because of his use of radiation in fighting syphilis, which earned him the recognition and friendship of Restif, and the hostility of the medical faculty, which pronounced his removal from the board. Jacques Louis Le Peletier de Morfontaine, marquis de Montmélian (1730–1799) was councilor of state, and holder of the office of provost of the merchants of Paris (1730–1799). It was at his home that Restif met the Marchioness de Montalembert on 30 April 1784, during a soiree that Restif later called "one of the most beautiful days of his life."

110. Marie-Joséphine de Comarieu (~1750–1832) was a woman of letters who hosted salons. She married the Marquis Marc-René de Montalembert (1714–1800) in 1770. He was an officer and engineer, and a member of the Academy of Sciences. In 1800, during her exile in London, she published a well-regarded epistolary novel entitled *Élise Duménil*.

111. It was in the buildings of Fort Kehl—on the right bank of the Rhine, in front of Strasbourg but on Baden soil to escape royal censorship—that Beaumarchais set up his workshop for the publication of the posthumous edition of Voltaire's works, for which he had acquired the typeface of the great English typographer, John Baskerville. Between 1784 and 1787, tens of thousands of volumes of this edition were printed by the Kehl presses.

112. The poet André Chénier (1762–1794) was sentenced to death by execution on 25 July 1794 for being complicit in a conspiracy hatched while he was being detained in the Saint-Lazare prison. Charles-Louis (1765–1794) and Charles-Michel (1766–1794) Trudaine were both guillotined on 26 July 1794, a day after their friend André Chénier. Louis-Sèbastien Mercier (1740–1814) was an admirer of Restif, whose works he repeatedly praised. Louis de Fontanes (1757–1814), poet and future Grand Master of the Imperial University, came to know Restif in 1783. Their good relations were spoiled when Louis took Agnès's side in their marital disputes. Louis Marie de Narbonne-Lara (1755–1813) was a Senior Officer and Minister of War from 1791 to 1792, a diplomat under the Empire, and the lover of Mme de Staël. Unless Restif is mistaken, which is not likely, the

Chevalier de Castellane, according to Jacques-Remi Dahan, is probably neither the marquis Boniface de Castellane-Novejean (1758–1837), a member of the nobility and a peer of France in 1815, nor the marquis Joseph Leonard de Castellane d'Esparron (1761–1845), a talented officer and painter, but instead a young nobleman of the old provincial house. Jean Mauduit, known as de Larive (1744–1827), was an actor in tragedies. He debuted at the Théâtre-Français in 1770 and was admitted as a member in 1776. Jean-Amable Foucault (1758–1827), known as Saint-Prix, was an actor in tragedies. He debuted at the Théâtre-Français in 1782 and was admitted as a member in 1784. Solemn and grave, he was initially Larive's understudy and only took off in the roles of kings and noble fathers after the latter retired in 1788.

113. A Bayard is a heroic French soldier.

114. Michel de Cubières-Palmezéaux (1752–1820) was a writer, poet, and philosopher.

115. Gabriel Sénac de Meilhan (1736–1803) was an administrator, publicist, and man of letters. He is the author of *L'Émigré* (1791), the first French novel of the Revolution.

116. Camlet, or Camelot, was a type of woven fabric that might have originally been made of camel's hair. In the eighteenth century, England, France, Holland, and Flanders were the chief places where the fabric was manufactured.

117. Pierre Jean-Baptiste Legrand d'Aussy (1737–1800) was a Jesuit and historian, curator of French manuscripts at the Bibliotheque nationale, and member of the Institute. He was also the author of *Fabliaux ou Contes des XII et XIII siècles* (1779–1781, 4 vols.) and *Histoire de la vie privée des Français* (1782, 3 vols.). Legrand d'Aussy, whom Restif nicknamed *Legrand fabliaux*, participated in a different luncheon, which occurred on 23 January 1787 with the "academicians of Amiens," not this one that was on 17 November 1789.

118. Louis-Abel Bonafous, known as the abbé de Fontenai (1736–1806), was a journalist and writer. He was responsible for Restif's invitation to share a meal with the "academicians of Amiens."

119. The Duchesse de Luynes: Guionne Joséphine Élisabeth de Montmorency-Laval (1755–1830). Married in 1768 to Louis Joseph Charles of Albert, Duke of Luynes (1748–1807), she was therefore sister-in-law of the Viscountess de Laval, and aunt and mother-in-law of Mathieu de Montmorency-Laval. A woman of letters, she translated Defoe, Gray, and Swift. She became lady of the palace to Queen Marie-Antoinette in 1775. She was very influential because of her friendship with the queen; she was suspected of having been at the beginning of the Revolution "guilty of democracy," and of having mediated between the constitutional party and the king.

The Countess of Laval in 1789 was the Princess Maximilian Marie Salm-Krybourg (1744–1790), wife of Duke Charles Jean Brittany Tremoille (1737–1792), who had probably followed her husband in his emigration. Restif means the Viscountess of Laval, Catherine Tavernier Boullongne (1749–1838), mother of Mathieu de Montmorency-Laval, salon hostess, and Talleyrand's mistress.

Duke Louis-Marie de Mailly d'Haucourt (1752–1795), a deputy for the nobility of the bailiwick of Péronne at the Estates General of 1789, was one of the "academicians of Amiens" at the meal of 23 January 1787; his wife, Marie Jeanne de Talleyrand-Perigord (1747–1792), was the cousin of Charles-Maurice de Talleyrand, and lady-in-waiting to the queen. After his visit to her on 15 December 1787, Restif said she was "a respectable woman."

Matthieu de Montmorency-Laval (1766–1826), officer and politician, was the deputy of the Bailiwick of Montfort-l'Amaury at the Estates General of 1789. Initially in favor of new ideas and a supporter of the philosophes, he emigrated to Switzerland, near Madame de Staël, at the end of 1791. Appointed to the Peerage in 1815, he was Minister of Foreign Affairs (1821–1822), governor of the Duke of Bordeaux, and member of the Académie Française (1825).

The Bishop d'Autun was Charles-Maurice de Talleyrand-Périgord (1754–1838). According to Jacques-Remi Dahan, Nerval concludes too quickly in seeing the latter as the "deaf man"; Dahan continues: "although the critic Pierre Testud remains perplexed about the personality of the latter, the 'deaf man' cannot be confused with Talleyrand since the latter is clearly identified by Sénac de Meilhan as 'a bit acrimonious, a little lame'" (*Les Illuminés*, 245). The description is from Restif's *Monsieur Nicolas*, where he describes the event in greater detail.

Emmanuel-Joseph Sieyès (1748–1836) was vicar general of Chartres and a politician. Since 1788 he had published numerous pamphlets in Paris in which he set forth his conceptions, the most famous of which was *Qu'est-ce que le Tiers-Etat?* [What is the Third Estate?]. Restif confirms, in *Monsieur Nicolas*, the participation of Sieyès in the hoax that occurred on 17 November 1789.

120. Charles-Irénée Castel de Saint-Pierre (1658–1743) was the author of *Projet pour rendre la paix perpétuelle en Europe* (1713); in the book he proposed an international organization to maintain peace. His *Discourse sur la polysynodie, ou l'on demontre que la polysynodie ou pluralite des Conseils, est la forme de ministere la plus avantageuse pour un Roy et pour son royaume* (1718) resulted in his expulsion from the Academy. In the book he attempted to show that polysynody, the form of government where each minister or secretary of state would be replaced by a council, would result in power not being concentrated in a single person, namely the king.

Claude Henri de Rouvroy, comte de Saint-Simon (1760–1825) was an economist and philosopher; he was the founder of Saint-Simonianism, a movement that believed industrialization would lead to a more productive society in which men would together engage in useful work; this would be the basis for true equality.

121. The hernutes are a Protestant sect of the Moravian Brothers of Bohemia. Some of the Moravian Brothers, who were refugees after the Thirty Years' War in the lands of Count Nikolaus Ludwig von Zinzendorf (1700–1760) in Upper Lusac, founded the city of Hernhut in 1722. Here they formed a new sect called Brüderunität (Unity of Brothers), under the protection and authority of Zinzendorf. The hernutes, bound only by the Lutheran faith in Jesus Christ, practiced the joint ownership of property, charity, and the humblest work.

122. According to legend, Buffon would only work in a beautiful setting, with jabots and embroidered cuffs with Alencon lace, after having been combed and powdered. The proverbial phrase "Buffon's cuffs" characterizes the style and manners of a person. Joseph Haydn (1732–1809) is credited with similar behavior. He, like Buffon, only wrote after being powdered, and dressed in cuffs, jabots, and with a sword at his side.

123. Francois Noel, known as Gracchus Babeuf (1760–1797), was the founder of the newspaper *Le tribune du peuple*, and a theoretician of a political doctrine prefiguring communism; he was condemned to death under the directory for wanting to overthrow the regime and restore the constitution of 1793.

124. Assignats were banknotes used during the French Revolution.

125. Charles Eugene de Lorraine, Prince de Lambesc (1751–1827). On 12 July 1789, the mestre-de-camp (colonel) of the "Royal-German" regiment (Lambesc supported Germany in France's war with Austria), ordered the crowd gathered at the Tuileries to disperse. The clumsiness of his command led the rioters to spread the most extravagant rumors about the "the atrocious conduct of the Prince de Lambesc," a charge of which he was exonerated at his trial before the Châtelet tribunal.

126. Jean-Marie Collot, known as Collot d'Herbois (1749–1796), was an actor, dramatist, and revolutionary. The following exchange is from Restif's *Drame de la vie* [Drama of life].

127. The intention of the book, written by Collot d'Herbois in 1791, was to explain the Republican constitution to the people. It was well received and became a bestseller.

128. The départements in France were originally created in 1790. They are the largest unit of local government in France, and also in some former French colonies.

129. Honoré Gabriel Riqueti, Count of Mirabeau (1749–1791), was a controversial figure in the French Revolution. He was involved in numerous scandals, which left his reputation in ruins. Nevertheless, after the Revolution, he rose to the top of the French political hierarchy and acquired the reputation of being a voice of the people. A powerful orator, he became the leader of a moderate position among the revolutionaries and supported a constitutional monarchy. After his death it was revealed that he had been in the pay of King Louis XVI and the Austrian enemies of France since 1790. As a result, historians are divided on deciding whether he was a great leader who saved the nation from the Terror or a disgraceful traitor to his country.

130. Louis Bénigne François Bertier de Sauvigny (1737–1789) was a public servant under the monarchy and the intendant of Paris from 13 September 1776 onward. One of his main objectives was to reform the taxation system.

131. The governor of the Bastille, Bernard-Rene Jordan de Launay (1740–1789), and the provost of the merchants of Paris, Jacques de Flesselles (1730–1789), were among the first notorious victims of the storming of Bastille on 14 July 1789.

132. During the storming of the Bastille, Bertier was beaten and stoned and taken to the Porte Saint-Martin. There he was shown the severed head of his father-in-law, Joseph Foullon de Doué (1715–1789), a member of the Parliament of Paris. Bertier was eventually hanged from a lamppost in front of the Hôtel de Ville.

133. Charles Philippe, count of Artois (1757–1836), son of the Dauphin Louis Ferdinand and grandson of Louis XV, and future Charles X. He emigrated on 16 July 1789 and traveled to the European courts to seek allies. Louis Joseph de Bourbon Condé (1747–1818), cousin to Louis XVI, was prince of Condé from 1740 to his death. During the Revolution, the prince supported the monarchy and was one of the principal leaders of the counterrevolutionary movement.

134. The Women's March on Versailles, also known as the October March, began in Paris on 5 October 1789. It symbolized the new balance of power that displaced the ancient privileges of the French nobility and favored the common people.

135. Louis Philippe Joseph, Duke of Orleans (1747–1793), was a cousin of Louis XVI. He actively supported the Revolution of 1789 and was a strong advocate for the elimination of the absolute monarchy in favor of a constitutional monarchy. He voted for the death of King Louis XVI; however, he was himself guillotined in November 1793 during the Reign of Terror.

136. According to Jacques-Remi Dahan, this is probably Josse, a bookseller in Paris who in

1793 produced an edition of the *Discours sur le gouvernement* by Algernon Sidney, and in 1794 produced an edition of *The Social Contract* by J. J. Rouseau. It is not known if he is related to the line of Parisian booksellers named Josse who flourished in the seventeenth and eighteenth centuries and ended with Jean-François Josse, active from 1719 to 1779, and his cousin René, active from 1722 to 1782.

137. *Peccata* refers to a sin or pity in Italian. In his book, *Les spectacles de la foire*, the French historian, Émile Campardon (1837–1915), reports that the *Peccata* referred to "the fight of a donkey against dogs." In his book, he also speaks of "a great fight between a vigorous bear of the Pyrenees mountains and the mastiffs, followed by an uproar or bacchanal, recreative of several Peccata, richly decorated with fireworks" (Émile Campardon, *Les spectacles de la foire* [Paris: Berger-Levault, 1877], Book II, 57). Nerval uses this term, *Peccata*, metaphorically to satirize the authors of the time.

138. The "mass graves" refers to the mass graves of the Holy Innocents. It was the largest intramural cemetery in Paris under the Ancien Régime. Located near Les Halles, the commercial heart of Paris, the cemetery was a meeting place where life came alive from dawn to dusk. It was where writers were called upon to falsify accounts or official documents. Some writers made it their specialty. These illegal activities were practiced secretly to escape the eyes of the informers who were prowling around the vicinity of the cemetery. Thus, the expression "writers of the mass graves" was a disparaging one.

Camille Desmoulins (1760–1794), a lawyer and journalist, was a fellow student of Robespierre. Barnabe Farmian Durosoy (~1745–1792) was a journalist and man of letters who wrote novels and poetry. Thomas-Marie Royou (1743–1792) was a political journalist and literary critic. Julien-Louis Geoffroy (1743–1814) was a journalist and literary critic. Jean-Charles Poncelin de La Roche-Tilhac (1746–1828) was a Doctor of Law, a printer, a bookseller, and a journalist in Paris. Jacques Mallet Du Pan (1749–1800) was a historian and publicist, and editor of the *Mercure de France* from 1785 to 1789. He was a supporter of the constitutional monarchy. Claude-Sixte Sautreau de Marsy (1740–1815) was a journalist and editor. He created the journal *L'Almanach des Muses* in 1765 and collaborated on it until 1789. Louis Dussieux (1744–1805) was a writer, journalist, and historian. Francois-Joseph-Michel Noël (1756–1841) was Robespierre's classmate at the Louis-le-Grand College, and a writer, journalist, and philologist.

139. Brother Jean des Entomures is the name of the character of a combative monk in Rabelais's *Gargantua and Pantagruel.*

140. Jean Siffrein Maury (1746–1817) was a celebrated churchman, panegyrist, and member of the Académie Française (1785). He was elected a member of the Estates General of 1789 by the clergy of Péronne and defended the property of the clergy in the National Assembly during the session of 30 October 1789.

141. François Chabot (1756–1794) was a Capuchin friar in Rodez, elected to the National Convention in the département of Loir-et-Cher, and a member of the Legislative Assembly in 1793; he was an informer and corrupt. He was sentenced to death on 5 April 1794.

142. Jean-Antoine Lafargue de Grangeneuve (1751–1793), a lawyer from Bordeaux, was elected to the Legislative Assembly in 1792; in a revolutionary act, he presented to the Assembly a report demanding the removal of the king. After he was elected to the National Convention in 1793, he adopted a more moderate position and sided with the Girondists. He was sentenced to death on 21 December 1793 by the military commission at Bordeaux.

143. Isaac Rene Guy Le Chapelier (1754–1794) was a jurist and politician. Suspected during the Reign of Terror of having had connections with the Feuillants (a political group of monarchists and reactionaries), he temporarily emigrated to Great Britain. He returned to France in 1794 in an unsuccessful attempt to prevent the confiscation of his assets and was arrested and guillotined in Paris.

144. No member of the revolutionary assemblies bears such a surname.

145. This is a literal translation. The word *plumassiers* refers to a "small, servile writer" ("plume" as in "pen"); a sort of a "penpusher-for-hire."

146. Pierre Jean Georges Cabanis (1757–1808) was a physician, philosopher, and friend of Mirabeau, who assisted him in his final moments and was even suspected of hastening his death to shorten his suffering, an accusation he defended in his *Journal of the Illness and Death of Honoré-Gabriel-Victor-Riquetti Mirabeau* (1791).

147. During the night of 20–21 June 1791, King Louis XVI of France, his queen Marie Antoinette, and their immediate family attempted to escape from Paris in order to start a counter-revolution with the remaining loyal troops. They escaped only as far as the small town of Varennes, where they were arrested.

148. Henri Le Fèvre d'Ormesson (1751–1808) was Controller General of Finances from March to November 1783. Administrator of the Paris département in 1790, he was elected Mayor of Paris against his will on 21 November 1792 but resigned immediately and retired to his home. Although he had been under house arrest and then detained during the Reign of Terror, his fame as a good man allowed him to survive the revolutionary period without damage. Michel Chamillart (1652–1721), Controller General of the Finances of Louis XIV, has already appeared in the *History of the abbé de Bucquoy*. He and Henri Le Fèvre seem to represent here the timorous decency that fails to fight victoriously against reality.

149. The Caveau café, located at the Palais-Royal, had a reputation for being the meeting place of many fine minds.

150. La Grotte Flamande was a café in the Palais-Royal, frequented by actors from the Montansier Theater.

151. The reference is to Robespierre's attempt to create a "Festival for the Supreme Being" in which a statue was created with a veil to represent atheism. The president had to burn the veil beneath which one would have seen the face of wisdom appear. Robespierre burned the veil, but the flame completely blackened the statue, and Robespierre claimed that wisdom thus remained dull.

152. In her study of Nerval, Bettina Knapp writes, "Napoleon was endowed with an unearthly aura and came to represent everything that was wonderful, powerful, and courageous—to a young Nerval who unconsciously may have considered himself to be just the opposite" (Knapp, 18).

153. Emanuel Swedenborg (1688–1772) was a Swedish scientist, philosopher, and theologian. His spiritual writings from ca. 1736 exerted a major influence on the French writers of the nineteenth century, Balzac and Baudelaire in particular. The works of Swedenborg had a profound influence on Nerval, who quotes his name many times in the following portraits. From sometime between 1746 and 1747 he worked on his magnum opus, *Arcana Caelestia* (Heavenly Mysteries), published posthumously in 8 volumes.

154. *Micromegas* is a philosophical novel by Voltaire (1752) inspired by *Gulliver's Travels*.

155. Quintus Ennius (239–169 BCE), poet and playwright, is considered the father of Latin poetry, although his work has almost entirely disappeared. Virgil is reported by the historian

Suetonius to have once been reading Ennius's poem only to be asked what he was doing; the poet replied that "he was gathering gold from Ennius's manure." (*Les Oeuvres de Virgil en latin et en francais* [Lyon: Amable Leroy, 1803], Book I, 38–39.)

156. Jean-Baptiste Santeul (1630–1697) was one of the regular canons of Saint-Victor in Paris, and a poet who wrote in Latin. Santeul's literary success was based on his series of sacred odes. He was mocked by La Bruyere under the name of Théodas.

157. The words Nerval cites suggest their meanings: *cythéréique* suggests "Cytherea," another name for Aphrodite in Greek mythology. *Mignonnesse* contains *mignon*, which is French for "cute." And *chimérais* contains the word *chimère*, which means "to dream" (and by extension, the English word *chimera*).

158. Jean-Françoise de La Harpe (1736–1803) was a writer who supported the revolutionary movement. He plays an important role in Nerval's portrait of Cazotte. Élie Catherine Fréron (1718–1776) was a literary critic and polemicist, founder of the journal *L'Année littéraire*, which he edited from 1754 to 1776, and an enemy of Voltaire. Often cited in *Monsieur Nicolas*, he gave an account of *La Fille naturelle*, which appeared in his journal in 1769.

159. Jean-Gabriel Mérigot the Younger was a Parisian bookseller who, along with other booksellers, produced several of Restif's works.

Pierre Vent was an advisor to the king and mayor of Verneuil-au-Perche, who began working as a bookseller in Paris in 1764. His son, Louis, succeeded him in 1794.

Jean-Pierre Costard (1743–?) was a Parisian bookseller who began working as one in 1769. He, along with other booksellers, produced several of Restif's works.

CAZOTTE

1. The adjective *humoristique* became common usage in the mid-1820s in reference to the English spirit of comedy. Michael Corvin, in his essay "Jean Genet in His Humour," writes, "In English, the word 'humour' evolved during the eighteenth century to designate the ability to present amusing, unusual, or sometimes absurd aspects of reality with a degree of detachment" (*Jean Genet: Performance and Politics*, ed. Clare Finburgh, Carl Lavery, and Maria Shevtsova [New York: Palgrave Macmillan, 2006], 23).

2. Pantomime spread throughout France and England from the sixteenth to the eighteen centuries, as an entertainment that took place during the intermissions of operatic performances.

3. Prior to the end of the seventeenth century, salon gatherings were usually held in the bedroom, which was considered more private than a drawing room: a lady, reclining on her bed, would receive close friends, who would sit on chairs or stools around her. The word Nerval uses is *ruelle*, which literally means "narrow street" or "lane," but also designates the space between a bed and the wall in a bedroom; the word was commonly used to designate the gatherings of the intellectual and literary circles that formed around women in the first half of the seventeenth century.

4. A reference to Voltaire's work *Zadig ou la Destinee* [Zadig, or the Book of Fate], first published in 1747. Its subtitle was *Histoire Orientale*.

5. The book by Cazotte is *Suite des Mille et une Nuits: Contes Arabes* (1788) [Continuation of the thousand and one nights: Arabian tales.]

6. Claude-Antoine de Choiseul-Beaupre (1697–1763), Peer of France in 1733, Count and Bishop of Châlons from 1734 to 1763, was the brother of Cardinal de Choiseul.

7. The prestigious rank of Commissioner General of the Navy was awarded to Cazotte only on 4 September 1760, with permission to withdraw from active service. At the end of his studies, on 1 March 1743, he had only obtained a certificate as an ordinary writer of the Navy. The writers of the navy (Les écrivains de la marine) are appointed by the king who grants them the certificate.

8. Appointed chief inspector of the Leeward Islands on 1 July 1747, Cazotte arrived in Martinique in the last months of the year for a first stay that lasted until June 1752; his second visit was from February 1754 to August 1759. The Leeward Islands are a group of islands in the West Indies.

9. In Pierry, France and now established in the Marne, Cazotte married, on 9 July 1761, Catherine Elisabeth Roignan (1731–1807), whom he had met in Martinique. She was the daughter of Simon Roignan, Counselor to the King, Civil and Criminal Lieutenant of Fort Royal.

10. This leave (1752–1754) was due to a serious eye condition the writer would suffer from throughout his life.

11. Bernard de La Monnoye (1641–1728) was a lawyer, poet, and critic, who was chiefly known for his carols.

12. The German poets are Goethe, Schiller, and Bürger, among others. Nerval devoted two anthologies to German poetry, one in 1830, the other in 1840.

13. Françoise-Joachim de Pierre, cardinal de Bernis (1715–1794) was a prelate, diplomat, poet, and member of the French Academy. The flowery verses of his youth earned him the nickname "Babet the florist."

    The poet Claude-Joseph Dorat (1734–1780) was one of the main supporters of *L'Almanach des Muses*, an eighteenth-century magazine that included his own poems as well as other lesser-known and some celebrated poets. One of its central attacks was against the *poésie galante* movement in poetry, whose aim was to "arrive at a pure and gallant poetry."

14. Edessa (Urfa, present-day Turkey) was the capital of one of the first Christian states founded during the First Crusade (1096–1099), under the sovereignty of Baudouin de Boulogne (~1065–1118), brother of Godefroy de Bouillon.

15. In the legend, Geneviève Brabant, falsely accused of adultery, and her child were sentenced to death, but their lives were spared, and they lived for six years in a cave nourished by the milk from a doe.

16. The full title of the work referred to here is *Le Lord Impromptu, nouvelle Romanesque, traduite de l'anglois* [*The Impromptu Lord, a New Romance, translated from the English*] (1767). It was purported to be the translation of an English work, but it was written by Jacques Cazotte. It was sometimes attributed to a Charlos and the letters "M. D." were stamped on the back of the binding.

17. A British Expeditionary Force, led by Major-General Peregrine Hopson and Colonel John Barrington, landed in Martinique on 3 January 1759 and fought the French near Fort Royal (now Fort Saint-Louis). Encountering French resistance, Hopson ordered his troops to re-embark; discouraged by the performance of his men at Fort Saint-Pierre, he returned to Guadeloupe, on which he launched a new offensive on 22 January. The surrender of the

British at Guadeloupe was obtained by Governor Nadeau du Treil on 23 April, after several months of combat and fierce resistance. Nerval's date is off by ten years.

18. On 8 May 1761, a judgment of the Court of Parliament condemned the Jesuits to pay the bills of exchange signed by Father Lavalette; the suppression of the Company of Jesus and the confiscation of its property on 6 May 1762 prevented the execution of the judgment.

19. Jean Charles Emmanuel Nodier (1780–1844) was an influential French author and librarian who introduced a younger generation of Romanticists to *fantastic literature*, gothic literature, and vampire tales. *Smarra, or The Demons of the Night* is his best-remembered work, the title of which is derived from the Dalmatian word for "nightmare." His dream-related writings influenced Nerval's later works. In her study of Nerval, Bettina Knapp writes of Nodier that "the supernatural, the world of dreams, the exotic, and the satanic held sway in his short stories and plays. . . . He was haunted by invisible but real forces, which seemed to surround him—by outer-worldly entities. . . . Nodier was a mystic. He did not represent the ideations of the ideologues or the Encyclopedists, but echoed the feelings and sentiments of the Illuminists, a type of underground movement that flourished as a counterpoise to empirical and logical reasonings. . . . Nodier's immense knowledge, his constant search into the world beyond the visible and the scientifically comprehensible, fascinated Gérard" (Knapp, 23–24).

20. *Le Cabinet des Fées* [The fairy library] is a collection of fairy tales and other tales of the marvelous compiled by the chevalier Charles-Joseph de Mayer (1751–1825).

21. In Nerval's dedication of *Les Filles du Feu* [The daughters of fire] to Alexander Dumas, he refers to "storytellers who cannot invent without identifying with the characters of their imagination" and counts himself among these, following Charles Nodier.

22. Jean-Baptiste de Boyer, Marquis d'Argens (1703–1771), was a philosopher and writer. Born of an aristocratic Catholic family, he led a life of debauchery when he was young. He joined the army and then escaped to Spain. On one occasion he attempted suicide. He spent twenty-five years in the court of Frederick the Great as a chamberlain. It was during this time that he wrote *Lettres cabalistiques* (1741).

The *Oedipus Aegypiacus* (1652–1654) was a major work on Egyptology by the German Jesuit scholar Athanasius Kircher (1602–1680).

23. The *Comte de Gabalis* (1670) by abbé Nicolas-Pierre-Henri de Montfaucon de Villars (1635–1673) is about an occultist who reveals the mysteries of the world to the author. The book was very popular in France and abroad and inspired the creation of many of the fantastic beings that would populate the European novels that came later. It was read by Charles Baudelaire and Anatole France.

24. Balthasar Bekker (1634–1698) was a Dutch minister and the author of numerous philosophical and theological works. He opposed superstition and did not believe that people could be possessed by devil; he went so far as to even question the existence of the devil. He was a key figure in bringing about an end to the witchcraft persecutions in early modern Europe.

25. The case is briefly reported in a biographical note by Bergasse (1813), before being reported in more detail in *La Famille Cazotte* (1846) by Anna Marie (Anna-Alba-Corniele de Beaurepaire, Countess of Hautefeuille). Nerval is referring to the latter; Bergasse was aware that the visitor is a disciple of Martinez de Pasqually, even though Madame d'Hautefeuille suggests that he is only a Master, "a man of high and vast piety." The veracity of this incident has some bearing to the narrative, but it would perhaps be better regarded as a symbolic visitation; the mysterious visitor, charged with inviting Cazotte to join the followers of Martinez, would thus be his "teacher" among the Elected Priests of the Universe, perhaps Jean-Jacques Du Roy d'Hauterive if we are to believe Saint-Martin. The Elected Priests of the Universe (*Cohen* is Hebrew for "priest" and *Elus* means "the elect" or "the chosen") was the first way to attain "reintegration."

26. Casuistry is reasoning used to resolve moral problems by extracting or extending theoretical rules from particular instances and applying these rules to new instances. Casuistry dates from Aristotle (384–322 BCE), but its high point was from 1550 to 1650, when the Society of Jesus used case-based reasoning, particularly in administering the Sacrament of Penance (or "confession"). The term *casuistry* quickly became pejorative with Blaise Pascal's attack on the misuse of casuistry. In *Provincial Letters* (1656–57) he scolded the Jesuits for using casuistic reasoning in confession to placate wealthy Church donors, while punishing poor penitents.

27. The assassination of Montfaucon de Villars on the road from Paris to Lyon was credited, in the minds of the people, to a Romantic idea of execution; Claude-Pierre Goujet, in his book, *Supplément au Grand Dictionnaire historique [. . .] de Mr. Louis Moreri* (1735), writes, "The laughing people [. . .] said that disguised Gnomes and Sylphs committed the attack, to punish him for having revealed the secrets of the cabal" (*Supplément au Grand dictionnaire historique, généalogique, géographique, etc. de M. Louis Moreri* [Paris: Jacques Vincent, 1735], Book II, 465). The circumstances of the crime, resulting from a family vendetta, were not clarified until the early twentieth century by René-Louis Doyon.

28. The Theosophist, Martinez de Pasqually (~1710?–1774), Master of Jean-Baptiste Willermoz and Louis-Claude de Saint-Martin, instituted the Masonic rite of the Elected Priests of the Universe, in 1766; the Order was particularly active in Bordeaux, the residence of Martinès, and Lyon. He set forth his doctrine in his book, *Treatise on the Reintegration of Beings in Their First Spiritually Divine Property, Virtue, and Power*, copies of which circulated in secret until its first publication in French in 1899.

29. *Le Magasin Pittoresque* [The quaint shop] was a kind of popular encyclopedia that, without neglecting important modern discoveries, concentrated on resurrecting ideas from the past. One of its issues dedicates an anonymous article to a certain grimoire: "a German manuscript of the fifteenth century attributed to Dr. Faust, *The Triple Constraint of Hell*, is a book of his occult art and his miracles, with which he forced spirits to bring him what he desired and to submit to his orders."

30. The Rite of the Philalèthes (which translates as "friend or seeker of truth," from the Greek) is the name given to a society of Freemasons involved in communications with the "spirit world" in order to establish a connection between man and god. It was founded in 1773 by the Marquis Charles-Pierre-Paul Savalette de Langes.

31. In the thought of Saint-Martin, the "Reparator" designates Christ.

32. All of the above tales were included in various volumes of *Le Cabinet des Fées*. *The Caliph of Baghdad* was a one-act comedy by Claude Godard d'Aucourt de Saint-Just (1768–1826) with music by F.-A. Boieldieu. It premiered in Paris at the Favart Theater on 16 September 1800.

33. Often present in *The Thousand and One Nights*, Eblis, according to Muslim tradition in the Koran, is the leader of the rebellious spirits who were driven from the paradise of Allah for having rebelled and refused to submit to Adam. In this respect, he is similar to the figure of Lucifer in Christianity.

34. Jean Terrasson (1670–1750), often referred to as the abbé Terrasson, was a French writer, priest, and member of the Académie française. His is best known for the fantasy novel *Life of Sethos, Taken from Private Memoirs of the Ancient Egyptians* (1731), in which Masonic ritual is linked with ancient Egyptian ritual.

35. This reference is to Jean Casotte (1611–1657), who was a lawyer in Dijon and an author of stanzas published between 1643 and 1648.

36. A blanc was a silver coin that was in use from the fourteenth to the eighteenth centuries in France.

37. *The Infante of Zamora* is a comedy in four acts with a mix of short arias by Nicolas-Étienne Framery; the music a parody of Giovanni Paisiello's *Frascatana*. The play premiered in Strasbourg in 1779.

38. Jean Françoise Rameau, nephew of the famous Jean-Philippe Rameau, is the narrator of Diderot's *Rameau's Nephew*.

39. *Les Sabots* [The clogs] is a comic opera in one act, with a mix of short arias, first performed by the Italian comedians of the king in Paris, at the Theater of the Hotel de Bourgogne, on 26 October 1768. The music is actually not by Jean-Francoise Rameau, but Egidio Duni (1709–1775); the libretto of the opera is attributed jointly to C[azotte] and Michel-Jean Sedaine (1719–1797) without either the name or initial of Benoit-Joseph Marsollier des Vivetières (1752–1817) appearing anywhere on the libretto. In his cultural newsletter, *Correspondance Littéraire* (letter of 1 November 1768), Grimm mischievously exposes by what scheme Duni convinced Sedaine to rewrite the entire libretto, "so that with the exception of the first tune, there is not a single word of M. Cazotte's play."

40. *La Nouvelle Raméide* by Jacques Cazotte was first published in 1766. It was a curious sequel to Rameau's eulogistic poem that came out in the same year.

41. During his stay in Paris from 1752 to 1754, Cazotte contributed to the "Quarrel of the Buffoons," supporting the partisans of French operatic music (that of the king) against the partisans of Italian operatic music (that of the queen) in anonymous publications, one of which was *The War of the Opera*.

42. Grimm wrote the tiny pamphlet during a heated debate on whether the opera should include French music or Italian. Grimm sided with the Italians and wrote *The Little Prophet of Boehmischbroda*. The phrase "diplomatic documents on the war of the Opera" refers to this heated argument.

43. Nodier writes: "his page." Emphasized by Nerval, the term *pays* (province, region) applies to a human being, and is rather ambiguous since, if it refers to an individual from the same region as another, it is also, in the vocabulary of companionship, the term by which one calls a journeyman worker working in a shop. Nerval may have been aware of this second meaning and played on the meaning of the words; in the latter case, this would then be a reference to Cazotte's affiliation with Freemasonry, as he was a kind of "journeyman" who binds himself to the work of Freemasonry, that is, to the legend of Hiram, builder of the Temple of Solomon.

44. The tricorn was a style of hat that was popular in the eighteenth century.

45. Jean-Francoise de La Harpe (1736–1803) was a French playwright, writer, and literary critic. Even though in the beginning he supported the revolutionary leaders during the brutal excesses of 1792 and 1793, he was nonetheless arrested and imprisoned; during his time in prison, he underwent a spiritual crisis and transformation, emerging afterwards as a Catholic and political reactionary.

46. The tripod is the one on which the Pythia of Delphi stood to utter her prophecies; the expression here is a direct quote from Nodier, who writes of Cazotte, "this worthy man was almost always on the tripod, and most of the things he announced were realized in their time in the most natural way" (Charles Nodier, *Contes* [Éditions Garnier Frères, 1961], 592).

47. Since the end of the eighteenth century, "Malvalsia" has designated less the wine originating from the Peloponnese than a Madeira wine or white port, made with the grapes of the Malvalsia variety.

Constance or Constantia is a sweet wine from around Cape Town (South Africa), which was very popular in England and France in the eighteenth and nineteenth centuries.

48. Sébastien-Roch Nicolas, known in his adult life as Nicolas Chamfort or Sébastien Nicolas de Chamfort (1740?–1794), was a dramatist, famous for his wit, whose aphorisms were very popular during the Revolution.

49. The great Hellenist Anne Dacier (1647–1720) attacked the abbé Jean Terrasson of the Academy of Sciences, who proposed in his *Dissertation critique sur l'Illiade d'Homèrie* (1715) "two thousand geometric demonstrations, which prove incontestably that Homer is a fool, and his poems, monstrous works."

50. Appointed librarian at the Royal Library in August 1792, Chamfort was briefly imprisoned in September 1793 and placed under surveillance because of his Girondin sympathies. Although surviving, thanks to his doctors, from a particularly atrocious suicide attempt the following November, he did not recover from his wounds and died on 13 April 1794.

51. Aimar-Charles-Marie de Nicolaï (1747–1794), first president of the Chamber of Accounts and member of the French Academy (1788), was sentenced to death on 27 June 1794 as an enemy of the people and an accomplice in the conspiracy that took place in the Luxembourg prison where he was detained; he was executed on 7 July.

52. Jean-Sylvain Bailly (1736–1793), writer, mathematician, politician, and member of the French Academy (1783), was sentenced to death on 10 November 1793 as a conspirator and convicted as one of the perpetrators of a plot to disturb the inner tranquility of the state; he was executed on 12 November.

53. Jean-Antoine Roucher (1745–1794), poet and political writer, was sentenced to death and executed at the same time as his friend, the poet André Chénier, on 25 July 1794, convicted of being an accomplice of an imaginary conspiracy in the prison of Saint-Lazare where he was detained.

54. Beatrix de Choiseul-Stainville, Duchess of Gramont (1730–1794), was the sister of the minister of Louis XV, a salon hostess, and a bibliophile. Sentenced to death as a counter-revolutionary, she was executed on 22 April 1794.

55. The Conciergerie is a former prison in Paris. During the Revolution, hundreds of prisoners were taken from the Conciergerie to be guillotined at a number of locations throughout Paris.

56. Nicolas Malebranche (1638–1715) was a French rationalist philosopher who sought to demonstrate the active role of God in every aspect of the world.

57. Félicité-Geneviève-Elisabeth de Jarente (1720–?) was the daughter of the Marquis de Senas and widow of the Marquis Valentin de La Croix, who was the captain-general of the artillery at the service of Spain and the Viceroy of Galicia. After a stormy youth, this great lady discovered in her husband's death a mystical vocation, establishing herself as a visionary and healer. She frequently visited Jean-Baptiste Willermoz, a highly regarded

Freemason and Martinist, soliciting him for admission to the order of the Elect Priests of the Universe, and in 1776 even offered hospitality to Saint-Martin, who wrote, partly at her home, the *Natural Table of the Relationships that Exist between God, Man and the Universe* (1782); but Martin quickly distanced himself from her. Cazotte, to whom she had opened her salon after the publication of *The Devil in Love*, welcomed her to Pierry in September 1789, where she resided until the arrest of her host, disturbing somewhat by her eccentric behavior the peaceful existence of the Cazotte family.

58. Jacques Scévole Cazotte, born in Pierry on 31 January 1764, was Naval Lieutenant in 1779, lieutenant of the guards of Frederick II and German prince of Hesse in 1785, and lieutenant of the guard of Louis XVI in 1791. He emigrated after 10 August and campaigned as captain with the princes of the Loyal-Emigrant Regiment and the Rotalier emigrants (30 November 1791). At the Restoration, he was appointed knight of Saint-Louis by Louis XVIII (27 November 1814), then ennobled and made battalion commander (5 December 1814). Librarian at Versailles from 1815 to 1831, Scévole Cazotte survived until an advanced age and devoted his life to maintaining and defending the memory of his father; he died in Paris on 20 June 1853. He is the author of *Témoignage d'un royaliste* (1839).

59. "To bind," according to Cazotte and his son, means "to reduce to impotence in order to prevent harm by magical operation."

60. In Scripture, pink represents lust. The French *rose* can also mean "red," which is another color associated with the devil.

61. At the Battle of Valmy (20 September 1792), with the expectation high that the Austro-Prussian counterrevolutionary troops, following the capture of Longwy and Verdun, were going to attempt another easy victory and open the road to Paris, the young revolutionary French army were determined to fight back under the orders of Dumouriez and Kellermann. Against all odds they forced the Duke of Brunswick's army to retreat.

62. Frederick William II of Prussia (1744–1797) withdrew from the Austro-Prussian counterrevolutionary alliance and separately signed the Treaty of Basel with the Republic on 5 April 1795, by which Prussia abandoned to France the Duchy of Guelders and the western part of the Duchy of Clèves, while France restored to it the territories conquered beyond the Rhine. A mystic spirit, Frederick William II was influenced by his private advisor, the Rosicrucian Johann Christoph von Wöllner (1732–1800).

63. The secretary of the king's civil list is responsible for the general management, as well as the management of human, financial, and material resources of the royal household.

64. This mysterious "Grimoire of Cagliostro" is one of the writings attributed to Cagliostro known as "the Gospel of Cagliostro": *Liber memorialis of Caleostro quum esset Roboreti* (1778) by Clementino Vannetti (1754–1795), which was translated in 1910 by Marc Haven (*L'Évangile de Cagliostro retrouvé*). In addition to writing *Rituel de la maçonnerie égyptienne* [Egyptian Rite of Freemasonry], Cagliostro is sometimes credited as being the author of *La Très Sainte Trinosophie*, a hermetic treatise whose manuscript was seized in his papers in Rome but which most authors concede was written by the Count of Saint-Germain.

65. Antoine Bret (1717–1792) was a prolific French writer and playwright, who dabbled in many genres.

66. The Convulsionaries (Convulsionnaires) were a group of eighteenth-century French religious pilgrims who exhibited convulsions and later constituted a religious sect and a political movement.

67. Clad in black and white robes, the Jacobins had a monkish appearance.

68. "Their knowledge will destroy them."

69. Brousolle is Suzette Labrousse (1747–1821), who is mentioned in the correspondence between Cazotte and Ponteau dated 27 December 1791 and 31 January 1792. She prophesied the fall of the clergy and the nobility, was close to the Jacobins, and, before Catherine Théot, received the protection of Dom Gerle and the Constitutional Bishop, Pierre Pontard; Saint-Martin, who met her in 1792, had many reservations about her.

70. Jeanne de La Rochefoucauld, Marquise d'Urfé (1705–1775), born Jeanne Camus de Pontcarré. This wealthy widow, fond of the occult sciences, opened her salon to comte de Saint-Germain, Cagliostro, and Casanova, the latter of whom mentions her in his autobiography, *The Story of My Life* (1822–1829).

71. Achille de Lascaris d'Urfé, Marquis du Chastellet (1759–1794), was the grandson of the Marquise d'Urfé. He was promoted to brigadier general on 9 March 1792, but unsuccessfully applied to the Ministry of War in February 1793: it is to this circumstance that Cazotte refers, abruptly summarized by Nerval. Arrested on 15 September 1793 and thrown into prison, du Chastellet was said to have poisoned himself in his cell at La Force prison on 20 March 1794, without waiting for his conviction.

72. In the morning hours of 10 August 1792, the National Guard, along with a mob of Parisians, invaded the home of the royal family (The Tuileries Palace). The angry crowd swept through Paris and destroyed all images and references to the monarchy.

73. Antoine Quentin Fouquier de Tinville (1746–1795) was a French prosecutor during the Revolution and the Reign of Terror. His activity during this time earned him the reputation of being one of the most sinister figures of the Revolution. His nickname was "Purveyor to the Guillotine."

Justin Huntly McCarthy writes: "The legend of the knights of the dagger seems to have arose in this fashion, according to the one who knew the palace and its people well in those days, the Count of Paroy: An old provincial nobleman, more than sixty years of age, Chevalier de Court, going one day to pay his court to the king, in very simple dress, carried under his coat a little hunting-knife that it had always been his habit to wear in lieu of a sword. A National Guard noticed this hunting knife, and in the fervor of his zeal arrested the old gentleman under the pretext that he was carrying a dagger. The mistake was recognized with the first explanation the Chevalier de Court made, but the opportunity was too good for the pamphleteers to lose, and the trifling event was magnified into the existence of a mysterious organization of knights of the dagger" (Justin Huntly McCarthy, *The French Revolution* [New York: Harper & Brothers, 1898], 540).

74. Ay (Marne) is a small wine-growing town five kilometers from Epernay. Givet (Ardennes) is a border town not far from Dinant (Belgium).

75. According to Jacques-Remi Dahan, the reference is perhaps to General Auguste Henri Marie Picot de Dampierre (1756–1793), an admirer of Frederick II, who took part in the battle of Valmy, pronounced himself in favor of the Republic, contributed to the victory of Jemmapes, and at his death received glorious honor by being buried in the Pantheon.

76. The function of office of the "archers of the poor" was to seize beggars roaming the streets and put them in the hospital.

77. This surname was probably the result of a misreading; perhaps it refers to the name Loë, which was that of an old Westphalian noble family and refers to the Baron Edmund von Loë-Imstenraedt (1749–1813).

78. What follows is from Cazotte's introduction to his *Oeuvres badines et morales* (1817), excerpted from the first paragraphs of a section entitled "Revelations."

79. The former would be Scévole Cazotte; the latter son was Simon Henry Cazotte, born on 12 April 1765 in Pierry and died in Dominica (Lesser Antilles) in 1810. He was attached to the infantry regiment of Poitou until 1791, and then emigrated and campaigned for princes as a lieutenant, before reaching England in 1793, then Martinique, where he settled.

Starting in the latter half of 1789, riots became a common occurrence in Paris. The violence resulted in an increasing number of members of the nobility emigrating from Paris to seek foreign aid or cause an insurrection in the provinces of the south. The French Emigration (1789–1815) was a mass movement of thousands of French people spanning various socioeconomic classes. While the violence in Paris was an immediate reason for their leaving the vicinity, they also fundamentally disagreed about the elimination of the old order, which offered privileges to which the nobility had grown accustomed.

80. Arnaud de Laporte (1737–1792) was Intendant of the Civil List, Secretary of State, and Minister of the Royal Household from 3 January 1791 to 10 August 1792. He was charged and brought before the Constituent Assembly after the flight of the king, where he attempted to read a letter explaining the king's motives. He was arrested after 10 August 1792, tried by the criminal court on the 17th, and guillotined on the 23rd.

81. Austria and Prussia threatened France with military action if their progression toward republicanism continued. As a result, in August the Prussian army, under the command of the Duke of Brunswick, invaded eastern France and captured the fortress cities of Longwy and Verdun. But in their attempt to invade Paris, they were stopped at Valmy by the French army, which was small compared to the Prussian army; this was viewed as a great psychological victory for the revolutionaries.

82. The Saint-Barthélemy's Day massacre occurred in 1572. It was caused by a number of assassinations and the violence of Catholics aimed at the Huguenots during the French Wars of Religion. The massacre began on the night of 23–24 August (on the eve of the feast of Bartholomew the Apostle).

83. The counterrevolutionary forces had invaded France on 18 August 1792. On 23 August, following a three-day bombing, Longwy surrendered to the allied armies of Austria, Prussia, and Hesse, who then marched on Verdun; On 2 September, Verdun capitulated, after the suicide of the colonel commander of the place. The next day, after Marceau's surrender, Charles William Ferdinand, Duke of Brunswick, took possession of Verdun in the name of the King of France.

84. Roch-Ambroise Sicard (1742–1822). After the death of the abbé de l'Épée, he succeeded him at a leading school for the deaf, which Épée had founded in Paris.

85. Stanislas-Marie Maillard (1763–1794) participated in the taking of the Bastille on 14 July 1789, and thereafter was known as the Captain of the Volunteers of the Bastille; he took an active role in most of the landmark revolutionary events, and was named captain of the national guard in 1790; on 17 July 1791 he signed the petition of the Champs-de-Mars, which proclaimed the creation of a republic, and was president of the improvised tribunal at the Prison de l'Abbaye. He seems to have encouraged the massacres, giving them an air of legality with his presence. Some credit him with playing an important and positive role in the affair. He also became known to posterity as "the grand judge of the Abbey" or "Chief of the Murderers."

86. According to the testimony of Jourgniac de Saint-Méard, a fellow prisoner of Cazotte, the

citizen Lavaquerie—who, during their imprisonment, fulfilled "the duties that humanity imposes on an honest man"—was not a turnkey but a concierge from the Abbey.

87. Jérôme Pétion (1756–1794) was a lawyer, mayor of Paris (1757–1792), and first president of the Convention.

88. Etienne-Jean Panis (1757–1847) was a member of the "Commune of 10 August," one of the administrators of the Paris police, and was elected deputy of the Paris department of the Convention on 12 September 1792.

Antoine-François Sergent (1751–1847), like Pétion and Panis, was one of the administrators of the Paris police and elected deputy of the Paris department of the Convention on 12 September 1792.

89. The lawyer who defended Cazotte and Arnaud de Laporte.

90. Jean-Charles Thibault de Laveaux (1749–1827), translator and historian, was head of the political and literary newspaper *Le Courrier de Stasbourg* (1791–1792), and then editor of the *Journal de la Montagne* (1793–1796). Laveaux, better known for his lexicographical work, was present in Paris between May and November 1792; after the day of 10 August in which he took part, he was appointed judge of the Tribunal of 17 August. Charles Monselet praises without irony "the wisdom of his conduct that produced answers which never veered from what we had the right to expect from his knowledge and experience" (Monselet, *Histoire anecdotique du Tribunal révolutionnaire* [Paris: D. Giraud and J. Dagneau, 1853], 74–75).

Nerval's conjecture about Laveaux's occult associations, to which Laveaux alludes, with regard to Cazotte, at the conclusion of his speech, is not sustainable: there is no reason to think that Laveaux had approached Martinist circles, or that he was even a Mason.

CAGLIOSTRO

1. Julian organized elaborate rituals and attempted to promote Neoplatonism as a rival to Christianity. In general, paganism was tolerated under Julian's rule.

2. The Serapeum, belonging to the library of Alexandria, is a temple or other religious institution dedicated to the syncretic Hellenistic-Egyptian god Serapis, who combined aspects of Osiris and Apis in a humanized form that was accepted by the Ptolemaic Greeks of Alexandria. In Nerval's *Filles du Feu* this temple is referred to as a "safe home."

3. Neoplatonism is a modern term (first coined in 1827) used to designate a tradition of philosophy that arose in the third century CE and persisted until shortly after the closing of the Platonic Academy in Athens by Justinian I in 529 CE. According to Plotinus, the three hypostases are The One, The Nous (intelligible world), and the Anima (the Psyche or Soul).

4. Clovis was the first king of the Franks to unify all the Frankish tribes under a single ruler, having changed the form of leadership from a group of royal chieftains to rule by a single king; in doing so, he ensured that the kingship was passed down to his heirs. He is considered the founder of the Merovingian dynasty, which ruled the Franks for the next two centuries.

5. Dom Bernard de Montfaucon (1655–1751) reports that a statue of Jupiter, supposedly destroyed by Saint Bernard de Menthon in the tenth century, "has been preserved up until our time [the early eighteenth century] in Savoie, at the mountain called the great Saint

Bernard, and at the monastery of Montjoux, *Mons Jovis*, so named after this statue of Jupiter" (Dom Bernard de Montfaucon, *L'Antiquité expliquée et représentée en figures* [Paris: Florentin Delaulne, 1719] tome II, second part, 418).

When the Bretons, who had preserved the Celtic language, expressed the day of Jupiter, which is Thursday, and in Latin *dies Jovis*, they called it *di Jou*. In other words, Jou is simply a shortened form of the name Jupiter.

6. Jacques du Breul reports that a statue of Isis, kept in the church of Saint-Germain de Près, was knocked down in 1514 by order of Cardinal Guillaume Briconnet, abbé of the monastery (du Breul, *Le théâtre des antiquitez de Paris, où est traicté de la fondation des églises et chapelles de la cité, université, ville et diocèse de Paris, comme aussi de l'institution du Parlement, fondation de l'Université et collèges* [1612]).

7. The "Venus de Quinipily," a granite statue of uncertain origin, originally stood on the hill of Castennec in the Morbihan, and was placed in the seventeenth century in the courtyard of the castle of Quinipily, now razed, near Baud. Both Morbihan and Baud are in Brittany, France.

8. The celebrated Abbé de Villars (1638–1673) was a French clergyman. He came to Paris in 1667, where he wrote several books, most of which have been forgotten or lost. He was assassinated in 1673 or (by some accounts) 1675 while on the road from Lyons to his native Languedoc, an event Nerval describes in the previous section on *Cazotte*. Villars's book *Comte de Gabalis* concerns an occultist who explains the mysteries of the world to the author.

Guillaume-Hyacinthe Bougeant, known as le Père Bougeant (1690–1743), was a French Jesuit and historian. Bougeant entered the Society of Jesus in 1706, taught classics in the College of Caen and Nevers, and lived for some years in Paris until his death. His *Amusement philosophique sur le language des bêtes* [Philosophical amusements on the language of animals], published in 1737, attracted the censure of his superiors, leading to his brief exile from Paris. The controversy surrounding his book was based on his claim that animals are extremely vicious by nature because the souls of beasts are rebellious spirits that have committed offences against God.

Antoine-Joseph Pernety, known as Dom Pernety (1716–1796), was a French writer. He was an intermittent Benedictine, and librarian of Frederic the Great of Prussia. Together with the Polish Count Tadeusz Grabianka, who had also been influenced by the Christian mysticism of Swedenborg, he founded in 1760 the secret society of the "Rite hermétique" or Illuminati of Avignon.

9. Milcom and Molech (who may be one and the same) are named in the Hebrew Bible as the gods of the Ammonites. These are gods associated with child sacrifice.

In the Hebrew Bible, Dagon is the primary god of the Philistines. They attributed their victories in war to him and offered sacrifices. This suggests that he played a part in doctrines about death and the afterlife. Usually portrayed as half fish and half human, Dagon is also seen as a god of agriculture. Within the Canaanite pantheon, Dagon seems to have been second only to El in power. He was one of four sons born to Anu. Dagon was also the father of Baal.

Typhon was traditionally identified with the Egyptian Set, who was also known to the Greeks as Typhon. In the Orphic tradition, just as Set is responsible for the murder of Osiris, Typhon leads the Titans when they attack and kill Dionysus, who also became identified with the earlier Osiris.

10. An Oread or Orestiad, in Greek mythology, was a kind of nymph that lived in the mountains, valleys, and ravines. They were associated with the goddess Artemis because when she went out hunting, she preferred mountains and rocky precipices.

11. The Druze are of an esoteric and ethno-religious faith that incorporates aspects of Ismailism (a movement within Shi'a Islam), Judaism, Christianity, Gnosticism, Neoplatonism, Pythagoreanism, Hinduism, and other philosophies and beliefs. From these influences they created a secretive theology. They are known to give esoteric interpretations of religious scriptures.

    An Ansarian is a member of a minority Shiite sect that practices a form of Islam that contains gnostic and animist elements. Like the Druze, their religious rites are based on the occult mysteries of initiation.

12. "La Philosophie" refers to the Knights Templar and their system of occultism. It also refers to the philosopher's stone of alchemy. I have kept the original French in this case since the full implications of Nerval's use of the word here are beyond the scope of a note.

13. Johannes Meursius (van Meurs) (1579–1639) was a Dutch classical scholar and antiquarian.

14. Plotinus (205–270 CE), Alexandrine philosopher, was founder of Neoplatonism and author of the *Enneads.*

    Proclus (412–485), Neoplatonic philosopher of the School of Athens, authored *A Commentary on the First Book of Euclid's Elements.*

    Porphyry (234–305) was a Neoplatonic philosopher, and disciple, publisher, and biographer of Plotinus. He is the author of a treatise *Against Christians.*

    Claudius Ptolemy (~100–~170), astronomer, mathematician, geographer, and optician of Greek origin, last master of the School of Alexandria, and author of the treatise *Almagest* in which he proposed a mathematical theory to account for the apparent movements of the planets. Ptolemy's geocentric system dominated Western astronomical thought until the sixteenth century and was supplanted only by Copernicus.

15. Gerolamo Cardano (Jérôme Cardan) (1501–1576) was an Italian Renaissance mathematician, physician, astrologer, philosopher, and gambler. He wrote more than 200 works on medicine, mathematics, physics, philosophy, religion, and music. His gambling led him to formulate elementary rules in probability, making him one of the founders of the field.

16. Louis René Édouard de Rohan, known as Cardinal de Rohan (1734–1803), was a French bishop of Strasbourg, a politician, cardinal of the Roman Catholic Church, and a cadet of the Rohan family (which traced its origin to the kings of Brittany).

17. The "Affair of the Diamond Necklace" was an incident in the 1780s at the court of Louis XVI of France involving his wife, Queen Marie Antoinette. The reputation of the queen, which was already tarnished by gossip, was ruined by the implication that she had participated in a crime to defraud the crown jewelers of the cost of a very expensive diamond necklace. The Affair was historically significant as being one of the events that led to the French populace's disillusionment with the monarchy, which joined other causes to eventually culminate in the French Revolution.

18. Lorenza Serafina Feliciani (1751–after 1797) was the daughter of a foundry worker. Giuseppe Balsamo, known as Count Alessandro de Cagliostro, married her in Rome on 21 April 1768; the testimonies Lorenza gave to the judges of the Inquisition in 1789 contributed to the sentencing and death of her husband.

19. Étienne-François, Duke of Choiseul-Stainville (1719–1785), was a French military officer, diplomat, and statesman. From 1758 to 1761 and 1766 to 1770, he was Foreign Minister

of France, and had a strong influence on France's global strategy throughout the period. He is closely associated with France's defeat in the Seven Years War and subsequent efforts to rebuild French prestige.

The abbé Voisenon was a famous man of letters in the eighteenth century who held salons and was a friend of Voltaire.

20. "Of all knowable things and some others": this phrase reflects the ambition of the humanist Pico della Mirandola and is meant sarcastically with regard to those who claim universal knowledge.

21. Agnès Sorel was the chief mistress of Charles VII.

22. Among the works of the "greatest masters" referred to here are *Hercules and Omphale* by Rubens, *Renaud and Armide* by Poussin, and several paintings of Agnès Sorel by Jean Fouquet, including *Madonna Surrounded by Seraphim and Cherubim*, and other painters of his school. However, Mark Antony and Cleopatra on the one hand, and Catherine II on the other, seem to have been painted only by minor masters: see, for example, *Catherine the Great Laying the Trophies of the Battle of Chesma on the Tomb of Peter the Great* by Andreas Caspar Hüne.

23. The Philaléthes (from the Greek meaning "lover of truth") were members of a secret society founded in France in the late eighteenth century, and influential in the Napoleonic era. Originally the Philaléthes Society consisted only of recognized Masonic authors. A Rite of Philaléthes was founded in Paris in 1772, devoted to the study of esotericism.

24. Jean-Jacques Duval Epremesnil, born on 5 December 1745, was a French magistrate and pamphleteer who was guillotined in Paris on 23 April 1794.

Johann Kaspar (or Caspar) Lavater (1741–1801) was a Swiss poet, physiognomist, and theologian.

Jean-Baptiste-Claude Delisle de Sales or Jean-Baptiste Isoard de Lisle (~1739–1816) was a French philosopher known for his multi-edition, multivolume work, *The Philosophy of Nature: Treatise on Human Moral Nature*, published in 1770. Sales challenged the claim that the Universe, the Earth, and all life on Earth were created by direct acts of God during a relatively short period, between 5,700 and 10,000 years ago. Instead, Sales believed, based on astronomical data, that the Earth was around 140,000 years old and that it took 40,062 years to cool down following its formation. However, he rejected the three-million-year-old date of the Earth that was taught in India at the time.

Information on Jean Terrasson has been provided in an earlier note.

Nicolas Bergasse (1750–1832) was a French lawyer, philosopher, and politician who was particularly active at the beginning of the French Revolution.

Jean-Baptiste du Val-de-Grâce, baron de Cloots (1755–1794), better known as Anacharsis Cloots (also spelled Clootz), was a Prussian nobleman and an important figure in the French Revolution. He was nicknamed "the orator of mankind" (citoyen de l'humanité) and "a personal enemy of God."

Antoine Court, who named himself Antoine Court de Gébelin (1725–1784) was a Protestant pastor who in 1781 began the interpretation of the tarot as an arcane repository of timeless esoteric wisdom.

Antoine Fabre d'Olivet (1767–1825) was a French author, poet, and composer whose biblical and philosophical hermeneutics influenced many occultists, such as Eliphas Lévi, Gerard Encausse, and Édouard Schuré. His best-known works are on the research of the Hebrew language and the history of the human race: *The Hebraic Tongue Restored: And the True Meaning of the Hebrew Words Re-Established and Proved by Their Radical*

Analysis, and *Hermeneutic Interpretation of the Origin of the Social State of Man and of the Destiny of the Adamic Race* (1815).

25. Abbé Augustin Barruel (1741–1820) was a French publicist and Jesuit priest. He is now mostly known for setting forth a conspiracy theory that involved the Bavarian Illuminati and the Jacobins in his book *Mémoires pour servir à l'Histoire du Jacobinisme* [Memoirs illustrating the history of Jacobinism], published in 1797. Barruel believed that the French Revolution was planned and executed by secret societies.

The book by Robinson is in fact titled *Proofs of a Conspiracy against All Religions and Governments of Europe, Conducted in the Secret Meetings of Free-Masons, Illuminati and Reading Societies, etc., Collected from Good Authorities* (1789–1799), by John Robinson (1739–1805). Robinson was a Scottish physicist, inventor, and writer of conspiracies.

Mounier's observations refer to the book *De l'influence attribuée aux philosophes, aux francs-maçons et aux illuminés sur la revolution de France* (1801) by J. J. Mounier, Tubingen, and J. G. Cotta. It is a refutation of the *Memoirs* of Barruel.

26. This was not Robespierre's father, Maximilien Barthelemy François de Robespierre (1732–1777), a lawyer on the Arrois Council, but his grandfather, Maximilien (1694–1762), himself a lawyer who appears on the institution document (1747) of a sovereign primordial chapter of the Rose-Croix in Arras, under the name *Jacobite of Scotland.* Such confusion was frequent in the nineteenth century.

27. Catherine Théot (1716–1794) was a French visionary, and a victim of hallucinations throughout her youth. Many years of religious asceticism in the convent of the Miramiones in Paris drove her mad and she was placed under restraint. Liberated in 1782, her early ideas concerning a Messiah took over her thinking. She became certain that she was destined to be the mother of the new Messiah; she described to her followers the marvelous aspects of the coming Paradise on Earth and was hailed as the "Mother of God." From the idea of the advent of a Messiah to its realization was but a short step; Robespierre was seen by some as this redeemer of mankind.

28. The feast of the Supreme Being, organized by Robespierre, was celebrated on 8 June 1794. Its aim was to cement the new society by stigmatizing atheism.

29. Metempsychosis is a philosophical term referring to the transmigration of the soul, especially its reincarnation after death. Its legendary founder, Orpheus, is said to have taught that the soul and body are united by a pact that is not equally binding on either since the soul is divine, immortal, and aspires to freedom, whereas the body holds it in fetters like a prisoner.

QUINTUS AUCLER

1. Julien Offray de La Mettrie (1709–1751) was a French physician and philosopher, and one of the earliest of the French materialists of the Enlightenment. His best-known work is *L'homme machine* (1748).

Claude Adrien Helvétius (~1715–1771) was a French philosopher, Freemason, and writer. In 1758, Helvétius published his philosophical magnum opus, a work called *De l'esprit* (1758). Its atheistic, utilitarian, and egalitarian doctrines caused a public outcry, and he was forced to issue several retractions.

Nicolas-Antoine Boulanger (1722–1759) was a philosopher and man of letters. He studied both mathematics and ancient languages and composed several philosophical works in which he sought discover naturalistic explanations for superstitions and religious practices, all of which were published posthumously. D'Holbach and Diderot published, in 1766, and without any profound changes, his book *L'Antiquité dévoilée par ses usages, ou Examen critique des principales opinions, cérémonies et institutions religieuses et politiques des différens peuples de la terre.*

Despite Nerval's claim, Diderot was uninterested in a "moderate deism," and evolved from pure deism to atheistic materialism.

2. Constantin François de Chassebœuf, Count of Volney (1757–1820), was a French philosopher, abolitionist, historian, orientalist, and politician. In 1782, he traveled to the East and reached the Ottoman Egypt where he spent nearly seven months. Afterward, he lived for nearly two years in Greater Syria, in what is today Lebanon and Israel/Palestine, where he learned Arabic. He returned to France in 1785 and spent the following two years compiling his notes and writing his *Voyage en Egypte et en Syrie*, which was published in 1787. One of his most interesting ideas was that the people of Ancient Egyptian Civilization were not Ayran, an idea that conflicted with the European prejudices of the eighteenth century. "Just think," de Volney declared incredulously, "that this race of Black men, today our slave and the object of our scorn, is the very race to which we owe our arts, sciences, and even the use of speech! Just imagine, finally, that it is in the midst of people who call themselves the greatest friends of liberty and humanity that one has approved the most barbarous slavery and questioned whether Black men have the same kind of intelligence as whites!" (quoted in Cheikh Anta Diop, *The African Origin of Civilization: Myth or Reality*, ed. and trans. Mercer Cook [Chicago: Chicago Review Press, 1989], 27–28).

3. Eugène Viollet-le-Duc (1814–1879) resumed, in 1846, the restoration of the Basilica of Saint-Denis, which was vandalized from 1793 to 1794; he took particular care in arranging the royal tombs.

4. Bettina Knapp relates this anecdote: "On one occasion, legend has it, Nerval brought a skull from his father's collection. It had belonged to a drum major killed in the battle of moskowa. Nerval exhibited it to his friends, then filled it with wine (or, by some accounts, with water from the Seine) and passed it around the table. Each one drank from it. Some may have been repulsed by the idea initially, but their revulsion readily disappeared when they heard that Hugo's monstrous character *Han d'Islande* always drank from the skull of his victims—and Han had become a hero figure for these romantics" (Knapp, 46).

5. The dalmatic is a long wide-sleeved tunic used as a liturgical vestment in the Roman Catholic, Lutheran, Anglican, and United Methodist churches; it is sometimes worn by a deacon at Mass or at other services.

6. Gothic ogive arches exhibit the divinity of God by using logic and reason (hallmarks of the Enlightenment) to create symbolic and precise angles.

7. Judging the first version of her funeral statue to be too macabre, Catherine de Medici refused it. The sketch by Girolamo della Robbia exists today in the Louvre. In the second version, he made her motionless, representing the queen asleep. This version can be seen in the Basilica of Saint Denis. For this second version the sculptor was inspired by a Venus from the Uffizi Museum in Florence.

8. Anteros was the brother of Eros and the avenger of unrequited love.

9. Count Montgommèry, a Protestant captain, accidently killed Henry II in a jousting accident in 1559.

10. The Artemisia from the Mausoleum at Halicarnassus. Artemisia II of Caria (?–351 BCE), built, according to Strabo and Pausanias, the Mausoleum, which is one of the seven wonders of the world, in memory of her husband and brother Mausolus. For Nerval, she symbolizes fidelity in widowhood: in the manuscript belonging to the poet Paul Éluard, the first sonnet of *Les Chimères* ("El Desdichado") carries, with the word "widower" (first line, verse 1), the note "once: Mausolus."

11. Lucian de Samosata (~120–~180 CE), already mentioned in the text on Cazotte and often considered the Voltaire of Late Antiquity, is the author of *Dialogues of the Gods*, a mocking critique of the Homeric gods.

12. The reference, according to Jacques-Remi Dahan, may be to the Scottish mathematician John Craig (1663–1731), vicar of Gillingham, who introduced Leibniz's differential calculus in England, and who applied algebra to the calculation of the probable duration of the Christian religion in his treatise *Theologiae Christianae Principia Mathematica* (1699).

13. Pierre Gaspard Chaumette (1763–1794) was a French politician of the revolutionary period. His ultraradical philosophies were regarded as excessive even by his contemporary colleagues. His belief that religion was useless was frowned upon by the deist Robespierre and many others and ultimately led to his execution.

Marie-Jean Hérault de Séchelles (1759–1794) was a French judge and politician who took part in the Revolution. Robespierre, who as a deist and a follower of Jean-Jacques Rousseau's ideas, resented Hérault and other followers of Denis Diderot's naturalism, which asserted that only natural (as opposed to supernatural or spiritual) laws and forces operated in the world.

Louis Marie de La Révellière-Lépeaux (1753–1824) was a deputy to the National Convention during the Revolution and he later served as a prominent leader of the French Directory. His policy was hostile to the Christian religion, which he proposed to substitute, as an agent of civilization, with the religion of Theophilanthropy, invented by the English deist David Williams.

14. At the Feast of Freedom and Reason, a cardboard installation had been built in the nave of Notre Dame—probably at the transept—and connected to the pillars by draperies that concealed the choir and the bottom of the cathedral, surmounted by a small temple in the Greek style.

15. Marie-Françoise Fournier, known as Sophie, was the wife of the printer Antoine-François Momoro (1756–1794). It was not Mme Momoro who represented the figure of Reason (or rather, Liberty) at the festival, but instead a singer from the opera, either Mlle Aubry or Mlle Maillard; Sophie would, however, represent Reason at a different "civic ceremony" at Saint-André-des-Arts.

16. The Theophilanthropists ("Friends of God and Man") were a deistic sect, formed in France during the latter part of the Revolution. On the altar of the Theophilanthropists was deposited, "as a sign of gratitude for the blessings of the Creator, a basket of flowers or fruits, according to the seasons" (Henri Grégoire, *Histoire des sectes religieuses*, [Paris: Baudouin Frères, 1829], Book I, 398).

17. Christophe Antoine Gerle (1736–1801) was a French revolutionary and mystic. During the revolutionary chaos, Gerle developed a strong vein of mysticism, mingled with ideas of reform. The ideas of Catherine Théot, who proclaimed herself the Virgin, the "Mother of God," and the "new Eve," were very attractive to Gerle; he recognized Robespierre as the new Messiah, and at the meetings of the Théotists he officiated with the aged prophetess as copresident. But the activities of Catherine and her adepts were short-lived.

18. In Goethe's novel, Werther wears a blue coat with gold trousers, typical for a ball, the night he meets Charlotte for the first time. Robespierre also wore a blue coat with gold trousers, along with the tricolor sash of the people's representative.

19. In ancient Rome, a flamen was a priest serving a particular god.

20. Delisle de Sales (Nerval misspelled the name) devoted a chapter of his treatise *The Philosophy of Nature* (1777) to the "Philosophical Evidence for a Supreme Being," which was published in his *Memoir in Favor of God* in 1802.

21. Any sacrilege that cannot be atoned for is an unholy act.

22. The book in question is *La Thréicie, ou la seule Voie des sciences divines et humaines, du culte vrai et de la morale* [The Thracian or the only way of the divine and human sciences, of the true worship and morality] (1799), by Gabriel André Aucler.

23. The palladium is originally a statue of Pallas-Athena, which the Trojans considered the surest guarantee of the safety of their city. According to legend, it was transported to Rome by Aeneas, where it would have been preserved in the temple of Minerva or that of Vesta and was not to be seen by anybody.

24. Iacchus was the solemn name of the Greek god Dionysos as used in the Eleusinian mysteries. In this version of the myth, he is the son of Zeus and Demeter. Jealous, Hera asks the Titans to get rid of him; they cut him into pieces and cook them, but he is later reborn as Dionysus. Iacchus was referred to as the third "Bacchus" of the Mysteries of Eleusis and likened to Christ.

25. "Who would have wiped the blinding mist from her eyes."

26. The Pythagorean Quaternary, or tetractys, consists of the celestial numbers 1, 3, 7, 9, whose sum is 20, and the terrestrial numbers 2, 4, 6, 8, whose sum is also 20. These two together form the Sacred Quaternary, 40. It is thought that these numbers and their mystical significance were derived from the Egyptians. In general, the Sacred Quaternary represents the nexus of all things, all harmony, and all number. The harmony of above and below is one Nerval's central ideas in *The Illuminated*: "If the earth emitted influences contrary to those it receives, nothing would happen in Nature; thus, the upper world continually creates the lower world; and the lower world is the reflection of the upper world, and it cannot be otherwise." This is a fundamental idea in the cabalistic system.

27. Ouranos (or Uranus) was the primeval god of the sky. For the Greeks the sky was a solid dome decorated with stars, whose outer edges enclosed the flat Earth. Ouranos was the sky and his consort Gaia was the Earth.

28. "Conscious of gods." The quote is from Virgil's *Aeneid*.

29. Ahriman is the god of evil and darkness in Persian mythology.

Shiva (Sanskrit: *Śiva*, meaning "The Auspicious One"), also known as *Mahadeva* ("Great God"), is one of the primary deities of Hinduism. He is the supreme god within Shaivism, one of the three most influential denominations in contemporary Hinduism. He is also one of the five primary forms of God in the Smarta tradition and has the aspect of the "the Destroyer" or "the Transformer" in the Trimurti, which is the Hindu Trinity composed of the main aspects of the divine.

30. Unitarianism is a Christian theological movement named for the affirmation that God is one person, in direct contrast to Trinitarianism, which defines God as three persons coexisting consubstantially in one being.

31. Codrus was the last of the semimythical Kings of Athens (r. ca. 1089–1068 BCE). He was an ancient exemplar of patriotism and self-sacrifice.

Decius was Roman Emperor from 249 to 251 CE. In January 250 CE, he is said to have issued one of the most remarkable Roman imperial edicts. Nerval may have been familiar with it, so I have reproduced it in full, as it has significance in the context of Quintus Aucler's words regarding the need for sacrifice to the gods. From the numerous surviving texts from Egypt that record the act of sacrifice, it appears that the edict itself was fairly clear:

> *All the inhabitants of the empire were required to sacrifice before the magistrates of their community, "for the safety of the empire," and by a certain day (the date would vary from place to place and the order may have been that the sacrifice had to be completed within a specified period after a community received the edict). When they sacrificed, they would obtain a certificate (libellus) recording the fact that they had complied with the order. That is, the certificate would testify the sacrificant's loyalty to the ancestral gods and to the consumption of sacrificial food and drink as well as the names of the officials who were overseeing the sacrifice.* (David S. Potter, *The Roman Empire at Bay AD 180–395* [London: Routledge, 2004], 241)

32. The lines are from Horace's *Odes* 1.2.

33. This invocation to Mars is the Orphic hymn LXII.

34. The Romans did not number days of a month sequentially from the first through the last day. Instead, they counted back from three fixed points of the month: the Nones (the 5th or 7th, depending on the length of the month), the Ides (the 13th or 15th), and the Kalends (the 1st of the following month). The Ides occurred near the midpoint, on the 13th for most months, but on the 15th for March, May, July, and October. The Ides were supposed to be determined by the full moon, reflecting the lunar origin of the Roman calendar. On the earliest calendar, the Ides of March would have been the first full moon of the new year.

35. In ancient Roman religion and mythology, Liber ("the free one"), also known as Liber Pater ("the free Father"), was a god of the cultivation of the grapevine, wine, fertility, and freedom.

36. In Greek mythology, the Curetes and the Corybantes guarded the infant god Zeus in a cave in Crete, uttering loud exclamations, beating drums and ringing bells, to prevent the cries of the little child from being heard. The Corybants were the priests of Cybele, who celebrated the worship of the goddess with a great reinforcement of tumult and screaming.

37. Floréal was the eighth month in the French Republican Calendar. The month was named after the Latin word *flos*, which means "flower." Floréal was the second month of the spring quarter. It started 20 or 21 April and ended 19 or 20 May.

38. Lares were guardian deities in the ancient Roman religion. Their origin is unclear; they may have been hero-ancestors, guardians of the hearth, fields, boundaries, or fruitfulness, or some combination of these.

39. *Lemures* was a name given to the *manes* of the dead. In ancient Roman religion, the Manes are chthonic deities sometimes thought to represent the souls of deceased loved ones. They were associated with the Lares, Lemures, Genii, and Di Penates as deities that pertained to the domestic, local, and personal cult, and belonged broadly to the category of *di inferi*: "those who dwell below." The ancients believed that the soul wandered the world after death and disturbed the peace of its inhabitants. The good spirits were called

Lares familiares, and the evil ones were known by the name of Lemures. They were said to terrify the good, and to continually haunt the wicked and impious. The Romans celebrated festivals in their honor, called Lemuria or Lemuralia, in the month of May. For three nights the temples of the gods were shut, and marriages prohibited. It was also customary at this time for people to throw black beans on the graves of the deceased, or to burn them, as the smell was supposed to be disagreeable to the wicked spirits.

40. The rituals of the Argei were religious observances in ancient Rome that were performed on 16 and 17 March, and again on 14 or 15 May.

The agonistic festivals were the Roman festivals in honor of Janus and others as Agonio.

41. Carna is a protective Roman Goddess, who brings strength of the physical body.

42. The festival of the Mater Matuta (the Matralia) took place on 11 June and involved several unusual customs, such as the fact that only free women in their first marriage might take part in them and their prayers must not be for their own children but for those of their sisters. The goddess was later identified with the Greek goddess Leucothea, who was also identified with Ino, protectress of mariners.

43. In ancient times, Roman feasts in honor of Vesta took place in early June.

44. In ancient Roman religious practices, the lectisternium was a propitiatory ceremony, which consisted of a meal that was offered to the gods and goddesses.

45. In ancient Roman culture, *sigillaria* were pottery or wax figurines that were offered as traditional gifts during the Saturnalia. *Sigillaria*, used as as a proper noun, was also the name for the last day of the Saturnalia, 23 December, and for a place where *sigillaria* were sold. A *sigillarius* was a person who made and sold *sigillaria*.

46. In ancient Rome, the Carmentalia was a festival that began on the day of 11 January, possibly also in February, in honor of Carmenta, a goddess of childbirth and prophecy, who was associated with technological innovation as well as the protection of mothers and children; she was also a patron of midwives. She was said to have invented the Latin alphabet.

47. Ambarvalia was a Roman agricultural fertility rite that took place at the end of May, and it was in honor of Ceres. During these festivals a bull, a sow, and a sheep were sacrificed; before the sacrifice, they were led in procession three times around fields; as a result of this the feast is said to have taken its name based on the words *ambio* (I go round) and *arvum* (field).

The *Amburbiales* were festivals dedicated to the purification of the city and celebrated with processions around Rome and the immolation of victims.

The *great Lustre* was an expiatory sacrifice that occurred every five years after the census.

48. The Semailles were festivals of celebration held in honor of Ceres and of Tellus; they were one of the conceptive feasts.

The Paganales were old rural festivals, so called because one celebrated in the villages of Pagis.

49. The *novembdiales*: from *novem* (nine) and *dies* (days), meaning "lasting nine days." A religious festival of nine days' length or the ceremonies honoring a deceased, which in ancient Rome ended on the ninth day of death with a funereal feast (the *novendialis*). The English word *novena*, for nine days of prayer, shares the same root.

The Lectisternes is a rite of the Roman religion, where the gods are invited to a banquet, to appease their anger.

50. Jacques-Remi Dahan has located the original spellings that Aucler used in *The Thracian* for "Boudda" and "Nair": Bouda and Naïr. He has also located an alternate spelling for "Ghervai" in the issue of *Revue de Paris* of November 1851, where "Quintus Aucler" was first published: Chervai.

51. The Greek form of the Hebrew word, *Yeshua*, from which the name "Jesus" is derived.

52. These were reported to be Julian's last words, expressing his recognition that, with his death, Christianity would become the Empire's state religion.

53. Literally, "the return of Saturn's reign," i.e., "and now justice returns."

54. The sense here is that the name of palladium is given to all things to which a state links its durability: in this respect, the "mystical palladium" of Rome, after the conversion of Constantine, is the cross.

55. La Pléiades was the name given to a group of sixteenth-century French Renaissance poets whose primary members were Pierre de Ronsard, Joachim du Bellay, and Jean-Antoine de Baïf. Étienne Jodelle, seigneur de Limodin (1532–July 1573), a poet and dramatist, was one of the group's members. His first play *Cléopâtre captive* was a great success. In honor of the play's good reviews his friends organized a little joke at his expense; his enemies brought a goat (sacred to Bacchus) garlanded with flowers and presented it to Jodelle. They also accused Jodelle of having sacrificed the animal to Bacchus, essentially accusing Jodelle of impiety.

56. Baruch Spinoza (1632–1677) was a philosopher who created the groundwork for the Enlightenment and modern biblical criticism. He came to be considered one of the great rationalists of seventeenth-century philosophy. Pierre Gassendi (1592–1655) was a philosopher, priest, and mathematician. He was one of the first thinkers to formulate the modern scientific outlook, based on moderated skepticism and empiricism. He also wrote two books forcefully reviving Epicureanism.

57. Theosophy, literally "God's wisdom," refers to systems of esoteric philosophy concerned with investigating and seeking direct knowledge of the presumed mysteries of being and nature, particularly the nature of divinity. Theosophy is considered part of the broader field of esotericism, which refers to the hidden knowledge or wisdom that offers enlightenment and salvation to the individual.

58. In Freemasonry, *Philalèthes* or *philalètes* is the name given to the Rite of Philalethes and its followers. Philalethes was a seventeenth-century alchemist and the author of many influential works. This regime of philosophic or mystic masonry was established in 1773 by the marquess Charles-Pierre-Saul Savalette of Diapers.

Historically, the Illuminati refers to the Bavarian Illuminati, an Enlightenment-era secret society founded on 1 May 1776. The society's goals were to oppose superstition, obscurantism, the religious influence over public life, and the abuses of state power. The Illuminati—along with Freemasonry and other secret societies—were outlawed by edict by the Bavarian ruler, Charles Theodore, with the encouragement of the Roman Catholic Church, in the years 1784, 1785, 1787, and 1790.

59. A spagyric is an herbal medicine produced by alchemical procedures, which involved the fermentation, distillation, and extraction of mineral components from the ash of the plant.

60. Politricon (not polithricon) or polytric (*Polyrichum commune*) is a large moss that was often used in ancient medicine and magic preparations.

61. I.e., mineral, plant, and animal.

62. *Elohim* (Hebrew: םִיהֹלֱא) can refer to either a "god" or "gods" in both the modern and ancient Hebrew language. According to the Pythagoreans, it was a term for divinity or the first being, or the totality of all beings, the Monad being the source or the One meaning without division.

63. Albrecht von Haller (1708–1777) was a doctor, naturalist, and Swiss poet. This important spiritualist anatomist, author of the important *Elementa physiologia corporis himani* in 8 volumes (1757–1777), was a determined opponent of the thought of La Mettrie.

Charles Bonnet (1720–1793) was a Swiss naturalist and philosopher. He is the author of *The Philosophical Palingenesis* (1769), which earned him Charles Nodier's boundless admiration.

64. Étienne-Jean-Baptiste-Pierre-Ignace Pivert de Senancour (1770–1846) was an essayist and philosopher. His first book was *Les Premiers âges: Incertitudes humaines* (1792).

65. Anne-Pierre-Jacques Devisme of Valgay (1745–1819) was an administrator and man of letters. He is the author of *Essai sur l'homme, ou l'Homme microcosme* (1805).

66. It was not the doctor Casimir Broussais (1803–1847) who assumed, by 1840, the role of leader of the Swedenborgian community of Paris, but his brother Émile Broussais (?–1852), lawyer and apostle of spiritual regeneration.

67. Lazare Lenain (1793–1877) was a textile worker, secondhand bookseller, and occultist from Amiens. He wrote only one book, *La Science cabalistique, ou l'art de connaître les bons génies qui influent sur la destinée des hommes; avec l'explication de leurs talismans et caractères mystérieux, et la véritable manière de les composer; suivant la doctrine des anciens Mages Égyptiens, Arabes et Chaldéens, recueillie d'après les Auteurs les plus célèbres qui ont écrit sur les Hautes Sciences* (1832), a heterodox compilation held in high esteem by the esotericists of the nineteenth century. The book, essentially Judeo-Christian in nature, hardly makes Lanain a successor to Quintus Aucler; however, Lenain makes three references to *The Thracian* in his book.

68. "Bard of Thrace," from Virgil's *Eclogues*.

69. Gabriel André Aucler, *L'ascendant de la religion, poème en 3 chants, ou récit des crimes et des fureurs, de la conversion et de la mort chrétienne d'un grand coupable, qui ont eu lieu récemment dans la ville de Bourges* (1813). A copy of this rare pamphlet appears in Paris in the collections, familiar to Nerval, of the Bibliothèque de l'Arsenal.

70. "The Misopogon," or "Beard-Hater," is the Roman Emperor Julian's satirical essay on philosophers. The cause of Julian's anger was that the people had built a Christian Church in Apollo's grove in the suburb of Daphne, and he saw that his attempts to restore the religion of paganism were failing.

Peter Valente is a writer, translator, and author of twelve books, including a translation of Nanni Balestrini's *Blackout*. His most recent book is *Essays on the Peripheries*. Forthcoming is his translation of *Nicolas Pages* by Guillaume Dustan.